RELEGATION

FORM

Marc Torkington.

For every Wanderer.
Home, Away, or nowhere to be seen.

CHAPTER ONE

"Don't go down there mate, they'll cut your fucking head off and show it on the internet." I warn Tom as he considers going off down a narrow and forbidding-looking side street. We've been joined by half a dozen other Wanderers fans now searching for a pub and a couple of them laugh nervously at my comment. It is *September 15th 2007* and we find ourselves in amongst an imposing lattice of rough terraced alleys in deepest Birmingham, an absolute shit-tip of a place.

The white girders on top of St. Andrew's Stadium can be seen looming above the buildings we walk past intermittently but they're the only remotely appealing looking thing in the vicinity because everywhere else is a mess and the gangs of scrotes hanging around street corners eyeing our Boltonian micro-invasion don't help matters either.

My name is Jamie Denham, I'm 24 years old. Through a combination of bad luck and frankly poor judgement I very rarely see us win away, it is a situation that constantly grates on me. I've somehow conspired to miss some of the great moments in our recent history away from home and it's time for a change, starting today against a team we really *should* be able to turn over.

I've travelled with Tom as usual, the lad I've been going to the match with for years, but he has an edge over me because the bastard has watched us win away a few times without me in the past and he's beginning to think I'm a bad omen. Some may suggest that being there to see us win at Old Trafford on your away debut couldn't be bettered anyway, but he refutes it.

The sun beats down on us, the last remnants of what's been a crap summer for the most part and now to help spoil the autumn, Bolton Wanderers Football Club are five games into the season with just three points to their name and sit second from bottom in the league.

No matter though because I'm convinced that this match is the turning point, been sure of it all week. The rest of September's games don't look too difficult to take some points from either and then we can get on with transforming into the brand new, effervescent, fresh and attacking side that Sammy Lee wants to build. We loved our time under Sam Allardyce, becoming more than we ever thought we could be but both parties have moved on; Allardyce to Newcastle United, whilst we had designs on trying something different to keep us at this level with more success in the league and then in Europe.

We would be led by the class of Anelka and the strength of Kevin Davies; supported by the skill and pace of Diouf, Wilhelmsson and Braaten, the quality of Nolan and Campo and kept secure by a mix of defenders. The tough and experienced Meite and O'Brien blended with the promising youth of Cid and Michalik, backed up of course by one of the best goalkeepers in Britain in Jussi Jaaskelainen.

Yeah. Well, that was the plan anyway. Allardyce brought his new team to Bolton on the opening day, they smashed us and it has been downhill ever since.

The pub we settle on suits the scene perfectly because it's horrible, resembling a converted old semi-detached house with grime covered windows and this gloomy, blackened interior. After sweating our way to the front of a six-deep queue at the bar we decide to drink outside on the pavement, I couldn't be arsed staring at the ancient meat pies in a yellowing cabinet sat on the counter inside, it was getting depressing.

Tom falls off the wagon within seconds of our arrival as he does seemingly every weekend after going a couple of days saying his drinking days are over and the fact that all we've eaten between us all day is a couple of bacon butties back home means that even this first pint is making us both a little louder and more brash. It is my first beer for six days after a long and frustrating week of work and it goes down in a matter of minutes, a special sweet taste all of its own not like any other pint I'll have again today or at all until the next time I go a while without drinking. The Seal Breaker.

    The pair of us down three each in quick succession as kick off grows closer and we're both well on the way by now, not quite as daft a haul as the six pints apiece in ten minutes we managed just before tumbling to our seats for the League Cup Final in Cardiff a few seasons back, but still pretty good going. I was wrecked for most of the first half of that game anyway and despite sitting just three rows from the front and dead-centre behind the net, I couldn't focus well enough to see Middlesbrough's two goals in the opening few minutes, then spent the second half feeling knackered and sick, I've been wise enough not to repeat that trick since. Empties discarded on the pub windowsill, we start towards the ground and pick up the pace, no easy feat with a gut-full of freshly introduced ale.

    I shuttle run across a busy road and catch the toe-end of one of my brown Gazelles on the curb at the other side, not enough to make me trip over but I stop for a moment and make sure I've not scuffed the suede which would go some way towards ruining the day if I had. For a half-second I mentally check myself; not too long ago I wouldn't have thought twice about it, I'd have been sporting worn out old trainers bought on the cheap, faded baggy jeans and a stadium jacket, not preoccupying myself with whether my carefully selected attire for the day had sustained any damage. Times are changing.

Once through the turnstiles we're directed down an alleyway which is sectioned off from the Birmingham fans by tall sheets of battered corrugated metal which some of them are kicking and hitting on the other side. I even hear one of them pathetically trying to get a chant of *"Zulu, Zulu"* going but he fails – it's just him – and Tom runs towards the barrier shouting *"Sharon! Sharon!"* in a pretty accurate Ozzy Osbourne accent which pisses them off, even more so when I and a few others join in, I can't help but laugh. A steward calmly moves us on and even he's smiling a bit too, Tom's struck gold with that one.

We move inside into a bleak space under the stands which has all the character of an abattoir and I head straight for the bar while Tom places his customary and surely doomed wager at the bookies. I nod to some lads as they pass me who are part of the regular away crowd and they do the same back, I don't know their names and never see them at home matches but have been at virtually every away I've been to that I can remember. That's as far as the acquaintance goes though, nod and gone.

Stadium beer is miserable at the best of times, even worse when served in floppy plastic pots with the awkward curved rims that often prompt me to spill half of it down my hand and clothes, but we manage to fit another one in before kickoff and then search for our seats amongst the obligatory sparsely populated away end. The teams come out, line up and kick off with little fanfare and the home side is serenaded from three sides of the ground by their club anthem *"Keep Right On To The End Of The Road"*, proud to be back in the Premier League and making a fair fist of it too. Wanderers don't exactly exert their authority over Birmingham and it's not long before there's hardly any noise coming out of our end other than complaints and hisses of derision.

I'm swaying in my seat and not paying an awful lot of attention to the action, my feet feel a bit numb as my body tries to decide whether I'm tipsy or just plain drunk and I spend most of the half scanning around the ground gawping at their supporters and taking the piss out of them with Tom. It's strange really. The start of the football season always feels a bit weird to me, like it's not really happening. After weeks away from it all and trying not to think about it too much and with no World Cup or Euros to watch I almost forget about what the match-going experience is like and the first few games don't feel real. Birmingham is beginning to bring home the reality that it's back; months of standing around watching crap football in pissing down rain and with countless pubs and hangovers to come. I love it.

The abuse directed at us by the Birmingham fans sat to the right of our section is predictable enough; *"wanky, wanky Wanderers…"* they chant, so we sing it back at them in both jest and agreement. Some of them start cheering and clapping as if they're responsible for suddenly convincing us we are shit, others further back from us start shouting *"Villa, Villa"* and a good proportion of our support joins in which they hate. I can understand their reaction though; they're apoplectic, what we're doing singing other teams' songs like that I don't know, embarrassing.

I look further up the stand to my right and there's a lad in an Aquascutum cap pointing and nodding animatedly at someone in our end mouthing "Yes, you. *You*" feigning a cut-throat movement with his finger and I shake my head, daft fucker.

I turn my attention back to the match just as a cross goes into our box and is headed home past Jaaskelainen. I drop down into my seat as the roar goes up and watch their fans celebrate across the way, Aquascutum's fury forgotten as he clambers over people to grab a mate and delightedly throttle him. As much as I don't like goals going in against us it is strangely enthralling watching the mass of arms and heads bouncing about in the opposition fans' end.

It's nearly half time when they score and before the ball even stops bouncing in the net the seats in the Wanderers section begin emptying rapidly, me and Tom join the masses moments later and head downstairs shaking our heads and cursing to eachother. Birmingham had offered very little yet we've gone and fallen apart again as soon as they put a decent move together. Once we get down to the bar though we are greeted with a scene of utter chaos.

No wonder our end had seemed so empty, it looks as if half of Bolton has piled into the bar area and begun chanting and dancing about. We duck and dodge our way to the bar queue then join in with the festivities ourselves. Despite the match still being in progress outside no-one seems to care, as virtually every song at Bolton I've ever heard is given a rousing rendition – anything from *"We're all going on a European Tour"* to *"Who needs Cantona when we've got David Lee"*.

There's a massed bunch of lads in a tight group in front of the bar bouncing up and down at this point jumping up as high as possible singing their hearts out, then someone launches a half-full plastic pint pot over the top of them and everyone else follows suit. It favours the front few rows of a music festival, dozens upon dozens of plastic pint pots whizzing back and forward over the group covering the lot of them in flat lager. A couple of lads slip over in the mass of puddles and grime on the deck but are simply picked up to rejoin the fray. Now there's just a wall of noise in the place, Tom pogoes into the middle of everything just in time for *"Walking down the Manny Road"* to get an airing.

Three stewards in yellow coats appear and randomly choose to grab one of us and take him out of the group but he's dragged back away from them with ease as the trio of very worried looking staff are surrounded by people chanting *"Who are ya?!..."* in their direction. They back off away from the scene, we aren't causing any trouble anyway we've just had enough of the "entertainment" on show out on the pitch so we've come inside to make our own.

The half time whistle must have gone by now because this place is rammed from back to front and yet still the group is in full voice, bordered by people filming the spectacle on their phones. On and on it goes, straight through the break and into the second half long after the bar is closed and cleared yet there's still a cluster of people springing about in the middle while me and Tom stand to the side drinking and laughing. The place is a mess with empty and crushed plastic pots covering the floor like a carpet and a few despondent bar staff standing nearby looking down at their clearly inadequate brooms and shovels.

A faint feeling of elation is flowing through me by the time I emerge back into the stands, it was quality down there and there's still a few lingering downstairs chanting, refusing to watch the game. It reflects what seems to be the current feeling amongst our ever dwindling travelling support, a sense of resignation and pessimism about our chances. I glance up at the scoreboard and it shows fifty-five minutes, we've been down there for over half an hour oblivious to the football and clearly we haven't missed much. If Sammy Lee gave them a bollocking during the interval then there's no evidence of it as we sit here through the rest of the half becoming gradually more and more deflated after the excitement of half time and depressed by our lack of fight on the pitch.

I look to Tom next to me and he keeps burying his head into his hands exhaling loudly, it makes me laugh because he's exaggerating it a bit but he's got a point. There's a brief moment of hope deep into the second period as Braaten breaks and darts for goal, but brief is most definitely the word as he gets snuffed out by a Birmingham defender within seconds and is summarily described as *"a bloody dickhead"* by an elderly chap next to me. There were high hopes for Braaten when he signed, one of those players that looked great on YouTube, but so far he seems miles off the pace. I stand up and lash my arm out towards the players and tell the lot of them to fuck off, surely our last chance gone. The bloke grabs my arm and chuckles.

"Hey lad, have a swig of that it'll take your mind of this shower." Then he prods a small hip flask into me. I laugh and thank him, taking a sip which burns a path down my throat like napalm and I hand it back.

"Garbage this ain't it mate?" I say to him between grimaces from the alcohol and he nods before having a slug of his own, that's the sum total of our discussion on the matter. We both sit back down and endure the final throes, they even nearly add a second which is the last straw for Tom as he gets up and heads for the exit without a word; I follow him and with a couple of minutes left there's a sad exodus away from the seats, down the stairwells, past the still devastated bar area and out towards the waiting coaches.

It's universally shit going to away games on official travel but Tom didn't want to drive down here and we weren't quite quick enough getting cheap train tickets after making a late decision to come. At least it's not too long a journey, but this is yet another unsuccessful away trip for me. We aren't the first onboard by the time we sit ourselves down and swap fleeting comments about the performance with some of the other passengers but no-one seems to care enough to get into a debate. I stare out of the window disinterestedly and finally decide I am actually a bit pissed. This is going to be a long season.

CHAPTER TWO

I'm confused by the weird numb feeling I've got in my teeth and gums after I come-to on the coach back to the Reebok Stadium, in a half-drunken daze with my eyes rolling all over the place and a cold trail of dribble leading out of one side of my mouth. My tongue can't feel my teeth properly when it touches them, it feels like face cramp. At one point I see a sign for Keele Services so I have a vague idea of where we are but I'm out like a light once more within seconds.

I jolt awake again sometime later and quickly try to pretend I meant to do it in case anyone saw me so as to mask any potential embarrassment, there's shouting and jeering from all over the coach and the sound of it woke me. Tom is standing up out of his seat mouthing off then he looks at me and laughs, telling me I've got a massive crease in my skin down one side of my face, probably from me leaning my head on my jacket using it as a pillow.

I rub my mouth on my sleeve to clear away the sleep drool and listen to what everyone's going on about, they're all shouting at the driver – he's taken a wrong turning. Sure enough, we've come off the motorway and are heading into Bolton Town Centre rather than carrying on towards Preston and coming off at Horwich for the site of our out-of-town stadium so he's taking some stick, even more so when someone asks if they can get off here because they're going into town anyway and he refuses.

A chant of *"You don't know what you're doing"* starts and spreads around the coach until we're all at it, followed by an improvised chant of *"We're lost, and we know we are"*. Some people are getting a bit abusive but there's laughing in amongst it though so no-one's that bothered… apart from the driver. Suddenly, instead of taking the easy and straightforward route from the town centre down Chorley New Road back towards the stadium, he revs the coach so we all get jolted back into our seats and heads up the Old Road which leads into the hills, a proper round trip.

  There are howls of confusion and anger at this, a man fully bedecked in the club shop's finest team wear and sporting a red face is out of his seat, arms flailing, demanding to know what the hell he's playing at but there's no response. The driver is clearly pissed off though because we're off down side streets and avenues from here on in, taking the longest possible time he can, in and out of country lanes and so the songs continue. Someone decides to launch a bag of sweets from the back of the coach down the aisle and they go absolutely everywhere, I get clocked on the back of the head by a stray M&M but catch it and eat it before it hits the floor. It's peanut, bollocks. At last we end up back on the right track and arrive at the stadium long after all the other coaches have emptied and left, there's a mad scramble for the door with M&M's pinging about all over the place at my feet.

  "Thanks a lot for that pal." I say sarcastically to the driver on my way off, he's got a face like thunder. Some suit from the coach company is stood outside moaning on that behaviour like this will lead to the coaches being stopped for good and another lad tells him with drivers like that it'd be a fucking relief. I join up with Tom who's already striding away from the scene towards the nearby supermarket. I know exactly what he's after: food and beer.

  It's not long before I'm munching a pork and pickle pie and swigging from a can of Fosters on the road to his house up the hill away from the stadium after a quick shopping trip, feeling quite awake now and ready for the night ahead. With a shirt and jeans strategically placed at Tom's house the night before I can freshen up and change before hitting town. He's practically skipping up the street spilling beer all over the place so I can tell he's looking forward to it too, the pair of us zigzag off pavements and onto roads, our arms aloft, belting out Wanderers songs and quaffing the six tins we got from Asda. He drop kicks a half-eaten pie at me and it whizzes centimetres past my face before disintegrating against a phone box and we both laugh our tits off.

  We arrive at his house; Tom lives up on the Brazley estate a few minutes' walk away from Middlebrook with his Dad, Ray, but he must be out when we get back because the door is locked and Tom spends a good while struggling to get it open, comically losing his rag with it in the process. Once inside I wait my turn for a shower while he's in the bathroom and drop myself into the old armchair he has in the corner of his bedroom, have a flick through the channels on his telly and settle on Sky Sports News which is always good for a bit of background noise and finish off the can of beer I've been cradling since we left the supermarket.

  His work ID hangs off the handle of his wardrobe next to me and I laugh at the outdated photo of him sporting even shorter hair than my buzzcut which he had for a while before deciding to grow it out into the almost shoulder-length black wig he obsesses over now. There's hair straighteners hidden around here too, I know it, I saw him mincing about with them once. *"Thomas Wheeler: Sales Assistant"* it says under the mugshot, the lad works in a bookies I don't know why they've called him a sales assistant like he still works in Burger King. Tight bastards.

  Before he returns to his room I have a quick mooch at what new gear populates the interior or his wardrobe. Ever the obsessive-compulsive, he's organised the rail into different types of garment from jackets to polos to t-shirts to jumpers, then there's a bit of a gap before the spot where a black Lacoste v-neck and a metallic grey Victorinox polo hang, this must be some area for as yet unused clothing as I can see they both still have their tags attached. I feel a hint of jealousy, Tom wears all this sort of stuff a lot better than I do and the trainer collection at the bottom of the unit puts mine to shame as well, I've much catching up to do.

I'm into the shower in no time to get ready, with the absolutely cracking *"Getaway"* by The Music firing out of Tom's bedroom and prickling adrenaline rises within me. A feeling that you can only get in anticipation of a top night out.

Bolton is trying to paint itself as this up and coming, prosperous centre of cosmopolitan opportunity to finally get itself recognised as a city rather than just a big old town but ask most people who actually have to live here about it and they'll tell you you're taking the piss. Case in point – the nightlife. When I think of going on a night out in a city I think of somewhere like Manchester; loads of options and areas, countless bars and clubs and a sense of vibrancy amongst tall buildings and bright lights.

For a night out in Bolton though now that places on the edges of town have been gradually closed down you're left with one street, Bradshawgate, the centre of the earth. The majority of these places are character-less dives where you often have to try very hard not to get a kicking in off some not-right and his mates for little or no reason. You might even get *really* lucky one night and turn up in a bar where the customers are encouraged to get up with a microphone and MC for the crowd to some butchered version of an old dance classic.

Despite this you make the best of it, it's a shithole but it's our shithole and this is where we hail from and where our infant piss-up steps were first taken, so it retains some perverse magic.

Tonight Bradshawgate is soundtracked by this electro-house stuff that's been doing the rounds a lot in the last couple of years and it frames the scene well; *"Perfect – Exceeder"* and Freaks' *"The Creeps"*, Fedde Le Grand and Eric Prydz. Beats pulsing, lads buzzing, dressed to the nines and on top note flowing in and out of boozers on this single stretch of brightly lit, dimly viewed thoroughfare.

My head is spinning by the time we join the fray after more boozing at Tom's; dizzily looking around at the crowds of people heading back and forward up the pavement, on duty, countless birds passing by in a blur of short dresses, high heels, tanned legs, bulging tits and hair extensions. Tom slaps me on the shoulder and pulls a letching face at some girl as she walks past wriggling her arse all over the place, then starts towards the nearest bar swaggering about.

I find myself propped up against a pillar after a couple of drinks trying to get my eyes to focus on one thing at once, standing outside in the cobbled area between Barristers and The Swan, losing all sense of time and how much I've drunk. My stomach feels massive after all the lager I've consumed over the course of the day and fleeting thoughts of calling it a night begin to enter my head even though it's not really been that long since we got into town – long warm day, shit result and all that.

I hiccup and then there's that grim moment where the taste of lager-infused bile fills your throat and know that it's going to come up no matter what. I wince, put my half-drunk pint on a windowsill and rush inside The Swan to the toilets which are of course all in use so I turn and immediately puke into the sink beside me, a fucking vile rush of sick that tastes exactly like Fosters heads straight for the drains and a man having a slash in the urinals behind me laughs. I spit out a couple of times and splash some water into my face then check how bad I look in the mirror. At least it doesn't look like I've been crying my eyes out like usually happens when I throw up.

    I rejoin Tom outside with a glass of water that I'll use to clean the taste away, all of a sudden the lights are being switched back on in my head and it makes me grin. The Second Wind has arrived.

    "Alright mate?" He asks, nodding towards the water I'm clutching.

    "Yeah I am now ta, almost had a major case of Pavement Pizza on our hands then though, we're lucky." I still feel proper pissed but the feeling of unbalanced bloating has suddenly been lifted and I'm ready to go again. We drink up and go back out into the street so I lead us across the way towards BL1 bar and head through the doors into the teeming mass of people inside, can barely hear myself think with Rihanna wailing on in the background. We push through towards the front and the crowds, coloured lights and loud music are bringing me back up to the right level again – I grin at a barmaid and she serves us promptly which I'm chuffed about considering how busy it is.

    Two bottles of Sol each, these won't last too long and I get to work on mine whilst glancing at the football highlights up on the screens hanging from the ceiling, that comfort blanket of seeing football on in bars regardless of the game, team or level is back. Familiar shapes and patterns of play dance across the lurid floodlit green turf.

    "Upstairs after these lad…" Tom shouts over *"S.O.S."*. I wink and do a camp pose.

    "Oh aren't you forward!" I reply, touching his arm and laughing.

"No you knob, Reflex upstairs it's well funny!" I nod and polish off the first Sol then go straight to the second; Tom's working just as quickly at his too. I've not actually been upstairs to Bar Reflex before but it's an 80's place so I'm expecting to see some fun and games on the dance floor, these beers are going down easy.

The ten minute queue back outside was not what I was expecting to get into Reflex however and it frustrates me as we stand there swaying and perving in the cold. Once inside though, climbing the steps and into the venue with *"I Want To Break Free"* playing the wait is forgotten, there's some absolute stunners in here. A lad stands in my way at the bar pretending to mince about miming the words in time with Freddy and he nearly goes over when I nudge past him to get served but he doesn't seem bothered in the slightest.

We get back onto the pints and just as I'm handing one to Tom I feel my arse get pinched and I'm hoping to Christ as I turn round to see who it was that it wasn't the lad doing the dancing. In the event, I'm not sure what would have been the worse option because I'm now confronted by a girl practically towering over me; I actually have to look slightly upwards to meet her eyes. Now, girls that are taller than me are usually a no-no for a kick off anyway, they make me nervous, but she's built like a St. Helens prop and she's got this mad smile on her face.

"One of them mine then is it?" She asks, rhetorically, I discover within seconds and I hear Tom stifle a bemused laugh behind me. Not quite sure how this comes about though, but minutes later I've bought another round in and she's trying to force her tongue down my throat with me pinned against a wall, while Tom tries to get stuck into her mate on the dance floor just as *"Eye Of The Tiger"* kicks in. I come up for air and reach for my drink, she's taking massive gulps of her pint but without taking her eyes off me, staring at me, sort of trying to scratch me through my shirt with her other hand. I can't help but think of scenes off *"Alien"*, actually.

I make an attempt at conversation, even just to find out a name and buy some time to fend her off at least, but she just wants to get back to eating my face off again so I oblige but it's not exactly enjoyable with someone basically just trying to get their tongue as far into your mouth as possible, I mean where the hell did she learn how to kiss? She must know this isn't how it's usually done surely, a thought momentarily drops into my head that if she's like this with her kissing then what must she be like in bed. It makes me shudder and I pull back for another drink.

The look of relief on my face when Tom finally comes back about five strides ahead of Facehugger's mate must be visible because he points and laughs at me. I do my best *"Let's get the fuck out of here, now"* face and he seems to get my drift because he tells me we're doing one even though we've barely been here half an hour. Then to my horror, he laughingly swerves for the toilet rather than the exit and I contemplate another few minutes' trouble with her, but amazingly and very luckily she trudges to the bog as well.

That leaves just me and her pal stood here looking like spare parts. Well, for about five seconds anyway. She walks over to me, one hand goes behind my head and another one squeezes my arse and now I'm kissing *her*. She's an infinitely better kisser than her predecessor and much better looking too, but clearly went to the same school of assertiveness because she's slipped my phone out of my pocket and is typing her number into it whilst letting me kiss her neck.

"Leaving are you?" She says once she's finished with my phone and I nod, she smiles and it makes her look really quite pretty actually. "Don't blame you…"

She goes, nodding towards the Ladies' and I laugh out loud, maybe she felt sorry for me, it makes me like her. Tom emerges first and gives me a weird look after seeing her hand still on my backside so I shift it away as if she's just done it and took me by surprise, but at last we're off and I can't get back down the stairs quick enough, even leaving a fair bit of my last drink behind.

I didn't mind the second bird at all really but the first one was a real rotter, so the feeling of cold fresh air hitting my face as soon as I step back onto the street is most welcome. We both get some cash out of the machine round the corner and we're basically left with only one option down this side of town. I tell Tom we're off to Ikon and he laughs, making an air horn sound as we start walking. Fair enough, there are a couple of other options for carrying on the night but he knows that trancing it up is a guilty pleasure of mine and it beats lurking around in some of the hovels down Bank Street.

Within minutes I'm standing next to the main bar in Ikon with two bottles of tooth-enamel-stripping bottles of Smirnoff Ice in one hand while I pump the other in the air to the beat of Rank 1's *"Airwave"*. I overhear Tom asking a lad called Paul who we've knocked about with at football a few times in the past if there's any coke he can get hold of, but he tells him he's out of luck and a brief shot of relief flashes through me in amongst my drunken shuffling. Been there, done that, Tom's got the grubby little T-shirt. Paul is stood with a group of serious looking characters and seems to not want to be disturbed. I get a nod of acknowledgement out of him but little else.

Tom shakes his head in disappointment then points up to the dance floor and I'm only too happy to oblige seen as the DJ is right on form tonight playing some proper classics and we edge our way into the mass of people right in front of the booth just as Underworld's

"Born Slippy" comes in which of course sends the crowd into raptures and I laugh out loud at the brilliance of it all. Drifting away in this historical bastion of a Bolton venue, watching the lasers break into a thousand green threads above us with everyone reaching up for them through the smoke as this absolute anthem for our generation booms out, we're at the fag-end of the clubbing scene now but these tunes are still majestic.

A small stream of spilt Smirnoff Ice runs through my fingers and down my arm as I look round to grab Tom and hug him in the way pissed lads do, my other arm strokes past the almost bare back of an impossibly thin blonde next to me and the sheen of sweat rubs onto my skin. She snaps her head round in my direction with a look of disgust across her emaciated face as if I've just touched her up on purpose but the moment is a fleeting one as I turn to Tom who is laughing with me and chanting along with the tune in delight, *"Shouting lager, lager..."*.

I've reached the stage of drunkenness where I don't care how embarrassing any of this looks anymore, it certainly *feels* like dancing to me and no-one's going to tell me otherwise. Tom's got his eyes closed with a bottle an inch or so away from his mouth, making it look as if it's a struggle to finally hoist it up to his lips, swaying and laughing, sporadically thrusting a hand skywards miles out of time with the beat and it makes me feel like my dancing must look even better. We are into some unidentifiable trance mix now and I can't place any of the songs, it's just a constant delivery of beats followed by breakdowns of melodic euphoria that has whoever is left able to once again raising their arms aloft as if trying to control a huge invisible beachball.

My drunken imagination is trying to convince me that I'm somehow spiritually connected with the music now, that I could go on like this all night, entering some altered reality where nothing matters anymore apart from these ethereal sounds – not even the fact that my feet are sticking to the floor and my shirt is wet through with sweat. I could have been stood here for hours for all I know. Suddenly, Tom's balance goes and he clatters to the floor, bottle spinning away through a forest of legs and I break from the music's spell.

    I must have fallen asleep or gone into some sort of daze for a bit because the next time I'm properly aware of what's going on is when I'm sat next to Tom on a rock hard couch set against a wall some distance away from the dance floor. He's sat back with his eyes shut mumbling profanities, a barely touched glass of water on the table in front of him and a smudge of grime up his sleeve. All of a sudden, wrenched away from the music and the moment I feel absolutely nothing for it anymore, gazing across the sea of still-waving arms in front of the DJ with a feeling of disinterest, that beat merely droning now.

    It gives me chance to check my phone for messages. There's one from a workmate taking the piss about the Wanderers result and another from a girl called Joanne who I met in Varsity a couple of months back telling me to come and meet her at a house party as soon as possible. She sent it over an hour ago but I ask her where to go anyway. I can't say as I was overly attracted to her last time but female company is female company after all. I get a reply within ten seconds at most.

    "Oi. Mate. I'm going to get off I'm going up to this bird's place." I say to Tom shaking his shoulder once I've been given a destination by Joanne. I think he means to nod but his head is listing all over the place. "You should get off home too pal, come on." I say, still grabbing his shoulder, but he shrugs my hand away and shakes his head.

"No it's reet man I'm staying here a bit, gonna fuckin' like… Get back on it." He stammers, wafting his hand at me to shoe me away. I'm not convinced, seen as he's in an absolute state but he's adamant that he's going to stay back, he can look after himself after all. I try him again telling him he should come to the taxi rank with me then get one home but he tells me to fuck off and that he'll be right in a minute, so I laugh and shake his clammy hand before making my exit from the pounding bass and drunkenly leg it across the road for a taxi, the cold air making me shiver after sweating constantly for the last hour or so.

I've got a headache coming on as the taxi speeds up Blackburn Road, miles north out of town – and miles away from home – to Bromley Cross. It takes some time to find where I'm supposed to get to, Joanne said she would meet me out on the main road to stop the taxi but even despite this we drive past her and have to track back a bit to where she meant. She didn't really help matters by taking refuge from the wind in a phone box instead of waiting at the roadside like she had first said.

Now to be honest, this is only the second time I've ever seen her and that first time I was pretty hammered from what I remember which seems to be the only state I can pull in at the moment and situations like this are what result from that. She reminds me of the girl I had the close shave with earlier in the night, Facehugger; similar look, similar stature, similar manic look on her face. Inside I'm wondering what the hell I've done to deserve this but also that now I'm here there's no way I can escape for a while yet so I tell her she looks nice through gritted teeth and ask where this house party is.

I was a massive fan of the film *"Human Traffic"* when I was younger, it ended up being one of the main reasons that I got into listening to dance music rather than just the likes of Machine Head and Slayer all the time.

One of my favourite scenes in it is the house party the group go to later in the film, I used to be amazed by the huge venue it was held in with its warren of rooms and always wished I could experience something similar. Well, the place Joanne leads me to comes somewhere close. We stumble up a potholed dirt track lined by hedges twice the size of me and it leads out into a gravel car park serving this absolutely massive building, it's a mansion. For a few moments I think about seeing her more often if only to come to places like this for parties all the time but it subsides quickly.

    One of her mates opens the door as we approach and doesn't even acknowledge my presence which I find a bit strange especially as she's letting me in with no questions asked. I follow Joanne into the hallway then we're led into a living room which must be the size of the whole ground floor of my house. It's dominated by a large fireplace in the far wall and luxuriously plump couches surround the rug in front of it. MTV Base is muted on a gigantic plasma screen which has a corner of the room all to itself and there's a very grand looking piano to my left in front of the bay windows.

    For all its grandeur though, there's no sign of a party. In fact other than me, Joanne and the girl who let us in there's only three other people here and they're all fast asleep on the couches, the room almost completely silent other than the ticking of a clock sat on the fireplace. There were livelier parties aboard the *Mary Celeste*. Joanne leads me over to a vacant couch and we sit down at opposite ends of it without a word said, the "host" goes over to one of the sleeping group – presumably her boyfriend – and shakes him till he stirs uncomfortably from sleep and she tells him she'll be in bed. I watch him grimace, appear to fall back asleep again, then suddenly scrabble up off the settee and lumber out of the room towards the stairs without so much as a glance in our direction.

Once the silence returns again I look over at Joanne and frown at her, scan around the room then back at her as if to ask her where the promised house party is. She just looks at me out the corner of her eye and says nothing. I'm confused now, not sure what I've got myself into here but I decide that since the only other time I'd seen her we spent a fair while kissing I might as well salvage something out of the evening by having an encore, so I put my hand on her leg and lean over to kiss her but she sort of half-turns away so I end up kissing the side of her mouth and cheek instead.

Unabashed, I lean in closer and finally make contact with her lips but to say she isn't very receptive would be a hefty understatement, I move my hand up her leg to her groin and she turns away again so I shuffle back to my original position and again she looks at me quizzically with most of her body twisted away from me. I look round at the other two people who are still sleeping then at the TV and I can feel a bemused frown forming on my face.

"We were supposed to be getting pizza soon." Joanne says after a couple of minutes of complete void and it makes me jump. Jesus, she actually talks. "But seen as everyone's gone to sleep there's not much point bothering. Are you hungry?" She asks, pointlessly, so I just say I'm fine even though I feel like I could eat a horse stuck between two mattresses. I can't wait to see what's in the fridge when I get home.

The headache is coming back now, throbbing through my dehydrated brain and I need an outcome from this night one way or another so I decide to go for broke and put my hand on Joanne's leg again and lean in to kiss her. I run my hand up to her admittedly magnificent breasts and for about half a second she responds, gasping quietly, letting me touch her and fleetingly I think I might be in here, but then as quickly as it came, she's gone again and I'm kissing cheek once more while she palms my hand away back to her leg. This time I sigh and glare at her, wondering what the hell she wants from me. Then she looks away towards MTV and with that I've had enough, I shake my head and sit there for a few seconds pondering what, if anything, to say before going for my phone and looking for a taxi firm.

"I think I should probably go. I'm getting pretty… knackered." I say to Joanne as the phone dials out, she turns back to me and infuriatingly just says "oh, okay" then goes back to staring at the mute television. I order the taxi and tell them to pick me up from the main road even though it's freezing and I can tell it'll take them a while to get all the way up here. I stand up and tell her I best be off, then motion towards the door so she can let me out. There's no way I want to be sat in here with her and this riveting conversation we're having waiting for a cab to find me off the beaten track in the dark, it'd be unbearable. She opens the giant front door for me and I give her a strange look, maybe something to prompt her to say something, anything of note, but she just wears a purely blank expression.

"See you later then, yeah." I offer, before turning on my heels and traipsing off across the gravel towards the main road with a howling wind coming in from the side and an eerie rustling sound passing through the trees around me. So, here I am, carefully hopping over puddled potholes with one hand over my left ear to cover it from the freezing gusts, in almost complete darkness save for the light from the mobile phone in my other hand that I'm using as a torch, miles away from home looking for a taxi which may or may not arrive where I asked it to, unsure as to how or if Tom got home okay, totally confused about what just happened back there with Joanne, starving hungry, drunk, cold and absolutely shattered. Got to admit though, Birmingham away certainly had its moments.

CHAPTER THREE

Barclays Premier League – Sunday 16th September 2007

		P	W	D	L	Pts.
16	Fulham	6	1	2	3	5
17	Tottenham Hotspur	6	1	1	4	4
18	Reading	6	1	1	1	4
19	Bolton Wanderers	6	1	0	5	3
20	Derby County	5	0	1	4	1

Bolton Wanderers' 1-0 defeat at Birmingham City leaves them second bottom in the Premier League table with just one win from their opening six fixtures. A 3-0 home victory over Reading provides their only points at this stage following losses to Newcastle United, Fulham, Portsmouth and Everton.

    I check my phone through barely open eyes and see that Tom tried calling me at just gone five in the morning, no doubt to tell me something absolutely nonsensical, but I was clearly well gone by then. It's nearly one in the afternoon now and I consider getting out of bed to confront what's sure to be a torrid hangover that will hit me as soon as I'm upright, but then Tom calls again so I put those thoughts off for a while longer.
    "Alright mate?" I say, finding out in that moment that I seem to have lost much of my voice.
    "Mmmurgh…" Comes the reply. Yep, he's a mess. I laugh at Tom, a phlegmmy and broken cackle that makes me sound like I've been a chain smoker for decades.
    "Haha, you sound wrecked where did you end up?" I'm still trying to laugh but it sounds horrible.

"No idea man, came out of Ikon, puked in a bus shelter and next thing I know I'm here in bed…" He stops mid-sentence and I hear him laughing away from the phone. "There's an open can of cider upside down sticking out of my underwear drawer mate. Dunno how that happened, I bet it fucking reeks." I laugh again, don't know how he finds that funny it would piss me right off and make me think about never drinking again – actually I'm thinking that right now anyway as I lie here in a sweaty, dehydrated heap.

"I ended up going to some bird's house party at this mad mansion in Bromley Cross!" I exclaim, still unsure of what the hell all that actually was and dreading remembering how much it cost for the taxi there and back. Tom laughs incredulously, but Jesus he sounds rough.

"Mint! Fit?" He asks.

"No." I blurt out immediately. "It was shit actually, was only about six of us there and people just fucked off to bed leaving us sat there on the couch. So I tried to have a dabble and she just froze up it was like kissing a mannequin. I just came home after a bit, honestly I was there all of twenty minutes." I wonder if I'll ever hear from her again, hope not.

"Jesus sack her right off pal, you want some action." My eyes painfully roll over to one side as he's talking to scan the pile of clothes on the floor that I left last night, this morning even, I can see already that my brown suede Clarks' look ruined and it annoys me.

"Too right, dizzy cow. Fucking good day though wasn't it?" He agrees, both of us paying little attention to the fact that Wanderers had been woeful against Birmingham. I spent a fortune with little to show for it but I've already mentally labelled yesterday as a fine awayday, despite most of it taking place back in Bolton.

"Tell you what though, I need a shit…" Tom tells me, he clearly likes to share.

"Oh nice, I don't wanna know." I've slid one leg out from under the covers now for the first stage of the get-up and it is freezing.

"I absolutely fucking guarantee you that whatever I produce can't be found on the Periodic Table either lad." He adds and I nearly piss myself laughing at that comment, the dirty bastard. "I'll send you evidence, speak to you later." He hangs up before I have chance to reply. I'm still chuckling as I finally drag myself out of my pit into the unwelcome cold light of day and just as I'm about to put my phone back on charge on the bedside table, a text comes through from Joanne saying *"Thanx 4 lst nyt, cnt w8 to av ma hands on u agen ur wel fit, Jxxx"*.

I'm unimpressed, both by the shocking text-speak and what she's saying – she never put her hands anywhere near me, I might as well have been trying to get into an oversized cushion. I can read this situation like a book, she'll tell me all sorts so I go and see her again and once again she'll just want to sit there looking at me out of the corner of her eye making me feel weird like she did last night. I shake my head and delete the text and her number immediately, another one scratched off the list.

I nip to the toilet, every bone in my body aching and I'm sure I can still feel beer swilling about inside my stomach which makes me feel awful. Nearly blow the back of the bowl away with a piss that's been brewing for about eight hours then go back to my bedside and there's another text, this one is off Tom entitled *"Bubonic"* accompanied by a picture of the dump he's just done for me to see, clogging up the toilet. I wince, delete it and decide to start the day.

For the most part I'm just the same as so many people I know my age, a graduate from a degree that ultimately meant nothing. Still living at home, working a miserable dead-end job, single, bored and stuck in a grey area of life between education and settling down where there seems to be no sense of direction or purpose – where living from weekend to weekend is everything – messing about, existing. In many respects I'm a bit of a loser; no beliefs, no convictions, an expert in nothing.

    I went to University more out of delaying a decision about what to do with the rest of my life rather than as part of some great design for the future, anticipating that I would surely find my true calling at some point during those three years. I didn't. When I graduated, with a 2:1 honours degree in Society and Conflict, there was still nothing there that I could see myself making a career out of, so I went travelling.

    For a couple of months I trudged around Europe with just a backpack for company and a lump of hard-saved £4.50 per hour wage for funding. I started in Amsterdam and made my way as far east as my nerve and travel pass would take me; taking the night trains from brilliant Berlin to Munich, from partying in Krakow to Prague, from relaxing in the forests around Ljubljana to Zagreb, from rainy Belgrade to Budapest. I opted out of going to Kiev in freezing November so doubled back on myself; bored senseless in Vienna, worried about money and sitting around internet cafes in Zurich and avoiding urban warfare in riot-blighted Paris before flying home in knackered clothes, skint and shattered but inspired by the adventures and my own self-sufficiency.

    I was convinced that I now knew what I wanted from life; a steady and fairly well paid job that would fund more forays into Europe and beyond in the future, sure that I would be able to pick one up easily with my degree and new-found life experiences and that a rewarding career in some form was just round the corner. It wasn't.

    I should have stayed away much longer and gone much further afield. Instead I spent the next few months on the dole then went in and out of a couple of utterly stultifying retail jobs listening to managers who could barely read and write telling me how to display Point Of Sale stands accurately and making it seem like a disaster on a global scale if the tills cashed up five pence short at the end of the day, like the multinational super-company I worked for had just been brought to its knees by my sloppiness with a few coppers. Finally it seemed as if I had been saved when the company I now work for decided to get in touch and offer me a job – an admin clerk in a Manchester City Centre office. It ticked all the right boxes at the time; alright wage, comfortable hours, based in a city that I love and crucially it took me out of the firing line from irate customers. I'm bored again now though, my mind has shut down.

      In its favour is that it's not one of those places that you take your work home with you and turn into an emotional wreck over it. It also just about funds my current lifestyle; I can go to one of my favourite shops like *Ran* or *Oi-Polloi* in Manchester, pick up a new pair of trainers or a jacket and still have enough left over for the month to go out most weekends watching football and going to the pub – I can pay my keep on time as well.

      That is basically how my life runs at the moment though; 9-5 Monday to Friday at work then massive blowouts on Friday and Saturday nights, with recovery time on Sunday and repeat over. I loved it at first too, with a bit of structure to everything and some freedom to do as I pleased, but multiply that over the course of every single week of the year and it has left me feeling stagnant now, like I need another change.

      It is mid-afternoon by the time I'm up and I've already had a smirk and shake of the head from my step dad, Martin, his usual greeting for me when I'm hungover. I'm in the kitchen slouched over the worktop slowly working my way through some bacon on toast and Mum starts moaning as a glob of brown sauce shoots out the opposite end of my sandwich when I take a bite and misses the plate. I try to tell her I'm nearly finished anyway so it doesn't matter but I can only muster a jumbled up sentence with my mouth full and my brain still in bed. I'm loving how the tang of brown sauce knifes through the stale alcohol taste in the back of my throat though. I wince when she then asks how yesterday was.

"It was alright." I say, polishing off the last corner of toast. "Wanderers were crap though and I spent a fortune. Got to stop doing that." I drag that line out every time either of them asks me about a night out I've been on, so I'm sure they believe that statement as little as I do. Mum just tuts at me, then comes up with the ridiculous notion that I might want to accompany her and Martin to the garden centre today. Not a chance. I widen my eyes and look away in disdain, sure, like I want to spend my Sunday with a hangover in a garden centre with my parents. Mum will be stopping for ten minutes at every display and Martin will be close to suicide before they even get through the doors.

"Absolutely nowt. I'll take the dog out then I'm going to sit in front of the telly all day and not move." Martin strolls in and kisses Mum, she tells him that she's sure he can't wait to get to Barton Grange and he tells her to bog off.

I get on well with my parents. I was never like so many people I met at Uni who couldn't wait to get away from theirs, convincing themselves that they'd escaped from horrible home lives to be able to finally flourish on their own from Freshers' Week onwards. All I came across were people living in bubbles; legends in their own egos, maxing out on angst and castigating every feature of their "previous lives", when in reality all they had was a family who were only wishing the best for them back home and slipping them extra funds whenever they asked.

There was no desperation to get away after Uni as I slowly saved up for my brief European trip and I don't mind living here now so long as they don't mind me being around; they give me as much space as I need, I give them as much rent as they need and I can talk to them both too, it's a comfortable arrangement. I'll not be here forever so I'll make the most of it while I can, my sister Carla moved out a few years ago and lives in her own place now – I'll do that myself someday but there's no rush.

I neck a couple of pain-killers then go to the collection of coats hanging up behind the kitchen door and as soon as I grab my old parka Holly, our permanently energetic Chocolate Labrador, comes careering in from the hallway barking and with her tail favouring a helicopter's rotor blades at full pelt – she's known for some time that as soon as I go for this coat it is time for a walk. I snatch the lead from the next hook along to my coat and loop the chain over the dog's head and secure it around her neck while she growls and frantically tries to lick me in excitement. She leads me out of the front door rather than the other way round and we head in the direction of some nearby woods at pace.

It's mild and sunny again today and the rays reach down in broken translucent beams through the trees to the floor of the small patch of woodland we have arrived in, I release Holly and watch her speed off ahead as soon as we are past the gate. There's a long-since felled tree trunk which lines part of the path through this area and I take up the same position as I always do when I'm down here with the dog, perching in a gently curving groove near what once was the base of the tree which could easily have been machined purposefully to match the shape of my backside, such is the way I fit into it so comfortably. I lean back, stick the headphones in and immerse myself in

New Order, my favourite band. I love the swirling mix of dance, rock, synth and design that makes me wish I was born in another era.

Holly returns supercharged and begins to busily scurry around in front of me trying to get my attention and then when I don't immediately look at her she thumps a muddy paw down onto my foot, tail wagging furiously. I laugh and attempt to ruffle the fur on her head but she ducks away from my hand with a bark and runs off into some bushes further up the gravel path that cuts the piece of woodland in two, a welcome enclave set in amongst the masses of terraced streets and main roads that dominate this area of Smithills in north-west Bolton, the area I've lived in for most of my life. I've played, ran, hid and contemplated in these woods for as long as I can remember.

Hangovers are getting more and more difficult to endure, who knows how badly they'll affect me in years to come and now I've got this time to myself I can concentrate on the fact that I actually do feel like death. My eyes seem to be operating in a slightly different time-zone to my brain because they are taking an extra half-second or so to catch up whenever I turn my head anywhere and it's making me feel dizzy. The throbbing headache that started towards the end of last night has returned too, so this, coupled with a lingering sickly feeling in my throat is leaving me sitting here wanting it all go away. I make a desperate promise to never drink again if I can just start feeling better straight away but as usual it doesn't work. *"True Faith"* and *"Your Silent Face"* – one of those songs so supreme that you wish it would never end – ram the point home mercilessly.

Holly emerges from the bushes and sprints over to me carrying a filthy branch in her mouth which she kindly drops at my feet, complete with a few streaks of drool. I pull a headphone from my ear and laugh at the clump of dirt stuck to her nose, reaching for the very end of the branch, the cleanest part I can find.

"You mucky sod, aren't you getting too old for this?" I say as I stand up to launch it back into the bushes it was retrieved from and Holly spins around to run after it. I return to my position and let the hangover consume me again, identifying the return of another feeling I often get after a night on the booze – paranoia. Fleeting suggestions keep dropping into my head that I've done something terrible and unforgivable, but I can't think what it is, texting all and sundry fishing for responses to see if I've pissed anyone off. This is another miserable by-product of drinking too much and like the headaches it is getting worse with each hangover.

I'm trying to analyse every detail of yesterday to see if there's something I should be worried about; Joanne keeps appearing in my mind but I'm sure it's not her, it's not like we ended up in bed and did something to regret, we barely even spoke. Maybe the stuff on the coach home from Birmingham will come back to haunt us, maybe they'll track everyone's names and ban us? I quickly disregard that too, it wasn't *that* bad and I'm not too bothered about the coach company either, it was a laugh. Tom didn't mention anything about being pissed off that I left him in Ikon last night. Maybe I spent too much. Maybe I spend way too much on nights out? I emptied my pockets this morning though and I came home with about fifteen quid in a heavy handful of change and it's not like I'm saving up for anything in particular anyway.

I can't figure it out and I know that's because there's nothing *to* figure out, but still I can't shake it. My skin seems to have a horrible dirty sheen on it too, especially my face which feels like it is covered in grease and I've got a couple of barely visible but painful spots appearing around my mouth. To complete the misery I feel a right bloater as well, the Michelin Man tyre doubling as my midriff that shows itself now I'm sat at the tree feels like it's about to burst through the stretched t-shirt under my coat and is not helping my mood in any way. Fearing slipping into some regret-infused malaise that could potentially last for days I search for something else to think about and settle upon remembering when supporting my team was a little simpler.

I was a late starter when it came to getting interested in football then beginning to follow Bolton Wanderers. At primary school all the kids would be into it and playing football at playtime in gigantic 40-a-side matches that spanned the whole width of the playground. Here, skirmishes for control of the ball would break out round a blind corner or down some path leading to the gates, totally out of sight of either goal as most of the players stood idle in the main area wondering if they would ever get a touch again before the bell went, or lurking on the goal line waiting to steal a decisive deflection on any shot that eventually came in. Meanwhile I would look on surveying the scene with my small band of outcasts from our vantage point in a deserted corner of the yard pretending to be army snipers picking out stray targets.
The first hint of interest in the game came when I happened to watch some of an England friendly on television at a friend's house on a sleepover. David Platt scored, that's all I remember. The others were watching it so I joined in, with no clue as to what was going on other than wondering why everyone still seemed so enthralled even though nothing was happening. Then came an event that finally stoked up some interest; Wanderers were on Sky Television for the first time in their history and there was a lot of coverage surrounding it – not that I could watch the game as we didn't have Sky but someone let me borrow it on tape days later – so I listened to it on the

radio in my bedroom amongst the military themed drawings on my wall and the books about guns and armies strewn about the floor.

It was Owen Coyle's 86th minute equaliser against Arsenal, a team I knew nothing about other than that they were bigger and better than us, in the FA Cup that got me hooked. I went crazy when the goal went in, jumping about in my room screaming and celebrating and did the same again once I had possession of the tape and I got to actually see my now Favourite Player In The World Ever, miraculously sweep the ball home to make it 2-2. At last I began to join in the epic footballing battles being played out at school every day, though by then at our place we had been forced to use only the foam balls that you couldn't get any decent purchase on after wayward shooting took out one hopscotching girl too many.

I suppose it was a bit of a false start though because although I now called myself a Bolton fan (I even cried when Oldham later knocked us out of the cup and they are still unforgiven to this day) I had no real urge to go to a game so I spent the rest of the season watching whatever matches made it onto terrestrial television and wearing through more and more pairs of school shoes due to my playtime exploits. Plus I still had virtually no idea about the game, I mean despite even watching them play against us on that borrowed videotape, I still spent months thinking Ian Wright was white and that Tony Adams was a striker simply because he scored a goal.

Then came Junior Whites, the youth club set up by Wanderers. I was encouraged to go down every Friday evening after tea with my cousin who was already well into the game and so we spent our Friday nights playing football on the sand-covered astropitch in the shadow of Burnden Park. The following season, 1994-1995, we started going to some matches organised by Junior Whites paying 50p each for our seats in the Great Lever End, but even these first few fixtures didn't quite give me the bug. Everyone goes on about their first match and how it had this life changing effect on them, well, as Bristol City made it 2-0 in front of me in August there wasn't a single hint of excitement, nor when Gerry Creaney was scoring for Portsmouth in September, or even as I watched my first Bolton Wanderers win against Notts County in November.

I took a while to go back after that, but I knew Wanderers were having a good season and we were getting a lot of news coverage after beating Norwich to get to the Coca Cola Cup Semi Finals so I decided to offer up 50p of my pocket money again and make it to another match to see if anything had changed since my last visit. Every obsession needs a spark – and this one was mine. Wolverhampton Wanderers at home on February 4th 1995; in front of our biggest gate of the season so far of nearly 17,000 as the away fans abused us and our mascot and as the rain came down, Wanderers had gone a couple of goals in front and I was already loving the noise and the racing of my pulse every time we came forward. However, as my cousin and I returned from the toilet at some point in the second half, running along the concourse at the front of the Great Lever End, we reached a point level with the corner of the goal just in time for *"The Moment"*.

Jimmy Phillips hit this shot from outside the box at an angle, our attention drawn to it by the hush of anticipation that suddenly descended on the seats to our right as we ran and I'm still convinced that the ball curled inwards, then outwards and back inwards again on its way to the top corner. Smashing against the stanchion in the back of the net just as we got level to it and getting a perfect view of the whole of Burnden Terrace turning into an instant scene of mania. Still running, I leapt up onto my cousin's back shouting and screaming, scores of Lever

Enders lunging forward off the front row to climb up the railings separating us from the pitch and both of us stood there hugging and jumping around, me in my Reebok shell-suit top and my cousin in his shiny yellow away kit from a few seasons earlier.

We added two more not long after that including one by the god-like – to me anyway – Owen Coyle, a 5-1 victory against one of our closest rivals in the league to send us top in the midst of a joyous Burnden Park and at least one absolutely smitten twelve-year old who didn't want the match to end. I've only ever seen that goal once since that day and that was on *"Endsleigh League Extra"* a few days after the event. Twelve years is a long time to go without seeing the goal that changed everything.

So then that's where it all began for me, still some way off being anything approaching a regular at home games and years before the first time I went to an away match but the bug had finally been planted. I spent the rest of the nineties supporting a team that became feared in the cups, known for playing good football and seemed to be quite popular amongst neutral supporters for the way we approached games even during a couple of relegations from the Premier League. I wonder if that shot from Jimmy Phillips really did change course three times in a 25-yard stretch between his occasionally lethal left boot and the top corner. Maybe it's better if I *think* it did.

CHAPTER FOUR

Barclays Premier League – Monday 8th October 2007

		P	W	D	L	Pts.
16	Sunderland	9	2	2	5	8
17	Tottenham Hotspur	9	1	4	4	7
18	Reading	9	1	4	4	7
19	Bolton Wanderers	9	1	2	6	5

| 20 | Derby County | 9 | 1 | 2 | 6 | 5 |

After the defeat to Birmingham City, Bolton Wanderers' UEFA Cup campaign begins with a fortunate 1-1 draw in Macedonia against Rabotnicki Kometal followed by a 1-1 draw at home to Tottenham Hotspur in the Premier League. A 2-1 win in extra time at Fulham in the League Cup sends them through to Round Four, before a 1-1 draw away to bottom club Derby County takes their points total at the end of September to five.

At the start of October, Bolton qualify for the UEFA Cup Group Stage with a 1-0 win over Rabotnicki in the second leg of their qualifier. However a 1-0 defeat at home to Chelsea proves to be Sammy Lee's last match in charge of the club, who leaves by "mutual consent".

    I'm slumped in front of my computer bored of the week already and it's only 10:00, Monday morning. I'm sort of half-sliding off my chair, shirt untucked, tie battered to fuck, trainers on instead of shoes and a face unshaven since last Friday. One of the other lads shoved a brew in front of me a bit ago but now I've finally looked at it it's gone all cloudy on top and I know it's going to taste rank. I'm going over the stuff about Sammy Lee getting sacked, leaving – whatever – and studying the league table in the Evening News which all makes for sorry reading, that's why my face has this fat-bottom-lipped sulk frozen onto it.
    We are in a right state and I doubt that we can get out of it this time. I see Spurs down there with us but there's no way they're going to still be there in a few weeks let alone at the end of the season, it's going to be left to us and the likes of Reading and Derby to fight for survival but I just can't see where our next win is going to

come from. Arsenal, Villa and United are all on the horizon and I can't picture anything positive for us from any of those games.

Sammy Lee's plan for us in my opinion was perhaps just a bit too much too soon. We've been a team that has played one specific way for years and as appetising as the thought of us suddenly transforming into a side that's not only solid at the back but that also attacks at speed with wingers and two proper strikers was, we just don't look like we know what we're doing, as if the concept is alien to all of our players apart from Anelka up front who would look class in any team.

Things haven't felt right all season and some of the players that helped us make such a force in recent years have either looked out of sorts or been marginalised; Kevin Davies has spent a lot of time dropped or playing out of position, Ivan Campo hasn't played at all and Gary Speed has been given a coaching role whilst also being a key player which can't be helping his preparation for games. Meanwhile some of the players signed in the summer who were supposed to help bring about this change of style are simply not up to it. All in all, it's a mess.

Whoever takes over in Lee's place has got a right job on his hands, as it stands I can't see us scoring enough goals and I can't see us keeping it tight at the back well enough with the players we've got. At least we made it through to the Group Stages in Europe though. The home game against Rabotnicki was about as unenjoyable as it could get but it was a win at least – thanks to Anelka coming off the bench to score the decisive goal almost immediately – and it's the draw tomorrow, I've been excited about it since the final whistle of that game last Thursday night. Anyway, work.

It's the done thing to whinge about how bad Mondays are; actually I can hear Jo Whiley on the radio in the office right now telling people to text in and tell her how they're surviving this horrific day. To be honest though Mondays are fuck all, you build up to it on Sunday night readying yourself for yet another new week so when you finally crash-land onto Monday your defences are up and it's usually over with quickly and fairly painlessly. Tuesday is the killer. Tuesday is where you know you're knee deep in a week filled with cold, early starts in the dark and late finishes also in the dark and weekend is well and truly over with.

"Bastards!" Comes a shout from behind me as I examine my cup of tea further, it's Graham, possibly the bitterest old man ever to walk the planet. He's just walked in late this morning and it has obviously pissed him off royally because he's hardly ever late, that's one of the things he likes to pride himself on and measures everybody up against – punctuality. "Enid fucking Blyton wrote those bus timetables, they're a work of fiction!" He continues, in his gravelly old Salfordian accent, as he rushes to his seat a couple of rows ahead of my desk and switches a monitor on while removing his anorak from his hunched back.

"Here he is, slacker Graham." I say, peeping round my computer screen to see what his reaction is. It's predictably harsh.

"Ah fuck off you. It was the fucking buses, I'm never fucking late. Fucking dogs they are!" Graham's got issues with his temper, you're lucky if you can get through a conversation without him kicking off about something and his choice of language makes mine look quite placid at times. Problem is, Graham's about sixty-two and he should be chunnering on about his grandkids or what happened on *"Last Of The Summer Wine"* the other night, not calling young girls he's seen in the street on his way in fucking slags or jumping around in front of the radio haranguing the presenter for talking about Pete Docherty for too long. He nearly threw the thing out the window that day, then looked like he was seriously considering launching it at me instead when I told him he was probably too old to even know who Pete Docherty is. The little silver-haired nutter. The funniest thing about it all though is that there's only us on our section who seem to be aware of this side to Graham because any time he talks to someone else from the office or anyone over the phone he sounds like butter wouldn't melt, like a nice old grandad as he should be.

  Five people work in our department which is cut off and secluded from the rest of the office floor, where all the archives and records for the company and its clients are kept. We are allowed a bit more freedom than the other sections are, it's quiet and orderly out there at the desks where the public can show up but in here it's got the same sort of attitude and atmosphere that I was used to in warehouses that I worked in during Summer Holidays at High School.

  Along with me and Graham there's Danny Anderson who's probably my best mate at this place; he's a couple of years older than me but we started in the same week and we are fairly alike when it comes to most things although he's a City fan so I'm slightly smarter and considerably more cheerful. We're not mates to the extent where we socialise much out of work other than on company do's but we do get on well and he's also a Uni graduate in a subject that's got nothing to do with the job he's doing and this place isn't a career choice so, like me, he doesn't take things here too seriously.

  Then there's Brian. Brian lists his interests as *"MCFC and tits"*. He's sound as well but he shares his club allegiance with the world on a daily basis with the volume set to eleven, so him and Dan often end up on my case about football. Fact is though Brian is fucking clueless when it comes to work so I can usually shut him up when I pull him on some of the absolute toilet he types in his letters to people about their account queries.

Finally there's Sarah, a nineteen year-old agency girl we've had in for a few months and I'm convinced she's still trying to come to terms with the reality of where she's found herself, in a daily shouting match between four blokes about anything from football to music to society in general and she spends most of the day with a horrified look on her face listening in to what's being discussed. She's a good egg though, I think she finds most of it pretty amusing but I can't see her being here for ages and I'm sure she will be the one laughing when she finally saves the money to go to Thailand and leaves us behind.

I can map out every work day before it happens, they're all the same and rarely offer anything overly challenging or out of the ordinary; spend an hour catching up on emails and chat, a couple of hours doing some filing, an hour typing out some letters, half an hour or so for lunch, then an afternoon doing the same as I did in the morning. Most of the time I can just cruise through the days but there are times where it hits me a bit and I sit there so bored and so uninspired that I can barely move off my chair to do anything.

My phone vibrates as a text arrives and it's from Facehugger's mate who I met in the 80's place after Birmingham a couple of weeks ago, I've since discovered her name is Felicity. She's been texting me on and off and seems fairly keen when she does so I've been trying to press her to meet up again but she appears to want to dodge the issue for now which to be honest I'm not too bothered by, I'm only looking for a bit of fun really. It's the usual stuff asking about how my weekend went and going on about how crap Monday is, of course. I just tell her it was alright, didn't do much, asked her how hers was, tell her we should meet up sometime, then stick the phone next to my computer and gear up for the filing.

Piles of documents to be filed away are stacked up on shelves at the back of our section, work that has been backed up for weeks taking it even further out of target than it probably already was, the company is struggling to keep up. I collect a bundle of forty documents from the top of the heap and glance at the date on the first letter; it was processed six weeks ago. There's probably another letter somewhere in this paper mountain dated a couple of weeks later asking what happened to the document I'm holding in my hand because when they phoned us about it our office had no idea what they were talking about and it was nowhere to be seen on their file. I'm not arsed, I just work here. I'm fairly confident in saying that everyone else in this place feels the same.

I unwrap the bundle and set about marrying up each piece of correspondence with the file it belongs to in amongst our vast library which sprawls off into dark and cavernous rooms and houses details of people's personal business dating as far back as the sixties. Graham is in one of these rooms somewhere and I can hear him complaining about something to himself, he needs to chill out. I can do my tasks with only the minimum amount of concentration on the job at hand so it enables me to slip off into daydreams which isn't always the best thing to do as time ends up slowing down considerably.

At the moment though my thoughts are consumed with the European draw tomorrow rather than the fact that we're managerless and in the relegation zone, I can't help but be excited about it. I think about trips abroad and foreign stadiums, drinking on the airport before we set off and seeing Bolton play against unusual teams and sure enough; this particular Monday takes an age to pass.

Tuesday 9th October 2007

Adrenaline begins to circulate as I log onto the UEFA website this morning to see who we got in the draw for the Group Stage, I'm desperate to go abroad to watch at least one of our away games now I can at last afford it, wherever it is. I've never been to a European away before but I'd love to get somewhere good, I don't think I could stand the stick I'd get from Dan or Brian because any time they mention being in Europe I like to remind them that the last time City were there they had the glamour of a game in Wales, one in Belgium and an inglorious exit in Poland.

I finally get to the page, hit the UEFA Cup section and there it is: UEFA Cup Group F – Bolton Wanderers against Sporting Braga and Aris Thessaloniki at home, not massively inspiring and Red Star Belgrade away which sounds like a bit of a nightmare. Then I feel a jolt as I see the final name… Bayern Munich. *Away*. My jaw literally drops; we couldn't have drawn anyone bigger or better. Bayern are usually in the Champions League year after year and are only in the UEFA Cup because of one freakish season last year where they finished out of the top couple of places in the Bundesliga.

"Oi lads, have a look at this!" I shout towards Brian and Dan, shaking a little with the excitement and they come over to read the screen. "Bayern Munich away boys, T.N.S. and Groclin, it ain't!" I exclaim, referring to two of the teams City played during their last European campaign.

"You going then or what?" Brian says trying not to look impressed and I get another hit of adrenaline – *hell yes*. I send a garbled text to Tom enthusing about the draw and Munich away and ask him whether he wants to go or not.

While I wait for a reply I start having a look around online for flight tickets and I'm surprised by the lack of Manchester to Munich services; there's all sorts going out to Frankfurt, Berlin, Hamburg, but very few to Munich and the ones that do are very dear compared to other German airports, surely they've not cottoned on to the fact that an English team has just drawn Bayern and they anticipate high demand for flights so they've hiked the prices within the last few minutes?

A reply comes from Tom; he agrees that the draw is immense but that it might be tough to get a lot of money together in a short space of time. He tells me to work some magic finding cheap flights and accommodation and come back to him with a price. Thoughts of work have gone flying out of the window for today I can barely concentrate hard enough on what websites I need to look at let alone put Mr and Mrs Skint's documents away correctly. I'm jumping with excitement on one hand but feeling sick about the sort of prices I'm looking at on the other, how fans of teams that get in Europe and then progress far every year cope I'll never know.

Spend half an hour or so doing some work while the Manager was hanging about the place and then get straight back to the websites I'd been checking on and already many of the limited number of flights I saw before have vanished from view. I phone Tom and tell him that it's basically now or never with these flights as they're going fast and then I say I'll lend him some money if he wants which I could end up regretting, but we need to sort something urgently if we're going to go anywhere. That seems to sway it, he again tells me to make the best booking I can and get back to him. I mean, we could fly with the Wanderers travel club as a last resort but that's an in and out job on the day of the game and I'd much rather get chance to enjoy the place a bit first.

  I snatch up the receiver to the phone on my desk and dial the number of the travel agents displaying pretty much the last flights to Munich from what I can see. Nerves increase as the dialling tone gives way to a Cockney sounding lad on the other end.

  "Alright mate, erm, I've been having a look on your website and I'm wondering if you can do me any deals on flights to Munich around the seventh or eighth of October?" The travel agent responds with a knowing chuckle.

  "Another Bolton fan I take it?" Jesus, how many of us have been calling up today?

  "Yeah, how did you guess? Have a lot of us been calling up?" I'm grinning at the thought of that.

  "Oh it's been absolutely non-stop all morning mate, I've lost count." Sounds like we are really coming out of the woodwork for this one.

  "Right I better sort myself out then as soon as possible, I'm looking for flights for two preferably on the Wednesday but I'll go Tuesday or Thursday on the day of the game if that's all that's left…" The agent tells me to give him a moment as he searches for whatever flights are remaining then comes back on the line.

  "Okay I'm literally down to the last three flights with two seats I'm afraid mate and one of them is late on Thursday getting to Munich at six while another takes you via Zurich, getting you in on Thursday early hours." I disregard both, they're nightmares. "The last one I have for you departs early Wednesday morning and will get you to Munich by mid-afternoon coming back in the early hours of Friday, flying British Airways, but I must tell you there's a change at Heathrow on the return and the price is £245, each." I feel sick instantly, I could go on *holiday* for that.

The lad has gone silent waiting for my response, he sounded almost apologetic when he gave me the options, no wonder. But it's now or never, take it or leave it. I've just about got enough money in my account to pay for both flights now and obviously get Tom's share off him as soon as I can but it's a massive outlay just for a couple of nights abroad. It takes me about three seconds to justify it; Bayern Munich away, UEFA Cup, sounds like loads of us are flying out there for it. *Once in a lifetime experience.*

"Right go on, I'll take it, I won't get anything else at this stage by the sound of it." He agrees with me, course he does, he's just made a ludicrous sale to some desperate prick looking for last minute flights to Germany and I'm sure his commission will be very healthy. I give him my card details and nearly five-hundred quid goes floating out of my account.

"Tom, it's booked we're going to Munich!" I shout down the phone moments after I finished up with the travel agents, he cheers back at me in response.

"Fucking beautiful mate I love it, go on what's the hit with the price?" He won't be laughing in a minute, I think to myself.

"You're not going to like it lad, you sitting comfortably? Oh sorry, you're always sitting comfortably at work aren't you?..." He calls me a dick then tells me to give him the bad news. "It's two hundred and forty five quid each pal, literally the last flights they had unless we wanted to wait overnight in Switzerland. I nearly fell off my chair when he quoted it but it's the best we'd get now, they're all being snapped up." He groans loudly on the other end and sighs.

"'Kin hell Jamie that's steep is that. I'm skint till the end of the week." I tell him not to worry and that as long as I get it back before the next Millennium then he's alright.

"It's going to be immense mate, better than anything else we've ever done watching Wanderers. Anyway balls to it, what else you going to spend it on?" I'm reassuring myself there as much as Tom, but it perks him up anyway.

"Haha yeah too right it'll be mad, nice one for getting it sorted. What about hotels?" Oh yes, the next issue. This won't be half as much of a problem though, that's already in hand.

"Don't worry about that I'll find us somewhere, it'll be piss. I stayed in this hostel when I went there a few years ago it was quality, it was just like a regular hotel only the rooms are shared with five or six people. But it's safe and all that, no bother." He sounds less than convinced.

"You joking me? A hostel? It better not be a shithole man…" If it's the same as last time then it's far from a shithole and quite cheap too considering it is right near the centre of Munich.

"Worry not my friend, it'll be reet. You're talking only a few quid per night too and after shelling out all that on flights, the cheaper the better when it comes to digs." That pretty much sells it to him and he sounds chuffed, so yes indeed, Munich here we come.

I come off the phone buzzing with excitement; I can feel it humming away in my guts already and it's still four weeks away. I raise my arms and cheer, job done. Dan walks past behind me and coughs loudly.

"Fuck me, you actually going to do any work today you lazy get? You've not done a tap all morning." He gets two fingers wafted in his face in response, but I stand up to go and do some graft, I sense Graham's angry gaze piercing two holes in my back. Just as I'm about to move away from my desk my phone lights up and I get a text from Felicity asking me to meet up with her tomorrow night after work and it makes me grin cheekily. What an absolute result of a morning.

CHAPTER FIVE

Wednesday 10th October 2007

I breeze into Barracuda on Bradshawgate, a day on from booking tickets for Munich. I'm still jumping with excitement and head straight past the bar towards the back of the building where Felicity had assured me she would be waiting. Sure enough there she is, sat tucked away in one of the booths with a bottle of fruit juice in front of her and she beams as soon as she clocks me which makes me smile too but also sends a quick burst of nerves shooting through me which I'm sure all goes straight to my cheeks, because they're suddenly on fire and the thought that now I must be blushing only serves to make it worse.

I throw my bag across the bench-seat opposite her trying my hardest to look confident and ask if she wants a drink before I even say hello despite the fact I can see she's barely started on her current one. She turns the offer down, still smiling, so I buy a pint for myself before rejoining her at the table.

"Hello again you." She says, instantly flirtatious and just as attractive as I had first thought despite my drunken stupor when we had met in Reflex, weeks ago.

"Hey, it's great to see you again." I keep eye contact. "You look gorgeous." Now it's her turn to blush, but she retreats to her drink momentarily which enables me to draw a pretty large mouthful from mine and it tastes great. She pauses for a second then smiles at me and leans forward.

"Anyway, where were we?..." She lunges almost full length across the table to my face and we kiss as if we've been lovers for years. Her tongue is freezing cold and comes with a sharp tang from the fruit juice but I like it and I run my hand through her hair as she lays hers on my burning cheeks. We embrace for at least ten seconds before she giggles and slides back to her original position.

"That's' the best ice-breaker I've ever had!" I gush, which comes out as cheesily as it sounded in my head moments earlier, Jamie you knob, but she giggles again and now her leg is stroking up against mine. Quite clearly she's just as forward sober as when she's drunk, my heart is racing, I fancy the pants off her instantly and unbelievably it seems like she feels the same about me. "Sorry I look a bit of a tip I didn't have time to get a change sorted this morning." I glance down at my now very slack tie and my shirt sleeves rolled up to the elbows, but she just looks at me still smiling and tells me I look fine.

Felicity, on the other hand, looks great. She reminds me a bit of Reese Witherspoon; similar features and blonde straightened hair which drapes lazily over her shoulders, only Felicity is slightly larger than your usual Hollywood actress but I don't mind that, in fact to be honest I prefer this over wafer-thin girls anyway, it's just more attractive and shows she doesn't mind enjoying herself.

"I like a man in a suit anyway." She concludes, stretching forward again to kiss me which gives me a brief but tantalisingly revealing glimpse down her cleavage and we are at it again with hands in eachother's hair, tongues grinding away. I want to be sat next to her, preferably somewhere completely deserted and it frustrates me but then again, this is a fucking great return from someone I've only been in the company of for about ten minutes total.

We drink again after we free ourselves and my mind is beginning to examine the situation and wondering how to play this; half of it is thinking about dates and seeing that smile of hers daily while the other half is thinking about fucking her stupid when I'm at a loose end and I'm not sure which I'd prefer but I'm fairly certain I wouldn't get very far if I just told her I want some sort of no-strings sex arrangement. A vision of her tipping the remains of her drink over my head quickly flashes by.

"I'm so glad you like me still even when you're sober." I say. Creep. My mouth seems to be functioning redundantly from my brain because even though I've not decided how I want to play things, everything I've said so far makes me sound besotted already and I mentally tell myself to get a grip – which comes out physically in the form of me reaching for my pint. I glance around the pub and at Sky Sports News on the television behind the bar which happens to be showing something about the UEFA Cup draw and it gives me chance to distance myself from the last comment and change the subject.

"Ha, I'm off to Germany in a few weeks watching Bolton, it's gonna be mad!" I enthuse, but Felicity does a mock yawn and smiles at me, obviously Wanderers talk won't be on the menu when I'm in her company.

"What's that in? Rugby?" She asks and leaves me hanging for a second with a look of horror on my face before poking her tongue out and giggling again which makes me laugh too. I look into her eyes for a moment before moving to kiss her myself this time and she doesn't back away.

"Fancy another drink?" I ask when I take my lips away from hers and she nods, gently pecking me again, so I return the gesture before leaving the table for the bar feeling flustered, heart still pumping. She's doing something with her phone when I turn back to her as I'm waiting to be served and her smile has gone, replaced by a faint look of concern but I brush it aside as the drinks appear and I take them to the table. I ask her if she's okay to which she just nods, so I take my seat again and there's a bit of a silence as she stares at her juice and I passively watch a lad struggle with the fruit machine.

"Jamie, there's something I should tell you." She says, cutting through the void in proceedings, my heart misses a beat and immediately feels like it's halfway up my throat. "Oh God you're going to fucking hate me now." She adds, which only serves to make me feel worse.

"Why, what is it?" I'm trying to compose myself because if she's about to tell me something terrible then at least it'll help me make my mind up about what to do. Felicity sighs heavily and shakes her head, looking away from me, almost looking like she isn't going to say anything further. "Come on tell me, what's wrong?" This makes her wince and sigh again, but she finally looks at me, makes eye contact and holds it.

"I'm not exactly single…" Heart goes again. "In fact I'm married." Then it drops like a lump of steel.

"You *what*?!" I blurt, my chin must look like it's hit the table my mouth is open so wide, I'm actually gobsmacked, tingles of nerves rippling up through my legs as if I'm scared her partner is going to walk in any moment. Her fucking *husband,* even. "So what the fuck are you doing here then?" She looks like she's about to get upset but this is one situation where I can honestly say I'm not the one who's fucked up, for once.

"Because I like you. I liked you in town the other week, you really make me feel good in your text messages and I like you even more here today." I try really hard not to break out into a massive smile, someone I've got the hots for saying that to me does not happen often, but I suppress it.

"Yeah, but you're married. You can't be doing this!" She nods and looks a little resigned.

"I know, I'm a bitch. To you and him for doing this. I just really wanted to see you again. I want you…"

She replies, leaving me in no doubt what she meant by the last bit, the way her look of guilt was replaced in a millisecond by those flirtatious eyes and the cheeky half-smile again. *"Fucking hell, she does want no-strings..."* I think to myself and a wave of lust rises up through me. The best of both worlds. I decide to at least have a go at holding out, try and convince myself that I do have some morals lying about somewhere.

"Well, I like you too you're hot and I want you as well. But, are you sure you should be doing this Felicity? It's *really* bad." My protestations are admittedly pretty flimsy and she sees right through them.

"I know..." She whispers and moves in to kiss me again. To my credit I do hesitate, if only for a beat, but then we are kissing once more, even more passionately and I'm beginning to make a right mess of her hair. "We will have to see when we're both free then, don't you think?" She retakes her position and teases at the straw in her drink, staring at me. I smile and nod. "But one thing okay, call me anything but Felicity, I hate when it's said like that. Always makes me feel like I'm in trouble." I consider telling her she *is* in trouble, in more ways than one, but I decide to avoid a potential misunderstanding especially when I'm on for a result as cracking as this.

"Alright then, Bob, whatever you say." I grin and she laughs out loud, kicking me under the table.

"No! You know what I mean silly, just Flick or something that's what most people call me, I just hate Felicity." Flick sounds good to me. I can tell she's beginning to rush her drink which must mean she's after making tracks soon. "I'm not sure when I'll be free next but I'll be sure to let you know." Flick says and I'm happy with that, even if all this just gets put on the back burner for a while it'll still be sat there like a bonus for somewhere down the line. "I better head off I'm afraid darling, he'll be wondering where I am." I could do without the references to the husband, even if he does remain nameless, it'll start to grind away at my conscience at some point I'm sure.

"Ah alright, well I can't wait to see you again..." Which is a massive understatement considering what will probably be on the menu on our next meet. I neck the remnants of my drink as Flick finishes hers. "I should go too, Mummy will probably be wondering where I am." I roll my eyes, even though I am actually looking forward to tea it's not something I'm going to let on about. She chuckles and we both stand up in unison, sharing another kiss when we're upright. I lead us out of the pub, she's a couple of strides behind me and we just say a quick goodbye outside the front door, no kisses now we're out in the open.

Then we part company, both heading in opposite directions on Bradshawgate and as a few drops of rain begin to float down onto the road I think about what's just gone on and shake my head disbelievingly, grin a mile wide.

CHAPTER SIX

Barclays Premier League – Saturday 27th October 2007

		P	W	D	L	Pts.
16	Sunderland	10	2	2	6	8
17	Middlesbrough	10	2	2	6	8
18	Tottenham Hotspur	10	1	4	5	7
19	Derby County	10	1	3	6	6
20	Bolton Wanderers	10	1	2	7	5

Archie Knox takes charge of the team temporarily in the wake of Sammy Lee's departure as Bolton lose 2-0 at Arsenal and begin their UEFA Cup Group Stage matches with a 1-1 draw at home to Sporting Braga. Gary Megson is appointed as the new manager of Bolton Wanderers.

"It's chained to the mirror *and the* razor blade, you prick." Tom goes, still glaring at me like I've just called his Dad a nonce or something. He takes another swig of the piss-flat Carling we're drinking and shakes his head as we sit here in The Toll Bar in Horwich in the early stages of what is sure to be a long session. Wanderers don't play until tomorrow so I'm going to crash at Tom's after this and save myself the hassle of coming back up here for the game.

"Nah, it's *like a* razor blade… sounds nothin' like *and*" I tell him, though I've said it with a grin to try and make light of the situation because I know how arsey he can get about stuff like this, was only supposed to be a throw-away comment anyway after hearing the song on one of the televisions hanging from the walls in here.

"Bollocks." He spits, with the pint half tipped towards his mouth but still staring at me across the table.

"Tellin' you!" My voice pitched high. I'm trying to take the piss now because I'm not sure of myself and I can't be arsed getting into an argument about song lyrics. Wish to fuck I hadn't said owt now.

"You talk some shit you do, not got a clue, *"like"* makes no sense!" At least he's half grinning now, although that might be because he's finished his drink. "It's about doing coke, off a mirror, using a blade. Look the lyrics up, you'll see." I hold my hands up in submission, fair enough. "Anyway, sup that let's do one." He stands up and straightens out his quilted Barbour jacket in the process – the one that makes him look like he's going out pheasant shooting – then gives me another look of disdain when he sees me take a full swig of beer but then discard the glass with some still left in the bottom. I fucking can't stand the shit you get left with at the end of a flat pint especially if it's been sat there idle for ten minutes while your mate grills you about *"Morning Glory"*. He shakes his head then makes for the door and I rush to catch up with him, we leave the pub side by side and the discussion about song lyrics drifts off into the ether.

We walk round the back of the Crown Hotel to get onto Lee Lane and more pubs. I've a lot of affection for Horwich and Rivington. I used to go to school with Tom here and it's very picturesque and still fairly quaint in some parts… it's a mint piss up in the village as well. I see a pub crawl on Lee Lane as a case of the quality of the overall experience being greater than the sum of its individual pubs; Toll Bar, Flea Pit, Bowling Green, The Albert, The Saddle, Sam's and all the others (that's a lot of pubs for just one street!), none of them are especially amazing in their own right in my opinion but they all come together in one short stretch of road to make a really decent line-up.

Our time is split between either talking about the girls coming in and out of the pubs we temporarily settle in for one drink or two, or about Munich. I've sorted out our accommodation now and so all we have to do is sit back and enjoy it; a Wednesday morning flight to Germany, quick bag drop and change at the hostel which is right outside the train station we'll use to get to and from the airport, then all Wednesday evening to sample the atmosphere and get plastered. Then Thursday; looking around town, the match, followed by a sharp exit back to the airport for a plane to London and a short hop back up to Manchester. £245 each still leaves me feeling a bit aggrieved but I wasn't left with much choice and seen as the hostel is costing less than a tenner each for the night, we haven't done *too* badly.

Into The Bowling Green for our next round, a place that will always hold some fond memories for me as it was the first place I ever got drunk in – so I guess "fond" isn't the right word seen as it concluded with me projectile vomiting up a wall outside and falling asleep next to the toilet when I got home – but regardless it's still an important venue from my past. An excitable Saturday evening atmosphere has descended upon Horwich with a lot of people out and about on the lane and many of the pubs pretty well filled, so I have to do a lot of shuffling and sidestepping to get to the bar to be served. Someone's got a birthday do on in another room and I can see Tom making his way over there to see what's going on while I get the drinks in and by the time I get back to him he's already chatting to the birthday girl, resplendent in her ill-fitting dress with a bin-lid-sized *"18 today!"* badge attached to the front.

Their conversation is awkward at best, she's going on that it was actually her birthday yesterday but she was in town on the lash with the girls and that tonight it's her family get-together, *"two parties for the price of one –*

can't go wrong, can you?". Meanwhile Tom's ignoring this and trying to convince her that they've been out before but I think all sides know this is a ridiculous notion and once she realises he's not interested in asking about her night out yesterday she begins to make her excuses.

All the while I'm helping myself to the buffet, greasy mini sausage rolls and dry ham sandwiches washed down with beer. I'm a spare part here while Tom speaks to the girl and I end up daydreaming about Munich, playing scenes over in my head, trying to picture what seeing Wanderers playing in Bayern's stadium will look like or thinking about being crammed into a beer hall with hundreds of singing English and German drunkards. The forums are alive with excitement and anticipation, it's going to be legendary I can tell already.

"Erm excuse me, are you enjoying that?" This woman taps me on the shoulder and I turn round to face her with some pastry from the sausage roll stuck to my bottom lip, she looks a right battleaxe. "You're not a part of this group are you?" She goes on, the *"are you"* part sounding more like *"aaayorrr"*. I don't get a chance to answer and I must cut a very guilty looking figure, gulping the last bit of meat down heavily. "No, you're not. So can I suggest you stop eating our food and fuck off please?" She raises her voice, the *"fuck off"* forcing a projectile of spit to fire off hazardously close to my face.

People start looking around at me angrily, I just pull an apologetic expression and lay my remaining roll back on the serving plate which she watches me do and looks a bit disgusted by it. It's a good excuse to break Tom away from the birthday girl and leave though so I neck the rest of my drink and exit back onto Lee Lane with the sounds of bitter muttering and over-exaggerated tutting at our backs. Jesus, I only had a couple of sausage rolls and the locals were reaching for their pitchforks and lanterns.

A whistle-stop pub crawl ensues with a single drink each in every bar on the stretch until we reach Sam's and I'm building up to being pretty merry by this stage. I fucking need to be too because Tom seems obsessed with the birthday bird from the Bowling Green, he's been on about her since we left and keeps suggesting we go back to extract her and a randomer from there and go into Bolton with them. Once I tell him to piss off and come to his senses and that she was as rough as a robber's dog anyway he quietens down about it, her type are ten-a-penny in town. The Bolton idea sticks in my head though, stupidly, as soon as Tom mentioned it some idiotic part of my brain was already deciding that we should end up down there tonight.

A couple of bottles each in Sam's keeps us at a level and I call a taxi for as soon as possible to take us into Bolton. It turns up in no time too and we speed off up Chorley Old Road with the windows down letting wind blast our faces and Tom does his best to ignore my tipsy ramblings about how top Horwich is for a drink and how I don't go out there enough. Bradshawgate is the aim, obviously, my legs numbing a bit through drinking by the time we reach the outskirts of Bolton so it will be a relief to get out and about. There's no plan to this evening now, no ultimate destination to aim for, so we'll just flow with it and hope that it doesn't land me in a Bromley Cross mansion again. I tell the driver to pull over outside a bar in town, not that I could tell him what it's called as it seems to change its name every other week but we can start here and work our way down the street anyway.

We barely last the contents of a bottle in there it was gash, then start criss-crossing the road hopping from place to place and continuing the one drink per venue policy which ensures maximum coverage for investigating the quality of the girls in each one whilst making sure we aren't exposed to the shittiness of each one for too long. Some of them are very sparsely populated but we're in luck with a couple.

    The music in the place we're in by about half eight is absolutely blaring, to the extent where it almost felt like a buffering force trying to repel us from entering the doors at first such was the noise and vibration, I've no idea why they've cranked it up so loud tonight and it sounds even worse as it's not packed.

    Tom insists on going in rather than skipping to the next one because of the cheap drinks, *"Destination Calabria"* is on at the moment and the accompanying video plays on a big screen nearby depicting all these naughty looking girls practically fellating musical instruments. I don't mind all this new electro stuff, it's just being played a bit on the loud side for me, as in making it an actual impossibility to speak to someone stood at arm's length even by shouting at them and it's making my fillings hurt.

    We've abandoned all hope of communication and are just people-watching over eachother's shoulders; he's staring blankly somewhere while I've fixed my eyes on two proper young looking birds dancing about in the corner next to the big windows looking out onto Bradshawgate. Both of them look like clones of eachother; long blonde hair with black streaks emanating from underneath the top layer, vest tops with tits squeezed up, out and on show, black hot-pants only just beginning to cover their thin milk-bottle-white legs and matching pairs of white high-heeled shoes which in my book don't really seem to suit their outfit but I might be wrong, I usually am with shit like that. The pair of them have stern looks on their faces as they dance, to suggest that they're fully aware of the number of males gawping at them and that they're not to be fucked with.

    Phone vibrates in my jeans and it's a message from Flick asking what I'm up to and I get a sudden jolt through my body thinking about her, an even bigger one when a quick flutter of texts reveals she's also out in town for a few drinks with her mates tonight. *"The possibilities are endless..."* she tells me with a wink at the end of the message, amazing. I've decided not to tell Tom about her for the obvious reason and also because he might remember it was her that he was trying it on with in Reflex after Birmingham although I doubt that he recalls much of that evening. I'll just see how the night pans out, if he ends up completely tatered and homeward bound early again then maybe I'll go and find her but I'd have to downplay it quite a lot with all her mates being out too and just act like an old work colleague or something. Anyway, that's for later there's still a lot of life left in this night yet, especially as I re-decorated another wash basin in the toilets of the last bar we were in so I'm right on it again.

    Time and money slips by, reaching over towards midnight and neither of us appear to be flagging; this just seems to be one of those nights where your body is able to withstand more of a beating than normal. Eventually we find ourselves heading down the slope at the end of Bradshawgate onto Bank Street and you know your night will be a messy one when you end up in this part of town. The possibility of meeting up with Flick seems to have gone as she's in a bar right at the other end of the road and returning home soon but it's not really a concern to be honest – when Tom's up for a laugh and up for sticking around then I'll gladly go with that and let Flick happen another time.
    Bergeracs it is, messiness confirmed. This place has an all night licence and I've been in here a couple of times until dawn, sat outside at the back until the sun comes up then taking the bus of shame with the Saturday or Sunday morning shoppers still in clothes from the

previous night and probably reeking of ale and takeaway. Heading home not with that sense of righteous exhilaration you might get on the way back from some amazing all-night session at a superclub, but with your head bowed knowing that the rest of the weekend is a write-off because you've just spent all night drinking in a glorified toilet listening to a donked-up version of the *"Baywatch"* theme tune six or seven times over.

  We duck inside and get stocked up on booze then find a spot to prop ourselves up against which gives us a good view of the dancefloor, it is jumping as *"Mr. Brightside"* booms out and people animatedly mouth the words to whoever they're on there with and bounce around excitedly. I spend some time looking around at the people in here and at the Wanderers memorabilia that hangs up behind the bar which seems slightly out of place in somewhere like this, moaning about how bad the beer tastes to Tom.

  Leaving him to stand guard over our position, I go for a mooch around and piss about walking into different areas of the club whilst swigging from my bottle. I head off towards the back of the place, into a room where doors lead to the toilets and it looks as if there's been a leak somewhere because the floor is flooded, leaving a greasy puddle across the ground and I tiptoe through it, avoiding what appear to be… yes, yes they *are*, actual turd particles floating about in it.

  The next door leads outside to the beer garden which is also busy and awash with noise but the atmosphere seems quite good natured which isn't always a given in here. For a while I perch on the edge of a picnic table swigging rank beer and looking over at random birds for just long enough until they look in my direction and flash them a smile, without much in the way of reciprocation. I discard my empty and go back to see what

Tom's up to and see if he wants another drink, it's just started raining now as well and cooled right down.

When I get back to our position he's standing with his back to me and chatting to a very attractive looking girl, he doesn't hang around. I come over and stand next to him, grin at her then ask if he wants another one.

"Oi, you..." His new companion goes, her pretty façade tarnished somewhat by a horrible, high pitched voice. "You look like you've got a disabled mouth you do, what's up with it?" She says, the shrieking bint. I'm quite taken aback by that actually; I've never heard anything like it, fucking *disabled mouth*?

"*Right*..." I look at her as if to say I'd like her to die immediately, but I'm not getting into a scene with her in here. "Drink, Tom?" I try again but he says no and actually appears to want to stay where he is – talking to her – and she's still frowning at me I can see out of the corner of my eye. Bollocks to this, I go over to the dance floor and mingle into the group, the ever popular *"Chelsea Dagger"* is in full swing, beer is splashing everywhere and bodies are bustling into eachother, even more so as the song reaches its bombastic climax so I'm laughing and pogoing too, getting into it.

The feeling of thin fingers reaching under my shirt and around my stomach from behind makes me jump and nearly spit a mouthful of Becks over an unfortunate lad's back but I keep it in and crane my neck back to see who's responsible for this. She's fucking *hot*, whoever she is. A slender brunette has both her arms wrapped around me and she pushes her firm breasts into my back, her hips grinding up tight against my arse, she smiles and moans as she does it. This night just gets odder. She can't be thinking I'm someone else surely and she doesn't look like she's going anywhere either, so I turn round to her and we kiss, absolutely going for it with my disabled mouth, she isn't shy.

Fuck me, she isn't shy at *all*. Now she's worked one of her hands down my jeans and under my shorts and here we are completely surrounded on a packed and smoky dance floor in the middle of a club and she's wanking me off to Kasabian. Well, trying to anyway, she's struggling to get the angle with her wrist. It's a red rag to a bull, that. Through her jeans I rub her crotch firmly and she loves it, moaning and kissing more and fumbling even more keenly through my boxers.

This is an absolutely bizarre and debauched situation but fuck it, she's mint. I'm starting to work the zip of her jeans down and I feel her lace knickers with my fingertips, which I then attempt to shift to one side, but as I drag her closer to me again I feel her other arm, just fleetingly, in the wrong place – deep in my fucking pocket. I swipe my hand away and pull hers out of my jeans to reveal my house-keys, cash card and a couple of tenners in her grip.

"What the fuck's this all about then?" I shout over the music, to which she smiles innocently and just hands them back to me. I look away to put them back in my pocket and zip myself up and even though she was clearly diverting me to empty my pockets I still in some idiot way think I can somehow forget about that and we can carry on molesting eachother here in the middle of the club. When I look back up to her though she's already seeping away into the crowd, I go to Tom and he's pointing a finger in the face of the tool he was with and looking pissed off, ask him what's going on and he tells me she was trying to get into his coat pocket while his back was turned.

I'm livid; this place is full of rats. I storm over to the doormen who look down on me with absolute disdain as one of their other colleagues smashes past me dragging a pissed up lad out of the club and launches him, airborne, out onto Bank Street. I struggle to steady myself for a few seconds, shaking my head in protest.

"Do you know there's birds in here robbing from lads?..." I splutter, feeling so aghast at what's going on in the club and also how I've just been nearly flung to the floor by one of the bouncers that I don't sound very coherent. I'm certainly not going to start explaining to them how I came to find her hand in my pockets either. "They're robbing from people, at least two of them in there, two girls..." Tom's stood behind me but not really saying anything to back me up and in front of me I've got these three fat bald bastards looking at me gravely.

"To be honest mate, I couldn't give a fuck." One of them replies, his cold words slam into me like an executioner's bullet and I look at them all helplessly. Balls to this, night's over for me and Tom concurs. We head out and up the street slagging the place, the girls, Britain and all of humanity off then go and get a doner calzone each from the nearby takeaway and carry on our ranting all the way to the taxi rank on the other side of town, walking through completely dead streets as the rain sweeps down heavily and starts to fill up the corners of our pizza boxes with water as we eat from them. The misery of winter is beginning to very visibly roll in.

CHAPTER SEVEN

Sunday 28th October 2007

The pair of us slouch solemnly in our chairs nursing a beer each in The Greenwood, our usual haunt for home games, while Ray – more of an occasional attendee at home matches these days – ridicules us to increase the misery, the tight old get. We both feel worse for wear after last night and still pissed off about the two girls in Bergeracs though we do laugh at the disabled mouth comment, it was totally random. This old building has hosted many a drunken session for us; its wooden bar, walls and features, stained carpeted floor and pool room round the side always feels comfortable and familiar to me but I'm definitely not fancying any of that for today's meeting with Aston Villa. We often hear stories of it shutting down imminently but it never quite happens, thankfully. Almost every time we come in here we bump into someone who has some "inside knowledge" about the place changing hands soon and the new owner wanting to bulldoze it but they're yet to be proven right.

  All the energy and enthusiasm I had yesterday has gone now and the pint is tough work to get down, I'm glad to get back into fresh air. We have to file past a group of fans outside the pub who are taking advantage of the fact they can still stand outside wearing only shirts or thin jackets before everyone's match day quarter-to-threes – or in today's case, 1pm on a frigging Sunday – revert to being spent huddled inside the pub grimly coming to the realisation that to get the match today they'll have to leave now and get piss-wet through and frozen or else miss kick off.

  We're off down a side street away from Chorley New Road then down by playing fields leading to the ground and gradually the spires of the Reebok's floodlights come into view over terraced rooftops, giant white pylons tilted distinctively towards eachother keeping watch over the pitch. Middlebrook, the retail park where the Reebok Stadium is situated, must be the windiest place on earth. All year round regardless of the season or temperature there's basically a gale running across the whole site coming down off the hills and over Red Moss so you're constantly fighting against it. Tom and I exchange expletives as the wind shoves us in the back jolting us forward while we pass disinterested shoppers on the last leg of our journey and cross the car park towards the ground.

There's not much of a queue to speak of outside our turnstile which is a worry seen as it's not long until kick off so it looks like we're in for a sparse crowd as if it's only the League Cup on a Tuesday night or something. Tickets are scanned in then we pass inside and Tom goes to the bookies while me and Ray hang back and stare up at the monitors looking for team news before he comes back telling me he's gone for a two-nil Wanderers win with Davies getting the first goal. His Dad tells him he's just wasted another two quid.

Our seats are right down at the front of Lofthouse Stand Lower – the East Stand – and have been for seven seasons now. We bought season tickets as soon as we both had jobs that paid enough to afford them which conveniently turned out to be our first season back in the Premier League, before then we just had to pick and choose which games we went to. They're fairly centrally located so we can see right across the length of the half way line to where the manager stands screaming out at the lads. We've seen some fucking great things in this stadium since then; my personal favourite is when the underused Jared Borgetti scored a stoppage time winner against Lokomotiv Plovdiv in our first ever proper European game a couple of years ago, if you don't count playing Ancona in the Anglo-Italian Cup in 1993 as our first, that is.

It felt like we'd genuinely arrived as a top level football club playing that first UEFA Cup match but we were far from our best and it looked like we were only going to scrape a 1-1 draw until Borgetti stuck one in right in front of where I was sat behind the net as a one-off for that game and it went crazy. I remember legging it down the steps right to the front where the players were celebrating and jumped up onto the barriers with loads of other fans clambering up with me, grabbing eachother and falling over seats, swinging shirts and scarves around in the air like a proper European crowd.

    Tom was with me too but he doesn't agree, reckons I only say that's my favourite because it happened so recently and we wouldn't have even been there to do it if it wasn't for beating Ipswich 4-1 in 2001 to keep us in the top division and that was his favourite match. It was a great day but I nearly melted it was so hot and so bright I couldn't even look down at my white shirt without squinting.

    Today seems a far cry from those heady days though. There's an underlying buzz around with people talking about the European games and the Munich tie in particular but other than that there's little to write home about yet again and there's a feeling that many people's minds are still in bed. Turns out there's only 18,000 on, less than we'd get at Burnden Park sometimes and there was no trouble at all finding a spare seat for Ray. It's one of those matches where you can tell within the first few minutes what sort of atmosphere it's going to be and today it is virtually silent apart from sporadic bursts of noise from the lads congregated under the big screen.

    There's stadium-wide apathy about our new manager Gary Megson, as there was at the Braga game midweek just after his appointment was announced and it only takes me a few minutes to have been fully briefed by people sat around me about his mostly uninspiring record managing other teams. It leaves me ashen faced and quiet while Tom gets into a debate with the people behind us about whether we should persevere with Sammy Lee's tactics or go back to what made us successful under Allardyce, but all that is going to be up to Megson.

Actually I love the two blokes who sit behind us, Tony and his son Anthony. They've travelled all the way up here from Shrewsbury for every home league game for the seven years I've had my seat and further still beyond that and always brighten up the day regardless of how crap the showing on the pitch is. Tony will without fail bring up his time playing football for the Army at some point in every game, usually after a player goes down like a sack of shit and starts rolling about as if he's mortally injured – because according to Tony, playing for the Army you'd get up and carry on even if you'd broken your leg otherwise they'd play on around or straight over you. Makes me laugh every time he tells that one.

Anthony meanwhile inexplicably blows a gasket at around the same point during the second half of almost every game even if we're winning; he ends up jumping out of his seat absolutely laying into the players for not clearing their lines fast enough after we defend an opposition attack. *"Push out you lazy fuckers! Get out now!"* He fumes, frantically sweeping his arm across the length of the pitch trying to shove the players further upfield as if they'd all become Subbutteo figures.

When he first started doing it I thought it was a bit weird and was amazed that his Dad didn't seem too arsed about his language but he's invariably right because over the years Wanderers have developed this mentality where the further into the second half we go the more we seem to get nervous and sit back, to the stage where I've lost count of the number of times we've given away goals and points in the last ten minutes. Anthony usually sees this happening around the hour mark and the players get it in the neck from him, it's brilliant.

We're finally roused out of our seats as Anelka curls home a free kick in the first half, a great finish right into the top corner, but it's one of those situations where because you've not been animated and up out of your seat all game you find yourself just clapping and waving your arms in the air a bit within seconds of the player beginning to celebrate his goal rather than going mental and grabbing everyone around you. I tell Tom after we sit back down that if we're going to do anything this season then Anelka is crucial to it all because he's on a completely different level to anyone else we've got at the club, hardly a revelation that, then just as I'm saying it he misses a sitter immediately after the restart and I look a bit of a dick but everyone knows it's true really.

    This is yet another match that I'm just coasting through this season, not living every second as has been the case in the past. There's just something not quite right this time around and I just stand there at half time in front of my seat listening to the other few scores coming through on the speakers and listlessly watching the substitutes have a kick about, seeing Stelios ball-juggling by himself wearing his woolly hat and wondering why he's not being given much of a look-in recently.

    At least something happens out of the ordinary this time though, the opposition don't leave it until the last few minutes to score against us. In fact it is only about ten minutes into the second half when Villa get a throw-in which should really have been for us, cross into the area and their striker equalises by chesting it past Jussi, the cheeky bastard. Anthony hadn't even had chance to get stuck into the players either and there's a feeling of resignation about the whole thing as we sink back into our seats with Tony assuring everyone that Villa will go on and get another one here no doubt.

    Thankfully they don't, it ends one each, but I'd lost interest long before the final whistle anyway so it's actually quite a relief to head off at the end, filing away up the hill away from the stadium as we've done so many times but just not talking about the match, it is forgotten already. There's a bus going towards Bolton and home very conveniently coming in our direction as we make it back up onto Chorley New Road so I get on it, wave Ray off who's already striding away and tell Tom I'll see him next week. The bus makes good pace, not an awful lot of traffic to speak of which is very unusual seen as a match has just ended, another indictment of the way our crowds are dropping and I'm glad to be going home.

CHAPTER EIGHT

Barclays Premier League – Wednesday 7th November 2007

		P	W	D	L	Pts.
16	Middlesbrough	12	2	3	7	9
17	Tottenham Hotspur	12	1	5	6	8
18	Wigan Athletic	12	2	2	8	8
19	Bolton Wanderers	12	1	4	7	7
20	Derby County	12	1	3	8	6

Bolton Wanderers head into their UEFA Cup tie with Bayern Munich still with only a single league win all season. 1-1 draws with Aston Villa and West Ham United in the Premier League sandwich a 1-0 home defeat to Manchester City which ends their League Cup campaign.

    It would be fair to say that I'm not the greatest flier in the world. I cack it when there's any heavy in-flight bumps and for some reason whenever there's an announcement from the cockpit I find myself panicking that the pilot is going to declare that the plane is going out of control and we are about to crash. It's only quite recently that I've started to feel confident about even leaving my seat during a journey because I'd convinced myself that any slight movement on my part would make the aircraft unstable. Returning from a family holiday in Corfu once when I was a kid, I sat frozen in my seat for the entire three hour flight grasping the napkin that came with the in-flight meal because I had told myself that if I shuffled about or let go of the napkin then we would crash. The sheet of tissue was absolutely ravaged by the time we touched down in Manchester.

Thankfully I've improved a little since then and ditched many of these kinds of pointless superstitions and rituals that I used to put myself through to avoid some sort of catastrophe as if my actions would dictate fate either way. Although as Tom and I step aboard the British Airways flight to Munich in Wednesday afternoon rain at Manchester I fleetingly touch the outside of the fuselage on my way past which I always told myself was another way to avert disaster. It is ludicrous.

Tom claims the window seat immediately and I listen intently to the stewardess giving the emergency demonstration but he doesn't bother watching because he says she isn't fit enough so he just sits there with his eyes closed, plugged into his iPod. I'm looking forward to getting to Germany and back to Munich for my second visit; everywhere I went over there impressed me with how clean, hi-tech and reliable everything was, only then I was there alone and inhibited whereas this time I'm going along with an estimated five-thousand other Wanderers fans for our biggest European awayday yet.

I squint to stare at the tall buildings nestled in Manchester city centre on our departure which is mercifully peaceful despite the wet weather and after all the build up we're at last bound for Germany. There are quite a few Bolton fans onboard plus one or two Everton as well travelling to Nuremberg for their game tomorrow and a lively, expectant atmosphere is brewing. The tiny cans of lager the airline sells are being worked through at a steady pace from the minute they're made available, even though two each for me and Tom come to nearly twenty quid and are small enough to finish off in three gulps. There's not actually much talk about the match that I can hear, it's all just about getting tuned in when people finally hit the fabled Munich beer halls that everyone must have been going on about from the moment the draw was made and my excitement about the whole thing completely eradicates any sort of flying nerves that may have been waiting to get to me.

Our approach into Munich after a little less than the advertised two hours' flight-time looks amazing out of the window as a clear winter's evening draws in and casts a deep red haze over the horizon. It provides a stunning backdrop to the Alps which we can see in the distance across the right wing, a sight enhanced by *"Supersonic"* and *"Rock 'n' Roll Star"* blasting through my headphones, winding me up. The landing is perfect and someone shouts *"Come on you White men!"* as we turn off the runway prompting a few cheers go up, I'm absolutely jumping inside and can't wait to get out into Munich, I look at Tom and I can tell he's feeling the same. Two coiled springs waiting to unleash into Munich and get in amongst the travelling fans.

I'll let the Dolph Lundgren look-a-like Passport Officer off for giving me a funny look when he examines my passport, I do look fuck all like I appear on the photograph with giant spiky hair and a stubbly beard of years ago so I just say a grateful *"danke"* when he hands it back and we go straight out into arrivals since we're only carrying hand luggage. There's a scene of mild chaos and frustration as the latest batch of arriving Bolton fans try to make sense of the ticket machines and gates that lead to the U-Bahn station – no staff in sight – and a bloke next to us considers jumping it but someone standing with him puts him off by telling him the Polizei will shove him in jail for the night if he does.

I quickly pay for two single tickets for me and Tom out of a machine round the corner before it gets overrun by people and we head for the escalators to the platform. Finally, one intrepid Wanderer finds out how to purchase tickets by miraculously converting the ticket machine's screen to English and all of a sudden there's Tageskarten aplenty and a mob of them are bounding down behind us, spirits raised again. A train sweeps in almost immediately bringing with it a huge gust of cool air down the tunnel and we pile onboard, knowing the locals are watching us curiously and it makes me feel we're in some way superior and untouchable.

But then there's a sag in excitement, an hour's train journey into the city through pitch black Munich suburbs punctuated only by the occasional outpost of a deserted station and everything goes a bit quiet with very little to do or talk about. Tom kicks me in the shin sitting opposite me just as I'm starting to feel my eyes getting heavy and I glare at him about to ask what he's playing at, but he gestures with his eyes at a bloke sitting adjacent to us. I look to my left and there's a smart business-type sitting typing away at a laptop on his knee, swigging from a can of Jack Daniels & Coke. A *can!*

"We are getting on those before we leave here mate!" We're laughing incredulously, JD & Coke in a can, never seen the likes of it. The guy polishes four of them off before we make it to our destination and I wonder how he's still able to do whatever he's doing on the laptop because I'd be more than likely on the way to being trashed by then. There's a hustle and the noise level picks up, people are getting up and starting for the doors, we must be close at last and sure enough we pull into the Hauptbahnhof which causes a mass exodus out of the carriage as soon as the doors part.

I've got the pocket map I printed off the internet before we left home with a red line drawn from the station we're in straight to our hostel a couple of streets away and I lead Tom out of the building to get our first taste of Munich, which on the evidence of this first glimpse is surprisingly dead. Tall buildings surround us on all sides but all of their lights are out for the night, a vast taxi-rank and bus station takes up most of the approach area but there's not a single vehicle present, no people moving about other than our train-load and certainly no distant sounds of hordes of chanting Bolton. This is all a bit of a let-down but I reassure Tom and myself that all the places we want to be are a trek from here so we don't have to worry that we've wasted our time just yet.

It is as if someone just powered up a sat-nav in my head, because the minute we emerge from the main doors of the station I remember exactly where I am from my visit two years previously and the route to our accommodation, the same place I stayed at last time, is clear as day to me. I eagerly stride to our destination; Tom a couple of steps behind less sure than I am that I know where I'm going, we hurry across a road that must be three times wider than anything back home, hurdle the seemingly abandoned tram lines and make it to the other side just as a lone taxi materialises from nowhere and hurtles by.

"Just round this corner pal." I say over my shoulder and sure enough just as we turn into a dimly lit narrow side-street, there is our hostel a few hundred meters further down with welcomingly bright lights emanating from its reception cutting an illuminated swathe through the still darkness of the alleyway. I remember it being a good laugh with all sorts of different people socialising in the bar which was of great comfort when I was here alone but now everything feels different; with Tom I don't have to get to know anyone else, we're just here for beer and football. The cheerful German girl at reception takes our details and hands over our room keys and Tom seems glad that we are in somewhere that actually resembles a good hotel, up until now I think when he heard the term "hostel" he conjured up images of stinking shit-tips full of cranks and foreign weirdos.

Our rooms are clean and tidy, the only apparent downside being that we are sharing with four other people in bunks but there's no-one else around when we drop our stuff off so it's no problem. I have a quick wash in the bathroom and come out to see Tom crouched in the middle of the room, his bag strewn all over the bottom bunk furthest from the door, lacing up his brand new blue adidas Gazelle Indoors; they look superb but we both bought a pair at the same time last week so I decided against bringing the same trainers as him along. I place my bag on the bed above his and start carefully unpacking the contents, hoisting off the sweaty t-shirt I travelled in and replacing it with a plain shirt and my aqua-blue Lacoste v-neck which I'm still enjoying getting a lot of use out of despite having it for ages and some of the shape beginning to fall out of it.

"Can't beat a bit of knitwear now, can you?!" I say to Tom laughing and take a look out of the window which only presents me with the same dark and deserted scene we saw upon arrival.

"Let's fucking get on it." He orders, springing upright and throwing his thin anorak on over his polo-shirt. I'm not convinced that combination will be enough to shield him from the temperature but anyway he's eager to get on with proceedings. I zip my jacket right up to the chin and we head out, literally bouncing down the corridors to the lift. On the way out I grin at the receptionist and shout *"tschüss!"* which makes some of the other guests sat quietly at the internet terminals look up at us, she smiles and waves looking slightly baffled. Out the doors we go, back onto the main road outside the station and start towards the centre of Munich in the cold darkness.

It's gone ten when I check the time after a few minutes of us both jogging down the pavement, trying to keep warm more than anything as the cold has suddenly become truly bitter. Now I can understand why there's not many people out on the streets, although as we finally close in on the squares in the centre we do see small batches of English wrapped up in hats and scarves cantering to wherever they're headed. We are aiming for the *Hofbrauhaus*, a world-famous beer hall well known for its lederhosen-clad oompah bands and gigantic beer steins, but we are struggling to find it seen as I've gone and left the map in the hostel. The only thing I do remember about it from the map is that it's on the same side as and nearby to the grandiose Town Hall complete with the very intricate looking Glockenspiel which I had spent over an hour gawping at in the sunshine in 2005, but now it will barely feature as a footnote in our plans.

I lead us away from the huge building into another darkened street that has the wind coming right down its path so as we turn the corner our faces are immediately slapped with cold gusts and daggers of rain that seem to be travelling horizontally. I swear and cover my face with my arm, shuffling across the street to the other side which looks like it will offer us a little more cover under some scaffolding.

"Fuck me, this is ridiculous." I moan to Tom who looks absolutely frozen. "First bar we see we are going in, yeah?" He nods with a look of relief and we continue up the street which has blue and white chequered flags hanging from high above, now being thrashed all over the show by the weather. We turn off as soon as possible to get out of the wind's path at least and a pair of easily identifiable Bolton fans are a few yards in front strolling away from us, a man with his arm around a woman walking slowly and huddled up.

"Scuse' me mate any idea where this Hofbrauhaus place is?" I shout to the bloke, breaking into a jog to reach them, they look a lot better prepared than we do with their matching woolly hats and club scarves. They both seem pretty cheerful, considering.

"Alright lads, yeah it's only down here and off to the left, it's massive you can't miss it. I think half of the

Reebok is in there too from what I've heard." The man says, chuckling to himself and his partner smiles at us.

"Oh thanks very much, was worried we'd end up out here all night looking for it. Are you going there too?" I'm unable to keep still trying to battle against the cold.

"No, no. Probably a bit too raucous for us, we'll leave that to you younger lot!" And he pats my shoulder. I laugh and thank them both, tell them to enjoy their evenings then me and Tom scoot off where we were directed, jogging again feeling renewed enthusiasm now we know where we are supposed to be going. Finally there are some signs of life, with a few people dotted about whilst the pavements are lined with parked cars and as soon as we turn left as told, there is our target, a huge white building that looks like the type of place you'd traditionally associate with Germany and bedecked with the same blue and white flags we saw before. Between bursts of wind I can hear familiar chants coming from the place, a rolling wave of *"White Army"* building to a crescendo. Tom cheers next to me and we both stride up to the doors.

"Raucous", the couple outside suggested. They barely came close. Our entry to the building is given a ceremonial feeling as we walk between rows of police dressed up to a man as Robocop, every new customer given a serious eyeballing by each one of them through their darkened visors and then rounded off by a cameo appearance through the lens of the final copper's video camera who is busy recording everything. Then at last we are through the main doors into the beer hall itself and it's a total riot in here; the whole place has been completely taken over by Wanderers fans, everywhere I look there's someone in a Bolton or an England shirt hopping about, singing and shouting, raising large beer steins skywards.

Some of them are stood up on the tables stamping their feet, one is even attempting to swing from the chandelier-type light fittings hanging from the elderly building's ceiling but to the relief of most of the people stood near him he can't get a good enough grip to stay attached. Giant England flags are rigged up to every available space, the initials of the team's name stencilled into each of the four white spaces upon the flag or a random district of our fine town emblazoned across the horizontal red bar of the St. George's Cross. The noise is huge and rattles around the whole scene, it is boiling hot and there isn't a single space to sit and drink anywhere, while if there is a bar I can't see one, nor can I pick out anyone serving drinks.

We move further inside and make our way towards the back of the room where there is a gap, past a boundary of people stood recording the party on their mobile phones, some of whom appear to be locals in awe at the spectacle. Or depravity. Whatever.

"Jesus mate where are we going to find a drink in this place? I can't see anyone serving…" I say to Tom, but he's not listening as he's seen someone he recognises in amongst the throng.

"Hey it's Greeny lad! Ha! Can't believe he's in here!" Tom starts forward to push back into the crowd to get to him. Paul Green, I haven't seen him since the brief meeting in Ikon after the Birmingham game. He's a fairly short and stocky lad from Westhoughton with a buzzcut and an accent that often seems to come very close to toppling over into full on Wigan. It has been a while since I've been in the company of Paul for any length of time, not that this is such a bad thing. Tom's known him longer than me as they're both Horwich regulars and we have ended up going to a few matches with him in the past but they only seem to hang around together these days when I'm not about. He's a proper coke head, pure and simple.

Each to their own, I'm not too arsed what people do to enjoy themselves of an evening but I'm just not down with the whole coke thing, it seems like every fucker's at it at the moment too, but from what I can see it just turns people into lunatics.

I know he was the one who set Tom up with some before an away last season and he went round the fucking bend; I mean proper *"Apocalypse Now"* stuff. It was embarrassing to see him literally *crawling* around in the back streets of Horwich in tears after we came back from a hammering at Old Trafford shouting that we were all twats for leaving him behind, which was bollocks anyway. But it got plain scary when he was jumping in front of cars on Lee Lane trying to pick fights with the drivers and kicking out at buses as they sped by, grabbing me to tell me he wanted to kill me one minute, then that he loved me like a brother the next, it went on for hours. Took Tom weeks to get over that night and I thought he was trying to keep away from Paul and all that shit but clearly I was mistaken. If he starts going down that route again then me and him have got a problem.

Tom shakes Paul's hand and they pat eachother's backs, starting a conversation as I stand at the back looking on, can't hear anything they're talking about but they point at me a couple of times and I nod towards Paul with a polite smile. Tom threads his way back towards me in a hurry shaking his head.

"Fucking stopped serving in here! Greeny lad said they're closing up because of all the trouble they've had." I swear loudly. I'm dying for a beer.

"You're joking, we've done nothing wrong. Fuck this we need another bar then." I'm already turning for the front door and out into the frozen night again to continue our search for a drink.

"Yeah man definitely, Paul knows this place with a load of bars, he's heading out there now let's get in a taxi with him." That wasn't part of my plan at all but Tom looks right up for it and it's not like my idea of coming here has worked out anyway so my opinion won't carry much weight right now. I follow on behind them, delayed a little by the mass of people still all over the place singing old Wanderers songs and seemingly not too bothered by the fact that they won't be getting any more booze out of this place tonight. Four of us leave the Hofbrauhaus and appear back onto the windswept street; Paul leading us towards a group of parked taxis, followed by Tom and one of Paul's mates, Chris, who I've not seen since the United debacle.

We're in a minibus within minutes, Paul sits in the passenger seat giving the driver his destination but I can't quite hear what he says.

"Fuckin' bang on this place, apparently there's a load of clubs on one complex. Can't go wrong really." We're told as we speed off towards a main road away from town. I'm frustrated that I've not actually had a drink here in Munich yet but at least we are actually heading somewhere and not finding our way around unfamiliar streets in weather that doesn't seem to be getting any better. Tom's chatting to Chris so I'm just looking out of the window at the sights as they speed by in a watery haze.

"So how've you been Jamie mate, not seen you in ages!" Paul goes, craning his neck over the seats again.

"Yeah not bad cheers, it's been months hasn't it." I'm not his biggest fan after all that went on in the past but there's no point being hostile, especially if this place he's got in mind comes good. "Desperate for a beer though pal, you know…" I continue, adding a bit of a laugh.

"Yeah me too, only had one in that beer hall it was impossible to get a drink in there. Don't worry though this next place will see you right." He nods excitedly at the taxi driver too as if he's part of the conversation as well. Makes me laugh, he seems alright Paul tonight, to be honest. The journey takes us quite far out of the centre and we alight outside what looks to me like a fairground that has long since closed down; stone walls surround the complex covered with overlapping rotten and torn flyers advertising forgotten club nights and events, while in front of us lies the entrance under a battered wooden archway. I hand Tom a few Euros to put towards the taxi and we proceed, not another soul in sight as yet. The scene opens out into a wide courtyard bordered by darkened and lifeless facades, but a faint and unmistakable dull thumping coming from somewhere signifies that there must be at least one of these places actually open.

    Some commotion to our right and a slice of light appearing grabs our attention and we turn towards it, a door has opened up and it illuminates a cabin that looks like some sort of box office and the silhouettes of a couple of doormen who must have been stood there all along, a gaggle of people stumble out into the night laughing.

    "I think we're on lads." Chris goes, already aiming for the light which to be honest could lead us into who knows what, but our options don't look too varied right now. We get to the doors, the bouncers are blank faced even when I acknowledge one of them but don't seem like they're about to turn us away and the four of us crowd around a small glass pane behind which an extremely pretty girl sits, she disinterestedly comes out with something in German, barely looking up at us.

    "Erm, we're English…" I offer dumbly, I mean my German is probably strong enough to ask for the four of us to go in at least or even to tell her I don't speak much German, but that's all I can muster. Shirking the chance to impress her or the lads with some local lingo when the moment of truth came.

"Ah, okay guys. It is ten Euro to enter, then all drinks are free with this token." She replies, I'm a big fan of her accent. Sounds like a good deal to me too as we produce the notes and swap them for a stamp on the backs of our hands and the said tokens, which are actually old beer bottle tops with a symbol painted on them. Inside we go, the sound of some unknown but competent dance music gradually getting louder. We pass through two pairs of blue fire doors and out onto steps leading down into the main room… populated by dozens of Wanderers fans. I'm a bit bemused really seen as there was no sign of life outside let alone Bolton fans but here they are, many of them wearing the shirt, some of them sporting "Campo wigs" and a few of them dancing around heroically on the dance floor in front of cheering onlookers.

More Wanderers flags adorn the scene too, including one that has found its way behind the bar. Paul looks pretty pleased with himself and finally we can get on it, straight to the bar we go and to our astonishment, *every* drink is free with the tokens so there's no time to waste. Two bottles of beer each and at Tom's request a shot of Jagermeister for the lot of us. The shot is downed within seconds of the liquid making acquaintances with the glass and I'm already tearing into the first beer to quench the frustrated thirst of the last couple of hours.

Tom spots somewhere to sit and we make ourselves comfy on a length of couch that stretches across the back wall of the place with some high tables in front of us, swap a few hellos with some of the other English lads around us then get stuck into the drinking. I've chosen to go with Tyskie in here and it's going down very nicely indeed, my opening barrage of two bottles and a shot lasted barely five minutes at best and I'm off to the bar again for reinforcements, same again please.

To be fair this place is a dive, I mean it makes the old Hawthorns look like Es Paradis; the furniture is battered, the floor is sticky and the dark blue walls drip with condensation as the techno pumps out and the punters, probably now hailing from as diverse a range of places as Munich, Warsaw, Little Hulton and Tonge Moor, shuffle about and drink themselves silly. Basically, it's just what we were looking for. I rejoin the other three and we're having a right laugh at it all, the craziness of being out in the middle of Europe to watch Wanderers and celebrating that fact deep in some hole in a forgotten part of Bavaria.

The quick drinking goes right to our heads which was the plan because we feel like we're playing catch-up with the rest of Munich here and our small table is rapidly filling up with empty bottles and shot glasses. Tom's latest return from the bar saw him with another couple of bottles and a JD & coke, we are going to be properly trashed tonight, it is one after another for some time.

Down at the bar a couple of lads look like they're trying to chat up two girls who've appeared from nowhere. Actually thinking about it, there's a distinct lack of females in here. Then I notice that these two chumps, muscle-bound and looking like right players, are actually both wearing little black leather bum bags. I snap my vision back round to the others who have just clocked it too and we fall about laughing, what a pair of tools. They even look like they might be in luck with the two birds too which is an absolute travesty. I break off and make for the loos while the others continue to cackle on about the scene at the bar.

I go into a cubicle for a piss, it's rare that I'll go to a urinal, I hate performing in public. My head is spinning quite nicely and the excitement about the rest of the evening, about tomorrow and the match continues to grow to the point where I've actually got butterflies thinking about it. My attention is grabbed by a conversation going on back out at the urinals.

"Ahh Bolton Wanderers hooligans, ja?!" One of the locals goes and I laugh to myself.

"Haha no just here for the match tomorrow mate, you a Bayern Munich fan?" Comes the reply, followed by a grunt of disgust made by the German.

"No way! I am a supporter of Koln. I hate those fucks. Go Bolton!" I finish off and go back outside, raising a fist and cheering at the Wanderers and the Koln fan, who both do the same in return, I love it in here. I emerge back into the club and clearly something's happened in the short time I've been away, as the two girls who had been at the bar being chatted up by the bumbag boys are now up on the tables in front of Paul, Chris and Tom, dancing. I rush back over to our area and rub my hands laughing my tits off; Tom grabs me when I get over there, also howling.

"Mate, this is amazing! How'd this happen?" I shout over the music, not taking my eyes off the two sets of bare milky-white legs now right at my eye-level in front of me as they prance about. One of the girls looks at me upon my return so I pull my tongue out at her and she does the same back, followed by a dirty little smile and a wink. Naughty girl.

"Chris went down there for a drink, butted into their conversation with the two clowns at the bar and told them to come up here. They just climbed straight up onto the tables and started dancing!" Tom responds, finishing off yet another bottle and discarding it on a table next to us. There are empties everywhere; good job there's no sign of trouble in here because it would be carnage.

"Result." I re-take my seat and just watch these two as they carry on dancing with eachother, bang in time with the music and posing for Paul who's taking photos and videos of them on his phone. They dance back-to-back for the benefit of the camera, it's all happening too; writhing up against eachother, stroking fingers slowly down tightly packed tops and flicking their long dark hair all over the place. They're up there for at least five or six songs, gaining quite a crowd as well, until a few of the onlookers climb up on the tables too trying to dance with them and they seem to lose the will to carry on so they lower themselves off their mounts giving everyone a full view of their tiny knickers in the process, a goodbye present to us all. Top show that, but now with a bunch of English lads up on the tables stumbling around and waving their arms in the air it's not quite as appealing, especially if one of them falls off in our direction.

We agree to drink up and return to the city centre, curtailing the night somewhat but Tom's right when he says the main event is tomorrow and there's no point getting too wrecked and ending up lost miles out of town. We wade through the empties and the Wanderers fans scrambling to get up onto the tables then thread our way back outside into the blustery darkness, over two hours was spent in there and the amount we consumed for the equivalent of about eight quid made it more than worth it. We walk back to the main road for a taxi discussing which of the two dancing birds was the better looking.

Despite us all being hammered as it is, the plan is for a swift drink back at the hostel before Paul and Chris go back to their digs for a few hours' sleep in preparation for meeting up again and really getting into Munich tomorrow before the game. Paul has surprised me tonight, he's being a right laugh and there's been no mention of narcotics at all during the night which is a bonus. There's a few taxis parked up outside the main gates of the complex and we pile into one, heading back towards the Hauptbahnhof close to our hostel.

The looks I get from the others as we return to the hostel to find the whole reception and bar area in darkness and everywhere closed down are grim enough to stop a clock.

"You've really shat out here Jamie mate, what the fuck?" Tom says, almost whispering as if he's going to wake everyone up.

"I don't believe it, I'm certain it was open most of the night last time." I protest, arms out-stretched and turning to the others, it has gone 1:30am now but I'm truly convinced that I was in here until the very early hours one night in 2005, though nobody looks like they believe me.

"Fuck this we'll serve ourselves, come on..." Paul decides and before anyone can say anything he's off towards the bar, skipping past the tables and striding round the side to the swing-door leading behind the counter. Chris laughs hysterically and runs around to join him; Paul reaches for a few pint glasses and starts pumping Erdinger out into them, making a real hash of it too. Me and Tom are stood on the public side of the bar, aghast for a few seconds and then cracking up too – especially as Paul serves me three quarters of a pint of froth and a quarter of furiously fizzing lager. Tom's is marginally better and we struggle to get at the liquid as our faces end up covered in foam. Paul loses his temper and swears at the pumps which has me laughing out loud, he gives up the attempts at pulling pints and turns his attention to the spirits, rattling the upturned vodka in the optics to no avail.

"Oi, oi, get on this..." Paul is all over the Jagermeister machine and manhandling a large green bottle of the stuff; Chris goes for the other one and yanks it away from its moorings. I can't believe we're doing this. Paul rips off the rubber seal, has a swig and winces then passes it to Tom who does the same. I take a gulp and it burns badly, Christ it tastes rank and I feel every last molecule of it heading towards my gut.

"Come on we can't stay here and drink these we'll get fucking banged up." I say, if someone catches us doing this then our Munich trip is well and truly over. Thankfully the others agree although Paul has one final attempt at the Erdinger with more success, he pours two almost passable three-quarter-pints and re-emerges with Chris, catching up with us as we venture back out into the streets carrying two pints of lager and – ridiculously – two full jumbo bottles of Jagermeister straight off the optics.

We stroll around in the streets of Munich swigging from the pints then taking a sip of Jagermeister, hiding them under our coats when anyone passes by. I take a long gulp of the sweet viscous liquid and it finally makes me heave, I've had enough of that now and offer it around but no-one wants it funnily enough so I set it down on the windowsill of the next shop that we pass – it happens to be a pharmacy which we all find hilarious. I wash down the taste of the Jager with the last of one of the pints of Erdinger and chuck the empty in a bin. The fresh air has really made the alcohol go to my head now and I'm starting to stumble all over the place, which nearly leads me to trip over the outstretched legs of a tramp who's lying up in the entrance to a closed down shop.

"Fuck me, sorry mate!" I slur at him and he mumbles something unintelligible back at me.

"Ey up pal, here have this." Paul moves in besides me and hands over the other container-full of Jagermeister which makes the tramp's eyes absolutely light up.

"Danke, danke! Vielen dank!" He beams, gladly wrenching the bottle from Paul's hands and taking a hearty gulp. The four of us laugh our heads off and our new friend does too, holding the bottle to the air. "Auf dich! Auf England!" He toasts loudly, then takes another huge slug of the stuff. Tom is leaning on Chris' shoulder unable to stand up he's laughing so much and probably as wrecked as me.

"If this chap survives the night drinking that then I'll be fucking amazed." I give him a thumbs up before turning away and carrying on up the street followed by the others, each of whom say goodbye to the bloke who must think Christmas has come early. Once around the next corner a Burger King looms into view and it's open too. Our laughing is replaced by cheers and sighs of relief as if four parched explorers in the desert had just stumbled upon a life saving oasis. We pace across the empty road and go straight inside the still busy restaurant and I find myself swaying as I stare up at the menu boards, drenched in bright light which makes my head spin and surrounded by a dozen foreign voices.

 A few minutes later I'm slumped with my head against the windows chewing slowly through a cheeseburger that appears to be filled with jalapenos, I don't know what I ordered or how as I'm in a total daze. The others are dotted around different parts of the restaurant for some reason, all of us extremely worse for wear and very slowly lifting burgers and fries to our mouths, unable to look up and face the bright, piercing lights. I think to myself that this burger would probably be really nice to eat sober as it seems to taste a lot better than ones at home but that is mixed in with thoughts of knowing that I'm truly wrecked here and a horrendous hangover is surely due tomorrow – but how the hell am I going to find my way back to my bed anyway and worst of all, am I going to get caught for helping to rob the bar when I do?

CHAPTER NINE

Thursday 8th November 2007

Opening my eyes only serves to let in a blaze of daylight and it feels like hell so I close them again and plan how to get through the next few seconds of my life. The headache is indescribable and it just seems as if my brain is trying to ram forward out of my forehead onto the pillow, eyes spinning listlessly behind red hot lids. I feel myself drifting back into sleep which would have been a godsend but just as my muscles begin to relax again I'm shook violently on the shoulder which jolts me up immediately, my eyes forced open so quickly that I can actually feel my pupils contract painfully to cope with the sudden influx of light. It's Tom, looking very worried.

"What the fuck are you playing at mate?" I feel truly miserable and want to return to my shell forever.

"Sssh! Get up, we're gonna have to get out of here pal." I look around and realise all the other beds are now occupied with sleeping folk. "If the staff find out about last night we are in the shit, come on let's go." He continues, I pull my phone out from under my pillow and note that it's not even eight o'clock yet so we've barely slept at all but he's right, we need to do one. I nod and get into action, throwing the duvet back and dragging myself off the bunk down to the hard floor, there's a heap of jeans, trainers and designer tops on the deck and I separate my stuff from Tom's before going to the bathroom.

In the mirror I'm confronted by a battered looking man who needs a shave and a man who also appears to have some processed cheese stuck to his lip, which he promptly removes. I spit into the sink and run cold water over my face, taking a quick wash before fumbling quickly to get dressed and emerging back into the room.

    Everything is done quickly and quietly; packing our stuff up, checking for anything we might have missed, double checking match tickets, cash cards and keys. We leave the room behind and go to the lifts, looking at eachother gravely, I'm swaying and I feel ill but we have to get out of here fast. The lobby is deserted save for a lad behind the counter who I go straight for and tell him we want to check out, I worry that he might wonder why we are going so early but I'm sure he's seen people check out at all hours in the past. I await a question about what we were doing stealing from their bar the previous night, or the police trashing down the front door to apprehend us but nothing comes, other than our returned passports and a thank you. A *thank you*. Had a look at your optics recently, mate?

    I hand the room keys over and we turn to exit, trying not to actually leg it out of there, then as soon as we're out of the building we are laughing, can't believe our luck, how the hell have they not noticed their depleted bar yet? Maybe they will later on, I'll try not to think about it. A misty cold air fills the city and hangs heavily so I'm shivering soon after we leave the hostel and stumble in the direction of the train station while Tom gets on the phone to Paul to see where he's at. Much busier in Munich today as the morning rush hour begins and the deserted road of last night is now host to an endless stream of vehicles travelling both ways at pace so we go down into a subway to take us to the other side.

    "Right, use your famous navigational skills to get us to Karlsplatz underground station, Paul's going to meet us there he says that's near where their hotel is, we can dump our stuff there too." Tom hangs up with a long sigh, a cloud of white breath rising up into the frozen ether.

"Oh, easy that mate we're right near it already, it's only down here." I reassure him and thankfully it is close to our current location because I don't think either of us is in good enough condition to go on a long mission across the city. I point down the main road we were jogging down last night which leads to the Glockenspiel in Marienplatz, the main square, we could even get a tube to the place but it's probably not worth the effort. My head still thumps with a vast hangover and the taste of Jagermeister hangs like a grim reminder at the back of my throat, a warning to never touch the stuff again.

"Hope that tramp survived the night drinking that crap." I offer as we trudge down the road, Tom sniggers back.

"Don't talk about that man, it was vile." He mumbles, burying his chin down into his coat, hands planted firmly in pockets and barely keeping his eyes open.

We get to Karlsplatz in no time and Paul stands out from the dense pack of drab winter-clothed commuters leaving the U-Bahn station in an ace bright yellow K-way cagoule. I want one. This is complemented by a pair of adidas Oslo on his feet and it is fair to say he looks fucking mint. He laughs at the state of us and guides us towards his accommodation as we fill him in on our swift and lucky escape from the hostel and he repeats my earlier comment about concerns for the tramp's wellbeing after our quite irresponsible gift to him.

Their place is a fairly basic hotel but at least the rooms are private and the warmth is heavenly. Chris is lying on one of the beds with his hoodie up and eyes closed but he says hello and sounds pretty wasted still, with a big vat of water on his bedside table. Paul tells us they're going getting some breakfast in a bit but that we can stick around in their room while they're out to get our heads down. It's still early and there's a full day ahead of us so I'm happy with that, it's good of them to let us stay. I dump my bag on the deck, go to the loo and make myself sick into the sink which takes the edge off before sitting down in a chair watching Paul and Chris get ready to go and get some scran. I slouch back, feel my eyes going heavy, make an attempt at keeping myself awake, shift positions a bit, then I'm out like a light.

    I'm awake first, still just about perched in the chair and I see that Tom is asleep face down on Paul's bed. The clock on top of the telly tells me that it's just gone eleven and I'm relieved that I wasn't gone for too long. Today is massive, historic. Head is still banging but that will soon shift so I get up and sort my gear out for the day, straighten out my jeans and top then lay them out on Chris' bed. I shake Tom awake then go for a shower and feel a bit guilty for using their only remaining dry towel but they'll get over it. I still need a shave but otherwise I'm fresh and ready, brand new Spezials tightly laced and the blue Lacoste on again which appears to have survived last night without any further damage or spillages. Tom's slowly waking up as well so we won't be hanging around for too long and I have a browse through a *"Welcome to Munich"* leaflet while he goes for a shower.

    The door locks itself as we leave and Paul's got the keys so we could do with sticking around with him after the game so we can get our bags back. Our flight is at half eleven tonight so there won't be much time to waste after full time, an extra night in Munich would probably have been a better plan but I wasn't exactly spoilt for choice with flight options. We rejoin Paul and Chris outside the Glockenspiel and I let them lead us around the city, happy to take a back seat rather than be a tour guide again this time and we wander off down back streets and alleyways on the search for beer.

We come across the Hofbrauhaus with a fraction of the trouble we had last night, a splendid sight in the daylight it is too as the blue and white chequered Paulaner flags adorning the entrance shimmer in the wind. Not so splendid is the look on the face of the chap stood in the doorway, or what he tells us: *"No football supporters."* Sure enough there's a piece of A4 in the window confirming it. It's a travesty, maybe the lad swinging on the lights last night was the last straw?

    There's another place further up the street, a Hard Rock Café, which is bursting at the seams with Wanderers fans, some of whom have spilled out onto the streets in high spirits. We file inside only to find that it is totally jammed with a sea of people from back to front and I'm sweating instantly with the sudden difference in temperature between here and outside. There's nothing doing, the four of us are just stood in a line with nowhere to go or turn to, certainly not to the closest bar I can see anyway seen as it's lined with people four or five deep so we basically reverse back out into the street. The walking begins again with no particular destination in mind, curving around back towards the direction of Marienplatz, looking for a more accommodating bar.

    I poke my nose up to the window of a small sports shop sandwiched in between a chemist and a closed souvenir stall and thoughts of stumbling upon some miraculous rare adidas trainer flash through my mind but unsurprisingly nothing unusual stands out. It's not 1984 anymore; there's as much chance of finding decent footwear on eBay or even in a few places in town now, no need to go traipsing around Europe with a Transalpino pass and an empty Head bag on the search for gear these days. More's the pity; they would have been exciting times. I see a pair of red and white trainers that look like Gazelles on a stand and they're okay just nothing too out of the ordinary. It would have been a different story if they were anything more exotic; I'd have been in there like a shot spending a large chunk of today's war-chest on them, but otherwise it's all running shoes and plastic shit-flickers so I turn away and carry on up the street.

We're out of luck. A traditional or traditional-*looking* pub nestled down one of the many tributaries to the main drag looks promising until we get to the small windows to see coats and sweaters pressed up tight to the glass, people crammed in again. I'm getting frustrated now, Munich's reputation as a beer drinking city is taking a beating in my eyes here at the moment and the others look just as cheesed off. Chris looks concerned that he might never drink again, between pained drags on another of the cigarettes he bought from a stall in Karlsplatz.

"Getting a bit desperate this ain't it? These are shit too." He nods down at the cigarette then spits as we carry on walking. We end up back on Kaufinger Strasse, the main road through the middle of town and approaching another busy bierkeller.

"Right, no matter how ram-jam this is we're drinking, yeah?" Tom declares and we all agree. "I'll sup anything, fucking parched." He was half dead not so long ago, a miraculous recovery. I'm definitely wanting a beer but could do with a sit down while I do, I've been feeling pretty bleak too and these cobbles are a nightmare.

The place we come upon looks like a scaled down version of the Hofbrauhaus, again it's jumping inside and it feels quite festive too with its warmth, steamed up windows and fairy lights hanging amongst the fixtures and potted shrubbery. Vaults lead off from the long corridor of an entrance; each one is full so we walk further back into a large hall adorned with Bolton flags and Germans filming the lads singing about John McGinlay in the middle. Through that and we're into another busy hall but one that happily offers us some empty tables. We slump onto thick wooden benches and within moments this giant of a woman appears before us to take our orders – *"vier grosse biers, bitte"*.

They're delivered in double quick time, four huge steins, her arms bulging under the strain but she handles them effortlessly. The glasses slam onto the wooden table and we're all straight into them. I watch the fraulein who served us ferrying six full steins a few minutes later, three in each hand so our quartet were clearly nothing.

"Jesus, she's got some power in those arms that bird."

"Oh you'd know all about that as well wouldn't you." Paul comes back at me instantly.

"You kidding? She'd rip the fucker off with those I bet she's like a cyborg." I laugh at his grimace. It's great in here, now we've finally got somewhere to set up camp and dig in for a couple of beers. Wanderers songs reverberate through the building, our glasses raised as we pitch in with our portion of *"White Army"*, then *"Ten German Bombers"* pipes up in the other rooms and spreads – Tom joins in at *"Eight German Bombers"*, Chris and Paul at *"Seven"*. I can't be arsed with it. The keller is packed out by the time they get to *"None... cos the RAF from Bolton shot them down"* and the songs follow on incessantly.

We're served again by the girl with the blonde pigtails and the big arms before our other beers are dead, keeping it flowing. *"Eyes right, foreskins tight..."* starts, our steins go up once more and again we're on top note, *"...bollocks to the front, we're the boys who make no noise and we're only after cunt..."*

Consistent drinking at last, interrupted only by singing and eating giant pretzels, whilst we're now sharing our benches in true Bavarian style with some other blokes who have been joining in with the chanting also. I make conversation with the one closest to me by saying how great this whole thing is, being in Munich and watching the Whites, but I soon find it's a bad idea – it turns out he's a European Away Snob.

"Well, it's okay I suppose…" He jumps in as soon as I finish my sentence, as if he's been itching to talk about this to someone all afternoon. "I've been on better, were you in Skopje?..." I shake my head then tell him this is my first European away and he gives me this look of pity mixed in with scorn. He informs me that he's a *"Euro Hundred-Percenter"* and starts going on about his trips to Bourgas, Guimaraes and Marseille during Wanderers' previous UEFA Cup campaign, telling me about how this Munich do has got nothing on those excursions and that he was one of the few who made it out to Istanbul to watch us against Besiktas that season too. A badge of honour, sure, but don't brag to me about it.

I can't be arsed listening to much more of this balloon, I'm personally loving my first European trip watching Bolton which incidentally is far from over with yet and I don't want someone telling me that it's nowhere near as good as ones that happened two seasons earlier. I think about telling him he should have tried Eastern European hostels on for size with nothing but a backpack and a million bed-bugs for company but rule it out because it would probably make him worse.

I decide I want to be away from this character as quickly as possible and I get up to go and follow Tom who's gone for a mooch in some of the other rooms to get a feel for the atmosphere more. We prop ourselves against a wall surveying the scene and *"Ten German Bombers"* starts up yet again.

With my stomach rumbling, a gaseous hollow in my gut, the decision is made to scavenge for food. While it is good to see Bayern fans mingling with Wanderers I'm not convinced they're appreciating some of the songs that Bolton's finest are offering up, with *"German Bombers"* now down to *"Five"* again, it is being belted out at the top of people's lungs in here, some younger lads have their arms outstretched like planes. I'm making a point of not joining in.

"Didn't actually pay for any of them beers in there, did we?" It dawns on me once outside, there we were continuing to order more drinks to our table and we were supposed to pay at the end. "They'll lose a fortune today in there playing it like that." We've saved ourselves a load of Euros doing that, it wasn't even *intentional* either. Oh well, we won't go back.

"What are we going to eat then lads?" Paul asks, his words accompanied by a gust of white breath. "I can't be arsed with more fast food, I want something proper." We concur, not that any specific ideas are forthcoming though and so we walk aimlessly in the streets of Munich once more with the light fading.

Why he picks it I don't know, but Tom spots somewhere after a few minutes' walking about shivering; it's just some railings and a gate with steps leading underground, there's a menu that no-one bothers reading but there's another Paulaner sign, so we go downstairs into an Aladdin's Cave of a place. There's no sign of football fans down here just a smattering of dourly dressed Germans eating and some of them stop to look up at us as we pile into their quiet abode in a blaze of brightly coloured windbreakers, knitwear and trainers. We shuffle off to a corner table, all dark wood and low ceilings with dim lights behind translucent shades.

"Oh nice one Tom…" Paul says deadpan as we sit down. *"Tom Tit…"*, but we're presented with beers promptly which is a good start and we get stuck in. Right, menu… not a clue what's going on there, I recognise a few words but not a lot; *sauerkraut, wurst, salat*, but nothing else and the others are stumped too.

"Tell you what, this could be anything this place, I've never heard of half of the shit on this menu. We'll end up eating the German version of black pudding." It's a worry.

"I like black pudding." Chris comes back, I mime being sick under the table. In the end we basically chicken out of ordering anything noteworthy and the lot of us end up with more giant pretzels which are good as a snack but I had hopes of tucking into a hot pre-match meal to take the edge off today's beer and yesterday's hangover, but our collective fears of being served something regretful just leads us all to selecting the easy option. I switch between supping lager and picking off the large chunks of salt on my pretzel to chew and let the taste fill my mouth before washing it away and repeating over.

We end up slipping into a haze of drinking and it doesn't do us any good. The first couple of beers are seen off quite merrily as we casually chat our way through them but then we all seem to seep off into our own quiet worlds. We must look an odd bunch from the outside; each of us slumped over our glasses offering the briefest of comments at best, before retreating again to silence. Tiredness, hangovers, burnout from all the excitement leading up to this experience perhaps, I don't know what it is but we all look seriously morose, it's not a pretty sight, yet the waiter just keeps on replacing empty glasses with full ones and we just keep on drinking them.

Our only saving grace is that they're much smaller measures than the ones we've been used to in Munich – not even pint-sized. Crucially though, no-one in our group is bothering to keep abreast of what time it is, I glance at Tom and he could easily be asleep as he sits with his head in his hands, Paul looks blankly at me when I turn to him and Chris is just slowly tapping his box of cigarettes on the table, staring at it emotionlessly. For a good while I can honestly say I'm not thinking about *anything* at all, I've no awareness of the other people in the building or any noise they're making and my mind is empty. I just sit there, my eyes so heavy.

With a jolt I come-to for no particular reason and sit up straight, shaking my head out of sleep-mode. The time, the fucking time. I grab my phone from out of my jacket and the others all reconnect with reality in unison, somehow it is twenty to six and a fearful rush attacks my senses. Kick off is at seven, I can't believe what we've done.

"We've got to go, like now!" I say dramatically. "It's twenty to six!" There's a melee of swearing and scrabbling for belongings and paying of bills as we piss about looking like The Keystone Cops, losing any image of effortless cool we may have gained upon entry to this place and we basically fight over eachother to get back up the stairs and to street level to run to the train station.

I'm fretting by the time we get to the Hauptbahnhof as I know time is seriously getting on and we're all wasted, there's not enough urgency from any of us. I don't know why but I just can't get my head around the train timetables and maps, it's usually something I'm really good at but it's just not happening. There's Bayern fans in here and so there must be a train to the ground but I'm needing a giant neon sign saying *"Train to Allianz Arena this way..."* but there isn't one.

"Taxi?" Paul offers and despite the probable cost it's a good idea.

"Yeah alright, probably for the best, where's Tom?" Paul points to a shop in the station just as Tom's on his way out of it.

"Check these out!" He enthuses and opens a carrier bag full of cans of JD & Coke as we had promised ourselves to get hold of yesterday but that feels like an age ago now and my stomach lurches, more alcohol is the last thing I should be consuming, how he still has the will to drink I don't know. Chris mirrors my feelings exactly, turning away with hands on hips, silently mouthing *"fuck's sake"* to himself.

The four of us cram into a taxi outside the station and ask for the Allianz Arena. Driver nods and we pull out of the waiting area outside the station. It's going to be tight this, I can't believe we were in that cavernous restaurant for so long.

The cans come out of Tom's bag and the driver frowns but I suppose he doesn't want to turn the fare down and kick us out so says nothing. I can see almost immediately that we're in trouble, the traffic is horrendous and we're stationary within minutes. It's stop-start all the way out of town, each of us exchanging concerned glances. I slip into a worried stare out of the window as we head onto a dual carriageway that is jammed with traffic. Tom makes short work of one of the cans and immediately goes for another and the sound and thought of that makes me start to need a piss urgently, the type of feeling where your whole midriff actually hurts because you need one so badly and it consumes every last ounce of will in your body just to concentrate on holding it in.

There's nothing for it, I give up hope of holding it in so I take off my seatbelt and get out of the car in the middle of the static carriageway before skipping off between cars, climbing over some railings and skirting off behind some sort of storage sheds to relieve myself, it's an incredible feeling. I return to the road and catch sight of some extremely scornful looks from drivers of other cars as I pass through their headlights and I can see that our taxi has moved a few meters further forward, how lucky I am that the road ahead didn't suddenly clear. Tom tells me I'm a mad bastard for doing that and hands me a can, suddenly I'm less averse to drinking again now.

Time ticks on still further, past half six and beyond and Chris who's sat in the front passenger seat suddenly starts kicking off and banging on the window.

"Oi, oi, driver what the fuck?! What are you doing, it's over there!" He's shouting and bouncing about in his seat, we look at what Chris is referring to and a sight from Hell greets us; the glowing red of the Allianz Arena by night... miles and miles away... in the *other* direction. The car erupts, all four of us are in absolute uproar screaming at the driver who has a look of pure fear and confusion all over his face and he's trying to speak but can't get a word in, when he finally does it's not what we want to be hearing. His English is broken, but we all recognise the word *"lost"*.

"Lost? Fucking lost, a taxi driver in Munich?" Tom shouts, his can shaking precariously in his hand.

"Yeah mate, how can you miss a giant luminous red stadium at night that you've probably driven to a hundred times?" I chime in but he probably doesn't understand a word, just our tone. He raises as hand in submission shouting *"yes, yes, sorry. I ask, okay?"* and then he grabs the radio and starts chatting on with someone on the other end, presumably asking for directions. He pulls off the still busy carriageway that I thought must have been match traffic but is clearly just rush-hour normality and we speed off up some other road, with the brightly lit stadium at least in front of us now, albeit very much over the hills and far a-fucking-way.

Kick off time comes and goes and we're still on the road, each of us is trading expletives and total disdain about the whole situation and as we turn a corner to finally be greeted with the stadium up close I look at the clock and see that it's gone 7.20pm. The driver drops us on a wide concourse that leads to a ramp leading up to the ground and we try to blag it but he's having none of it and starts yelling so Tom runs back and literally *throws* some money at him through the window.

"Fucking hell it's 1-0! We've scored! Wanderers have scored!" Paul starts shouting as we show our tickets to a gang of blokes manning a metal fence who let us by and we leg it up this *"Krypton Factor"* ramp to the stadium. He's waving his phone over his head and cheering, must have had a text or checked online, but I'm not as chuffed, in fact I'm gutted that I've missed it and now I'm at a loss as to where we have to go to get to our seats. The way the stadium is set out is totally alien to what I'm used to, you can actually get into the ground from any position around the stadium it is all open and I can see some of the crowd inside, there don't appear to be turnstiles in the same form we have back home but I see a letter attached to a wall which must mean which block it is... and we're on the wrong side of the fucking ground.

"I don't believe this we're at the wrong end it's on the other side..." Chest pumping, lungs desperate for air. With that, Tom starts to sprint with everything he's got and pulls away from us so we follow, me lagging behind notably, cold and thin Bavarian air taking its toll on me as soon as I pick up the pace. The letters on each block tick by agonisingly slowly until we reach ours and then we realise that we have to get to the third tier, with numerous flights of stairs curving up before us like some sick Dali painting.

A gigantic roar bursts out from within the stadium virtually as soon as we get into the building followed by booming music that rumbles through the floor which must signify an equaliser for the home team and I curse angrily, we are missing all this. Tom begins to stride up the stairs, his speed belying someone who has drunk so much so recently. The climb is torture, every step a major hurdle and my legs are screaming at me to stop, my stomach in knots, so when I reach the top at last I'm gasping for breath and doubled over but Tom tells me to follow him, as Chris and Paul go off to find their seats somewhere else amongst our supporters, too knackered to say bye.

    I'm absolutely shattered by the time we reach our seats; a sick concoction of knowing we were missing a large chunk of the first half sat in that fucking taxi, then knowing we'd scored against Bayern bastard Munich and I'd missed it, then having to run around the perimeter of the stadium, followed by having to leg it up a seemingly never-ending staircase to the top tier of this gigantic arena. My legs are utter jelly as I finally find my seat; Tom is leaning against the stairwell exit catching his breath, looking out at the scene ahead of him. I find the seats and admire the view – and *what* a view.

    This is a stadium like no other I've ever been in for a game; three tiers jam-packed with people and not a single seat free, overlooking a playing field on which the participants look miniscule from all the way up here. Wanderers fans are congregated across the length of a curve in the stadium in the highest section plus another segment below us in the middle tier, the noise the English contingent is making is pulsating and incessant.

    I can't shout myself because of the bilious pool that's now cramping my abdomen and the pain I'm feeling in my lungs from the running and fretting a few minutes earlier. Finally Tom appears next to me and neither of us says a word as we both study the scene, I switch my vision from the pitch then to the Bolton support, then to Bayern's as sporadic bouncing and cheering rises up from different areas in their vast crowd, then back to the pitch.

    Right now for me this has ascended beyond anything to do with the actual football match taking place, the fact that we are fielding what is almost a reserve team away from home against one of the strongest teams in Europe means virtually nothing. I'm too pissed and tired still to really take note of mislaid passes, of tackles and shots and certainly way too overwhelmed to take stock of anything tactical down there.

 We've barely been at our seats for fifteen minutes when the half-time whistle goes and I sit down at last, head dropping into my hands and I shut my eyes just trying to gather my thoughts. The team are cheered off and the songs begin again once they disappear down the tunnel, as the Bayern fans disperse to fill themselves on bratwurst and pretzels the Wanderers end remains pretty much full, awash with raised arms and prolonged chanting. There's no doubt in my mind that regardless of anything that happens in the second half, for many Bolton fans this will be the very pinnacle of anything they witness following their team – me included.

 White shirts spread out onto the pitch as we come out for the second half, followed by the black of Bayern Munich. By now I've pretty much got my act together and spent most of the break taking photos and filming every corner of the stadium, chatting with Tom about how amazing the place is, I've seen this stadium many times on TV but nothing has done the true scale of it justice, it is a masterpiece of a ground.

 Now I'm fully alert I can actually see what's happening in the game and we begin the second half being ripped apart by Bayern's French winger Franck Ribery, he is absolutely shredding us, haring all over the place and we have no answer. It's not the first time he's done this to us either; Ribery was responsible for putting us out of the UEFA Cup in our last campaign when he played for Marseille so we've seen all this before. Bayern weave together a flutter of lightning quick passes within minutes of the restart and all of a sudden the ball is fired into our area low and fast, then there is their striker Lukas

Podolski to put us to the sword from close range. He taps home to make it 2-1 and the Allianz Arena erupts, a monstrous roar directed at the goal scorer and us. The rout begins, surely.

Podolski's name is announced over the speakers and the crowd repeat his surname three times as loud as they can muster, it's an awesome sound and again it feels like the gravity of the event is overtaking the reality of us now trailing in such a massive game. Tom just tells them to fuck off and lays into our defence for not closing Bayern down while they passed us to pieces.

Their fans quieten down almost as soon as they finish their last blast of *"Lukas... Podolski!"* shouts and it's left to us to fill the void in sound, so we do just that – every single Wanderers fan up on their feet chanting *"We are the one and only Wanderers..."* as Bayern continue to carve us up, a continuous wave of chanting from our supporters. They're murdering us on the pitch but their fans have nothing on us no matter how many they outnumber us by.

Not ten minutes later though Podolski is being taken off only to be replaced by Luca Toni, a World Cup winner and one of the top strikers in Germany. I shake my head at how good their squad is, he's going to score with his first touch, I'm certain of it. Within seconds Bayern get through us yet again and Ribery hits a peach of a shot which is nailed-on to go flying into the top corner, it's a goal without a doubt, 3-1 and no way back from this. Somehow though Al-Habsi gets a hand to it and tips it over the bar, I've never seen anything like it he came flying out of nowhere, must have had about a second to react to it – at most – and he made it. I'm clapping and shouting and whining all at the same time, an amazing save. I look over to Tom and his mouth is hanging wide open, speechless – and that's as rare an event as you can get which says it all.

Then, inexplicably, as the ball goes out of play the boards go up at the touchline for another Bayern Munich substitution and this time it is Ribery to be replaced by an unknown reserve player named Kroos. There's an audible gasp from many people around us, Ribery has been a class apart all game and I consider clapping him off but no-one else looks like doing it so I scrub that idea. A rumble of noise begins in our section again following this new injection of belief *"Come on you Whites... Come on you Whites"* slow and loud, without their two best players on the night we are still in with a chance here if only we can hang on.

Bayern's fans have gone deathly silent and they must know surely that they've just been severely blunted by the two substitutions. We suddenly begin to look more solid, more confident about attempting even the most basic of passes which we didn't earlier on – fair enough we're not exactly going at them like an Arsenal team on the break but we've put our foot on it at last, stopping Bayern Munich in their tracks.

Twenty more minutes of battling to stay in it ensue and Wanderers' mostly second string players have done us proud; men like Gerald Cid, Mikel Alonso, Lubor Michalik and Daniel Braaten have barely shown anything noteworthy all season yet they all look tonight like they're worth another go to me. Well, maybe not, I have been pissed for two days.

Another regular bench-warmer Andranik trots over to the touchline to take a throw as the clock dribbles over into the final ten minutes, right up the other side of the pitch seemingly miles away so I'm straining to get a good enough view of what's happening, it feels like I'm watching it through a living room window on someone else's telly. He throws it before Bayern really get chance to turn and face, a looping ball that lands in the Munich area and bounces to Nolan who flicks it up over one defender which has the Bolton fans screaming out with nervous encouragement, then he manages to shift it past another but both players are left off balance and out of position as a result. The ball falls loose about ten yards away from goal, no Bayern players nearby and only Kevin Davies in any position to do anything with it. There's a backdraft of silent anticipation that sucks downward from the Bolton fans and back again, suffocating the screams of milliseconds earlier as our legendary Number Fourteen connects with a half volley and fires it right through Oliver Khan, low into the Bayern goal.

    The Wanderers end explodes into life at the astonishing sight of the ball striking the back of the Munich net. I can't even scream, I just jump up making this ridiculous moaning sound with my fists raised, snatch a glimpse of Davies running off to celebrate, then look to my right across the stretch of Bolton fans and all I can see is a scene of pure delirium. A mass of squabbling arms and bouncing heads, white shirts swinging around in some places, a couple of flags going like the clappers in others, but mainly just bodies and noise. So much noise. A maddened rush from the collective screams of thousands and now here comes Tom, all arms and legs – he clatters into me shouting into my ear absolutely delighted – I finally find my voice and shrug him off, clamber up onto my oval-shaped seat, raise my arms again and bellow out with everything I've got.

    So here I am; stood up on a plastic chair at the back of the third tier of a giant and packed out super-stadium, my arms aloft and screaming in delight, surrounded by over three-thousand of my comrades all of whom are utterly elated. My team has just scored a late equaliser at one of the biggest clubs in world football – and I could stay right here in this moment forever.

CHAPTER TEN

Barclays Premier League – Friday 30th November 2007

		P	W	D	L	Pts.
13	Reading	14	4	1	9	13
14	Tottenham Hotspur	14	2	6	6	12
15	Bolton Wanderers	14	2	5	7	11
16	Birmingham City	14	3	2	9	11
17	Middlesbrough	14	2	4	8	10

The 2-2 draw in Munich maintains Bolton Wanderers' unbeaten record in UEFA Cup Group F and is followed three days later by another draw, 0-0 at home against Middlesbrough in the League.

A fortnight later, Bolton record their first home win over Manchester United for thirty years, beating them 1-0 at the Reebok Stadium. However, a 1-1 home draw with Aris Thessaloniki in the UEFA Cup leaves Bolton needing to beat Red Star Belgrade in their final group game to qualify for the knockout phase of the tournament.

Our office doesn't really claim to have a "local", there's so much choice around us that everyone has their own preference. The Moon Under Water on Deansgate isn't anyone's preference though yet still here we are mixing with the hordes of city centre drunkards, the lost stragglers from stag parties and lads from Salford spoiling for a fight in the toilets. Who chose to come in here I don't know but they deserve a talking to, I'd have much preferred Corbieres, the Nag's Head or the Rising Sun which aren't far away but not here, it's a heaving mass of menacing characters. I'm stood slightly away from most of my colleagues, a couple of steps up the large curving staircase that eventually leads towards the second floor of the building, leaning over the banister next to Dan with a pint nestled between both hands.

  We are looking down towards the group from our office who are arranged in a loose circle stood, sat or leaning in the bar area below. I can see that Steve from Accounts has got his head pressed into some bemused and much younger looking girl's ear, letching while someone else from his section looks on laughing nervously. Graham is nigh on paralytic now, still in his work shirt and tie, crumpled against the wall and probably still moaning about the smoking ban to anyone who can be arsed to listen. Al meanwhile – a shambles of a lad from Admin who fancies himself as a sharp dresser yet still insists on coming out in this oversized Evisu t-shirt, a yellow Livestrong bracelet on each wrist and baggy jeans with all that ridiculous spilt paint effect crap all over them – is arsing around in front of everyone shouting and spilling his drink all over his hands and the floor.

  "So Dan, would you say it seems there's a bit of a drinking culture in this office?" I actually find the scene of turmoil in front of me pretty funny but I'm mockingly pulling a solemn and concerned face.

  "Oh does it lad, *does it*." He grins, shaking his head as he surveys what's going on before us. "You sound like you've cheered up anyway, finished moping about now have you?" I take a moment to think, then nod and take a swig of beer.

  "Yeah, yeah. It was nothing anyway just been feeling a bit off, you know? Seeing some of these mugs like this would put a smile on anyone's face though." I point down to some of the clowns I work with each day, wasted and enjoying themselves.

  I hadn't actually noticed that I'd been visibly miserable recently but I wasn't going to let on that the reason I'm fed up is because I'm still on a comedown from Munich – some three weeks after the event – and on a downer about football in general. The whole Munich experience was unforgettable from start to finish and wasn't even spoiled by a nightmare journey home after a delay into the early hours in Germany and a laborious transfer in London before flying back to Manchester. By the time I finally crashed into bed I'd been awake for something like 42 hours and was destroyed for a couple of days after. The memories only seem to get better and better the further away from the event we go, it still dominates chat between me and Tom and we'll struggle to beat it in future. But, like a brilliant holiday, it takes time to come to terms with it being over with, I just seem to be taking longer than I should to achieve that.

    Added to this there's a nationwide depression about football at the moment as the post mortem continues over England's failure to qualify for Euro 2008. Croatia beat us at Wembley last week and there has been collective soul searching ever since. I'm a fan of England, I know most of the Mancs I work with – Red or Blue – aren't fussed about the National Team but I always get behind them. Euro '96 was the first tournament that I took great interest in and although it did attract a lot of hangers on in the following years, the effect it had on me at thirteen and still newish to the game was huge, every England game felt like life depended on it. I enjoy pissing Dan and Brian off by going on about it whenever they whinge about England and their fans, Euro 96, France 98 and Euro 2000 hold some great memories for me. I'll still watch every game at Euro 2008 if I get chance, I love watching international tournaments anyway, but it won't quite be the same without England there.

    My glumness about the game has continued despite Wanderers' quite unbelievable win over Manchester United at the Reebok a week ago. I've waited my whole life for a home win over them. We've played far better against United and not won in the past but they were rank awful and missed some real sitters in the process as we hung on to our single goal, scored of course by Nicolas Anelka. I stayed in the ground celebrating longer than I ever have after the final whistle in that game and maybe, just maybe, we can somehow survive this season and perhaps, just perhaps, Megson is the right man for the job after all.

  He must be laughing himself to sleep at night at the moment after the Munich draw and the United win, there were people singing his name and even chanting *"Ginger Mourinho"* at him at both of those games, it was bizarre. Maybe it's just me being negative about things though, but despite those two results all I see are dark clouds hanging over us; lumbered with a load of weak signings and with a number of defeats already, the damage might have been done.

  Finally at least, our stay in the Moon Under Water appears to be coming to an end as a number of colleagues are busy putting coats on and preparing to move, so we come down the stairs and see what's next. Off we go back down Deansgate to a couple of other bars, our numbers dropping as time passes, including Graham who sloped off back to Salford without saying a word to anyone after leaving the Moon. Even fewer remain as I follow Dan's lead and descend into South; a subterranean indie club down a wind and rain swept back street, these parts of Manchester always look better to me when the weather is grim.

  It's not long until I'm bopping around daftly in the busy darkness to some of my old favourites, on the march with the Boon Army; *"This Is The One"*, *"Pounding, "Voodoo Ray, "The Only One I Know"* and the rest of it, right in the middle of the dance floor but at least it's packed out so I'm not centre of attention. Well, to everybody but one person anyway. As I look around me to see what else is going on I realise that I've been joined by one of the women from the office, Steph, who's dancing right behind me and she laughs when she sees me notice her. I laugh too, she's probably taking the piss out of me but it's harmless enough, though as *"Pacific State"* comes in and I get into it again, she appears next to me and wraps an arm around my midriff so we're dancing together. Then as the smoke descends and the lights cycle round illuminating random smiling faces and hands in the air, one arm around my midriff becomes two and now my colleague is stood right before me and leans forward for a kiss immediately.

    I put my free arm around her while the other one goes over her shoulder awkwardly as I try not to lose grip of my Red Stripe and we share a lager fuelled kiss for a few seconds, before she breaks off and looks at me with a mixture of surprise and embarrassment. I don't think she really knew what she was up to there. I shrug my shoulders and smile which makes her giggle and then she leaves the dancefloor back towards what remains of our group, all of whom saw what just happened and they're pointing and laughing. Steph doesn't appear to be seeing the funny side anymore though, I watch as she shakes her head at a mate and pushes past someone else going towards the toilets. She initiated it, daft sod. I wave two fingers up at my colleagues then carry on acting the fool on the dancefloor into the night.

Sunday December 2nd 2007

    We just seem to get battered every year at Anfield now. In our first season back up in the Premier League we managed a 1-1 draw there and of course there was the famous win in the League Cup Quarter Finals a few years ago but in the league the hammerings are becoming depressingly commonplace. That's why I can't be arsed spending a daft amount of money on a ticket to go and watch us there this season, no doubt from a seat that you can't even see the entire pitch from as is often the case there. Instead I meet Tom and Ray who despite coming to games now and again, more often than not ends up here watching it on pirate TV in a pub up Horwich, probably spending the same amount as he would on a ticket anyway.

    I joined them here at just gone two and as kick off approaches I'm still nowhere near the end of my first drink, nursing a pint as for some reason the hangover from the piss up in Manchester two nights ago lingers on, I still feel lethargic and a bit spaced out even now. Wanderers go a goal down on seventeen minutes; a free kick goes into the box and Hyypia heads it home, it's all so predictable. Liverpool's fans don't even celebrate that much there's just a short blast of almost apologetic cheering as the net bulges and as I finally get to the bottom of my drink I sit back and shake my head, same old story.

    I go and sort us out with another three beers and bags of fanny fingers which we get stuck into as the game plays out, the pub with its curtains closed shutting out a cold and grey Sunday afternoon with Winter Hill totally obscured by rain-laden clouds. I love scenes like this; feeling tucked away from the elements in a dark, warm haven with an assortment of old village drinkers – the type of dyed-in-the-wool, career pissheads that you despair of but strangely admire at the same time – and people in the know about the pirate telly watching the game, this sort of thing makes winter bearable.

    Suddenly my passive viewing of the match is shaken back into life; Reina and Carragher make a complete balls-up of a clearance and Anelka ghosts in beyond them, the ball at an angle to the goal but with the Liverpool net gaping and the pub erupts with a huge, simultaneous *"Go on, go on!"* directed at the screen as the Frenchman makes contact… and puts it wide. Desperate yelps from around the room greet the miss and the camera zooms in on Anelka who can't believe it, that was absolutely ridiculous.

They show replays of it over and over just to rub it in more as the minutes pass, we could have gone in at half time all square and maybe have something to hold on for in the second half. I'm listening to Ray explain once again how it should have been put away when up on the screen, Gerrard puts Torres through on goal with only Jaaskelainen to beat and he despatches it brilliantly, chipping it over the Finn and into the net just before the break and that is that for today now without a doubt. Sure enough the half time whistle goes within seconds of the restart and a hum of resigned voices takes over the pub, surely most of the people who came here to watch this knew we wouldn't get anything today anyway, but Anelka's miss just twists the knife a little bit more.

The second half is just a formality and I watch it merely half-heartedly whilst chatting to a couple on the table next to ours about the team. The few drinks I've had this afternoon have also not only shaken the hangover off but have also made me get the feeling that I could go on a session but I'm back in work tomorrow so I need to make sure I'm off pretty soon after full time. These Sunday matches are really starting to get on my tits this season but it comes with us being in Europe and playing more games so it's to be expected and accepted by the modern football fan.

Ten minutes into the second period Liverpool are given a penalty and it's a joke of a decision, the sort that teams like Liverpool get at places like Anfield and the sort that teams like Bolton never get anywhere. Again, it all just feels like the same old story. Gerrard sends Jussi the wrong way routinely to finish us off with over a third of the game still left to play. I've long since emptied my last pint and zipped my jacket up to leave for home as Ryan Babel makes it four in the dying minutes so I do one even as he turns to celebrate, saying bye to Tom and Ray and rushing out to catch a bus in the direction of Bolton. Beat United one week, struggle against a Greek side at home and get thumped by Liverpool the next, we are nothing if not unpredictable this season.

CHAPTER ELEVEN

Monday 3rd December 2007

"Yep… Yep… err, *yeah obviously*… Nah… Yep…" I'm halted from continuing my Monday morning appraisal of the girls in next year's Hollyoaks Babes Calendar that Brian's brought in to put up on his locker, by Steph who's appears from nowhere and stands at the door to our section.

"Here she is!" Dan goes, stood nearby as if he'd been expecting her to show up. She beckons for me to go over and see her so I give Brian his calendar back and he hits me on the shoulder, winking at me so I shoot him a smirk as I walk off. I follow Steph out the door and she closes it behind us, I can see she looks nervous.

"Listen…" She starts, brushing back her short brown hair away from her face. "South on Friday night, sorry about that I was just drunk." She sighs, this looks as if it's quite a difficult situation for her actually and she seems genuinely embarrassed. "I don't want you to think I'm, you know, after anything…" My laugh does a reasonable job of hiding my slight discomfort at being stood here while a woman in her mid-thirties tells me she's sorry for sticking her tongue down my throat.

"Hey, don't worry about it I was pretty well gone too. Are they giving you a hard time about it?" I nod my head towards the direction of her department, hands in my pockets, my faded shirt that I bought about a year ago in a multi-pack from Next untucked, looking a tip to be honest but it's alright I'm not trying to impress anyone.

"Yeah just a bit" I can tell it's an understatement. "I don't think they'll let me forget it in a hurry." I laugh and she smiles back at me. Steph's not the best looking and I've definitely never thought of her in any romantic sort of way, what with the age difference and all, plus I thought she was engaged anyway but clearly not. At any rate she's not even really my type; she's always seemed a bit up her own arse and the way she has come over this morning and talked to me as if she's letting me down gently or something only serves to reinforce my opinion. All this is fine by me, I kissed her while I was pissed, so what?

"Oh well anyway, no harm done. Just tell them lot to do one they love a gossip don't they?" I start to back off towards the door and she says thanks before turning away, I mentally note that actually she *does* look pretty good in heels. Dan and Brian are stood pointing and laughing at me as I re-enter our department and I shake my head at them.

"Knobheads! She came over to say sorry for going with me on Friday night." I roll my eyes as I say it.

"Aww poor Jamie." Brian says, sticking his bottom lip out.

"I know yeah, what can I say hey, I'm clearly not good enough for her." I reply, taking the piss. I return to my desk and start rummaging through some papers to do some work with and the others drift off back to their jobs also. I gulp down half a cup of tea which is at that blissful optimum temperature stage that only lasts an elusive minute or two in one go and log onto my computer to finally get this week started.

Tuesday 4th December 2007

Monday passes by and terrible Tuesday oozes in, my commute into work again a catalogue of frustrations; standing at the stop near home in a freezing rainstorm waiting for a bus that ends up being quarter of an hour late, to take me to a jam-packed Bolton Train Station where I have to give up on getting on the first train that comes because in their wisdom the train company sees fit to send one with just a single carriage. Eventually I end up on the following train where I have to stand up and overheat all the way to Manchester in amongst loads of ill people, sneezing and coughing, steaming the windows up with their germs. So I'm into work late and with wet socks on all day, trudging around the office feeling thoroughly fed up, which isn't helped by the Agency girl Sarah moaning that she can smell my feet every five minutes.

    For someone who said they thought South last Friday was a drunken mistake and I shouldn't think anything more of it, Steph seems to be finding a lot of excuses to come over to our department, she only really needs to come over once a day to drop off some of her finished work for us to file away but while I'm eating my lunch I realise that as she stands there handing Graham a bundle of paperwork and quickly glancing over to me that this is the *fourth* time she's been over today.

    She makes it five visits late on in the afternoon and this time I make her double-take when she again glances over at me because I'm staring at her too, making a point of it. Instantly she goes red and spins away to briskly walk off which makes me laugh, even Graham has picked up on all this now and he tells me he thinks she's got her eye on me. I tell him I think he's right as he ambles off into the file library and over his shoulder he shouts *"stupid bitch!"*. Cheers for that, Graham.

Wednesday 5th December 2007

	Steph is conspicuous by her absence from our area all morning today and I'm pissing myself off by constantly looking out for her appearance too, it's not like I fancy her or anything but when you get the impression that someone is interested in you it just makes you look out for signs of it more, no matter who they are, but making a habit of going round to the front of the office to see if she's turned up isn't doing me any favours. I make sure I don't go back unless I need to and do a good job of it, getting myself involved in a re-organising job right at the far end of the library which takes me right through lunch and deep into the afternoon, clearing space out for 2008's files when they start to arrive in less than a month's time. Tasks like this are real day-killers.

	I waste more time by standing around with Brian who once again takes great delight in picking out old stories from his awaydays following City; I've heard them all many times but it's always a laugh seeing how he delivers them, loud and animated, prancing about doing impressions of Gerard Wiekens heading in at Wrexham in 1998, or Kevin Horlock scoring at Wembley a year later. I mentioned to him earlier on about how we always seem to get dicked at Liverpool after our 4-0 trouncing on Sunday and so today's offering of anecdotes includes how he went to Anfield twice in less than a week in 1995 and saw them lose 4-0 in the Coca Cola Cup and 6-0 in the league three days later. He also finds a way of getting onto the time he went to a game at Rotherham with some mates and ended up getting chased by a load of Sheffield United's firm whilst waiting for their connecting train, then chased once again through the streets of Rotherham by "about fifty" Neanderthals. They add ten to their number each time he recites that story to me, it cracks me up.

	"Go on then, who've Inbred Wanderers got this weekend?" He asks as I return to my desk for a well earned sit down and a brew and when I tell him Wigan on Sunday he instantly starts giving me nuggets about their old ground, Springfield Park. Sounded like an absolute shithole that place, it certainly didn't look the best on the video I've seen on YouTube of the 92-93 season where Tony "Zico" Kelly rips through Wigan's defence and scores in front of our travelling fans, caged in and pressed up to the front of a tiny grass embankment going mental. Once he's finished I open my emails up and wade through all the ones from different clothing companies offering me discounts on crap looking gear, then I come upon one from Steph, unbelievable.

"Hey James, god this is a bad idea..." It begins, which makes my heart pump a bit harder, mouth drying out. *"Do you fancy going for a drink after work tomorrow? Meet me at five outside. It's fine if not. I feel like an idiot now."* I snatch glances to my left and right in case anyone's looking, feeling shocked. I'm totally thrown really, especially after what she said on Monday and I still maintain that I'm not interested. But all of a sudden the same curious, mischievous urge I had when Flick had confessed all to me before Munich envelops me again and the voice of reason in one part of my head telling me that Steph's right, this is a very bad idea, gets swept aside by the one telling me I'm single and I should be doing stuff like this and the fact that it is a bad idea makes it all the more exciting. So, I quickly fire off a reply before I give the voice of reason chance to make its opinion sink in. *"Yeah, sure..."* I say. *"Why not!"*

Thursday 6th December 2007

I couldn't sleep last night as I thought about all this with Steph, telling myself that I really shouldn't be doing this with someone I work with, particularly someone I'm not at all looking to start doing anything serious with and especially someone who is a good few years older than me. But the nerves about all that are mixed in with a fearful excitement; fantasises have been whirling around in my head about being involved with an older woman and the fact that she's the one who has done all the flirting and made all the moves here, not me. I somehow reason that because that's the case, I can deny all interest at a later date if need be, to get myself out of all this if the shit hits the fan.

    Again Steph doesn't appear on our department at all today, instead one of her colleagues brings over her stuff and if she has told anyone else about our date tonight then they haven't let on about it. I'm a little gutted that she suggested tonight actually, as Wanderers are in Belgrade for our last UEFA Cup group game and it is massive, we must win and I was looking forward to watching it with Tom at his house but I've told him I'll see him at the Wigan game on Sunday instead and asked to keep me updated with the score if he can. The anticipation for the night ahead makes the day drag badly, my stomach churning and my legs feeling sore with adrenaline.

    I feel quite sick by quarter to five which is stupid of me as I shouldn't be getting so worked up about this, if only for the fact that it will make me look exactly like the type of love-struck young lad she must have expected to find on Monday when she came over to apologise for kissing me. I get changed in the toilets when the time finally comes and being away from the office seems to calm me down a little as I quickly throw on my navy blue Fred Perry knit with its red and cream trim and a pair of 501's, then splash some water over my face and compose myself for a few seconds stood in front of the mirror.

Steph is loitering away to the left near a corner of the building when I come outside and as I near her she's already starting to head off away from work and looking quite shy.

"Oh I didn't know you were going to get changed, I feel overdressed now." She says quietly and I tell her not to worry, I seem to be doing that a lot.

"So where are we going then, have you got anywhere in mind?" I'm looking slightly upwards to her as her heels make her just a little taller than me and I can see that she's tarted up a bit but looks alright for it.

"I don't mind, wherever you want." I knew that was coming, but despite a list as long as my arm of places I like to drink in Manchester I end up suggesting the Printworks, it just seemed like a fairly neutral place to offer. Steph seems keen though so we walk through town not really saying very much to eachother aside from the odd comment about someone we see walking by or about how eachother's day in work was, it's a pretty uncomfortable ten minutes' journey in truth.

Of course, drink one goes down in no time and so does drink two, so by the time she gets round number three in as we nestle ourselves into a dark corner of Waxy O'Connor's basement we are both tipsy, particularly as neither of us has eaten since lunch. We are at least finding more to talk about now although a discussion about what's going on here or why we are doing this remains absent, perhaps she's just flying by the seat of her pants with this one like I am. Turns out she's a United fan although she seems like the type of United fan that doesn't know an awful lot about the game so I tease her for a bit about us beating them the other week which she doesn't seem too aware of either and also give her some stories from Munich which she laughs at and seems quite shocked by the bar robbery we carried out. Work talk fills up a good portion of the evening too, I don't know why people do this; discuss at length with their colleagues about why they hate the place while they're not even in the building, but it acts as good polyfiller between the quite noticeable gaps between conversation.

  When I stand to go and get a further round in she grabs the front of my top and kisses me, so this propels the evening into the next stage, forgetting about inane conversation and filling the gaps with kissing and groping. She has this look in her eye each time I look at her, I can't describe it, it's like a tractor beam anytime I catch her eye I end up drawn in again and again. The drink has worked into me very quickly and now not only am I quite into the frequent kisses we are sharing but I'm horny as fuck for her and she knows it.

  I'm trashed and have lost all sense of time as I keep looking over to the screen with Sky Sports News on to see how Wanderers are doing in Belgrade but we haven't even kicked off yet, turns out is barely half seven. We move on to another bar in Printworks and it has filled up for a busy Thursday night, in fact the second place we go in feels more like a club and is already bouncing when we arrive so I move onto drinking bottles of some fluorescent blue shite whilst doing shots with Steph and dancing. It turns out I know more words to Girls Aloud songs than I would usually care to admit; camping it up big style as we dance and sing *"Biology"* to eachother, getting close as the crowd grows and the volume rises. Right now, I'm not thinking about what I'm doing at all.

  Checking my phone between drinks shows Tom has been in touch saying that Wanderers lead at half time in Belgrade and my spirits rise up twice as high as they were in the first place, I'm loving it, kissing Steph even more and making no secret of the fact that I want her. She necks her drink and tells me to come with her, tractor beam eyes doing their stuff once again and we head out of the bar and out of Printworks into the cold night, me a step behind her as she leads me away from the building and the crowds into a back street and against a doorway. We are all over eachother, my hands down her blouse and hers working at my zip, kissing and touching in the shadows. She drops to her knees once she's got my jeans down slightly and I look down at her dark hair pressed against my midriff and laugh to myself; this week started off with her trying to forget about that kiss and it is ending with me standing in a rainy Manchester back street looking out for passers-by as she sucks me off.

    For a few moments I stand and enjoy the pleasure and forget about who she is, where I am, what we're doing. But, it seems, she doesn't forget. Almost as quickly as she got down there, she suddenly stands up and backs a half step away from me looking absolutely mortified. I stuff myself back into my pants and zip up, stood in silence looking like a prize tool for a few seconds.

    "You okay?" I ask, frowning. She straightens her clothes up and brushes her hair back quickly, not looking at me. "Steph?" As soon as I say her name she swears to herself under her breath and shakes her head.

    "Sorry, no. No this is wrong, I'm going, I've got to go." She mumbles, looking totally lost and with no hint of the drunken flirtiness she was showing not ten minutes earlier.

    "Alright, okay. You need me to walk with you or something?" I offer, sounding like a right patronising bastard in the process. She shakes her head, repeating that she has to leave and she begins to walk away, shuffling with her first few steps then finding her feet and striding away with the popping sound of her heels echoing against the walls of the narrow alley. I watch her walk the entire length of the street and turn the corner without once looking back at me. I check my clothing again and start to walk off in the other direction towards Victoria Station, not feeling drunk anymore but certainly not feeling good at all. I feel a little guilty and a little dirty, but my overriding feeling is that I desperately hope that no-one at work finds out about this.

Friday 7th December 2007

I'm tired and drained sitting in work this morning but fortunately not too hungover. Again I didn't sleep too well last night as my head spun whilst watching Sky Sports News tell me that Wanderers beat Red Star and made it to the next round but not feeling very much about it or anything at all really, just so nervous that I'd walk into work today and be greeted by lines of colleagues taking the piss out of me. There's been nothing though, no mention of what happened last night and no sign of Steph near this part of the office either but the suspense about wondering what she thinks of what happened is tearing away at me. I'm still not interested in wanting to go out with her or anything, despite the signals I was giving out pissed up last night and if there's some way I could tie this off and walk away knowing I had one evening with her and *that* happened, then it's a success.

Brian and Dan go on about the result but I can't concentrate properly with all this going on and I'm a bit short with them. Fuck it, I decide to email her just to at least test the water.

"Hey, hope you're okay. Last night was a bit mad, hope you're not upset in any way. We can just forget about it as if nothing happened if you would prefer?..." It is cobbled together and I know it will read quite emotionlessly but I also don't want her to start thinking I'm pining for her or going to start acting weird with her. As soon as I send it I feel a slight weight lift from my shoulders, feeling good that I'm trying to move away

from what happened last night and this week. There's a reply from her in under a minute.

"Fine." Is the sum total of her message and that's it. I smile wickedly. As far as I'm concerned, sitting here behind the safety of my monitor adopting a kind of selfish and fairly cold-hearted attitude that I've rarely felt before, that is the end of the matter. Finished.

CHAPTER TWELVE

Barclays Premier League – Saturday 22nd December 2007

		P	W	D	L	Pts.
14	Middlesbrough	17	4	5	8	17
15	Birmingham City	17	4	3	10	15
16	Bolton Wanderers	17	3	5	9	14
17	Sunderland	17	3	5	9	14
18	Fulham	17	2	7	8	13

Bolton Wanderers qualify for the last 32 of the UEFA Cup with a 1-0 win in Serbia against Red Star Belgrade. In the Premier League, they beat Wigan Athletic 4-1 but are defeated in successive away games; 4-0 to Liverpool and 4-2 to Manchester City.

Football during the festive period is massive in Britain, far bigger than anywhere else in Europe. While our continental counterparts are taking winter breaks or travelling to warmer climes for friendly tournaments, we embark on one of the busiest parts of the entire campaign in league and cup, with the kind of schedule that used to be commonplace throughout the whole season in bygone times. The games come thick and fast. It is great to watch on telly from the armchair but actually attending a reasonable number of these matches can be a ballache; with expense, disrupted transport and generally miserable weather mixed in with all the usual engagements and responsibilities that Christmas brings really taking their toll. It's not a popular opinion but I'd be in favour of a winter break here, not some daft month-long shutdown but just maybe two weeks right at the end of the year, I think it would be good for all concerned.

Today we face Birmingham to hopefully try and avenge the dismal defeat at their place early in September. There has barely been any daylight at all today; the Reebok Stadium's floodlights, LED's and scoreboard give the pitch an almost fluorescent green quality as they beam down onto the grass in front of the glum darkness of the stands. Players and supporters alike shield themselves from the bitter cold that envelops the stadium whilst Birmingham's small and patchy groups of travelling support stand around in the South Stand. They took great delight in mocking our poor turnout down there but they've hardly covered themselves in glory with their numbers here today either.

No repeat of the post match shenanigans seen after that game for me this day however as I'm due to head straight off after full time for a family meal at my sister's tiny flat in town. Tom meanwhile mentioned that he might see what Paul is up to and join him at the pub if he's going after the match, it would have been good to go too but I'll be seeing everyone on Boxing Day for Everton away anyway and I'll save myself for then.

I finally shook off my gloomy mood following Munich and the United win and it was helped by getting other plans sorted to look forward to – which include Paul and Chris again now as well – and especially as our European adventure continues after the impressive victory over Red Star Belgrade. Into the Last 32 we go, with the draw to be made in the coming days.

"He's still staring at me that tosser..." Tom elbows me in the ribs and nods his head over towards a steward manning the nearest stairwell to us. "Get a fucking proper job you gimp!" He shouts and I jab him back, telling him to calm down. We don't need any more trouble from the orange warriors; in our previous home game Tom had numerous disagreements with them over the standing/seating arrangements at the ground, they were on our backs all game for persistent standing and came very close to chucking us out. A mitigating factor surely was that we were in the process of hammering Wigan 4-1 but no, we were spoiling the view for others. Everyone else should have been on their feet too, some local derby.

The steward doesn't have much to bother himself with today though, we have played for over an hour and it has been a competitive battle but hardly anything to have us out of our seats every few minutes. In fact the most notable thing was the absolute nightmare of a game Ivan Campo had, he looked so sluggish and managed to make almost every pass go astray. He almost capped off a shambles of a performance with an own goal too. I love the bloke but him being subbed off early in the second half was the best thing that could have happened.

"Should start sitting with Chris and Greeny lad, it's shit down here, proper boring." Tom carries on moaning after craning his neck to glare at the steward for the umpteenth time, first time I've ever heard him complain about our seats I thought we were in agreement they were near perfect. Chris and Paul are right in the corner under the scoreboard and though standing for the full 90 minutes in that area is never questioned, the downside is some of the chumps that populate it.

"Give over you don't want to go down there, you'd despise it."

"No, it's decent." He says, going against everything he's ever said on the matter. "I'll probably look into shifting my ticket after Christmas, wanna come?" I know this is something he's never going to do, the likelihood is he won't even remember saying it by the next home game but it's still a surprise to hear him going on about it.

That's as far as the discussion goes though as first Wanderers have a goal disallowed for offside then minutes later as we're still debating that decision, we do at last take the lead and it is a belter. A cross goes into the Birmingham area and their defender makes a hash of clearing the ball with a total air-shot, but right on his shoulder is Diouf who controls and sidesteps him in one movement, takes another touch then fires it into the goal. Off he goes to celebrate; festively bedecked in gloves, a long sleeve shirt and a polo-neck top under that, with the crowd in relieved raptures. Breakthrough.

Our lead and Birmingham's bluntness in attack makes me feel fairly comfortable about the outcome now, we are quite steady at home at the moment and I can't see the away team coming back. My mind begins to wander onto other things; I sneak a look at my phone to stare yet again at a photo Flick sent to me a few days ago of her in a Santa hat and not much else. Got to sort out a meet with her sometime soon, some of the texts she sends me are outrageous.

I must admit as I've walked around the Christmas Markets alone at night after work in the last couple of weeks amongst the massive crowds wrapped up in hats and gloves, soaking up the atmosphere under twinkling lights and the giant Santa Claus perched on the Town Hall that I've pondered what it would be like to share it with someone. Bratwursts and hog roasts, mulled wine and German lager in large wooden huts full of life, it's a proper couples' paradise that place. It was good to be able to work through my entire Christmas shopping list in the space of about an hour's lunch and avoid the turmoil of a prolonged shopping session, but then there were only about six people to buy for. I stare blankly out at the pitch as I weigh up whether I would have preferred to have spent the money I used on the thick beige Barbour crewneck I treated myself to on a girlfriend instead.

I pull the cuffs of said jumper down over my hands to add some more protection from the cold. It *is* a fine garment, money well spent.

From nothing Bolton are gifted a second goal which shakes me from my daydreaming. Birmingham conspire to balls up a throw in and give it straight to Anelka instead, bad move. He advances on Maik Taylor who must be fuming at such a sloppy turnover of possession especially to someone like Anelka and our striker simply shifts the ball away from his grasp, skips round him and taps home. Any memories of his shocking miss at Anfield are banished, that was clinical and sure enough the keeper absolutely does his nut while we toast the strike with clenched fists and bear hugs.

Now Birmingham really are done for, they're frustrated and hopeless which shows in some of their challenges as we revel in an unassailable lead and pass the ball about comfortably – unheard of scenes these really. Just to put even further gloss on what was at one stage looking like a keenly fought stalemate we turn it into a rout; they give up possession cheaply yet again which allows Nolan to send Anelka clear one-on-one with Taylor and we are celebrating before he's even taken the shot. He slides it effortlessly into the net and trots away nonchalantly doing his inexplicable crossed hands celebration, the man is ice cold. We have to marvel at such a finisher playing for Bolton, he's as good as it gets.

"Merry Christmas pal..." I shake Tom's hand on exiting the ground following more of the same best wishes shared with Tony and Anthony and glares exchanged with the steward. "See you Boxing Day, no getting leathered the night before!" He has drawn the short straw and will be driving us to Everton – well he didn't have an awful lot of choice, only two of the four of us can actually drive – and he reassures me that he will remain sober and that I am a fool for doubting him.

"Have a good one, sure I can't talk you into a trip up H-Town tonight?..." The temptation is there but I certainly wouldn't be making any family meal later on if I did. Instead I wish him well and get on my way leaving Tom to join up with the others. Happy crowds in blue and white *"Santa Is A Wanderer"* hats stream away from the stadium safe in the knowledge that we won't be in the bottom three at Christmas.

CHAPTER THIRTEEN

Barclays Premier League – Monday 31st December 2007

		P	W	D	L	Pts.
14	Middlesbrough	20	5	5	10	20
15	Birmingham City	20	5	4	11	19
16	Bolton Wanderers	20	4	5	11	17
17	Sunderland	20	4	5	11	17
18	Wigan Athletic	20	4	4	12	16

The 3-0 victory over Birmingham City at the Reebok Stadium is all that keeps Bolton Wanderers out of the relegation zone as they record two more away defeats; 2-0 at Everton and 3-1 at Sunderland.

     I can't remember the last time I spoke to someone that actually rates New Years Eve, seems I'm not that only one who can't be arsed with the added expense and crowds of pricks getting just that extra bit trashed for the sake of it. New Year for me doesn't represent a fresh start it just means the end of a holiday and back to work again, maybe that's why I can't get too excited by it. None of my admittedly small band of friends enjoy it either, hardly anyone mentioned it at work and my parents are just staying in watching it on telly with the dog whilst my sister is having a quiet one with her boyfriend at their local.
     Meanwhile Tom's introducing a girl he met in Horwich the other week to his own brand of New Year merriment at home and everyone else I know has no plans. So I'm sat alone in my room with the lights out steadily working my way through a load of San Miguel that I got off a relative for Christmas and some beers I

cadged from the fridge downstairs whilst listening to an old Tiesto set on the internet which is making me think about going away for Summer 2008. The driving, epic brilliance of *"Suburban Train"* giving way to *"Flight 643"*, then into his remix of Paul Oakenfold's *"Southern Sun"*. A trance pinnacle for me, a vocal you could get lost in. Magnificent.

It's the endless supply of long, dreamy breakdowns and uplifting trance that is conjuring images of watching deep red Mediterranean sunsets on a beach with a beer in one hand and a gorgeous girl from down south, Newquay or somewhere like that, who I'll definitely only spend one night with in my life in the other. Jan Johnston's *"Flesh"* comes in, framing this fantasy perfectly.

She'd be called Sophie or Harriet or some shit; a little blonde bundle of energy on her first holiday away with the girls, shoulders a furious shade of pink, she's been pickled in an immeasurable amount of vodka mixers and cocktails all day every day for the whole week that she's been out here in the Balearics. It's her last night here so she's feeling emotional and wants a send-off that she will dream about all year until she returns again and meets some other random lad from a Northern backwater town. I duly oblige; splitting away from each of our groups of mates, sharing drinks on a terrace bar in the warm evening haze then going down to the beach in time to watch the sun make contact with the watery horizon before going back to her apartment and having amazing sex in amongst the half-packed suitcases and strewn underwear.

Mental images which are completely out of sync with the reality I'm surrounded by. I finish another can and peer out of my bedroom window into the inky night, street lights illuminate rain hammering down in amber globules onto terraced houses and the tree in our garden is being heavily buffeted by a wild wind coming in right against the glass. I messaged Tom a while ago to see how his night is going but I've had no reply as yet and seeing his name in my contacts list has made me begin to think again about Wanderers.

The draw for the UEFA Cup Last 32 was made a few days ago and it just gets better and better for us, next up is Atletico Madrid in mid-February. I'm running out of ways to describe how big some of these fixtures we've had this season are and it's strange to see the very name Bolton Wanderers alongside the likes of Red Star Belgrade, Bayern Munich and now Atletico Madrid. I was quicker on the draw in securing flights for this one than I was for Munich and I've managed to get me and Tom a belting deal. We fly from Manchester the day before the game down to Malaga, have a few hours on the airport there and then get an internal flight up to Madrid, all for the cost of £110 each and I feel pretty pleased with myself about that, it's great being able to construct trips into Europe on the cheap. No accommodation sorted yet however, Tom seems determined that we should stay in a proper hotel this time not a hostel so that's going to take the price up a bit more. Proper cannot wait for it, but it's a while off yet.

In the league though we've carried on being consistently inconsistent, relying on our home form at the moment to keep our heads just above water. Sweeping aside Birmingham 3-0 in the way we did late on made us look more than capable of staying up but in our last two games we've lost 2-0 away to Everton – a game that has now also convinced Paul and Chris that I'm a jinx at aways – then 3-1 at Sunderland. I've not a clue where we'll finish up this season and each time I start to see a glimmer of hope for us we dash it all by looking like a barely competitive side and getting well beaten all over the place.

I decide I've had enough of sitting around alone so I gather my remaining drinks and go downstairs to see midnight in with Mum and Martin. As the clock nears twelve I'm sat on the sofa in the living room with my parents flicking through the channels, skipping Jools Holland as they do every year, watching various television presenters standing in the piss rain being wracked by gale force winds outside Edinburgh Castle or on the banks of the Thames. I've enjoyed my Christmas; been off work and spent time with the family, walked Holly for miles almost every day and seen Tom a couple of times to watch some football on telly although he seemed a bit quiet last time and not himself.

We'd been watching the defeat against Sunderland on a feed from a dodgy website and fair enough it wasn't exactly enthralling viewing especially seen as we were two down after half an hour, but Tom just sat there slouched deep into the couch the whole time barely saying a word. I tried to cheer him up by going on about the Newcastle trip we've got planned in a few weeks but he just shrugged and said it would be pretty good, the old faithful ploy of bringing up Munich didn't really coax any sort of reaction either. Even as Diouffy surprisingly got us back into it at Sunderland with a goal before half time and we had a bit of a pre-break surge to get an equaliser all he could say was that it wasn't going to happen. He was right about that at least.

I got a taxi back home, didn't really feel like asking him for a lift while he was looking so miserable and after he told me he was having a girl round on New Year's Eve I just said I'd see him at the Derby County game a few days after. I know he doesn't usually have a great time over Christmas what with his Mum not being around but he's never been like that before, he looked fucked too as if he hadn't slept for days. I told him to look after himself and get some rest in before this girl came round otherwise he'd fall asleep on her after half an hour, but he just sniggered. I told myself not to bother too much about it once I got home and returned to the warmth and all the food and drink I could ask for, I'm more of a worrier about stuff than Tom is anyway so he'd probably just tell me to do one if I made anything more out of it.

As we hit midnight we go back to BBC One and Mum gives me a hug and kiss, whilst I shake Martin's hand and give him an awkward hug then we watch some more telly, quaffing cans and picking at the remains of a buffet that's lasted all Christmas in the fridge, turkey butties all round for the next fortnight. We last till about one then they go to bed and I return to my bedroom and back online to eye up a decent looking adidas Parka on Ran's website but it's ridiculously expensive for what it is and I end up deciding against it. I've also had no luck sourcing a K-way cagoule like Paul had on in Munich so instead, in between swapping flirty emails with some randomer on Facebook who's seemingly not doing much on her New Year's Eve either, I put an order in for an absolutely mint olive-green Telemark winter jacket by Fjallraven and some jeans. Christmas money – and more – waxed in a matter of minutes.

A few years ago all this time devoted to looking for clothes and footwear would have been totally unheard of, it just wasn't important to me at all. I seem to be a late starter when it comes to most things; football obviously, girls didn't figure in my thoughts properly until quite late on at High School, I didn't get drunk for the first time until I was seventeen, I left it until half way through my first year at University before I really started to go out regularly, I don't drive and of course I still live at home. Feeling the urge to dress decently and spending serious money on myself is just another thing that has taken its time to interest me, while the other lads were saving as much of their part-time wages as they could on a new jacket or a pair of trainers I was still slumming it in combats and band t-shirts, so now it feels like I'm making up for lost time.

    I suppose it suited what I was into though for a while, through college and early University it was metal all the way and with it came the "uniform" to suit. I don't regret it; I had some of the best times of my life at the dark, sticky-floored clubs and the gigs deep in the slam pits and feeling double-bass trying to rip my innards out. I'll still put some of my old music collection on now and again – there's always room for metal – but with growing older, hanging around more with Tom and being around the football crowd, came a desire to smarten up. Few birds in town are going to take a lad wearing 20-inch bottomed baggy jeans and a Dimmu Borgir t-shirt seriously anyhow.

    It was Tom who started it all off for me; he's been into dressing sharply for a long time and anytime we'd meet up he would always just look the part, especially when thoughts began to turn to not just going watching Bolton play but to turning matchdays into proper events and nights out afterwards. First, the baggy pants had to go. I wasn't too bothered about all the snide comments and barely disguised laughs I'd get off people when I was turning up at the Reebok dragging soaking wet and torn denim behind me but finally I decided for myself that I just looked a bit ridiculous and I went for something more subtle and practical, ending up with the straight-legged dark indigo 501's that I wear the hell out of now. Then the offensive t-shirts went shortly after and finally the massive skating trainers were banished as well, after never setting foot on a skateboard, each item of clothing slowly replaced by stuff I now considered to be bang-on gear, invariably costing what felt like to me an absolute fortune too.

Trainers have become a bit of an obsession – adidas in particular – but I'm only now beginning to really appreciate the back story of some of the classic models. I'm a novice when it comes to finding out how to get hold of some of the rarer editions and yet to come to terms with the amounts I'll have to spend if I want to finally lay my hands on some of the really vintage stuff. I regularly spend hours of my time scouring the web for any scrap of information I can find to expand my knowledge about my fairly recently-discovered obsession; I had to start totally from scratch with this one, no hand-me-downs from family members to treasure, no old stories to be told by a father or uncle that shared the same interests, just the sight of Tom one day turning out in a pair of pristine blue and white Spezials and telling me that it was just the tip of the iceberg.

I've mentally built up a list of what I'd consider to be the Holy Grail of trainers, that I'd love to own, wear and be seen wearing some day; legendary names from their "City" series such as München, Köln, Berlin, Brussels, Dublin and Malmö among others populate the list with this bright aura illuminating them in my mind anytime I picture them. Exotic names, aspirational destinations.

The München, ideally in red and white colourway and complete with these thick, high soles that make them look like they could well be designed by an orthopaedic surgeon and would make me feel like I'm floating off the floor. The Berlin, simple yet brilliant with their dark blue suede and lighter blue stripes, or the black and orange Brussels that never fail to look stunning in any photo I see of them. Then the grail of grails for me, the Malmö; a vivid yellow suede trainer with blue stripes and laces and a gum coloured sole that in my ridiculous sounding logic, wouldn't go with any item of clothing so therefore they would go with *everything*. It's a train of thought I've tried to explain to people when showing them photos of the Malmö before and they've recoiled, telling me I'd look like I'd have bananas on my feet. I struggle to make them understand, but I know they look class so it doesn't matter.

At any rate, none of these or any of the other of the myriad of great names from the past I often read about are realistically attainable because I'm hampered by freakishly big and flat feet, size 12. A lad who's into trainers but has feet too big to find anything available in his size half the time, *brilliant*. Frequent trips onto eBay confirm this for me, it is rare I see anything come up in a 12 and then I'm not about to spend many hundreds of pounds on a pair of trainers that could well have been manufactured in the mid-eighties and be crumbling to bits beyond what's shown in their photographs, I'd be too scared to even put them on. The Malmö and another City classic the Athen were even reissued as recently as 2005 yet coming across pairs in my size has been impossible so far.

For now I attempt to appease my obsession by getting my hands on what I can from the latest general releases but it's mostly Gazelles or Spezials in some form or another that I own at the moment and I'm desperate to expand my collection. A few days ago I read on a forum about a rumour that at some point in 2008, adidas are going to re-release a number of classic models including the Dublin, London and Stockholm and the thought of that kept me awake for most of the night. Trainer insomnia as a result of an online rumour, I need my head seeing to.

As for other types of clothing, sure there's stuff I see and get a hankering for and spend time hoping to get hold of if possible – Paul's K-way for a start – but I always feel that when it comes to clothes I can find "best fit" colours and styles to achieve what I'm aiming for but it's the footwear that does it for me, in specific designs and colours and there's not much compromise. I like feeling as if I go my own way when it comes to how I dress and how I act and always have, I'm not interested in being part of a scene or being labelled as a certain type of person, though I know that is actually probably a cost of looking the way I do – I mean come on, you go to the match wearing a Lacoste jumper, straight jeans and brightly coloured adidas and you're going to get labelled.

I actually used to go around thinking I was a "Casual" not so long back, now even the term itself makes me cringe as does the attitude I had then; *"I've spent £80 on a jumper and gone to the match wearing it, so I must be one"*, fucking embarrassing. I've quickly come to the realisation that I'm pretty far from it. "Casual", for the genuine ones at least, is a full time lifestyle – a state of mind – about taking pride in striving to always be ahead of the masses in terms of fashion, music and culture, as much as trying to evade a police escort and take the piss on enemy territory. I'm none of that, I couldn't keep up with the week to week, month to month changing of what's in and what's not for a start, let alone me having no interest in getting involved with any confrontations, I'm a self confessed pussy.

I just like what I like and do what I do; I love going to football, doing the aways, going out enjoying myself and the "Casual" thing is obviously an influence and an interest but so are many other things. I'm quite happy being stuck listening to my cheesy late 90's/early 2000's trance and Euphoria albums as much as my Stone Roses and Oasis, dreaming about Summer, travelling and moping around in cheap scruffs from TK Maxx on my off-days as well, it's no big deal.

Fair enough I say all this but some chap who sees me dressed as I do, thinks I'm game and gives me a good slap isn't going to know any different is he? That's just a chance I have to take I guess although I'd much rather stop and have a chat to him about where he got his jacket from rather than run for my life. Who knows, it might all change again in a few years' time and I'll start obsessing over something else instead of what I'm wearing but for now as the first morning of 2008 begins to unfold and fatigue sets in, I congratulate myself on my latest sartorial additions.

Time for bed and I sign off my conversation with the contact on Facebook with *"perhaps I'll see you around sometime?..."* and she replies that she's got a feeling that I will.

CHAPTER FOURTEEN

Barclays Premier League – Saturday 19th January 2008

		P	W	D	L	Pts.
13	Reading	22	6	4	12	22
14	Middlesbrough	22	5	6	11	21
15	Bolton Wanderers	22	5	5	12	20
16	Birmingham City	22	5	5	12	20
17	Wigan Athletic	22	5	5	12	20

Bolton Wanderers begin 2008 with a stoppage time 1-0 victory over Derby County, but travel to Newcastle United on the back of a 2-1 home defeat to local rivals Blackburn Rovers. Their FA Cup challenge is halted at the first hurdle with a 1-0 loss at home to Championship side Sheffield United in the Third Round.

It's a feeling I love, that slow, steady rumble of adrenalin that increases as time drags on leading up to The Day. As the arrangements slot into place; coming together to form a plan, times are agreed, tickets are collected, clothes selected and collated, any thought about what's coming prompts another prickling rush to course through my veins. There's an edge to it – not just another match, not just another night out, it's a trip into something unknown. You begin the day in your own bed and it's that certain knowledge as you lie there wide awake and raring to go at stupid o'clock that you could end up *anywhere* tonight doing *anything*, via football and your mates – and nothing else matters. You go to a home game or a local away, have a few beers, a night out then go home, but you travel miles to an away with a bag of gear for an overnight stop and the whole aura of it changes.

Cold wind cuts down across the platform at Manchester Piccadilly; a freezing January morning that's making me tremble into my Desert Treks, their brown suede stained by countless spilt drinks, but I'm buzzing with excitement, we all are, a tight bunch of four lads now. Paul and Chris are back on the away game trail with us after the great time we had in Munich and a decent day at Everton despite the score, we had a laugh and it has helped to restore some trust in them both. All the ingredients are here for something special, a train-ride to a Saturday night in Newcastle and a 17:15 evening kick-off so there's drinking time before and after the game.

We take a group of four seats, two facing eachother across a table, with our holdalls stowed above us in luggage racks and carrier bags full of cans displayed in front of us. Tom's already had a couple of tins on the way to Manchester but I prefer to leave it a bit, early drinking will only leave me half asleep or sick by night-time and I decide that I'll only open my first as we're leaving the station. I unzip my new jacket that I'm delighted with and fold it up in the space above which prompts a wail of shock from Tom, I look over at him and he's pointing at my top.

"Jesus Christ, what's going on there?" He goes. I'm wearing a burgundy sweater with a pale blue Lacoste polo underneath it. "What's with the claret son, have you gone out of your mind?!" I roll my eyes and sigh, I knew this was coming.

"It's burgundy…" I offer, deadpan.

"Is it fuck, it's claret. Claret and blue, you look like a Villa fan." Tom comes back.

"Burnley…" Paul chips in – laughing – and I shoot him an unimpressed glance. Someone will shout West Ham in a minute, I'm sure.

"It's burgundy. Claret's a different shade. Besides, *you* can talk, Begbie…" I glare at Tom. I've got a point as well, he came out in a lemon coloured Argyle v-neck jumper once and the mocking he got was so intense that he wore his coat for most of the day. He laughs and sits back, looks like I've won that one but at least he seems more cheerful after how he was over Christmas. The train finally begins to move so I reach for my first beer and crack it open, looking up out of the window as the roof of the station passes by and gives way to leaden skies. Our journey takes us out through the arse-end of Manchester, past City's ground and towards Huddersfield with the four of us chatting and drinking the time away, again there's a mood of excitement between us at what lies ahead.

"Absolutely gutted Anelka's gone, man. There's no way we'll stay up now, where's the goals coming from?" Chris ponders, shaking his head as we discuss Wanderers with the Pennines flashing by outside.

"I know yeah, feels like everyone else around us has a striker they can rely on to score a few as well. I wasn't surprised though, he's mint." I reply, it has been a week now since Chelsea came in and bought Nicolas Anelka off us which has left us looking seriously blunt up front and as much as I love Kevin Davies, he's never going to run a defence ragged and finish one-on-ones all day like Anelka was doing for us.

Anelka scored over twenty goals for Bolton which for a team in our position is impressive, I feel I'm pretty safe in saying that even though he only stayed with us a matter of months he was one of the greatest ever strikers to wear a Wanderers shirt, not in terms of achievements or medals won but for his sheer brilliance in front of goal. A cult hero but not in the traditional fashion; not the chest-beating, bloodied shirt type, he never pretends to love the club he's playing for he just scores a load of goals then goes off into the sunset. He had a slow-ish start after joining from Fenerbahçe but once he got into his stride the man was lethal. I'll never forget his first goal for us against Arsenal, an unstoppable shot from outside the box that went in off the bar, it was brilliant. We'll miss him desperately in the next few months.

"It's who we get in his place though ain't it, we've obviously just made some good money off selling him. If we're serious about staying up we should be going out and getting someone with pace who can get us some goals, can't rely just on Kev." Tom joins in, reinforcing my opinion whilst striding through the beers smooth and steady.

"Tell you what though; I'm well happy with Matt Taylor I want to see him smashing them in from all over the place!" I exclaim, making a scything motion with my free hand, it was actually a surprise that we got someone like Taylor in for me to be honest because from what I've seen in the past of him it looked like he could go to a better team than us but I'm not complaining. Chris reminds us all of a goal he scored for Portsmouth where he volleyed it in from just inside his own half and it excites me to think we could have a player who can do that sort of thing in our side, something different and unpredictable. I look over at Paul to see what he thinks but he just offers a nod, sat back in his chair looking disinterested, I think he's more looking forward to the piss up than the game which I suppose we all are really but Wanderers are the reason for us being here and I'm genuinely excited about going to St. James' Park for the first time.

"What you reckon today then? Can we get something?" Despite the burst of enthusiasm over Matt Taylor, we all retreat and say no.

"What, with Keegan going back there? They all think they're going to win the league now those daft pricks." I've never seen a more delusional bunch of fans than Newcastle's, there's optimism and then there's total

Fantasy Land, Kevin Keegan has come back to manage them after they sacked Allardyce off a few days ago and I saw one lad being interviewed on telly saying they'd get into the Champions League this season now, *without a doubt*. Without a doubt! He was standing there in front of the ground with the obligatory striped shirt on and beer gut hanging out, alongside hundreds and hundreds of other Geordies.

    It never ceases to amaze me that. Anytime anything of note happens at Newcastle no matter what time of day it is they all just pile down there en masse and balloon about in front of St. James'. They all must have some sort of clause in their job contracts saying that if anything goes on with the club then they're all allowed to just down tools, get the replica shirt out of the emergency cupboard and march to the stadium in either vicious protest or wild celebration. If I was one of them I'd obviously love feeling so partisan about my home team, but from the outside looking in it's absolutely ridiculous.

    Well past Leeds now and out into the sticks as farmland passes by, sodden and looking sorry for itself in the winter gloom but our spirits are high and even Paul has perked up now the conversation has turned to our plans for the evening. None of us has ever been to Newcastle before but each of us seems to have brought some inside knowledge from somewhere about where to go for nights out. The plan settles on checking into the Travelodge we've booked as soon as we arrive in Newcastle, having a few drinks pre-match then going over to the Tyne Bridge to some bars down at the riverside afterwards before making our way up into the centre. Not that anyone knows where that is but it's just something we'll find on the beer scooter no doubt.

    Our cans are done with by the time we're pulling out of Darlington and the final stretch of the journey into

Newcastle ends up dragging on, it is a longer slog than I thought getting up here but as soon as we emerge into the cold North Eastern air any lethargy that was beginning to build up is quickly blasted away, it's bang on midday and that gives us plenty of time, this is going to be epic. Thankfully there's a line of cabs waiting outside the station so we can pile straight into a taxi and head off with no messing around. It takes a while for us to get out of the centre of town with traffic and roadworks everywhere but once we finally get out onto a stretch of road that leads just out of the city to our digs it clears and the panorama of the Tyne Bridge and the imposing high stands of St. James' Park that greets us once we're away from town is quite stunning in truth.

"So where are you lads from then?" Our driver shouts back to us in his thick Geordie accent.

"Bolton!" Comes the unanimous response and he laughs.

"Oh, for the football? You boys gonna get hammered tonight, Keegan's the messiah." He goes, quite seriously too, I was right they are all deluded.

"Bollocks mate you shouldn't have got rid of Allardyce, we'll do you tonight." Tom says and our driver guffaws more, to the point where it looks like he's going to lose control at any moment.

"Alright man, calm down." Paul says deadpan, first thing he's said in ages and we all have a laugh at him, whilst he just smirks at the attention.

"You lot off out round the Toon as well afterwards or back off down to Bolton like?" Tom tells him we're here overnight and calls him "pet" as well, mimicking the driver's tone which cracks me up but I don't think the he clocks it.

"What's it like for a drink then, Newcastle? As good as it's made out to be?" Pretty much knowing the answer anyway.

"Oh aye, superb man, down the Quayside next to the bridge or up the Bigg Market and you can't go wrong. Really good do as well like, no trouble at all either." Our target of going down to the riverside sounds like it was a good plan, but the no trouble part sounds dubious.

"No trouble? Come off it, everyone's a pisscan up here aren't they?" Tom goes and the driver shakes his head animatedly.

"Oh aye we like a drink for sure but you nay get any trouble, you know why that is? No blacks!" I nearly choke to death I start laughing so much, what a statement that is, the others are rolling about in the back of the cab too. Brilliant. Driver keeps looking back at us in his rear-view-mirror as well, frowning wondering what he's said that's set us off. Jesus, I need a drink.

Our hotel finally appears just a fraction of time before I was going to start asking Tom just how far out of town he'd organised our digs to be, there were no cheap rooms left in the middle of the city and he said this was the best he could do, but it's definitely not stumbling-distance from town. We dump our bags in our two separate rooms which are only a couple of doors away from eachother then go straight down to the bar and sort out a few beers and some food after persuading Tom to scrap the idea of straightening his fucking hair again. The bang-average burgers and chips are thrown down our necks and we're back out in a taxi into town within the hour which drops us right in the middle of it all, virtually in the shadow of the stadium.

It reminds me a bit of Printworks back in Manchester the venue we end up in, a large glassy complex with a cinema, restaurants and a few bars in it and we go into the first place we see which is almost full and has a fair few lads in Newcastle shirts around, not a single Wanderers one in sight. We again follow the well-trodden path of commandeering a table, loading up on beers and gawping up at screens showing *"Soccer Saturday"*, swapping comments about what's going on now and again without saying much else.

We are in after kick off for the Premier League fixtures but haven't missed much. Most of the games eventually go our way at least; the ever-hapless Derby are being given a going over by Portsmouth, whilst Fulham, Reading and Birmingham are all being beaten too so I'm in a good mood watching the afternoon pass by in the company of the program's distinctive screen layout and over-excitable pundits. There's not quite enough time to stay to the end of the three o'clock kick offs as we want to get across to the stadium in good time but just as we sup up and make our way out, more goals go our way and I return to the streets on a high. The four of us group up and begin the relatively short journey over to St. James' Park, joined on the streets by hundreds of others.

This is how matchdays should always be; at a ground set slap-bang in the middle of the city centre and our walk from the bar to the stadium takes all of ten minutes, in the January darkness through tight little streets in amongst the masses on their way to the game. No wonder they all love the club up here with that stadium acting like a talisman in the middle of their city towering over surrounding buildings reminding them of their priorities any time they look skyward, the feeling around the place is electric too.

The walk up to the away end rivals Munich for exertion though with a horrible series of staircases rising steeply upwards before opening out onto the concourse. There's time to spare before kick-off and I spend it raiding the kiosk for a couple of Chicken Balti Pies which taste excellent. These pies constitute one of the highlights of the season for me, I love them and it is gutting whenever they run out at the Reebok, they compliment pints quite brilliantly. With those scoffed, enough of the orange-coloured filling spilt over my face and onto the floor and a final pint each emptied we can go up to our seats. It is a great arena for football this, not quite the Allianz but the home support are much louder and it's a cracking atmosphere with thousands of Geordies bouncing about singing Kevin Keegan's name.

 A huge roar from the home fans just before kickoff makes the hairs on the back of my neck tingle and our small slither of support tries to play its part but any noise we make in here tonight will be easily swept away by the 50-odd thousand locals who I don't expect will shut up all evening. All that pre-match bluster and volume lasts the best part of five minutes though, then Newcastle's support remembers that their team is actually a pretty woeful outfit right now. Save for a section to our left giving as good as they get when some Wanderers fans sing songs about Allardyce over to them, including one very angry looking bloke who's about five-foot-two with a black and white scarf wrapped around his face making a good contrast against his livid red skin, there's very little else in the way of noise.

 Very little in the way of action too and as I shift my weight from one foot to the other and clap my hands together firmly to try and fend off the cold, the match descends into a dour affair. Our debutant Gretar Steinsson looks impressive at least and I make that point to a very bored Tom who nods passively, he's spent the early stages of this game in Paul's ear about something and basically leaves me to it, stood on an almost deserted row of seats joining in with the sporadic Wanderers songs. It's no good when you can hear your own faltering voice during a chant, though.

 I feel every one of the forty-five minutes in the first half, time most definitely is not flying by and come half time I gratefully take my leave of the giant arena to retreat to the bar.

"Well that was inspiring wasn't it lads?" I say, addressing Tom, Paul and Chris who are stood around in front of me and I don't get so much as a murmur in response. "How can a team with Milner, N'Zogbia, Duff, Owen and Ameobi in the side be so short of ideas?" I'm not getting anywhere. I don't know what's up with everyone, sure it's cold and crap and they're all more looking forward to the piss-up than the game but we're here and might as well make the best of it, they had seemed quite enthusiastic about the football back on the train too. I say nothing though, no point getting anyone's back up so I just leave it and stare blankly out the windows at the rear of the concourse where everything is pitch black save for a smattering of amber lights in the far distance beyond Leazes Park.

The Newcastle supporters give it another good burst with the vocal encouragement once the second half gets underway but again it doesn't last too long and again the match settles down although with the home team pressing a little harder. Steinsson continues to impress me, I like how he comes across as a no-nonsense hard man, we need that sort of player right now away from home and he's doing a good job of seeing off the Newcastle attacks that come his way. They don't look overly dangerous, but they look more likely to do something than we do.

As always, we hammer the ball into the sky towards Kevin Davies and as always he does his best to get his head to these bombs coming down from Jussi's clearances or our defenders' long punts. But as always, with him being the only Wanderers player in Newcastle's half, his knock-downs are useless. I'm sat down by the time Megson makes three substitutions deep into the second half, I can't be arsed standing anymore and I've not heard a single word out of Tom or the others in the entire second period so I'm actually feeling fairly bored. Campo comes on first followed by Tamir Cohen and then JLloyd Samuel, changes that aren't really going to do much harm to this deadlock.

    It's a relief to see the board go up to show the amount of stoppage time being added on because I'd be half asleep if this was to go on much longer, there's virtually no noise coming out of any part of the stadium so everyone else must feel the same. Then we win a final minute corner and it drops into the middle of the crowd in the box, right where we would want it to go. A scramble ensues and Samuel swings a boot to connect with the ball at point-blank range. It looks a certain game-stealing goal and I leap out of my seat to begin the celebrations but Shay Given somehow keeps it out with a flailing leg that directs the shot away from goal and I slap the seat in front of me in frustration.

    It would have been an absolute robbery for us to have won the match but it wouldn't have mattered in the slightest. Nevertheless, the referee blows up for full time and I laugh my head off as I hear some of the same home fans who were acting like they'd won the World Cup before kickoff, actually booing their team off at the end. Newcastle supporters, ridiculous to the last.

CHAPTER FIFTEEN

I feel much livelier by the time our group is back at street level in the cold darkness and just minutes away from the resumption of ale. I decide to keep my thoughts about the football to myself as they're obviously not going to get me very far; I'm bringing up the rear anyway. For what it's worth, despite it being a shocking match I feel encouraged that we've come here and faced down a hostile crowd, nullified an admittedly poor Newcastle team and come away with a point which could prove invaluable to us. My word though, we don't half look desperate for a striker now Anelka has left.

Sam Jacks is our first port of call, a big, pounding, heaving venue full of mirrors, chrome and bright lights emanating from beneath the many bars and high tables. This will do nicely and once we get past a couple of sets of doors the whole place opens out into a huge and cavernous piss-up centre, Calvin Harris rattling through the place as we wade in. The downstairs area is packed to bursting point so on Tom's lead we head up some steps which puts us onto an upper tier comprising of a couple of bar areas and more seats with everyone seemingly back on form.

I lean over the steel and glass balcony to survey the scene below once we've stocked up and it's an epic mass of people crushed in waiting to be served, dancing or queuing up to view or participate in a dentist's chair set-up, complete with three barely legal looking birds feeding shots to the willing victims. Above the bar a girl dances wildly on a podium, hair windmilling viciously around and her shiny knee-high boots glinting in the light from blue strobes trained on her while the *"Blade"* theme tune blares out, banging.

We're all on bottles – two or three each – and by the time I'm just starting my second, Chris is in the queue for the dentist's chair, by my third he's actually in it and we stand up on the level above looking down on him. He gives us a thumbs-up then this stunner with long blonde hair, black bikini and hot-pants straddles him and begins pouring some green shit down his throat. We three voyeurs are all laughing our heads off, the music is hammering and the crowd is cheering, I can see the liquor glistening as it spills over and runs down the sides of his face as he lies almost horizontal. The blonde pulls back and with no time for Chris to recover, another one appears behind his head, giving him a great view of her tits as she gets to work forcing some blue stuff into him.

"This doesn't actually look much fun does it?!" I exclaim, watching more alcohol go onto his face than actually into his mouth.

"Fuck off man, it looks top, what's up with you?" Tom goes and he's pointing down at Chris hoping he looks up at him but to me Chris looks like he's doing his best not to drown during this alcoholic water-boarding session as a third girl, a brunette with a ridiculous pair of legs on her adds the coup de grace; a clear shot, right down his throat followed by a kiss on the cheek for the benefit of the first girl who has now got a camera, a few more quid for a copy of the photo no doubt.

Within seconds of a sweaty-faced Chris coming back to us and following handshakes and back-slaps all round, he's off to the toilets to clean up. He's got a white Armani shirt on and the collar has fluorescent splashes all over it – ruined surely. He doesn't appear to be too arsed about it though, Tom goes into the loos with him too.

"Your turn lad?" Paul asks as we're left on our own but I refuse in no uncertain terms and he doesn't look too keen either. Already someone else is in the chair being mock-fondled by the trio of beautiful but wicked assailants down below. As Chris and Tom return we get another beer down us swiftly, watching from above as the place gets more and more crowded.

We move on after the next round, a cab takes us down near the Tyne Bridge to the riverside and we are giddy with excitement, rushing towards another place as a bitter wind crashes in against us off the river laced with sleet. The next establishment is a Spoons, in a rustic-looking place with stone walls and something approaching a courtyard in the middle of it that would be brilliant in the summer but it's just a deserted bowl of fierce swirling wind tonight. I'm straight onto a pint once we are inside and up a flight of stairs to a warm but ultimately disappointingly quiet drinking area and I commandeer a place next to some windows looking over the river whilst the other three go to the toilets together like a bunch of girls.

I catch sight of a group of women struggling past outside in the wind and one of them makes eye-contact with me as she looks up in my direction, without thinking I blow her a kiss and it looks like it made her fucking day, she's absolutely beaming. Mint. I watch her for a few seconds as they walk on but she doesn't look back again and I'm grinning to myself as the others come over to our spot. They've each got themselves a short but can't seem to stand still once we're grouped up again, especially Tom who continuously fidgets with his top and starts looking pissed off when he can't seem to keep the bottom of it straightened out. I've seen this sort of thing before but I'm not going to dwell on what's going on for now.

Our bar-hopping continues for another couple of stops along the river as we seemingly try to see inside as many places as we can in this large city in one night until we decide to move back up onto a busy road just behind the line of venues and the pavements are crowded with people on the piss. It's a great scene, so busy and alive and from what I've seen, peaceful as our original taxi driver had promised. Into a vodka bar we go and wait an eternity to be served. I snatch a glimpse of the Jagermeister sat up on the optics at the back while my drinks are finally prepared and give it a small but knowing nod of the head, acknowledging an old foe. I must be seriously hammered if I'm trying to interact with bottles of spirits, Jesus.

    I seem to have lost the others again, or they have lost me, but fuck it they're off doing their own thing so I stand in the middle of the dance floor surrounded by strangers shuffling about and necking my shots. A hen party is in full swing over to my right and the girls are hopping around doing the conga and generally fooling about, they are gaining numbers as people latch on to the back of the line and I join too as the huge human snake encompasses virtually the entire floor. I certainly didn't imagine when I was stood at Piccadilly this morning that I'd end up doing the conga with a hen party in Newcastle while my mates are off somewhere else without me, but then again I guess I was looking forward to the randomness of it all anyway. I'm not at the back for long as more join in, someone goes down further up the line but they're picked up rapidly and we continue.

    It goes on for the entirety of a Britney Spears song, girls screeching with excitement and people stood at the side doubled over laughing, then just as the song ends the snake fragments into a sea of sweaty bodies who immediately return to their original activities, seeping off towards the bar or back into the crowd or standing around dancing, strangers once more. My head is spinning once it's over and I stumble around aimlessly for a few seconds as I debate whether to get another drink or just have a sit down to gather my thoughts, but as I do so I come face-to-face with The Hen, well, more like bump into her as she prances about laughing. We make eye contact and I apologise, she smiles and says "no problem"… and we kiss, right in amongst this mass of girls on her own hen night, just going for it for a good ten seconds or so, a fantastic kisser she is too. Then off she goes with barely an acknowledgement of the event, turning away back to her friends as I leave the dance floor.

    There's no response from Tom or the others when I try to call them and I've had no texts from them either, so for all I know they might not even be in this bar. Once I round off my last bottle I go outside into the street and walk over the road into a takeaway for some cheesy chips. The polystyrene tray they're served in consists of roughly 60% chip with an apology of cheese on top and 40% grease swilling around in the bottom but they fill a gap for now, I just leave the last layer of chips in the bottom so I don't end up consuming too much of the deathly goop.

    Still, after ten minutes I've nothing off the lads and the homing beacon in my head suddenly activates and zeroes in on bed. There's not an awful lot that can be done or said to reverse it, I'm pissed and knackered. Taxis wait right outside the doors and I duck into the one at the front of the group and set course for the hotel. The ride back is a long one and goes by in a haze of bright lights from bars and clubs, none of which I'm remotely interested in as my heavy head rolls from side to side and I'm thankful that the driver isn't into making conversation because I'd no doubt talk complete guff.

    By the time I've paid my fare outside the hotel in heavy rain my pockets are left almost empty, this has been one long and expensive day. It's only when I come to put the key in my door that it dawns on me that Tom is supposed to be sharing this particular room with me and I'm the only one with a key between the pair of us, but in a bout of anger and frustration at the way the night has turned out I enter the room, lock the door behind me and crash into bed.

Sunday 20th January 2008

    I'm awoken by loud banging on the door and my instant thoughts are that I must have only been out an hour or so before Tom came back, but as more thuds hammer down on the wood I check the time and it's actually nine in the morning and I finally notice that it's actually light outside.
    "Alright?" Says Tom when I open the door and see him stood there in just his shorts and polo shirt, with his jeans over his shoulder and shoes in hand. "Crashed on the floor in their room didn't I, I'm fucking hammered mate." He pre-empts my question and walks past me into the room to where his bag and unused bed is.
    "Fuck me, what time did you get back? I just came back here once I couldn't track you down."
    "Not a clue." He croaks. "We went to some club with these lasses we met. My phone's fucked, battery's run out. I came looking for you in that shots bar we went in but couldn't find you so I didn't know what to do really." That's almost certainly a lie so I'm instantly less bothered about leaving him to sleep on the floor of Chris and Paul's room.
    "Oh right, thought they might have tried belling me then. I was in there ages but didn't see any of you and I texted all of you from in there." I'm actually quite pissed off now because it's starting to look as if they consciously binned me off at some point during the night, but it's a choice of making a scene out of it and saying something to him and leaving a shit atmosphere over today when we're supposed to be in Newcastle until the afternoon and sharing a train home again, or scooting over it. So I take the easy route and laugh it off, *laugh it off,* just to

complete the image of me being a bit of a walkover once and for all.

Regardless, it doesn't coax any further comment out of Tom either way and he gets on with having a shower and tidying himself up. We're out of the room in time for check out and the four of us reconvene in the lift on the way back to reception and although we all have a brief exchange about them "losing touch" with me and not getting back till about four, I can see amongst the three of them that they're bullshitting me as Tom stands there with his head bowed looking leathered and in Chris' eyes especially I can almost see a look of *pity*. But on the surface I just take them at their word, not believing any of it, them probably not believing that I believe it either, but I just get on with it – resigning myself to knowing I'd look a right knob if a group of four lads were walking around and one of them was moaning and arguing with the other three all day. What a cop out.

Breakfast in a café back in town is a sombre affair but it would have been anyway I reckon. Despite how last night ended up going down I am still badly hungover myself so I hover over my Full English with shaking limbs and sweaty skin very slowly negotiating my way through each component of the dish one at a time as if to gradually introduce the greasy sausage, bacon, eggs and beans to my body and not infuriate it any further. The four of us sit in silence round the table, each a picture of macabre morning afters, only Chris says anything for the duration of our time sat here and even that was just to let us all know that he could quite easily go back to bed for the rest of the day to which we all mumble agreement.

With no prospect at all of any of us wanting to go looking round town we settle on a pub opposite the station and spend another quiet hour until our train is due to leave slumped on couches next to the window looking out into the street. Paul braves a beer but leaves it barely touched and I opt for a coffee but the other two don't move from their positions until we get ready to leave. Right now from the outside we could well look like absolute strangers to eachother and I'm left to my thoughts about all this, just a one off where alcohol – and whatever else – took over for a night, but back to Munich-style adventures after this? Or a warning of a return to times that I thought we were past and that Tom had put behind him months ago?

Whatever, as our group silence continues once we take up our seats on the train back to Manchester and we each stare out of the windows leaving Newcastle behind us at last, deep down I know that the latter case is going to be closer to the truth. As sad as it is to admit, becoming immersed with the alcohol induced paranoia, I spend the duration of the journey home beginning to feel really quite lonely.

CHAPTER SIXTEEN

Friday 25th January 2008

I've found myself thinking quite a lot recently about an ex of mine, well, *the* ex – Chloe. Pining for someone is never healthy, especially when they're long gone and I know it does me no good but it's hard not to. We lasted about a year and it all happened during a blissful time for me, the kind that times where when I'm feeling down like this makes me look back on them with glowing memories and the sort of daydreaming, slow-motion scenes you'd see in a melodramatic film montage.

At the same time we were seeing eachother, Wanderers were busy completing one of the most successful campaigns in their history; we'd beaten the likes of Liverpool, Arsenal, City, Newcastle and Tottenham and ended up finishing sixth to qualify for Europe. *Sixth*. I'd also not long since returned from travelling so I was buzzing and still filled with the glee and enthusiasm about making it through unscathed after seeing so many amazing sights and she seemed genuinely enchanted by some of the stories I'd prattle on for ages about, going back out there together was mooted too. Well, for a bit anyhow.

She just one day broke down in tears and came out with the old *"it's not you, it's me"* line. There was a mention of being in her final year at Uni, some talk about her feeling like we were "drifting", she even tried to make out *I* deserved better which was bullshit but probably just a way of making her feel better about it. I don't know what I did wrong. We broke up and I never heard from her directly again. Took me ages to get over her and until maybe this past week I thought I was doing a good job of it, but feeling lonely and out of the loop after Newcastle left me dwelling on it again.

So to clear my thoughts I've gone on a bit of a mad one, but it's not exactly working out. It is clearly bollocks when people spin yarns about shagging virgins who are ridiculously naughty, up for anything and know exactly what they want from you – because this one is absolutely clueless. It turns out a girl I've been chatting to on Facebook for a while was not only single and *very much* looking, but that she was also keen to meet up for basically nothing other than no strings sex which suited me down to the ground, so we set about trying to make it happen. With both of us living at home we decided to sort out a cheap hotel for the night to keep us out of the way of anyone and it seemed like quite a straightforward enterprise. About a week into our flurry of emails though she told me that she was actually a virgin and that she hoped that hadn't put me off (it hadn't), but that she was desperate to still meet up for the night.

She's eighteen, we're both single and both wanted it so I decided to just go for it, it's been well over a year since I last actually had sex as well, despite all the recent encounters with girls I've had. I'm sure my parents would be aghast, hers too, that not only was a one night stand in a Travelodge being arranged over Facebook but that also she was willing to give away her virginity to a complete stranger. I guess when it's put like that I don't feel as up for it either, but it teased at some sordid fantasies of mine so I pressed on with the meet.

Three weeks of planning, emails, texts, second thoughts and numerous attempts from me to almost talk her out of it as doubts began to set in later, I went to meet her at a pub in Bury. For the first time I felt a bit nervous but with all of our cards on the table and knowing what our intentions were rather than completely stepping into the unknown I didn't feel as bad and when she showed up she didn't seem too bothered either. She's alright looking and nice enough so I'm not sure why she felt the need to use the internet as a way to hook up with someone but whatever.

    We had a couple of drinks then walked to the hotel for the night, which is right about when she froze up completely. After dozens of filthy texts from her describing what she was going to do to me, what she wanted me to do to her, spelling out exactly how she wanted things to go – it ended up with us sat next to eachother on the bed not really knowing what to do or say. She banged on about being into listening to Duffy for a while which bored the shit out of me and I talked about watching Wanderers which I'm sure did the same for her...

    Which is why I find myself here; eventually naked, eventually with her naked, on top of someone who had promised me the fuck of a lifetime, uncomfortably fumbling around and constantly asking if she's alright. She doesn't say very much and doesn't do very much and the night culminates in an almost apologetic sex session, then a truly excruciatingly awkward couple of hours sat next to eachother on the bed watching television in almost total silence and definitely not mentioning the sex at all. She falls asleep at about midnight and I lie there struggling to drift off too as I watch the news feeling guilt beginning to seep in.

    Next morning we go our separate ways swiftly after a couple of kisses at the bus stop and she tells me she had a good time, she's on her own on that one, it was crap and rather than fulfilling any exciting fantasy about being with a virgin it has actually made me feel like a dirty old man. I sit on the bus back to Bolton staring out the window running my mind over it all; trying to suppress the guilt with the knowledge that we are both consenting adults and that at any rate I can keep it all a total secret at my end. No-one's going to find out about her, or this.

Saturday 26th January 2008

Wanderers have no game this weekend with us being out of the cup already so instead I've arranged to finally meet up with the girl I was talking to on Facebook on New Years' Eve, they should rename it Fuckbook. Once I got home from seeing The Virgin in Bury I told myself that I'd have a quiet night in but with it playing on my mind so much about how badly it all went and looking for ways to suppress my guilt and hold off any further pining for the ex, I sent her an email asking if she wanted a drink tonight. We've also been swapping emails frequently for most of January now and just like The Virgin, she has been as explicit as me about what we want out of this arrangement. An hour after I send the email she replies positively while I watch the afternoon's football scores roll in and a meeting time and place are set. The joys of modern technology.

I find her in The Swan and it is heaving as usual on a Saturday night. She stands off to the side near the entrance wearing a stripy blouse as she said she would be and we recognise eachother straight away even though we've never met. We say hello to eachother, I lie and tell her she looks great, then get our drinks in before going to sit on some rancid couches over near the bogs.

Amy she's called and although I'm showering her with compliments which are turning her into a blushing mess, she's pretty fucking far from alright, I'm just seeing how far I can push the boundaries of what I say to her. As

I found out last night it's alright giving it the big one via email about how naughty you are, it needs to be backed up in person otherwise it's pointless. She's quite short and very big, with greasy shoulder-length black hair, plus there's something about her that makes it obvious she's a bit rough. Could be the chunky gold earrings and multiple sovvies on her fingers, perhaps. It takes less than ten minutes for her to start telling me where she wants my cock and before long we're kissing and groping. At least it's an improvement on last night.

Sure enough we're away from town within the hour and into a taxi up to hers which is up on the Johnson Fold estate, not a million miles away from mine. Her hand doesn't leave my crotch during the entire journey and we rush to her house across the street excitedly. The lights are on I notice as we come down the path and a youngish looking girl stands up in the living room before coming to the door to greet us.

"Don't worry, this is my mate Tasha. She said she would look after th'kids while I'm out, I bet she didn't expect us back so soon!" Amy giggles as the door opens for us. Kids, I should have known, no wonder she wasn't doing anything on New Year's Eve.

"Fucking hell you didn't hang around, did you?" Tasha says, giving me the once over in the process. "I'll make myself scarce then! Kids are fast asleep so don't worry about waking them. I'll bell you after Amy, yeah?"

"Yeah babe, nice one I'll speak to you soon." Amy replies and off Tasha goes up the path and round the corner. She knows exactly what's going on here, I think to myself and was as casual as that about it. Maybe Amy has done this many times before, or even done the same for her mate – probably both. I should be astounded really, or in despair about the state of society, but I'm horny as fuck and I don't give a shit.

Curtains are closed and onto the couch we go; kissing frenziedly, her hand desperately trying to undo my belt, while I unbutton her blouse and slide the bra strap off her left shoulder, she's already moaning loudly and we're still almost fully clothed. Within seconds of her finally finding a way to open my belt, the zip is down and so are my jeans and she literally launches herself at my knob. She is absolutely wild, kneeling on the couch sucking me off and squeezing my balls in a vice-like grip, sucking hard, nibbling and spitting all over it like we're on film or something. I sit back and enjoy, stifling an incredulous laugh as well, it's fucking *mental* this. For just a second or two my mind goes back to Newcastle with Tom, Paul and Chris off doing their own thing and them obviously not wanting me around and I think fuck them, look at what I'm doing now, *look at this*.

By the time I manage to get my hands down her thong to play with her while she continues to devour me she's howling the place down, actually shuddering as I touch her and surely there's going to be a house-full of newly awakened screaming kids kicking off anytime soon.

"Right that's it, I want you in me, *now*." She orders, cheeks red from exertion and hair strewn all over her face. "Follow me." So I have to waddle off out the room with my battered knob out and my jeans around my ankles looking an absolute picture, I'm sure. Amy leads me upstairs once I pick up my trousers and hold them to my waist and to her bedroom, she jumps onto her bed and hurriedly removes her clothes as I do the same, the place cloaked in darkness save for the light coming from the landing.

I spread her legs out and eagerly climb on top of her and she gasps then moans loudly as I begin to push into her which is quite a struggle at first with her gut in the way, then fast and relentless.

"I want you to strangle me, hit me." She rasps, the nutty cow. "Hit me!" There's no way I'm hitting her. Amy wraps her legs around me and again tells me to strangle her but it's not my bag that. I move my hands to her neck for a few seconds which she appears to like but it does nothing for me. Instead I just compromise, hold her down firmly and absolutely go for it, I can barely class last night as a fuck, so for me this is the first time in ages I've had anything and it's amazing. I go on like a machine as well to be fair, in fact it's ridiculous. Covered in sweat, I carry on ramming in and out of her for ten minutes at least, surely. Her moans and pleas for violence died down a few minutes in and she just lay there taking it and grunting, yet now I feel like I could go on forever with no sign of me wanting to finish off.

It slowly dawns that Amy actually seems to be *asleep* though. I've fucked her to sleep! I stop and pull out, which makes her groan and her eyes open slightly.

"Jesus, you alright?" I whisper to her, I'm panting and dripping with sweat. She nods tiredly and it's impossible to imagine that this knackered looking girl nearly asleep on her bed was not half an hour ago acting like the Banshee Of Bolton. "Erm, do you want me to go?" Fishing for an answer along the lines of "No, please carry on", but most disappointingly she nods again and squirms about on the bed getting comfy.

What a letdown, I sigh and start to feel chilly. "Okay, I'll let myself out. Don't get up it's alright." I whisper and kiss her a couple of times on the lips. There's no danger of her getting up anytime soon, that's obvious. I clamber back to my feet and drape the duvet over Amy, now quite clearly sleeping, then start to put my clothes back on. As I bend forward to reach for my top, the light from the landing illuminates the varnished outline of a wooden cot on the other side of the bedroom. The kids have been asleep in here the whole time, grim.

I creep downstairs and let myself out, the Yale lock snapping shut as the door closes behind me and I decide to walk home seen as it is dry. I take a look back at Amy's house from the end of the path, the lights still on behind the closed curtains in her living room. She's asleep up there and so are two evidently young children, with her front door not properly secured and – until moments ago – with a total stranger hanging around in her house with his hands around her neck. Such things don't bear thinking about.

Tuesday 29th January 2008

We should be ahead here against Fulham on this cold and wet Tuesday night but we're deep into the second half now and scraping a win is looking increasingly unlikely. It's always toss against Fulham, always. They used to come here and do a job on us before we were in the Premier League and now up in the top division it's still a major grind to get anything out of them, even a measly goal. We've been on top most of tonight, I'm impressed again by Matt Taylor and especially Gretar Steinsson who is getting forward from defence and causing problems whenever he can but it's just not falling for us and whenever we do look like making something happen, their centre backs are right on top of anything we can produce.

"Not heard from you for a few days mate, what you been up to?" Tom asks as we gaze on at the action before us, drawing a blank yet again. I'm quite pleased he's asked, I left him to it after Newcastle and got on with my own thing.

"I've been getting into some birds haven't I! Met a couple of them on Facebook. There's a girl in work that's after me as well." He looks in my direction with a scrunched up look on his face.

"Fucking hell you're not hanging around are you, three in a week?" I feel pretty pleased with myself.

"I know yeah it's been mad, it all just happened really. This one from work has been pestering me for ages to be honest and you can't turn that down really." Embellishing the Steph thing admittedly, we've only really just began swapping emails again but it's only going to lead to one thing.

"Shitting on your own doorstep there pal, very dangerous." Tom comes back, just then we're both almost out of our seats as a chance goes begging at the far post from Kevin Nolan, but it's all half-hearted stuff from us anyway.

"Yeah I suppose you're right, but she's not bad. It would be no strings stuff so it'll be reet." Even I'm unconvinced by that as the moans and grumbles carry on in the stands around us.

"It's never no strings at work, work *is* the strings..." Tom laughs.

"Very philosophical Thomas. Nah it's alright, she's a grade above me anyway, she's not about to start going round spreading that sort of news. We haven't even done anything yet."

"What about these from Facebook then you dirty get?"

"Jesus, one was a fucking virgin, man..." He cackles wickedly, reeling back as he does so.

"Oh my god Jamie, you fucking mentalist, how old?!"

"Eighteen. But honestly it was rubbish mate, proper awkward." I shake my head thinking back, yeah that really was a crap night.

"I'm not surprised, it's not going to be like a porno is it? I bet she just fucking lay there shitting it you mad bastard." We're both laughing, though I'm unsure if I should have said anything about it, maybe should have left the virgin thing out of it. "So how about the other one, she a granny or something?" I elbow him in the ribs.

"Come off it you dick, no I met her on Saturday she lives in this council house near mine... Two kids." He starts guffawing again, looks like he can barely take any more revelations like this. "One word though mate. *Feral.*"

"That's worse! Two kids? Oh man, she's lining you up for a third!" I bury my head in my hands groaning, I'm laughing too but that thought makes me feel a bit ill. "Please tell me she was fit at least, come on." I slowly look round at him and hold the dramatic pause for a second.

"She had a face like a melted welly." We both crumble into fits of laughter, she wasn't *that* bad – okay she was pretty bad – but I love that expression, had to use it at some point. Saturday night was mad though, I've never had it like that before, it was good for a short while until the sleeping part, obviously.

"You're a sex pest mate." Tom informs me, all interest in the game now completely dead. "Oh well, as long as you're bagging up there's nowt to worry about is there..."

Fuck, that's a point.

Wednesday 30th January 2008

Of course, when I told myself at the end of last year after our brief encounter that the whole Steph situation was finished, it was never realistically going to stay that way. We ignored eachother for a few weeks after my email saying we could just forget about it if she wanted, then got talking about work, then began flirting again and eventually in dropped the email from her asking if I wanted to go for a drink. Naturally I said yes, going for the nothing to lose and nothing else better to be doing angle and so just a few days after the sorry night with The Virgin and the encounter with Amy I go for a drink with Steph after work down in Castlefield.

    Castlefield is one of my favourite areas of Manchester; a mix of industrial past and hedonistic present manifesting itself in the form of old factories and warehouses converted into modern apartments, trendy bars and open spaces of land to be used for gigs and festivals. Into the mix goes a constant army of people enjoying these amenities, all interjected by the Bridgewater Canal and a tangle of viaducts overhead carrying trains and trams around the city. There's always a great atmosphere around here and me and Steph have a couple of pints each at Dukes 92, one of the bars overlooking the canal. I watch a barge slowly make its way towards the lock which will deliver it further down into the Basin and because I've started on beer straight after work it's taking effect quicker.

    Steph is feeling naughty again tonight I can tell, in much the same way as she did that night in Printworks she's being very flirtatious and tactile, we're kissing in no time at all. I buy us a third drink but they're hardly touched because after only a few sips we escape into the dark streets looking for somewhere deserted, stopping often to kiss and whisper filth to eachother. I lead us under the viaducts and into the Roman Ruins that populate this area, there used to be a fort here and some of it was reconstructed as part of the regeneration of Castlefield to be a kind of outdoor museum.

    It presents us with a very useful blend of cover and seclusion, we run up some stairs taking us away from the street and over to some bushes lining the building laughing cheekily, she pushes me against the wall, kissing frenziedly as she goes for my jeans which she has round my ankles in no time. I want more this time though, more than what occurred outside Printworks last year. I begin to take her pants down too as she plays with me and produces a condom from her pocket just before they're off and slips it on me. As soon as the trouser legs are finally free of her heels, she drags me down to the floor and I'm fucking her almost instantly.

    A tram rattles by in the dark just yards away from us on one of the bridges as I pound into Steph and I wonder if the driver has any idea of what's going on below; two work colleagues creating what would be a century's worth of office gossip, shagging in a patch of wet, muddy ground with only a couple of bushes for cover. It's not the best really, half of my mind is on worrying about getting caught and it's freezing cold and filthy around here, I dread to think what's crawling around us and those thoughts put me off quite a bit. I'm stood up and yanking my jeans back up seconds after finishing off and wanting to get out of there, Steph recovers her clothes and she leans on me as she puts them back on.

    Steph kisses me again as we walk back towards life and I'm looking around sheepishly hoping there's no-one about, but she wants to hold hands and kiss me again, no wanting to walk away this time. When we pass into the light I notice that her back and arse are completely caked in mud and my knees are as well, jeans soaked, we look a proper state, there's even shit in her hair too. I can't believe I've just fucked someone in some bushes in the middle of town; it is debauchery of the highest order. I make my excuses sharpish and tell her I should be getting my train back to Bolton straight away and I do so, though not without her pressing for more kisses and intimacy before I leave. Something with her seems to have changed, she wants more I can tell.

CHAPTER SEVENTEEN

Thursday 31st January 2008

It is Transfer Deadline Day today so we can finally discover if Megson is going to manage to bring anyone in to fill the chasm left by Nicolas Anelka's departure. He can never be replaced but we need someone decent drafting in to score us some goals and keep us in the division. At the other end of the pitch we've signed a central defender, Gary Cahill; young, English and very promising from what I've seen so he's a decent acquisition. Work takes a back seat in favour of frequent visits to BBC Sport's website to see who has gone where and what the latest rumours are. The signs aren't promising though, I don't see many strikers linked with us, whilst my personal hope that we might somehow lure former hero Eidur Gudjohnsen back to us is fading fast.

Interestingly and very tellingly we have let Christian Wilhelmsson leave for Deportivo La Coruna, one of Sammy Lee's pre-season signings that was meant to be central to that new era of exciting attack-minded football, allowed to go after barely featuring and looking far too lightweight when he did. Leaving with him were Gerald Cid and Lubomir Michalik over the course of this Transfer Window, two more failed signings and no great losses. The only other player apart from Anelka that I have been sad to see leave in the last month was Gary Speed. Our midfield will be a weaker place without him in it, a top player and scorer of some massive goals in his time with us. There is no doubt that for better or worse, Megson is beginning to make his own mark on the squad.

I see Steph coming to my section more often than usual today, just as she did when we first started messing about. A couple of times I see her from where I am and she ends up blushing, each time she visits it's for very minor reasons too, to find out things she could easily do from her own desk. I'm still yet to fully understand how I'm feeling about last night, just as I was the with Amy I can't decide whether I should feel ashamed of myself for participating in such a depraved act or feel exhilarated that I'm doing things with women that I never imagined I'd get chance to do. I wasn't keen on how clingy Steph seemed to get afterwards either, that was a change from previously and I hope she isn't pining for something more. I decide to try and keep things light hearted when on her latest visit I actually speak to her.

"Hope you can get those pants clean..." I say with a chuckle but she turns a shade of crimson, looks at me for a second or so longer than I think I'd like her to, then walks off without saying anything. Fucked that one up, clearly.

I return to my desk feeling frustrated, I wish last night could have just happened and then I didn't have to see her again for ages. Shitting on my own doorstep, as Tom had warned. I need a different girl to think about to take my mind off it so I decide to text Flick and see if she finally wants to meet up after all this time and all these texts we swap at regular intervals. A prickle of sweat appears instantly when a few minutes later she replies, telling me to see her later tonight.

Flick gives me the details of where to go and when so we can finally follow up on the last time we saw eachother way back in October in Barracuda; since then we have kept in touch, a couple of times *almost* met up, but never actually gone through with it. Tonight is different. Flick works at a small nursing home in town and often has to stay on call through the night so she has her own living quarters nearby and it's at the front door to that small bungalow that I find myself, illuminated by a dim amber security light that probably needs replacing and battered by strong and freezing winds, my brand new mountaineering jacket coping admirably with these conditions however. I press the bell, hear it ring inside and I see movement towards the door through a small oblong window in the middle of it almost immediately. My chest is pounding, I hadn't given much thought to how nervous I'm feeling about this until this second and I wish I hadn't done so at all.

Flick opens the door and for a few seconds my nerves are completely swept away by being taken aback at just how *gorgeous* she actually is. She smiles widely at me, looking hot in Ugg boots, black tights, short skirt and a beige polo-neck jumper, with her straightened blonde hair and pink, glossy lips.

"You found me at last, about time!" She lets me in as I continue to try and mentally pick my jaw up off the floor. Once the door is closed we kiss passionately, as if we were two lovers finally reunited after so long apart. My arms wrap around her tightly and the embrace goes on for minutes, she's seemingly oblivious to the fact that my coat is soaking wet and my hands that are holding onto her tightly are actually freezing. Eventually we release eachother and still she wears a huge, beautiful smile.

"I was kind of expecting you to open the door wearing a white uniform and a pair of nurses' clogs..." I say to her as she leads me through into the living room, which just looks like any other save for the large whiteboard on one wall depicting a chart with various names and notes on and a few boxes of medical equipment stacked up in the corner.

"What, with a load of vomit on my apron and smelling of piss as well?" She goes.

"That's some kinky shit is that." I reply and we both laugh together, my nervousness has lifted from me entirely. We kiss again then she tells me to sit down while she makes us a brew.

Then, after all these months of me expecting our next and only meeting to be all about sex, we spend the following couple of hours just talking. Sat close and occasionally kissing and cuddling, but mainly just chatting about ourselves and our lives and I absolutely fancy the pants off her. The fact that she's married is obviously a major talking point and that detail cannot be forgotten regardless of anything that we say, but Flick explains to me about how she knows she got married way too young at nineteen – she's now twenty-three – and that there's no love or passion in the marriage anymore already, that all it has done is make her miss what it was like to be single again.

Even the husband has thrown in the towel she says, always either away working or can't be arsed moving when he's not. I can't help but ask why she doesn't just get a divorce then but she says no and seems to agonise over the very thought that it might come to that. It confuses me, but there's not much in this whole situation that I do understand, so many girls that I've come into contact with one way or another in the last few years, yet I've not been as instantly infatuated with *any* of them in the same way that I am here with Flick. She goes on to tell me that when we first met in Reflex she did fancy me but that she only decided to meet up again as a bit of harmless fun, yet when we saw eachother again in Barracuda a couple of weeks later she ended up really liking me and really wanting me.

We go through numerous cups of tea each and she ends up in my arms sitting on the couch. It is her that ultimately makes the first move. She strokes her pointed nails up my chest beneath my shirt which makes every hair on my body stand up and we kiss over and over, it's not long before she is forcing my jeans down as well and she moans as soon as she feels how hard for her I am. I help her lift off the jumper and immediately kiss up and down her cleavage, cradling one of her breasts firmly in my hand as I run my tongue over her skin and across her collarbone. She squirms and gasps and strokes her nails up and down me which turns me on to a ridiculous degree. I can sense I won't hold out for too long if she carries on with that, so I go for her skirt and at the first sign of me struggling to force the top button open she quickly stands up, tears off the Uggs, loses the skirt and then turns the act of rolling her tights down to her feet into one of the hottest things I've ever seen.

 Flick comes back over to me, watches intently for a moment as I bag up, then straddles me on the couch and lowers herself down onto me. We kiss and hold eachother as she begins to rise and fall atop me. She moans out with each stroke and I feel her back arching, her arms releasing me to run them through her hair which makes the long blonde locks flow out all over the place and I use the chance to move in and kiss her neck slowly and gently, working my way up to her ear lobe which I begin to nibble and she loves it – moaning louder and grinding herself down onto me harder.

 I tease her like this for no longer than a minute or so before she pushes me back and presses down as hard as she can as she climaxes, staring into my eyes as she wails so loud that I'm sure it'll wake up every Phyllis and George sleeping soundly at the far ends of the building. It's all I can take too and I cum just as she does, the most fantastic feeling in my life, with this beautiful blonde woman writhing on top of me and staring into my eyes with a look on her face as if she's never felt so fulfilled.

 We stay in that position for as long as we can before we're both freezing and cramping up, me telling her she's beautiful until she begins to blush far too much for her liking. There is obviously no graceful or sexy way to get out of the position we are in on the couch, but we both roar with laughter as she stumbles over trying to free herself from me and I find out only as I try to stand up that my legs have ceased up after having her sat on me for so long, so that I basically have to crawl to the bathroom wearing just my socks.

    Once cleaned up though we return to the couch and cuddle up again getting warm as I stroke her hair and kiss her forehead. We act, for the next hour or so, like any normal couple and for just that short while I manage to take my mind off the giant, inescapable elephant in the room and just enjoy the here and now, something I've always in the past struggled to do and yet here with the most unattainable girl in the world I feel totally at ease. She cuts into the blissful silence and tells me I better hop it as the clock nears eleven because she has to go on her rounds, cue more jokes about vomit and piss while I slowly and mournfully put my coat on.

    "See me tomorrow, please..." She whispers with me standing at the door ready to make my exit. "I'm not working, let's go somewhere and do something together. I'd like that." She smiles and I agree to it, a *date* with Flick.

Friday 1st February 2008

    I'm a washout in work today, thinking about Flick and how beautiful she is and I spend all day struggling to focus on anything else, I'm totally blown away by her. I even manage to completely ignore Steph on the couple of occasions that I see her. At the very least however, it stops me from dwelling on the fact that in the end the only striker Wanderers brought in to replace Anelka just before the Transfer Window closed was a proven stump from the lower divisions, Grzegorz Rasiak, absolute pants. Now in the evening, I'm due to meet Flick again at a retail park just outside of Bolton for a couple of drinks and a trip to the cinema and I'm as excited and nervous as a kid on his first date. I've taken extra care to wash and freshen up and dress smartly, all ready to meet her in shoes that have recently had their suede cleaned and knitwear that I only removed the tags from today.

 Once again she turns out looking incredible in tight jeans and high-heeled boots, which unfortunately do make her taller than me for tonight but I'll let her off and a revealing black top. I want her again badly. We manage a single drink at the bar in the cinema, it's snowing so we sacked off the plan to go to a pub across the way and went straight into the giant Cineworld instead. We chat and laugh and get to know eachother like any normal couple just starting out and I'm loving how easily it seems I can make her burst out laughing, I've not felt this comfortable with a girl in a long time.

 We choose to watch the newly released *"Cloverfield"* and I'm surprised by how much I enjoy it as I wasn't expecting much, though the way it's filmed with hand-held cameras does make me feel a bit nauseous at times. Flick enjoys it too, telling me she much prefers things like that to bobbins romantic comedies and that's another box ticked for me. What a woman. The snow has turned to sleet by the time we emerge and we brave the conditions to go to the pub and end the night with a couple of drinks in a cosy corner of the building, holding hands and cuddling more.

 It feels a great shame to have to end the night with just another kiss in the taxi before she gets out and it depresses me to see the door close and watch her disappear, but the reality of the situation is brought home again as I remember why she had given the wrong address for the taxi to drop her off at. One that is two streets away from her house to minimise the risk of someone who recognised her seeing her get out of it after kissing a strange lad goodbye.

Saturday 2nd February 2008

Me and the other lads watch Wanderers' game at Reading on Arabic television in a pub up Horwich and to our amazement, surprise and great relief we somehow come up with a 2-0 victory. Where to start? Three clean sheets in a row and five points from the last three games, Gary Cahill slotting in at centre back and playing like a man possessed, Heidar Helgusson at last managing a goal, the whole team looking like a decent unit for once and all this despite us missing a penalty in the first half. Of course this starts the boozing off in earnest and after a few in the village we end up in Bolton.

There's an absolutely buzzing atmosphere in town tonight too as we pile into various venues on Bradshawgate, everyone seemingly on good form and having a top time. I could let myself believe that the euphoric feeling permeating through the bars is to do with the Reading victory but I doubt the fortunes of the team dictate the mood around the town as much these days. Probably not in the same way it would have done in the past anyway, it's more likely that everyone's just delighted that another shitty week in shitty jobs in a shitty town has passed and it all converges into these streets for a few hours' worth of drinking and fooling about.

As time passes though the twin forces of the other three lads quite blatantly going off down the same path as they took in Newcastle and a series of very tempting texts from Steph begin to tear me away from the plan to end up on yet another full night of it in town. The familiar pattern of toilet visits in pairs, sometimes even all three of them at once and the way Tom of course manages to start turning into a dripping mess in a very short space of time leaves me in no doubt that he's being led back into doing coke again by the others just as he was in the past, he said those days were over with. I'm rising above it tonight though because I'm floating around atop a wave of deep tipsiness and these messages from Steph. By eight o'clock I decide to make a break for it and go for the train to meet her in Manchester, the other three show little interest when I tell them I'm off.

As I often do when I'm cruising towards drunkenness and in a good mood I talk to all and sundry on the train as they travel to the city on nights out, probably annoying the hell out of many of them in the process. Then I meet Steph in her car at the pick-up-point and I drop into the passenger seat, both of us knowing what the plan is and giving no thought to the usual dose of embarrassment we'll no doubt feel after it all. Once again I'm drunk and taking chances as they come, not thinking about the consequences, showing Tom that I can do mad shit when I want to as well, he can go off with the others if he wants.

Steph drives us to her house out towards Prestwich and little is said, nothing much *to* say really I'm just hoping we get there before I start thinking seriously about what I'm doing. Her place is a terraced house a stone's throw away from Heaton Park and she offers me a drink when we get there, a jumbo sized bottle of Stella which I begin to hammer through gleefully as she knocks back vodka and coke by the glassful. We sit on her couch as some oft-repeated shit on Dave plays in the background, our hands and lips all over eachother, coming up for air only to take on more booze.

I'm through the bottle fast and then we're scrambling upstairs to her bedroom. I stumble around all over the place feeling pretty well leathered by now but I find my way onto her bed and she jumps on top of me, pinning me down and setting about it like the world is about to come to an end. What transpires is nothing short of an unabashed romp, the pair of us going for it big time and trying all sorts out. But as the acts continue and the time passes I begin to both sober up and also realise that I'm making one huge mistake here. The post-sex regrets hit me like a wave before they're even in the past tense and it makes me feel sick, filthy and disgusting.

I pull out abruptly and Steph looks round to glare at me, startled but pissed, not really knowing what's going on and I blurt out a whole load of garbage about me suddenly not feeling well and really having to go. I shuffle to the end of the bed and recover my clothes, doubled over; feeling like a victim and Steph suddenly appears with her hands around my shoulders asking if I'm okay and sounding genuinely concerned but I shrug her off, I simply have to get out of here. My word I suddenly find her deeply unattractive. Once again I reiterate that I'm not feeling well but I also drop in that coming here was a mistake and that seems to hit her like a rock. She slides back against the pillows as if some sort of invisible force has just grabbed her and flung her backwards, a bit of an over-reaction I'd say, but she seems lost for words, her mouth hangs open.

"I'm sorry..." I say. "Just shouldn't be doing this, can't do it anymore." I stand up and go to use her bathroom feeling terrible but not about Steph, not at all, in fact perversely it feels like I've cheated on Flick. It was the image of her face that dropped into my head as I had Steph on all fours and began fucking her from behind whilst yanking her hair back and that image managed to rip away all the drunken lust from me in an instant. I just have to get out of here right now. In my frantic and desperate need to get as far away from Steph's as I can I phone up and order taxis from two different Manchester firms, whichever gets here first wins my custom.

I'm scurrying out of there in no time, with a half-dressed Steph stood at the door looking very sorry for herself but I can't make eye contact with her, I know what I'm doing is a twat's trick. I hurry into the taxi and tell the driver to take me to Piccadilly and just as soon as the wheels start moving the second taxi comes into view in the rear window and I try to make myself as small as possible on the back seat.

"Say mate, is that taxi for you as well? It looks like it's going to the same address." My driver asks and my face flushes up with an embarrassed warmth.

"No pal..." I very quickly snatch a glimpse out the back trying to act as innocently as I can. "No idea who that one's for at all." Lying bastard, but he doesn't press me any further, he's about to get nigh on a tenner out of me for this ride anyway.

I arrive at Piccadilly at just gone half past midnight so I'm in good time to catch the last train back to Bolton. Gone are the days when you could count on one final escape route home arriving at three, but still even getting to the station at this time means I have to sit in the freezing cold on the platform feeling ashamed of myself, so I accept this discomfort as a punishment for how I behaved tonight. I've probably done irreparable damage to any sort of reasonable atmosphere between me and Steph after this, plus I still feel like I've let Flick down in a big way, the irony of that situation totally lost on me obviously.

I think I fall asleep at some point unless my mind goes totally blank for a period of time on the void that is Platform 14 in the early hours of the morning. At any rate, I'm stirred up from whatever it was by the arrival of my train at last and I climb onboard barely awake, totally shattered.

 To my complete and utter life-shattering dismay, the next thing I see when I decide to look of the window is a sign saying Poulton-le-Fylde passing by at considerable speed. Then to compound matters I'm accosted by the ticket conductor who doesn't believe for a minute that I must have fallen asleep and missed my intended stop and proceeds to charge me a fortune for a ticket. So, I spend the next four or so hours what can only be described as grieving; lying across some benches in Blackpool North train station which at first is fairly busy with people going home from nights out but then quickly ends up being perhaps the most desolate and depressing place on Earth, completely deserted and so cold that it reduces me to a few moments of helpless and rather pathetic sobbing.

 I must drift into some form of sleep again but they're spells interrupted by the cold and fear of being mauled by some seaside villain, eventually I get myself on the first Manchester bound train of the day – the Sunday 5:20am service. A horrible frozen mist hangs over everything and throughout the whole journey back to Bolton I sit zombified in my seat, looking and feeling very grey and so exhausted, head throbbing painfully.

 It is past seven by the time I finally crash my crumpled body down into bed, even Mum and Martin are up by this time having *breakfast* before they go out for the day with Holly. They had just thought I had decided to stay at Tom's so naturally they're as horrified as I was when I explain to them that no, I ended up in Manchester (true) to have a drink with Dan from work (false) and fell asleep on the train back because I was so tired after such a long day (half-true), meaning I had to wait in Blackpool for the first train back home. So that's Sunday pretty much wiped off the map for me, out of it as soon as head makes contact with pillow.

Sunday 3rd February 2008

  I spend what remains of the day dazed and confused, moping about the house with nothing to do until I check my computer to see that this time it's me who has been propositioned by one of the various girls I've been in contact with on Fuckbook. She wants to meet me tonight as we don't live too far from eachother, nothing too full-on just a *"walk and talk"* as she calls it. So later in the evening I journey out to the agreed meeting point wrapped up heavily against the cold and still with my head feeling quite clouded after a bad night and little sleep. Thoughts of Flick still linger but it's not healthy having her on my mind all the time.
  Now, this girl's profile photo didn't really give too much away and was fairly blurred which should have been a dead giveaway that she wasn't up to much but I decided to meet her anyway, after all, she *did* ask. I approach from behind her and startle her with a *"hey!"* which makes her spin round and it's fair to say I am pretty startled too to be immediately struck by the very visible signs of a beard around her chin. I struggle to take my eyes off it as we start walking and make small talk, she has a dirty mind and an equally dirty mouth I quickly find out and after no more than ten minutes' strolling about aimlessly we end up behind a tree in on the periphery of a deserted park where with absolutely no encouragement from me she sucks me off. It's alright, but she *does* have a beard. I'm back home within the hour.

Monday 4th February 2008

    I stay off work today, I genuinely don't feel too great but it still does sound as if I'm lying when I phone in and speak to the manager whilst exaggerating an ill voice. I leave out the fact that I still feel battered after my impromptu sleep over in Blackpool North on Saturday and just say that I've got some sort of head cold. I shouldn't worry about having to cry off for a day though seen as Sarah phoned in sick not so long back because she had a spot on her face – she even told them that too – and nothing was done, so I stop feeling guilty as soon as I put the phone down and relax.

    Eager to put last night's bizarre rendezvous behind me and bored of watching back to back episodes of *"Curb Your Enthusiasm"* in bed I text Amy to find out what she's up to. Turns out she's not doing anything as she only works three days in the week and she invites me round for some fun, so by early afternoon I'm fucking her in her front room. It's a flying visit really; in, very little chat, bag up, shag her, clean up and fuck off. At least she didn't fall asleep on me this time which is always a positive sign and I enjoy the walk home back through Smithills which looks great on such a clear and crisp a day as this. Back to work tomorrow.

CHAPTER EIGHTEEN

Wednesday 6th February 2008

Well, I've been screwed over at work. Somehow everyone knows I've been shagging Steph, it is the hot topic in the office. I walked in yesterday morning feeling better and wanting to get stuck into normality but instead I've spent the last two days fending off constant questions and piss-taking. First off, everyone sat at their desks as I passed by them towards my section went quiet as soon as they saw me and as I looked up to see them all staring, a couple of them sniggered to eachother. Then I was treated to a full morning's worth of a grilling from Brian, Dan and even Sarah – each one of them has their own take on it; Sarah thinks it's all a giggle and that Steph's nice and we'd make a good couple, Dan can't believe I'd go with her and Brian thinks I'm a disgrace.

Perhaps my only saving grace from the two lads though is the fact that it's the Manchester Derby on Sunday and also the fiftieth anniversary of the Munich air disaster so they're currently embroiled in very tedious bickering with United fans in the office, arguing about who stole who's songs and which is the "real" Manchester club. Thank fuck I come from a one team town, I couldn't be arsed with all this. Meanwhile anytime I have any dealings with other colleagues in the office I'm pressed for more details even from people I barely ever talk to, digging for information and asking how long we've been carrying on for. *Carrying on?*

It turns out that Steph was so cut up about how I left things on Saturday that she confided in her best mate Karen about her feelings for me, but this mate happens to work in the same office as us and also happens to be known as Gobby Karen, as in she can't keep it fucking shut. So basically her section was first to be told how much of a bastard I am for leading Steph on for so long, embellishing it all by making it sound like we've been dating for months, then of course another section heard about it and another and so on, all within the course of an hour or two early on Monday morning while I was still happily fast asleep in bed in Bolton.

    It has been a whirlwind of gossip, pointed fingers and rumour ever since. Some people just think it's funny, others might as well walk around with t-shirts on saying *"Team Steph"*, they've well and truly gone for the idea that I'm a love rat, looking at me like something they've stepped in and the more that Dan and Brian play up on it the worse it gets. I know they don't really give a shit and are taking the piss but they've spent the last two days telling me I've broken her heart and that I should be ashamed of myself and it has been playing on my mind, not really Steph's feelings in truth – I find the whole idea that she really liked me a bit preposterous anyway – but how I've been the last few weeks with all these girls and especially how I feel about Flick.

    This afternoon I told Flick I needed to see her tonight and it turned out she was working the night shift so I could go and visit her again. I was so desperate to see her face, listen to her speak and just be near her again but I also felt like I somehow needed to bring *us* up at some point. All this scandal at work with people finding out about Steph would be a tiny drop in the ocean compared with what would happen if anyone else found out that I've been seeing a married woman, lives would be literally ruined, it has put things into perspective.

    So I went to see her at her work and of course we ended up having sex again, few words were said between us when I turned up and we made a beeline for the bedroom. Unlike last time though we were absolutely rampant, yanking eachother's clothes off and throwing eachother around on the bed, we were wild with one another, it felt to me like one desperate last stand and she was incredible. So now we are lying here opposite eachother in the bed, knackered and talking quietly.

"I really like you Flick." I say, pulling up the duvet over her shoulders, we are both naked and I can see her skin is covered in goose pimples. "In fact, I think I like you way more than I should." A shy smile flickers across her lips for a second as she hears the words but she's struggling to make eye contact with me and I can see that she's having trouble with her feelings too.

"I really like you too Jamie you know, I really do..." She places her palm on my cheek and strokes me with her thumb. "To the point where it feels like it's *you* who I'm with and it's *you* who I'm looking forward to spending time with." That makes my insides turn in all sorts of directions, a wonderful and horrible thing to hear. Again though she can't look at me and I know there's a huge "but" coming here, part of me really wants there to be a huge "but" too. There has to be.

"I just feel like we're on some sort of runaway train though, do you know what I mean? This crazy ride that we're loving but that we have to get off at some point. It's hard to describe..." No it isn't, she just summed it up perfectly.

"No, I feel the same. I feel brilliant but terrible Flick, I don't know what to do." I wriggle in closer to her and put my arm around her and finally she looks at me. "You are an *amazing* woman, everything I could ever want and more." She beams beautifully. "But deep down I know what we are doing is wrong, so wrong – and you do too." Her smile fades and she nods. "I don't know what damage I've done already, but I feel like we should stop." She gulps then slowly nods again.

"I know, you're right. I've always known it's wrong all this and I just felt that if I could just see you one more time, then one more. You make me feel like I'm, I don't know, wanted. But we should stop, I know." I feel – and she looks – like we can't decide whether to be relieved or devastated. Thing is though if me and Flick somehow in some mad way did get it together, one of two things would happen: one, she would crush me like Chloe did and move on in the end or two – let's face it, as amazing as she is, she's a cheat – she would end up fucking around on me at some point. Either way, *I get fucked around*. Again. There's no doubt that getting out now is the best thing I can do. We lie there staring at anywhere but into eachother's eyes for a couple of minutes in this warm and comfortable bed, totally silent, the only contact between us being our knees just gently touching one another's under the covers.

"Anyway, you can do better than a woman up to her knees in vomit and piss." She suddenly breaks the silence and we both laugh. "Come on, let's get up." We get dressed again whilst chatting and laughing away like mates, it's artificial but we need to do this if we're ever going to get out of this room without either bursting into tears or ripping eachother's clothes off again. I decline the offer of another cup of tea and get ready to leave once we are back into the living room, Flick comes to the door with me to see me out.

"Please don't make this the last time you see me Jamie." She says just as I'm heading back outside and it halts me in my tracks. I turn around to see her looking downhearted in the doorway. "I'm working again on Friday, come by for a brew and then..." I smile at her, I could fall in love with this woman, I really could.

"And then that's the end of it you mean?" She forces a nod after a few seconds but isn't smiling.

"Well I didn't want to say that but, yes. Then that's the end of it." I reach forward and touch her arm.

"Okay, I'll see you on Friday then. Hey, cheer up it's the right thing." I say to her, then turn around again and head off. It *is* the right thing for us to do, albeit after working through a whole catalogue of wrong things.

Friday 8th February 2008

I once again stand at the door to Flick's living quarters in the dubious gaze of the faltering security light and listen to the *"poc, poc, poc"* of the rain as it hits the surface of my jacket. I linger here in the wet for a prolonged few seconds before I finally summon up the courage to hit the doorbell for the final time. She comes and lets me in promptly and I have to say I'm glad she wanted to see me one last time because I've missed her despite only seeing her two days ago and the sight of her gorgeous face and that wonderful, voluptuous body has my insides doing somersaults like nothing else. She looks delighted to see me too, I peck her on the cheek.

"See, my behaviour is already improving." She laughs at that and seems in good spirits. Once she's made us a drink we sit down on opposite ends of the worn out old couch and chat about nondescript things, acting like civilised friends. I also note that she is wearing her wedding ring tonight too, the first time I've seen it since we met.

"So when do you go out to, where is it, Madrid?" She asks, I tell her in a couple of weeks and talk a bit about where we are staying over there. "And how are things at work? Still shit?" I nod and go into one about the latest goings on until I start to bore myself.

"What about you?" I turn the tables after I've finished moaning about the office. "How's this place treating you?" She winces and takes a long gulp of her tea.

"Oh don't get me started, Head Office has told us..." She stops mid sentence and sighs. "Fuck's sake we're talking like a pair of old biddies catching up down the Bingo, I can't do this." She lays her mug down on the floor then slides over to me and she places her lips on mine. I take her in my arms and we kiss over and over, it of course leads to the bedroom and we have sex.

We both know it's the final time, it has to be, no more discussions about that. The knowledge that this is the case though means it's one of the most intense experiences of my life. I kiss and touch every inch of Flick's body savouring these last few moments with this forbidden woman and as we spend these dying moments together she lies there beneath me sweating and moaning and gripping me tightly. Afterwards we stare into eachother's eyes and I thank her for making me feel the way she has and that I will never forget her. It makes her cry and as I let myself out of the building after getting dressed and leaving her wrapped in the bed sheets I feel like I could do exactly the same. Time to let Felicity go.

Saturday 9th February 2008

I'm profoundly gutted as I come away from the Reebok this afternoon, more gutted I think than I have been about football for a long time and miffed in an almost child-like, *"it's so unfair"* sort of way. We have been beaten many times this season but rarely so unjustly;

Wanderers had all the play, a load of chances and really seemed like a half-decent side at last against Portsmouth yet fell victim to a sucker punch of a goal that looked miles offside near the end and a 1-0 defeat.

I'm not exactly full of cheer later on either; once again a virtual passenger as Tom, Chris and Paul get on it in Horwich, but as was the case with the Reading game last Saturday I feel as if I've ultimately got the upper hand, an ace up my sleeve, as I've been told by Amy that she's got a free house after 8 tonight so I should pay her a visit. Again I feel like I'm making the conscious decision to put myself out of control once more by doing this but I feel the need to draw a line under Flick as quickly as possible and show to myself I'm not too hung up on her... by going with the first person that comes my way. Added to that, drinking that started in The Greenwood at lunch today and this increasingly familiar scene with the other lads developing in front of me means that going to Amy's seems like a decent idea.

At around eight I make a slurred phone call for a taxi, shouting over Basshunter which is on at an insane volume. *"Now You're Gone"*, seemingly a hit on every kid's mobile phone that I hear being played out loud on every bus and train I get on at the moment – well, that or Cascada – sounds so out of place to me in this old fashioned village pub, but they've thrown a disco ball up on the ceiling and shoved some coloured lights in the corner so it has become a legitimate destination to be added to the pub crawl list for the youth of Horwich. And us, it seems.

The look Tom gives me when I suddenly pipe up that I'm off is one of surprise and *disappointment*. That couple of seconds is exactly what I've been hoping for and building towards since Newcastle, for once I'm doing something *he's* not part of. Of course after that fleeting moment he's gone again, back into Tom-mode, not arsed, flowing with it and back all over Paul and Chris who incidentally didn't flinch when I said I'm going. Fuck them.

So I taxi it to Amy's, the kids being looked after by her accomplice Tasha for the night, the curtains are closed again and it's not long before she's straddling me on the living room floor as I play with her. We're still fully clothed but Amy leapt at me within seconds of my arrival and this is where we've been since. I'm determined to make this last longer than the last couple of times and I'm not having her fall asleep on me again either so fully clothed is good for now, albeit with my hands shoved far up the tiny red and black tartan skirt that's she's wearing. The fact she's dressed in that, knee-high striped socks and a tiny black blouse with her hair in pigtails and minus any underwear is driving me wild and we maul eachother for a good half hour here on the floor. I could never be with this girl, she's far from pretty and definitely not what I'd consider to be my type – I doubt I'd be hers either if we ever got to know eachother but that's not going to happen – but right here and now we certainly want eachother desperately and I can't wait any longer.

I manhandle Amy's considerable frame off me and we go to the bedroom, her blouse gaping open and one sock scrunched down around her ankle by the time we reach the bedside and she goes down on me, gorging before my jeans even hit the deck in a frenzy of lips, tongue and teeth – but mainly teeth. I can only stand the gnawing for a minute or so then I push her back and climb on top of her, legs wrapped over my back and her face pressed into mine. I know instantly there will be no repeat of last week's epic romp – for better or worse – and sure enough I last all of two minutes' worth of extremely fast and extremely loud sex complete with my back scratched painfully from neck to arse.

Literally the moment I finish off though, like being hit by a train, the horniness completely vaporises and the realisation of what I've done slams into me at breakneck speed. A full body cold sweat instantly envelops me as it dawns that I didn't even consider using a condom, sure enough a couple of unopened packets lie on the drawers next to the bed. I just cracked on and threw it right up there as soon as I could. I pull out of Amy and reel back horrified, she thinks it's a game though and hooks me back towards her with her legs before holding my head down to hers to kiss me.

"You know what I think I'm going to do?" She growls playfully. "I'm going to bite you..." So she proceeds to go for my ear, chewing on it for a few seconds as I lie there atop her like a corpse, worried that I've just basically ended my life. I let her continue for a bit, I can't just up sticks and fuck off, but what the hell am I going to do though? I kiss her for a bit and try to make it look like I'm going with the flow and Amy tries to turn me on again but that is definitely not going to happen now my stomach is churning terribly.

I last another couple of minutes at best before getting up, grabbing my jeans and going to the toilet without saying anything, leaving Amy sprawled out behind me. Fear courses through my body and I can see it in my face when I look in the mirror, large beads of sweat on my forehead and my eyes wide. I know for a fact that I'm shaking violently because I'm scared stiff, not because I'm naked. I wash my face and knob and put my pants back on.

"What's wrong?" Comes a voice from behind me, Amy stands there with a dressing gown on. I've nothing clever or funny lined up to say in response, she means nothing to me, so I just come out with it.

"That was fucking really stupid of me, I shouldn't have just done that without using a condom. I can't believe I just did that." She sniggers and shrugs her shoulders.

"Oh well it's no big deal is it. Besides you didn't use one the other night either." That only serves to double my anguish really.

"No, no it is a big deal for me, a massive deal." I push past her and retrieve my top from her bedroom floor.

"Well it can't be that big a deal, there's condoms there next to the bed and you chose not to use one." Amy goes as she comes back to the bedside. That comment riles me, but she's right obviously. "I *am* clean you know, you don't have to worry about stuff like that." In fact that was the least of my worries but her using the word "clean" nearly made me vomit right here in front of her.

"It's not that I'm bothered about." Even though it patently should be. "I just, I can't..." Worry and shock convulse up through me as I try to find the words but I fail to form a coherent sentence, instead I point over at the two vacant baby cots. "I don't want, I can't do that, no." I must look and sound like a total loser, I certainly feel like one. Amy's features harden as she realises what I'm getting at, at first she must have been quite forgiving thinking I was worried about STD's but now there's a lad stood in front of her nearly crying at the thought he might have knocked her up.

"Oh I see. Right, well if that's happened then it's my problem isn't it." I glare at her, horrified.

"Er, no it's my problem as well obviously. It's absolutely one hundred percent definitely not what I want, at all." I can't believe that just a couple of hours ago I was at the match on the piss and now here I am on a council estate talking about the threat of potentially becoming a father.

"Oh come off it, there's very little chance of me getting pregnant again anyway, not that it's any of your business. I wouldn't worry about it, trust me." She replies, with a tinge of anger.

"But I am worried, petrified actually." She shakes her head at me, looking pissed off now.

"No you're not, you can just disappear like the last one did and leave me to it can't you. It's me that should be worried." I start to feel quite frantic, ashamed of myself that I don't possess enough knowledge in this subject to make informed decisions and comments about it. Up until this very second my life consisted of work, football, clothes, mates and beer and now it feels like all that is about to be ripped away from me forever.

"Is there anything you can take, you know, a pill or anything?" I'm woefully ill-informed here. Amy frowns at me and shakes her head.

"No actually, I'm not on the pill." A huge fountain of worry is beginning to completely take over me, I have so little experience with things like this that I just don't know what to say, other than to want to blurt out something obvious and stupid like *"Please don't get pregnant, please, I beg you, I'll do anything."*

"What about the morning after pill, how about getting that?" I offer and now she looks decidedly angry at all this.

"I've just told you there's not much chance of me getting pregnant again, I don't think I'll need the morning after pill." Sweat trickles down my back as I stand here in Amy's bedroom scared stiff and clueless listening to her barking her response at me.

"I'll pay for it if you want, it's no problem." I say, desperately.

"Excuse me? Who the fuck do you think you are? I can pay for it myself thank you very much – not that I'll need it." She looks absolutely disgusted with me. "Look at the state of you fucking standing there whining, it's your fault this you should have thought about this before you had your pants off." There's little I can say in return to that, she's right of course and that comment pretty much sums up the last few weeks as a whole.

"I just... I just really wasn't expecting to have to be worrying about this sort of thing we were just having a bit of fun. Look, I should go you don't need me hanging around here like this." She seems to soften ever so slightly with me.

"I've told you not to be worrying about it, like I said the chances of me ever getting pregnant again are very slim. I'm not going to tell you why, but that's how it is. Do not worry about it." She orders me, but worry is exactly what I am doing. I want to be out of here and out of this right now. We go back downstairs and Amy pours us both a glass of water as we stand in her kitchen talking.

"Lads make me laugh, so up for shagging one minute then a nervous wreck the next." Amy doesn't sound angered or upset as she talks, just world-weary I guess, that's the best way I could describe it. "You're all the same you know, hang around for the fun then run for it when it gets heavy." Now, I get what she's saying but fuck me, we met up for no-strings sex after swapping emails on Facebook, there wasn't supposed to *be* anything heavy. I'm in no mood to argue over the fine points of the arrangement though, the last few weeks' debauchery have come back to haunt me and I've been caught out.

"Yeah, we seem to do that don't we." I could stand here and tell her that we're not all like that and that actually I'm a pretty decent person but what would the point be in that? Last thing I want her doing is starting to like me anyway.

"Yes, you do." Amy smiles wryly and sighs, staring down at the floor for a few moments silently. "Listen." She goes over to the unit to set her empty glass down. "Phone a taxi to take you home but tell it to go past the supermarket on the way and I'll go to the all-night pharmacy and buy the morning after pill if it makes you feel any better." It would look ridiculous if I jumped up and down on the spot cheering, but I have to say her uttering those words felt better than Munich.

"Really? Are you sure? If you want me to pay..." She glares at me before I finish the sentence.

"Yes, I'm sure. No, I'll pay for it myself." She replies matter-of-factly.

"Okay, well then yes it would make me feel a lot better." Amy smiles when I tell her this.

"I know it would, you look like a nervous wreck. It's pretty pathetic you know." I'll accept the jibe, in fact I'd probably accept a beating right now if it meant she would go and sort out the pill for herself which I have in my mind as some sort of "Magic Bullet" to cure this problem in one shot.

So Amy joins me in the taxi back to my house, gets out at ASDA on the way and tells me she'll walk home so there's no need to wait around. There are no goodbyes shared between us or anything, she just turns her back and I watch her walk across the car park at the supermarket heading towards the doors, the last I'll see of her I expect, I don't think either of us will be up for meeting again. Then I'm driven home and I'm back before *"Match Of The Day"* starts but I can't concentrate on it and after ten minutes I go to the bathroom and vomit a couple of times into the toilet, then sit there on the cold tiled floor with my head in my hands and my mind in bits.

CHAPTER NINETEEN

Barclays Premier League – Monday 12th February 2008

		P	W	D	L	Pts.
13	Newcastle United	26	7	7	12	28
14	Sunderland	26	7	5	14	26
15	Bolton Wanderers	26	6	7	13	25
16	Wigan Athletic	26	6	5	15	23
17	Birmingham City	26	5	7	14	22

Bolton Wanderers record scoreless draws away to Newcastle United and at home to Fulham in January and these results are consolidated with a 2-0 victory at Reading, their first away win in the Premier League for 10 months. However, a 1-0 defeat to Portsmouth in their following game still leaves them in a precarious league position. Home and away ties with Atletico Madrid in the UEFA Cup loom in February.

Settled sleep was very hard to come by over the weekend as the events of Saturday night played over in my head continuously. I've been overcome with worry about it all especially when I let my imagination go off on its own and speculate about whether Amy simply turned back out of ASDA as soon as the taxi was out of sight and didn't bother going to the pharmacy. I can't control that anymore though and I just have to take her at her word, I've deleted her number and won't be bothering her again. When I return to work on Monday morning Dan can see that I don't look good and we chat over a brew and two massive Danishes, breakfast of champions. I've felt like I needed someone to talk to about all this and the fact I've decided to confide in Dan and not Tom is quite telling.

I decide it would be better to just tell him everything; fill in the gaps about work-mate Steph that haven't been covered by Chinese whispers in the office, The Virgin, Flick and of course Two Kids Amy and the unprotected romp that occurred on Saturday night. Plus everything in between; Newcastle, Tom quite clearly getting back into coke, Fuckbook, falling asleep on the train and waking up in Blackpool, plus how I pretty much fell for Flick.

Dan is rarely surprised when anyone tells him anything, that's just how he is, but once I've finally laid it all out before him and he understands why I've been so up and down in work lately he seems genuinely shocked. He tells me I'm a totally different person to what he thought I was – more like him in fact – which shocks me as well as I always had him down as a bit of an introvert. To find out that he had the majority of the same experiences as I've had leaves me surprised but strangely reassured.

For the rest of the day we discuss various situations and crises we've been in and talk eachother through them. Dan's wildest exploits came while he was at University so they're a few years ago now but he tells me it was only after he graduated that the gravity of some of the things he used to do really hit him once he was out of the bubble of Halls and shared student houses. What he tells me really resonates, about how it's all very well going with the flow of things and doing crazy stuff just because you can but not everyone is lucky enough to get away with it. Most of all, he implores me to go to the sex clinic to help put everything that has gone on out of my mind. *"The best clean slate you'll ever get"* he describes it as.

Wednesday 14th February 2008

With Dan's advice in mind and after mulling it over for another day I decided to take the Wednesday off work citing an urgent family problem and so today I find myself en route to the Sexual Health Clinic on the other side of Manchester. I could and probably should have simply gone to the one in Bolton but I convinced myself that someone I know would see me so instead I get a bus to the train station, a train to Manchester and another bus up Oxford Road to the clinic. I'm scared shitless.

This is a huge day. Wanderers play the First Leg of their monumental tie with Atletico Madrid tonight but my mind isn't on it at all, my thoughts are entirely taken up by this visit to get my comeuppance. I've never been to the sex clinic before so my head is full of all the rumours and urban legends that you hear about going here, about probes being stuffed down your bell-end and fit nurses messing around with your balls trying to coerce a hard-on out of you so they can all have a laugh about it on their breaks later on. Pissing themselves about your tiny, terrified knob while they dunk their Rich Teas.

I feel like a dead man walking as I enter the building and give my details in at reception, the woman behind the counter tells me to go and wait my turn in the next room, she's totally expressionless and I wonder what she must think of me. I shuffle next door into the waiting room and there must be about thirty men in here; they look like they come from all walks of life, a couple in suits, one bloke in a high-visibility jacket, another in what looks like a Burger King uniform but each one of them united in looking very sorry for themselves. I quietly take a chair at the back with my stomach turning in knots and my throat bone dry.

The room slowly empties as each man is called up by a nurse and then my heart jolts severely as finally my name is called out, time to steel myself and get through this. In the event, my forced burst of confidence is premature as I'm led into yet another waiting room but there's only three other people in here and I sit back down again. Ridiculously, they've got *"Jeremy Kyle"* on the telly too as if to rub our predicaments in it a little bit more, but no-one's watching.

A name is called out and the lad in the high-vis gear stands up, his turn to be examined and as he walks in my direction past my seat he starts laughing.

"Right then, let's get this over with! Got fuck all to worry about me anyway." High-Vis winks at me and walks off towards where the nurse is stood, trying to crack jokes with her too as he does so but she's not interested. His bravado only makes me feel worse. While he's away I assess where I'm at with all this; the unrelenting nerves making me promise myself that I'll never sleep with a girl again, that once all this is over I'll sort my life out, become more respectable and honest and stop fucking about. I consider what if I have got an STD, something that will fuck me up good and proper, it makes me feel filthy.

I've been literally sick with worry the last few days over Amy, at one stage with her on that Saturday night I was certain that I'd basically got her pregnant and my life was over with and I've never been so thankful for anything in my life when she told me she would go to the pharmacy for a morning after pill. My utter physical and mental ineptitude when it comes to sex education was laid totally bare. I'll probably never speak to her again. My mind is screwed over Flick, I really like her very, very much and I think she feels the same too but it's a total car crash of a situation that and I definitely do not want to be responsible for breaking a marriage up. The line we drew under it last week has to be final. With Steph, everyone at work knows what went on, minus a few details such *as "Roman Ruins"* and *"behind the Printworks"*, but for the most part it's all out in the open and I'm just going to have to accept all the stick I've been getting. I consider it part of the price to pay for this quite ridiculous couple of weeks I've just embarked on.

    High-Vis returns after about ten minutes still looking pleased with himself and he takes a seat a couple away from mine, leaning in towards me once he's there.

    "There's four of them in there, four nurses, proper fit too and they all stand there staring at you with your cock out while they mess around with it. Mad as fuck. At least I've got no problems in that department, if you know what I mean." He hits me on the shoulder very amused with himself, the prick, I wish he'd keep his mouth shut. The temptation was there to ask him what it's like and what they do to you, like you did in your final moments before being taken in for an injection at school trying to get as much information as possible off previous victims, but I barely even react to him, I'm proper bricking it now.

    My name is called out next and I follow the nurse through a couple of sets of doors then into a examination room, shaking a little as I take a seat as instructed at a table. As promised there are four nurses in here but three of them are stood at the back just observing, they're probably students, I guess. The lead one asks me for some basic details then suddenly she comes straight out with the sexual questions and their directness takes me back a bit.

    "When was the last time you had sex? How many partners have you had? Are you gay or straight? Have you given or received oral sex? Have you given or received anal sex? Did you use a condom each time you had intercourse?" I feel deeply ashamed as I tell her I only used protection on some occasions and I want to lie but that will get me nowhere. I expect some sort of scorn

but she just nods impassively, ticks a box and moves on. Next she asks me to remove my trousers and lie on the bed so they can take a swab, but there's absolutely no danger of the infamous and feared erection, if anything it's trying to shy away as much as possible but I'm too nervous to even be embarrassed.

    I stare at the ceiling as something is inserted into my penis which stings a fair bit but it certainly isn't excruciating as was previously made out and it only lasts a few seconds, then after a quick prod around of my balls it's over with and she says I can put my jeans back on, still the three onlookers barely make their presence felt. Then I'm handed a plastic cup with a lid and she tells me to go to the toilet and urinate in it. I struggle like hell but I manage to force a piss out which of course goes on the floor, on my hands, in the toilet but also into the beaker and it stings infinitely more than the probe did.

    I wash profusely until my hands are red then return to the examination room and give her the sealed cup of piss, good job she's wearing gloves. Finally she asks if I'd like to have a blood test to look for things like AIDS. Fucking AIDS, I feel sick again. I say yeah, may as well have a full MOT while I'm here seen as I've never been in this situation before and I look away as she injects me which doesn't hurt too badly. I suppose having zero time to have my mind thinking about an impending injection makes it easier to get through.

    Once that's over with she tells me to go back to the waiting room and they'll have the results of the swab and urine sample in about fifteen minutes though the blood sample will take longer, but if there's any problems I'll be contacted in future. That would be the dreaded *"you're required to come back to the clinic"* text, but I'm virtually certain the blood test will turn up clear anyway so I'm not overly worried about that. I go back to the waiting room feeling numb but glad the examination is over, ready to face whatever they tell me. Almost as soon as I sit down, High-Vis is called back in for his results and he springs off through the doors again. I actually take notice of what the topic on *"Jeremy Kyle"* is today and sure enough it's an unwanted pregnancy, not even funny.

    The doors open about five minutes later and almost like a climactic scene from a comedy sketch show, the money-shot, High-Vis comes back into the room looking down at the floor, his face a shade of scarlet, shoulders hunched and he silently, slowly takes a seat at the back of the room, the news clearly bad. I'm in no position to gloat, but I bet he feels a right prize tit now. My turn comes around sooner than expected and I return to the examination room which now just contains the one nurse, I sit down and she smiles.

    "Okay Mr Denham, I'm pleased to say the results of the swab and urine sample came back negative, the blood test will be a while longer but we'll let you know in due course if there are any problems." I'm absolutely beaming and I thank her, grinning widely. "I can see you're pleased with the outcome James..." She smiles at me and I theatrically wipe my brow.

    "Oh, definitely, it's a huge weight off my mind, huge. It's a turning point for me this it really is..." I stop myself there, I could have gone into one saying how I'll be more careful from now on, that the last month has been totally out of character for me and that it won't happen again but I'm sure she's heard it all before anyway and I'm sure she thinks it's nothing to do with her. I just thank her again and make for the exits, sweeping past High-Vis on my way out and feeling extremely lucky to not be in whatever position he's in right now.

    The stroll onto Oxford Road for the bus back to the train station is one of the most pleasant feelings I've had for a long time, with all that worry and strife lifted from my shoulders I feel as if I'm bouncing down the pavement, like I could stop and say *"Good Day to you!"* to everyone I pass. It's cold but it's bright and fresh, a glorious and crisp February day and I can't stop smiling. Almost like a light being switched on, my thoughts flip onto Atletico Madrid at home tonight and the sheer magnitude of the game I'm just hours away from attending and a massive pool of excitement wells up inside me, my head tingling with nervous anticipation. *Come on Whites!*

Few times in the past have I gone to the Reebok looking for Wanderers to give me a break from goings-on in my life quite like this, I've never really thought of going to the match in that way before. I've read all sorts of articles by "experts" describing how the young male goes to watch football to give him a short, priceless release from the stresses of work and the wife and that it is his chance to be whoever he wants to be for ninety minutes, to cuss and shout and get everything off his chest among like minded males in a way that he never could anywhere else. I don't know where that leaves the many females that go too though. The fact is I attend a modern and sanitised all-seater stadium surrounded by families, where it is forbidden to stand up for longer than a few seconds, where you can only drink alcohol downstairs, where smoking is totally outlawed and where attempts at prolonged chanting are met with tuts and sighs from behind. I've rarely seen going to the match as my "release".

Tonight though I've never been so relieved to walk out of the stairwell and go to my seat, with my phone switched off and safe in the knowledge that after this morning's all clear I can think about something else at last. It's a freezing cold night but the crowd is brilliant, building the type of atmosphere that has been missing for years now, helped albeit by thousands of inflatable plastic tubes that have been given out in pairs so when they are hit together they make a loud smacking sound. A good portion of the home crowd has them and all over the place the white sausage shaped objects are being frantically waved about and slammed against eachother.

The whole stadium is awash with noise and chanting, sections of lads in the East and North stands bouncing about trying to get *"We're the one and only Wanderers"* going but finding themselves almost drowned out by the hollow metallic droning rising from the countless plastic tubes. I stand next to Tom and Ray with my arms out wide and head pointed skywards, eyes closed, screaming *"Wanderers, Wanderers…"* as the teams pose for photographs at the touchline, quite a few of us doing the same as me in our area but I doubt there's many around me feeling so much bottled up tension being released as I am. I feel like with every shout of my beloved team's name I'm blasting away one more day of anguish that I've put myself through recently, that tonight marks the start of a new me, no more messing about.

The sight of Atletico's players fanning out onto our pitch brings home to me how big a game this is, many of their line-up are the type of players you see taking World Cups by storm or grabbing headlines in the brilliant Spanish league yet here they are at Middlebrook in the rain with Dioufy and Kevin Davies staring them out in the centre circle waiting to kick off. Still the noise crackles out of the stands; I'm absolutely jumping inside, nervous and excited, desperate to be able to go out to Madrid next week with something still left to play for.

I needn't have worried. Straight from kick off we go for them, people still haven't sat down when we have our first shot in the opening seconds and although it's not a major threat to their goal a massive *"oooh!"* rumbles out from the crowd then screams of encouragement from the masses, then more chanting, every last person in the stadium is right up for this one tonight.

Atletico just can't deal with us, we're all over them, another shot goes in from Taylor and their goalkeeper Abbiati decides to smash the ball out of play with his fists rather than catch it and we're on his back already trying to unsettle him. There's nothing better than being treated to an opposition team fielding a dodgy keeper and watching him make a right tit of himself all game, we sense a calamity in the making. Still many of us haven't sat down yet; Tom grabs me and excitedly tells me we're going to do them, starts screaming out some crazy garbled incantation towards the action on the pitch about going to Madrid and drinking all their beer and ripping up their stadium and that we won't stop until we get to the Final in Manchester. I let out a massive laugh and wrap an arm around his back and we start jumping up and down together initiating another chant and all around us we're joined by people following our lead, at the top of our voices telling all and sundry that we are by far the greatest team the world has ever seen.

Matt Taylor continues to look like the signing of the season, running the show, shooting from all over the place like he used to do at Portsmouth. Still their goalkeeper is using his forearms and fists like a baseball bat, slogging our efforts anywhere other than into the net and every time he denies us there's laughs and shouts from the crowd expecting a mistake, we are loving this. At the other end Jaaskelainen pulls off an unbelievable save to deny former United striker Diego Forlan, stretching right into the top corner to stop a certain goal and more cheers cascade from the crowd, I've not seen continuous encouragement like this for ages, shivers rush up my back every time another wave of noise begins.

The first half is so pulsating that half-time arrives in a flash, the Whites go off to a standing ovation and more batterings of the plastic "Banger Stix". Tom and I look at eachother and puff our cheeks in mock exhaustion, still smiling and with every passing minute the excitement about Madrid grows because barring something ridiculous in the second half we will be able to go to Spain and still have a chance of qualifying for the next round. Tony throws an arm each over our shoulders and is beaming.

"Absolutely murdering them out there! I might even grab a couple of these fucking numpty balloons and join in!" He shouts, he's not been this excited since he thought one of the cheerleaders winked at him at half time last season. I still maintain she was looking at me, Tony's closing in on seventy. Resisting the urge to switch my phone on and see if I've got any horrific text messages from Flick or god-forbid Amy telling me she had actually lied about going to the pharmacy and that she hopes I'm proud of myself, I read the match programme and marvel at Atletico's impressive squad, telling Tom that we're done for if they bring Sergio Aguero on because he's another "New Maradona" and Andy O'Brien will never catch him. He tells me to give it a rest.

"Please welcome out for the second half, Bolton Wanderers..." The announcer goes and a blast of noise greets them again just as it did an hour previously, I close my eyes for a couple of seconds and hope we can see it through. A couple more shots test Abbiati but it seems we are slightly less frenetic than the first half, perhaps even in danger of slipping into a lull which is when we usually get caught out. Maybe most of the kids have knackered themselves out too because there's not half of the noise coming from the "Banger Stix" that there was previously and the nerves begin to surface, remembering we're actually playing a top quality European team. Then they put on Aguero who I had hyped up at half time and now I've gone totally quiet, sat bunched up in my seat watching the game balance out and seeing Atletico beginning to take control.

Time is getting on when play stops down the other side of the pitch and a melee starts between the players, the crowd on that side stand up and point at something, the sound of their outraged cries reaching us a half-second later. Then all of a sudden a red card is raised and Wanderers fans' arms go up too, its Aguero, sent off. I shake my head at Tom's frown, not a clue what happened but with that event our belief is replenished just like it was in Munich when Bayern took off Podolski then Ribery who had been ripping us to pieces all night.

"Come on Whites, we can do these!" I bellow towards the pitch, shaking my fist furiously and we get play started again before Atletico can sort themselves out. Stelios finds some space out wide to put a cross in, me and Tom are still stood up and others behind us follow suit to get a better view of the outcome. The ball loops into the area, Taylor tries to head towards goal but it hits an Atletico defender and there's a groan from the crowd, but the ball drops dead to the ground and in swoops El Hadji Diouf.

A quick flash of yellow and purple coloured football disappears behind flailing legs. Abbiati sees it late, then there's that clichéd but very real momentary silence in the stands, as the ball reappears, wide of Abbiati's left boot and into the bottom corner. *In!*

Utter pandemonium ensues. My face contorts as I let out an inhuman roar, leaping as high as I can muster, eyes maddened and wide. All I can see is a mass of arms flying about all over the place, unbelievable noise, a mighty and almost desperate sounding communal scream of delight. Diouf races off joyously towards the dugout chased by white shirts, Tom leaps onto my back shouting into my ear so happy that it almost sounds like his voice is cracking with emotion. In front of me there are groups of people hugging tightly, people thrusting fists skyward and for a split second I catch sight of Ray hanging over the gates at the front, must have legged it out of his seat and gone for the barriers, his arms aloft also, rolling back the years and loving it.

    Finally Tom releases me and we hug for a moment and then I shout in delight again as the scorer's name is announced, the Reebok Stadium is buzzing. Not a single person is sat down in their seat and for a few seconds there are three different songs emanating from the stands overlapping eachother until they're unintelligible, just a prickling haze of sound, I can safely say it hasn't been like this here for years. Gradually the celebrations tail off, long after the game has restarted and the goal has refreshed everyone's spirits so the songs have begun again and any plastic tubes that survived the seismic reaction to Diouf's goal are now back in use.

    The goal went in with fifteen minutes left and we spend the rest of the game flitting between should have scored moments and should have conceded moments. Atletico finish up looking more dangerous than us so come stoppage time, with everyone out of their seats again and desperately calling for the final whistle, I can barely watch. But at last as the referee blows up for full time and the cheers rise from the home crowd, elation flows through me not just because of the result but because tonight, surely, is the dawn of a much more positive future for me.

    Nothing can be as bad as the last few weeks.

CHAPTER TWENTY

Wednesday 20th February 2008

    This colossal European adventure begins, for me, huddled up miserably against a pillar outside Bolton Interchange at half two in the morning awaiting the arrival of Tom in a taxi from Horwich in freezing temperatures and with a relentless drizzle arrowing down from the darkness. I feel wretched. All the worry of the last few weeks has caught up with me and worn me down to the point where I've ended up with a horrible shivering fever. My head is full of whizzing and popping sounds, pain crackles through my brain and my throat has almost completely closed up, each attempt to speak or swallow heralds a jutting soreness in my neck. Being ill turns me into half a person, my confidence and energy has been smashed away leaving me as this pathetic shell of a human being, just wanting to be safely in bed and away from it all.

    This Madrid trip was supposed to be legendary, one to rival or better Munich with Wanderers on the verge of progressing into the later stages of the UEFA Cup, in fantastically uncharted waters with a mass of fellow supporters in tow having the time of their lives. Unfortunately I feel like I'm at death's door. I knew it was coming, the morning after the victory in the First Leg, a whole load of tension and anguish lifted away from me only to be replaced by this cold which has got worse and worse with each passing day.

    Last night I woke up and got changed out of sweat sodden clothes three times and this morning I was up at 1:45am to get ready for today. The last things my body wants to be doing are flying, getting pissed up and going to football. It's not as if our passage to Madrid will be swift either; though my quest to find cheap flights was very successful, it means we will have to travel to Malaga on a 6am departure, wait for a few hours there then board an internal flight up to Madrid and do the same in reverse a couple of days later. It seemed a lot more appealing when I booked it.

    I enjoyed none of the pre-game build up that I usually look forward to almost as much as the actual experience; the researching of the stadium and the city, the browsing of supporters forums to share their excitement and the process of deciding what to take and what to wear. I look down solemnly at the Spezials I purchased a couple of weeks ago especially for Madrid – brown with mint-blue stripes – their suede already covered with a sheen of rain and shake my head, coughing up stones from my diseased lungs and spitting it away into a puddle as I rue exposing the trainers to this sort of weather. I hover my small holdall over them to try and shield them from the rain, my only luggage for this trip, but the damage is probably already done.

    The figure of Tom emerges from the murk the next time I look up and he comes over to me looking knackered as well but on far better form than I am.

    "Morning Jimothy. What the fuck is up with you?!" He starts.

    "Feel like death, been ill for about a week it's horrible." My voice croaks and struggles under the weight of all the radioactive phlegm that populates my throat.

    "Come off it you pussy. I brought these..." He raises a carrier bag full of cans and my heart sinks but the fact is I can't act like a leper for two days, I've got to try and forget about how bad I feel and make the most of this otherwise I'll regret it in future.

"Alright hand one over. You'll kill me off you will, have you any idea how many tablets I'm on for this shit?" He just laughs and breaks one of the cans of Strongbow he's brought with him from the 4-pack and passes it to me. Everything about it has my body screaming at me to stop, as we stand here swigging cider at arctic temperatures from cans that are dripping with rain waiting for a rail replacement coach to turn up to transport us to the airport, but at least the freezing liquid momentarily sooths my throat with each gulp.

The coach finally appears and we are the only ones to get on. I know there are a few thousand Bolton fans bound for Spain but clearly they've all found better methods of getting there that don't involve travelling at this early hour. The can does not go down very well at all, in fact I'm still attempting to take swigs from it well past Manchester Piccadilly by which time it is warm and flat but I persevere. Tom is onto his second but at least the fact he is in a good mood has taken my mind off the fever somewhat and on the journey I fill him in on my recent misdemeanours which he sounds pretty disgusted at, but we don't dwell on it for too long.

Ignoring the obvious risk to his health, Tom and I quickly share the fourth and final tin outside the doors to Manchester Airport, passing it amongst ourselves to take huge swigs before going inside. We both spend the next couple of hours dropping in and out of sleep in Departures waiting for our turn to board and when that does arrive; we are both out of it again not long after takeoff.

The next time I open my eyes the foreboding mist and darkness of Manchester that I last saw through my little porthole window has been replaced by a scene or near perfection; the shining sun and down below, the east coast of Spain with calm looking waters and sandy beaches. Certainly does not look like February down there, I think to myself. I look at Tom and he is still asleep, I'm very glad that a large chunk of the journey has passed by without me knowing anything about it.

Though I still feel like shit, the excitement of the trip and the summery scene down below has perked me up and once Tom wakes up we are both in high spirits, looking around the plane and realising that we must be the youngest on it by at least thirty years, old couples on their way down to their retirement homes in Malaga. Mad to think that we've already passed by Madrid though and it will be some hours before we move on back up to the capital.

The heat hits us full on as soon as we make it to the top of the steps down onto the apron. The pilot told us on arrival that it's a balmy 21 degrees in Spain right now and it is wonderful, to think that back home is suffering the full effects of mid-winter yet down here it could easily be a British July. This is all the invitation we need to get on it and for now all thought of being ill has been disregarded. Once through Arrivals we find ourselves a place in the bar right up at the windows overlooking the parked aircraft and order a round of drinks. Me and Tom idle the time away watching the planes landing and taking off on the other side of the glass and the army of vehicles busy scurrying around the tarmac; tankers, mobile stairs and luggage trains everywhere. High, rolling hills form the backdrop to the scene dotted with white cottages and bathed in bright sunshine. The San Miguel is cold and sharp, it's warm, sunny and I'm on holiday. I'm beginning to feel like my old self.

I see a couple of other Bolton fans sat in the bar too as I scan the area and we exchange smiles and nods, one of them raises his pint towards us as he does so in salute. They're both wearing our new black away shirts with "Anelka 39" on the back, outdated already. I'm not keen on them really, they remind me too much of one of

City's from a few years ago. Actually I used to know a couple of lads at Uni who supported Bolton but had a soft spot for City just because they like Oasis, what is all that about? Things like that do my head in, I love pizza but I couldn't give a fuck about Lazio. I dislike City just as much as United; though that's probably exasperated by the fact I'm stuck at work with a load of their most vocal fans day in day out.

This is more like it, I think to myself, all of a sudden I'm up for this big time, that fizz of lager that begins to do its thing to your brain within the first sip is already hitting the spot and back comes my confidence.

"It would be ace being a football fan in Spain, do you not think?" I say, after a silent few minutes during which I've sunk the majority of my pint.

"How do you mean?" Tom's slumped to his left across the big chairs we are sat in letting the sunlight cover as much of him as possible.

"Well think about some of your away games. Barcelona and Real Madrid, Nou Camp and Bernabeu some weeks, then on others you've got Tenerife, Mallorca, Valencia. It's a holiday every other weekend that!" Tom remains unmoved for a few moments to the point where I think he's not even going to reply.

"Nah it's not like that here you're thinking about it from an English fan's point of view. They barely travel here, I watched a Barcelona game on telly the other week and I'm not joking there were 25 away fans there, the commentators counted them." I laugh incredulously.

"Piss off, who was it?" He shrugs and sits up to grab his beer.

"Dunno, Deportivo or something, but they just don't do aways, it's different." I round off my drink easily, I'm going to end up leathered probably. "Fair enough you might get more in your derby games and that, but they're not packing planes out and flying all over Spain to watch matches."

"Dear do as well I suppose. Anyway who needs Tenerife when you've got Middlesbrough?" I reply and we both grimace. He gets up to go to the bar for another round and I throw some Euros across the table telling him to double up. Why not?

By the time the alarm on my phone goes off telling us that it is time to board our next flight we've managed to get through six pints apiece and so I am, as expected, coasting towards being trashed. The pair of us make our way shambolically through the various corridors of the airport, counting down the gates on the way to our own but it's some trek and a relief that we had hours rather than minutes to spare to make it to our connecting flight. We pass through a set of doors into a large open area with a tangle of escalators snaking off in all directions and I study the signs and arrows to see which one we need.

"Right this is the one we want..." I say to no-one, because when I look round for Tom he's making a beeline for an empty children's play area. "What you doing now?!" I shout over and follow him over. He climbs up onto the tiny slide and bursts out laughing as he reaches the top, waving his arms about.

"Well fucking come on then you White Men!" He screams out and careers down the slide but as he's totally oversized for it he falls off half way down, ending up in a heap on the deck. I nearly fall over myself laughing at him, people have stopped dead in their tracks around the terminal seeing what the noise is about. Next, he's up and manhandling the Spring Rider next to the slide which he straddles and begins a mental series of twists and 360 degree swivels pushing the metal spring to its absolute limits. I whip out my phone and record a video of him on there, this mad looking wooden horse being pulled in all directions by what looks to be a black-clad giant, until his drunken grip goes and he's flung away to the side by it. Tom shouting *"Come on Whites!"* is rivalled for volume only by my howls of laughter, I'm doubled over whilst trying to film.

A woman in a blue airport uniform comes running over and starts shouting at Tom, it's in Spanish but I get the gist and she's not happy. I go over and grab him as he lies flat on his back and tell him we better go otherwise we won't be getting on any more planes today and he scrambles up, chuckling away, I can see in his eyes that he's already wankered. We move on at pace, not daring to look back at the woman and take our place on the escalators swaying and stumbling all the way to our waiting aircraft.

It's a tiny pencil of a Spanair plane that will fly us to Madrid and we take our seats in the cramped interior, the last onboard and our departure begins only a few minutes later. As we taxi out and once I've done my ritual examination of the emergency procedures I delve into my hand luggage stuffed down between my feet and pull out the throat medicine that I should have taken much earlier, but I forgot about it once I started feeling better as a result of steady drinking. I may as well have a blast on it now while I've got chance, so I place it on the pull down table with its small plastic spoon.

"What's this then?" Tom goes, suddenly roused from staring blankly at the seat in front.

"Throat medicine from the doctors, forgot I had it." I reply, unscrewing the top.

"Balls to that, you'll get all the medicine you need in Madrid." He shoots back, sounding disgusted and without taking another breath he swipes the bottle up off the table and necks it in two seconds flat. I'm absolutely aghast, he slaps the empty container back down and grins at me.

"I can't fucking believe what I've just seen, are you mental?" I half expect him to suddenly collapse or have some sort of seizure but he just sits there smiling.

"No, I'm tired though. Wake me up in Madrid, Jamie lad." With that he sits back in his seat and closes his eyes as I look on with my gob hanging half open. "Tasted decent that actually." He mumbles, looking pleased with himself.

The shuttle flight is done with in just over an hour but I'm fatigued and rough again by the time we get into a taxi to take us to the hotel. Tom slept through the majority of the flight and is asleep again in the car while I watch the Madrid suburbs turn into the hectic centre of the Spanish capital with our driver treating the congested roads like a rally course, how we don't hit anything I don't know but we must have come perilously close on numerous occasions, leaving beeping horns in our wake. I'm relieved to get to the hotel in one piece. We check in and drop our bags then make our way to a bar where Paul and Chris are supposed to be waiting for us; they sorted their flights out separately and have come over with a group of other lads who we are going to tag along with.

We meet them at an Irish bar called O'Connell Street and the place is already packed with Bolton fans, Wanderers flags hanging from balconies all up the street that it is situated on and even more in the bar. Paul and Chris are stood on the periphery of a big mob inside the wooden tavern and give us a warm welcome when they see us, well, Tom mainly and they introduce us to a couple of their group. Shorts and t-shirts are everywhere, it doesn't take much for the English to get into the summer wear. Everyone to a man is hammered and on top note and I'm back on the beer again as well, though there's no getting away from the feeling that I'm miles away from my best, as we stand here all my joints are aching and my back hurts just through the sheer effort of being on my feet.

Before I know it, it is dark outside which initially seems surprising seen as it's only about seven but then it is still winter, it just doesn't feel like it. The group decides it is time to move and we file out onto the street, there must be around twenty of us, being led by this tubby clown of a lad who doesn't seem to have a clue what he's doing and clearly doesn't get abroad much. I don't know what he is looking for but we find ourselves turning off down back alleys or into dead ends, dusty car parks and forgotten streets with no-one saying very much. All I know is that I'm in agony and have drifted to the back of the group while Tom and the others are somewhere near the front loving all this like it's some big adventure, we have passed countless bars that looked decent enough as well so fuck knows what the plan is.

I set the end of the next street as a mental deadline for jacking this in unless we find somewhere to stop before then, but sure enough we pass that with no sign of a halt so I shout Tom over.

"I'm off mate, I feel like shit." He screws his face up at me.

"Ah don't talk wet, we're on it here!" He responds, but I've had enough.

"Are we fuck as like, this lad hasn't a clue where he's going, I mean what is the actual plan?" Tom shrugs his shoulders but still looks enthusiastic. "Anyhow I'm really struggling I'm going to go back to the hotel and save it for tomorrow, I'd rather have a decent day tomorrow than knacker myself out tonight doing this." He tells me fair enough and that he'll catch me later then turns and jogs back to rejoin the group that are about to disappear around yet another corner leaving me on my tod. I retrace my steps back to the last busy road I saw to find a taxi, glad that we both have a key each for the hotel room this time. Thankfully there's no shortage of the white cabs with a red stripe on them buzzing about on the streets and I'm into one in no time.

    We sweep past sights that on any normal city break I'd be making a beeline to go and visit; a large fountain surrounded by bright strobe lights in the middle of a busy plaza, cafe bars with people sat outside looking very civilised taking advantage of the warm evening and a long road lined with palms and busy shops. They pass by quickly though, my head spinning and throat throbbing painfully each time I swallow.

    Instead of retiring straight up to bed though as I probably should, I find myself enticed into the hotel bar. I buy a coffee and dump myself into a comfy chair, immediately liking the atmosphere in here and again wishing I didn't feel so ill. A group of Spaniards are sat at the bar commenting animatedly on the Celtic v Barcelona Champions League match being shown on a screen high up in the corner of the room, whilst a member of staff shears away at a giant Serrano ham that wouldn't look out of place on The Flintstones, clamped into its metal stand on the bar before arranging the pieces on a plate for the people watching the game to tuck into. I imagine it being salty and chewy which makes me feel hungry but I know I can't eat feeling like this, it's only going to end up coming straight back up again.

    I sip my way through the coffee but there's no doubt I need to crash out and soon so I go back up to the room bouncing off the walls and trying not to concentrate on the stairs for too long as the patterns on the carpet seem to be swirling and spinning around. By the time I get back and strip my clothes off I'm covered in sweat just through the effort of it all and I feel my temples pulsing, I'm going under here.

    I was hoping to pass out as soon as my head hit the pillow but of course nothing of the sort happens; I spend an eternity shifting from one position to the next, turning the pillow over to the cold side countless times, lying on top of the covers to cool down then beginning to shiver so going back under the duvet again. Attempts to stretch and bend to stop pains all around my body only serve to give me muscle strain, my nose and throat have almost totally closed up now and all the while the room spins anytime I lie still for a moment. I will sleep to come with everything I've got.

Mental dreams about being chased by a giant Pacman whilst being stuck inside a bright yellow electronic maze like something out of *"Tron"* are ended abruptly as my upper body is shook by a huge, god-like force and for a few seconds I don't know where the hell I am or what is going on. I jolt upwards, startled, then finally realise the god-like force was actually Tom grabbing me and shaking me awake. I hate him instantly. I bury my clammy head in my hands for a few seconds trying to gather my thoughts then look up at Tom who is utterly wasted.

"Alright Jamie lad!" He slurs, then I'm given the shock of my life by Paul who shouts "Oi!" at me from the other side of my bed, I had no idea he was there and my chest feels like it's about to burst. They both fall about laughing.

"What's the fucking time?" I mumble, can't reach my phone it feels like it is lying a million miles away.

"Fuck the time!" Paul goes. "Fuck the time! Fuck the time!" He repeats over, then skips to the bathroom. Meanwhile Tom goes to the mini-bar sat beneath the dressing table and rips open the door violently, making every single item inside it tumble out onto the floor, bottles and cans roll around everywhere and a pile of chocolate bars arrange themselves at his feet. Again he finds all this hilarious, we're probably going to end up getting charged a fortune for all that stuff, I will definitely not be contributing to that. I lie back on the bed again with my head in a ridiculous amount of pain and I watch with my eyes half open.

The bathroom door re-opens and Paul shouts Tom in who swipes up a can from the floor and joins him inside. The door swings open fully and I see the pair of them on their knees around the closed toilet lid going at a load of lines on top of it with a rolled up note then Tom swearing as the recently unsettled can explodes everywhere when he opens it.

Almost as soon as I've closed my eyes and seemingly found peace, Tom is back again and shaking me just like he did before.

"What?" I moan, looking up to see the pair of them leering over me.

"Going back out, smell you later." They disappear and I drop back off to sleep wondering why they even came back in the first place.

Once more I'm torn from bizarre dreams at some other point during this marathon torture session of a night by the sound of Tom fucking about loudly with the door. My throat has dried out so I sweep the floor next to the bed with my hand and find a bottle of water which I take a few massive gulps from, the first couple of which hurt terribly as the liquid sears down. He clatters into the room alone this time but now looking even more of a mess.

"Yes Jamie, yes!" He shouts at me and grabs my arm yet again.

"What? What the fuck do you want?" I snap at him, majorly pissed off, but it doesn't register.

"You man, you're like a brother to me, you know that?" Oh not this shit again.

"Fuck off."

"No man you are, you are, you know that?" Then he fucking *hugs* me and I feel his soaked shirt collar against my face. Next, all of a sudden his mood changes.

"Me? I'm a fucking addict me man. A fucking addict, Jamie." He shouts aggressively, I roll my eyes and push him off me.

"Do one you dickhead, fuck's sake." I may as well be talking Chinese because he's on a different plane now, nothing anyone says will get through to him, just like the old days.

"I'm dirty inside, this is what I am mate. I'm an *addict*." Fuck me, he sounds like Jimmy Corkhill on a mad one, I wonder how much of that shit he's had tonight. Finally he leaves the bedside and goes into the bathroom and the next thing I know he's stripped naked and stood in the bath with the door open so I can see everything hanging out. Why he climbed into the bath I don't know, because he climbs back out again about ten seconds later, backwards though, arching his legs over the side and I look away from the scene of his arsehole being displayed. He grabs one of the bottles of beer that are still lying about all over the floor then opens the door and walks out into the corridor, naked.

"Tom, fucking hell what are you doing?" I have a go at shouting but it hurts and it's up to him if he wants to be a twat like this anyway, he can get fucking deported for all I care. He's only out there a minute or so at least and I heard no hysterical screaming so I don't think he was seen. "Tom, you're being an absolute knobhead, fucking go to sleep will you. I feel like shit here just leave me in peace? Fuck off to another room or something if you have to but, please, leave me alone." He at last seems to react to my rant, but starts advancing towards me again and there's no way he's hugging me with his cock out like that. "No, no, fuck off stay away from me." He looks hurt. "Stay the fuck away from me. Look at the state of you,

you're fucking naked. You ain't touching me, you twat." He actually looks devastated that I've told him that, the div.

"Jamie though, you're like my brother." I shake my head, brain rattling around inside my skull.

"Yeah and you're an addict and dirty inside, nice one, now fuck off." Finally he gets the message and backs off then goes over to the windows which he opens and places the bottle of beer on the ledge.

"Spain man, fucking Madrid. What a view. *What a view.*" He exclaims, sounding genuinely awe inspired, even though I know from looking through there earlier all you can see is a plain brick wall from the building opposite.

I shut my eyes and must drift off, though I'm not sure for how long. When I come to I look over to the other bed which remains empty so I struggle up onto my knees to look around and see Tom flaked out on the floor, still naked. I stare at his chest for a minute to check if he's still breathing, see that he is, then collapse back to bed and at last I'm out for the count.

CHAPTER TWENTY ONE

Thursday 21st February 2008

I creep around Tom's body and the still strewn contents of the mini-bar to go for a shower, trying to be as quiet as I can so I don't wake him, not through any care for him catching up on his sleep, more because I can't be arsed speaking to him. I feel much better than I did last night although still snivelling and snotting everywhere but I'm glad the queasy and unbalanced sensation has passed now.

Once dressed I leave the room and go outside onto the Madrid streets, warm already even though it's not that long since breakfast time. I decide to find a shop to stock up on some water but it takes me a good twenty minutes to actually find somewhere and by that time I'm sweating and rough again, but at least returning to the hotel quaffing ice cold water from one of the four bottles retrieved from a freezer in the Spar.

I find Tom awake in his bed by the time I get back, so I must have disturbed him on my way out and I dump the bottles on the table between our two beds.

"Still alive then? Thought you might need some of this." I gesture at the water and bend down to pick up the stuff on the floor to move it near to the mini-bar so it's at least out of the way and note the three-quarters-full bottle of beer still perched on the windowsill. "If you think I'm paying for any of this then you've no chance." He tuts and sighs loudly.

"Fuck's sake, we won't get charged for it calm down, I'll put it all back after." He groans, hands on his head.

"Course we will, you've drunk some of it and if it's one of them ones with the sensors in it to check for things being moved then we really are fucked. Well, you are. Like I said I'm not paying for any of it."

"All right, all right! Fuck me Dad, sorry." He snaps but I don't react, I'm pissed off with him for how he was acting up but it's too far from home to be having an argument with him with a full day and night together ahead. He messes about with his phone for a bit then begins to get up.

"Paul and Chris are going back down to that Irish bar again in a bit, you coming or what?" He asks stroppily with an angry tone of voice.

"Yeah, I'm coming. I feel a lot better than I did yesterday, still not great but at least I'm not about to keel over." I decide to try and keep the tone light, if he's in a mood then that's his problem. He goes for a shower and change which as usual takes fucking ages then we're back out onto the streets again, swapping only brief comments about what direction we are heading in as he stomps off towards the O'Connell Street pub a few paces ahead.

This time when we turn onto the street it is on, the pavements and road are jam packed wall to wall with Wanderers fans. They, like the numbers of England flags hanging from all possible fixing points, have multiplied massively since last night and the whole scene hums with the sound of hundreds of voices in jovial spirits mixed together with laughter and shouting. The road is on quite a steep angle so we have to trek upwards to reach the pub and I note that a line of Spanish police in black uniforms are top and tailing it, keeping a watchful eye over everyone including one with a video camera pointed in our direction.

It takes a while to meander through the masses and get into O'Connell Street, which is hammered inside as well and we find Paul and Chris together with a selection of the group from last night drinking in a back room.

"Morning fellas." Paul waves from his position at the bar and he clears a space for Tom and me to join him, which is a surprise. "Feeling any better Jamie? Sorry about last night, you looked fucked." That was a surprise as well.

"Er, yeah. Not brilliant but far better than I was, yeah I was a bit of a mess." The barman comes over so I order a couple of pints and Tom is into Paul before either of us has a chance to say anything else. "Alright Chris, where were you last night while these two were making my life a misery?" I say, in a joking manner. He sniggers, shaking his head at Tom.

"Told them not to go back there I said to leave you to it. I stayed out with this lot but we all ended up back in here till stupid-o-clock. Some of the others still aren't up yet they are in shit state today." I take a huge drink from my pint which I'm relieved to discover goes down without too much of a fight from my body.

"Jesus, all that walking around was a waste of time then in the end wasn't it?" I knew we should have stayed put.

"Oh that was fucking JB that." Paul laughs, I guess that would be the big fella who was leading us through the streets to nowhere. "Said these lads who are supposed to be sorting us out with a load of bing were going to meet us at some bar, but he didn't have a fucking clue where it was. We were out there for ages." With that revelation I'm even more relieved to have called it a day when I did. "In the end we couldn't find them so came back here but they should be meeting up with us today at some point. Miles better than Germany this is, no-one could get anything in Munich but here it's gonna be on tap!" As he says that, something seems to twig in his head as if he's remembered something so he tells me he'll be back in a bit and then turns to a group who are sat down at some chairs behind him and speaks to them.

"... Especially when this miserable twat is in a mood with me here." I hear Tom say to Paul as I turn my attention back to the bar and my drinks.

"You what? I'm not in a mood with you. Just didn't appreciate you waking me up with your cock out trying to hug me, that's all." I come back immediately and he appears to visibly retreat with embarrassment as Paul laughs his head off at him. Hopefully that'll shut him up for a bit.

I manage a full English breakfast and like everyone else who sits and eats it at the bar, wash it down with multiple shots of tequila complete with salt and wedges of lime, videoing Chris on my phone as he's encouraged to lie on his back on a table as one of the staff pours a long slug of it down his throat straight from the bottle serenaded by loud cheers.

The action moves back out onto the street as the pub gets way too hot and busy to stand and there's a festival atmosphere with everyone standing and drinking. I look down at the bottom of the street and note that the number of police watching over us has at least doubled since we arrived. There's a commotion behind me as a car attempts to drive down the packed out and surely pedestrianised street, which forces the group to part and crush together to avoid the clapped out old SEAT. Lads drop their heads down to the level of the driver and passenger windows to shout abuse in, I can see a cocky looking arsehole in a vest at the wheel laughing at them and mouthing something in return, the back seats are filled with bags and holdalls and a crate of beer is perched on top of it all. It seems that Paul saw this too and he emerges from the group of bunched up Wanderers fans.

"Spic twat!" He shouts towards the vehicle, scurrying behind it and lifting open the boot. For a few seconds there seems to be a slight hesitation amongst the masses as they watch Paul at work, then a frenzied mob as he extracts the crate of beers and tells everyone to help themselves. "Now go on, fuck off!" Paul screams into the car before slamming the boot back down. The driver isn't smirking anymore and he isn't hanging around either, sure enough he makes a swift exit down the street and away.

Chris manages to secure a couple of cans from the crate which is being set upon by a huge gang like the unfortunate victim of a zombie movie, 24 cans of beer completely vanishing from a cardboard box in seconds. It's warm and not at all refreshing but it is one less drink to pay for so I sup it gleefully as Paul is congratulated by Tom and some of his mates. Once these are finished we go on the march looking for more bars, Tom is in the group somewhere too but he's not speaking to me.

So, I am back to following a group through the tight and winding streets of central Madrid looking for beer but this at least feels different and more fruitful than last night's escapade as we are being led by people who seem to be more clued up. Local residents stand and watch us from doors and windows of their tan and beige coloured buildings, I am quite certain they don't like what they see but on this type of do I'm not fussed what they think. Backpacking alone and learning about places and people, then no, I'm nothing like I am today but here mixed in with a throng of football fans I'm shouting and ballooning as much as anyone.

We pit-stop at any pub we come across that looks big enough to accommodate us, sparing the tiny little cafes and tapas bars our presence. At one place the owner at least seems happy enough to see us and we grab him in the middle of our group and have someone take our photo, beers aloft and smiles aplenty. A round in here is quaffed then back into the streets we go, eventually finding our way into the massive, stunning expanse that is the Plaza

Mayor, Madrid's central square. Here it seems the majority of the Bolton fans that have descended upon this city have congregated and I smile broadly at the sight of it; even more flags hanging from balconies and walls, a gigantic one stretched out across the floor, lads taking part in a large and sprawling football match in one part of it, groups drinking and chatting in others, wonderful.

Our refreshments are provided in the form of a number of crates that Chris and a few others returned with after some of us chucked in some Euros and they went looking for a shop while the rest of us stayed guarding a position we acquired on some steps. They aren't away for very long then we are able to pick up where we left off. Someone definitely turns the oven up while I'm sat here, it is roasting and there's very little shade on offer as the afternoon continues, many are beginning to look very red and the football game dies down to barely a laboured kick about. I start to wish I'd have worn shorts but they weren't something I was thinking about back in Bolton where I'm sure it will be just as cold and wet as it was when I left. My jacket is off and I've pulled the sleeves of my polo up to my shoulders so I can feel the sun on my upper arms. Tom still hasn't spoken to me since I shut him up in O'Connell Street and I watch him for a few moments as he hangs around a group of people I don't recognise, hamming it up yet surely suffering in this heat whilst wearing a thick cable-knit Paul & Shark jumper.

I work my way through my drink and watch the world go by, actually feeling quite contented and excited about the match for the first time since pretty much the end of the First Leg, chuckling to myself as I watch a couple of topless Wanderers fans trying in vain to chat up a girl covered head to toe in silver paint at work as a living statue. I see her just about cracking a smile but she manages to keep her composure and they throw some coins into the pouch she has laid out on the floor. Soon after, some buskers show up with accordions and start playing songs. Before long I'm up along with a few others dancing about with them and singing *"When The Whites Go Marching In"*, loving it and loving the attention from the men and women stood around clapping and cheering us on as we do our jig.

Time rolls on, deep into the afternoon, hundreds of people cramming into the square building up towards the game and it is another sight that will stay with me forever. I weave through a mass of them to get to one of the packed bars so I can use their toilet and I'm hit pleasantly – if briefly – in the face by the cool air conditioning as soon as I enter the building, then turn left to head towards the stairs leading down to the toilet. I get only half way down the dim staircase before I'm stuck in a queue to get in, everywhere a blur of noise and laughter. It is slow going to even get into the area where the toilets and sinks are but once in there it becomes clear why there is such a delay; each of the four cubicles is fully populated by handfuls of lads snorting cocaine, the doors are open and I see some hunched over the cisterns, others sorting lines out on top of the toilet roll dispensers and others looking on anxiously to get involved. Even around the urinals lads are sniffing off keys, edges of cards and one is desperately trying to arrange some on the back of his hand.

One or two in the queue look on at them in disdain but the majority appear to be just waiting their turn to do the same. Down here the air hangs heavy and thick with heat and aggression, the noise of shouting and talking at speed about rumours of mobs lurking around the alleys or war parties going on the hunt is relentless, the walls are brown with damp and rot and the floors are filthy – it is a depressing scene. I finally get my chance to use a cubicle and shut the door behind me to gain just a few moments' space away from sweaty and charged up blokes while I have a piss. Returning to the surface when I leave the bar and go back into the searing heat of the square is as refreshing as any drink I've had all day.

By the time I return to our position, Tom is there too and he at least acknowledges me as I swipe another beer from the dwindling supplies. The decision is made to move on once the crates are finally empty and this comes round in no time. So we make a move in the direction of the hotel where a bulk of the people in the group are staying so they can sort themselves out before the game, it's not what I want to be doing really but seen as I am trashed it seems the best thing to do rather than go off alone. I had fancied a trip to the Bernabeu for a tour of the stadium when coming to Madrid first became a reality, but that's out the window now.

"Oi, oi, get on this!" Tom shouts from up near the front of the dozen-or-so strong mob we are walking around in. He splits off from the group and skips over to a tramp who is lying apparently asleep beneath a sheet against the wall. He then proceeds to boot the poor bastard in the midriff as he lies there and a few of the people I'm with howl with laughter. In a flash though the tramp springs up to his feet and rushes at Tom with his arms raised, who is taken aback and jumps away a few paces. Some of the lads storm in and grab the bloke and move him away from Tom who laughs and sniggers back at him, the tramp looks seriously pissed off and I can't blame him, I feel like a right twat for just being in the vicinity of this. Paul sits the man back down amongst the cardboard squalor he was sleeping in and I can see him saying something into his ear and whatever it is, the bloke looks crestfallen.

Finally we move on with Tom laughing and joking about the whole thing, making our way painfully slowly to a hotel which turns out to be only a stone's throw from our own accommodation, not before all of us stop in the middle of the road to halt traffic and let everyone know that we are Bolton, we are Bolton, we're the football kings with much shouting and Latino hand-wringing in return from the frustrated drivers stuck in the street. They weren't going anywhere fast anyway, Madrid is at a standstill as we enter rush hour and every street we enter is full of cars and people, this place is alive.

All of us end up going to one of the lads' rooms once we make it back and cram in there; I collapse down into a chair in the corner and take a beer that is offered to me out of a box on the floor. Then I watch on as all of the others hammer the coke with a vengeance; lines of it are set up and snorted from everywhere, off tables, keys, rails, the toilet seat, the sink, upturned ashtrays, the lot. One of them opens the balcony doors and does some off the railings overlooking the street, it is an absolute frenzy in here, bags of the stuff are everywhere. It is here where I feel like the odd one out and totally out of place, am I the boring one here? It's like cocaine is the new lager or something, it is rife every time I go away and watch Wanderers, but this is something else. I just sit drinking my beer and study each person as they find their own ways of setting up a new line.

I look over at Tom who was one of those who found a place at the edge of the bath and see him sat there on the bathroom floor with blood all over his face.

"Oh fuck me, Tom!" I shout and I'm out of my seat and over to him in a flash, the room descends into silence and everyone crowds round the door to see what's going on.

"Get off me I'm fine you mad head!" Tom moans as I grab him and stand him up, he shifts my hands off him. A long stream of blood is oozing out of his nose and has been spread all over his face by his hands which are also covered.

"You fucking nutter Tom." Someone shouts. "Well in!" Another goes and with that and a wave of laughter, they all go back to what they were doing. Not a single one of them gives a fuck, I can't understand what is going on, there's blood everywhere.

"Tom, what the fuck, have you seen yourself? What are you doing?" I say with my voice low as if I'm trying to hide it from the others. We both look at our reflection in the mirror as we stand next to eachother, but his eyes are nowhere. "Are you alright?" I ask the reflection and he just laughs.

"Honestly it's nothing, I'm fine." He wipes the blood away which seems to have stopped now at least with a tissue and runs some water over his face and hands then laughs again. I watch him for a few more seconds but he just glares at me then goes back into the other room with barely so much as a look from anyone else in his direction. I see Paul sat in the corner momentarily unoccupied and go over to him.

"Did you not see that? His fucking nose just exploded." I'm trying to not sound too concerned but not doing a great job of it. "What's going on? He needs help." Paul stands up and just sniggers at me, with the same look of pity on his face as I saw at Newcastle, as if I'm the sad act missing out on one big party.

"Don't be such a fucking mard arse, it's only a bit of blood. It's normal, *it happens*." He sniffs a laugh at me again and walks off towards the balcony and I'm left to stand here feeling like a right tool.

Thankfully we don't spend much longer in the hotel room. Finally the decision is made to get taxis to get to the stadium with kick off less than a couple of hours away and I am glad to be away from there and back outside, darkness has fallen upon Madrid now too. Taxis are easy enough to find but the drive is slow and frustrating through the packed traffic crawling in all directions around the city, it takes ten minutes just to get off our street. I am sat in the middle between Tom and Chris, with Paul in the passenger seat, each of us is steaming through the effects of alcohol and/or narcotics, but none of us are doing much talking.

CHAPTER TWENTY TWO

It takes an eternity to get to the stadium far to the west of the location of the hotels and by the banks of the Manzanares River; every road is a battle to travel down. We eventually tell the driver to drop us off nearby the ground as once we finally get into view of the place it is clear that there's no chance of getting any closer without running up an even bigger fare than it already is. The three of us on the back seat each muster up some coins to hand over to Paul, then Tom opens his door and promptly falls out back first onto the busy road, it is a miracle he isn't cut in half by passing traffic. I just laugh at him as he struggles to get to his feet, the dick, if he's not arsed about his own safety then I'm not being responsible for him either.

The road leading up to the ground is bathed in amber light and is extremely busy with people everywhere, along with a large police presence including a number of them on horseback. We spend a few minutes having a look around the market stalls set up outside the turnstiles selling all sorts of club tat and Chris buys a small pin badge depicting Atletico's and Bolton's badges on a white background. We are then chaotically thrust into the ground as crowds gather at our gates, bottlenecked by their narrow openings and the noise of discontent and frustration grows around us, I can hear shouts of protest and anger from people behind me but I've no time to see what is going on as I suddenly find myself inside.

We climb some concrete steps up towards the away end, just following the crowds really, bare brick walls to my right, railings and an open gap to the street below to my left. I look over the railings and see a mass of people outside still stuck at the turnstiles, with the mounted police accosting them in some areas and Wanderers fans having a go at them, it's an ugly scene.

"You can stick your fucking Ultras up your arse! You can stick your fucking Ultras up your arse..." I start chanting at the top of my voice, I'm not sure why, but others join in too including Tom and Chris who are busy pissing against the wall half way up the steps. Police completely bedecked in riot gear greet us at the top of the steps, then again through another small doorway leading to the expanse of the stadium and they look like vicious bastards. They glare at us when we pass them by and finally I have arrived in the grand old Estadio Vicente Calderon.

A cursory glance at it reveals a very Mediterranean looking two-tiered open bowl of a venue with fetching red, white and blue striped seats beneath bright white floodlights but as soon as I turn to find out where our seats are it becomes clear that it's an absolute death trap of a place. Steep knee-high concrete steps with plastic arse-bowls bolted to them constitute the away end and right at the back of the top tier, it doesn't feel entirely safe, like one jump would see me easily clear about ten rows in front.

We are in long before kick off while the teams are still going through their warm up drills down below us and aside from our end the rest of the stadium is virtually deserted. Paul sees some faces he recognises amongst the crowd of people being herded in and he goes to speak to them followed by the others, leaving just me at our "seats" so I use the time to take some photos of the place. I keep trying to get a better view of what is going on at the concourse entrances as most people are turned towards them rather than the ground and I feel a horrible jolt rush through me when for a fleeting second I see a police baton being raised and hammered downwards, the outcome shielded by masses of people. I dread to think what is going on over there.

My attention is not fully on the match as we kick off in this momentous fixture, I continue to try and see what is going on in the crowds but at least I haven't seen any more batons in use. No sign of the other three but to be honest I'm not missing them as I spend the majority of the first period chatting to an extremely pretty girl stood next to me who explains in her rather grating generic Uni accent that this is actually the fifth day of her holiday, that the first four were spent with her friends *"larging it"* down in Valencia before flying up here for the game. All of her friends thought she was just crazy to do it but, like, being such a big Wanderers fan she couldn't miss it, then she will catch another flight in the morning back down south to finish her holiday. Can't be bad.

She laughs about the fact that it is winter yet she has a tan and about how mad it is that she's taken time out from her girls' holiday to come here and watch football, but it's okay because they take two or three holidays a year together so it's only just this once, the questioning intonation in her voice going up a notch with every remark. I can't decide whether to fancy her or despise her. She looks younger than me yet is doing all this. I'm jealous, though not of her daft looking Atletico Madrid bob hat.

Meanwhile behind the goal to our left the home Ultras are busy kicking off amongst themselves and the stand which originally was full, with red smoke bombs going off and all sorts, begins to resemble a mosh pit as a large gap appears in the crowd. It expands out of nowhere like grease parting on water when washing up liquid is dropped into it and now and again a couple of figures emerge into the middle for the very briefest of melees. They're egged on by many of our supporters who for a while forget there is a game on, cheers when it looks like it's going to go off and boos when they melt back into the onlookers at the side. *"Get stuck in you soft sod!"* A woman a few rows in front of me shouts when someone else ends up skipping back over seats the way he came when confronted, she's loving it.

Unbelievably we almost take the lead early on in the game as Stelios has a shot parried away for a corner, backed by huge noise from our support and very nearly a surge forward like something from the terraces of old – leaving some people on their arses and needing to be helped up after tumbling down onto the next step in front. In the main though the game is not much of a spectacle but I'm delighted to see us defending so solidly, conceding only a handful of shots which Jussi deals with well and of course it is all serenaded by non-stop singing from us, high up to the side of the pitch.

Wanderers reach half-time unscathed, just another forty-five minutes to survive to keep this brilliant and most unexpected European run going, but Atletico are surely going to go all out the longer this goes on. I venture downstairs at the break and buy a French stick crammed with salami which I devour in no time, it tastes like shit but I'm ravenous.

"Here he is, the twat!" I hear Tom shout from over my shoulder and I turn to see the trio approaching me, Tom's face looks grey but he's smiling.

"Alright, where have you all been?" I ask them. "Not had any run ins with these Robocops have you I hope?"

"Nah but they're battering people left, right and centre it's fucking sick." Chris shakes his head animatedly.

"I must have spent about ten Euros already in that first half launching coins at them spic fuckers next to us!" Tom goes, though I'm not as amused by this as he is, he's going to end up getting lamped by someone if he carries on.

"Fuck me, you'll be getting batoned next..." I tell him pointlessly. All around us Wanderers fans pass by going to and from their seats but it's very clear to me that many of them look shaken rather than excited. I'm beginning to think I've had a lucky escape from something here, there are one of two people actually in tears in amongst the crowds and I spot one man with a bloodied face and jacket, it hits me that we're in a grim situation with the police tonight.

We return with the second half underway and I stand at the back with the others, far away from the girl I was talking to in the first half but that's no great shame really. The same story from the first half repeats itself, Wanderers do us proud defending everything Atletico throw at them, Gary Cahill in particular is playing out of his skin and looks an absolute hero down there tonight. Ivan Campo is brought on later and we cheer him loudly, drowning out the whistles from the home end as they see a former Real Madrid player enter the fray, he claps up to us when he comes on, the fucking legend.

I feel strangely detached from all this though, what with seeing the look on some of the travelling fans' faces at half time and listening to Tom giving it the big one constantly about having a go at the Spanish fans and police. I'm shouting and singing with everything I've got of course but there is no doubt the event has been soured by what I've seen. It doesn't help that the contest itself has petered out into a very dour game; virtually *nothing* happens after the Campo substitution.

Atletico come at us a little more into the last few minutes but somehow it doesn't feel like they are really going for it and we manage to hold up play and run the clock down very well. People around me are in a right state, some unable to watch, others actually biting their fingernails and tugging at their own hair through the stress of it all with the game entering stoppage time, whistles and pleas for the game to be up stream out from our end, Tom entering a new level of mental as he pushes past us to berate the referee from the steps. I'm just stood here though, arms by my side, making no noise just watching the referee's hands rather than the game, it's going nowhere anyway. I feel a weird peace while everyone around me is completely losing it. Though that doesn't last very long...

At last the final whistle is blown and the whole end erupts in mass celebration, arms and heads bobbing about as if we've just scored a winner. I raise my arms skywards and give a short shout of celebration followed by a very unexpected little blub, quite amazed at our achievement but thankfully no tears, I'd never live that down. A random man gives me a massive bear hug and we jump up and down together, grabbed by unseen hands and patted on the back, the scene repeated everywhere as three thousand Bolton rejoice. One of the greatest results in our history.

Inevitably we are kept in after full time, though we continue to sing and celebrate regardless while the rest of the stadium empties out including the tiny batch of Bolton fans housed in the opposite stand who must be getting special treatment. There is no announcement about how long we will be held in the ground for and many are restless, mobs of people are crammed up near the exits but are unable to move anywhere. Then I shudder as down at the front of our end I see the police wading in again, but this time there's loads of them and they aren't holding back. A line of the black-clad riot cops are lashing out at anyone in striking distance and bedlam breaks out down there with people running for cover, I can clearly see individual police smashing their batons into the heads, backs and limbs of our supporters.

I'm totally sickened and livid, joining scores of others hurling abuse down at the attackers while people run past me covered in blood. More beatings are dished out then the police hold the line once the area they had moved into is cleared, I want out of here as quickly as possible, if they decide to come into the next section up then that's right on top of us.

Some of our players emerge from the tunnel long after full time to do their warm-downs and they're given a loud and warm welcome, including Gary Megson himself and the *"Ginger Mourinho"* song makes another appearance. I wonder if they can see what has happened to some of their supporters from all the way down there, surely some sort of official complaint will be made over this.

At last we begin to move, some forty minutes after the final whistle, back up the steps and onto the concourses, shepherded down and out of the stadium by the thugs dressed as coppers and one or two people give them some abuse though not too loud, fearing a whacking. I exit the ground with Tom, Paul and Chris, happy to be out of there.

"That was fucking horrible wasn't it?" Chris says as we are herded into a convoy of people leading towards the city centre. "I've never seen anything like that, it was brutal." I agree, this crowd is full of extremely angry or upset men and women. Next minute, Paul darts to his right past a couple of people and emerges with his arms around the considerable frame of JB, the lad who led us a merry dance last night, but his face is covered in blood and the top of his head looks a mess.

"This is what you get for telling a copper to fuck off over here!" He enthuses, seems to be in a better mood than I'd expect him to be. "Got smashed over the head, sent out to see someone with a staple gun then got put back in the ground." He tells us and a group of shocked onlookers, tilting his head forward to show us a huge gash that has been very roughly stapled back together; I can see jagged pieces of metal sticking up out of the wound.

"Fuck me I feel sick. What are you going to do about it? You need to get it sorted properly surely?..." I'm wincing looking at that, it's a proper shit job they've done on him there. There's no chance for a reply though, further along the street far ahead of our group it is kicking off and JB forgets his injuries to scurry off and get involved. It is quite a way up the street away from us but I can see at least one person on the ground having the shit kicked out of them with a couple of people sticking the boot in to their head and midriff, can't tell who is who though.

"Yes, yes let's have it!" Tom starts, bouncing up and down but not going anywhere fast, I just leave him to it. Our journey away from the stadium is taking us up some deserted roads between tall concrete apartment blocks and under a blanket of amber light which all looks quite menacing especially with the thought that a mob of Ultras or police could confront us at any moment. The fight ahead of us has broken up and moved on by the time I get another decent view of it and there's no sign of JB either but at least Tom and the others didn't attempt to get involved, I'm in no mood to accompany any of them to the station or hospital.

Out of nowhere to my left, two older blokes emerge from a tiny alleyway at pace, one wearing a long green parka covered in patches and the other, a bald and barrel-chested character wearing a fucking England shell-suit from about 1990.

"Keep your shape Steve! Come on, keep it tight!" The chap in the parka says to his Italia '90 mate and they rush on past us towards the front, accompanied by the sound of rapidly rustling polyester. I catch the eye of some of the other lads near me as they watch the pair move off and we burst out laughing, one of the most random things I've ever seen.

Once we get past another block of tall apartments we at last see more signs of life with some shops and passing cars reassuring me that we were not going to be in the ghetto for very long. I follow Tom into a small shop and get a drink from the fridge while he causes all sorts of chaos trying to ask the shop keeper where he keeps his porn DVD's, the poor bloke looks totally bemused.

Eventually we return to the O'Connell Street bar where a large group of Bolton fans has gathered swapping war stories and comparing wounds, many of which look just as badly tended to as JB's. Tom fucks off to the toilets with Paul and Chris to get *"binged up"* again, not even hiding it anymore and I've had enough of him acting the prick. I go and get myself a bottle of beer and take it outside to talk to some lads about their experiences, it seems they were part of the large group outside Gate 21 after we first got inside and they were charged by the mounted police. Absolute animals.

Our flight leaves for Malaga in the very early hours and I'm eager to go back to the hotel to pick up my bag from the holding room and head on to the airport so we can be there in decent time for the plane. Before then though I have to endure over an hour of Tom hanging off me describing me as his "brother" again and putting his arms around me every five minutes, interjected by bouts of him suddenly fuming and kicking off with me, himself or random people stood about in the street. Paul and Chris, after seemingly supplying him with the coke, clearly decide that they don't want to be seen with him now and make their excuses. They have another night here and don't leave till tomorrow afternoon and Paul is adamant that he is in with a Norwegian bird he's seen a couple of times at their hotel, so they're off, leaving just me and Tom.

I give it up after I finish the beer off and start back to the hotel with Tom in tow talking complete bollocks. I'm embarrassed to be seen with him, particularly in the hotel when I get our bags from behind the reception and he struggles to get through basic sentences with the bloke helping us. The fact that no extra charges for use of the mini bar are mentioned is a shock but I'm glad it saves us a potential scene here in front of everyone. Tom does at least conk out in the taxi to the airport though and I manage some sleep too after a very long couple of days.

Once dropped at the terminal we have a long walk to our check in desk but I'm on a mission once I find out which direction we are supposed to go in, I want to get there as quickly as possible so I can crash on a bench somewhere and get my head down. As I briskly make my way towards our destination however, Tom mopes on miles behind me looking like a right sorry bastard. I glance behind me to check that he is still in tow and he looks a dead ringer for *"Shameless'"* Frank Gallagher with his greasy dark hair all over his knackered looking face and stumbling about everywhere, pointing at nothing and tripping over his own feet.

"Here, that's your boarding pass and your passport, you can sort yourself out if we get split up." I tell him once we're done at the gate and he tries to kick off but he's far too fucked and slumps into a sulk as I collapse onto a bench and stretch out with over two hours to go before we have to board. I close my eyes and shut Tom out, I don't give a shit what he wants to do with himself now. I've been used to sort out our flights and (eventually) accommodation, then to carry his passport and tickets around for him so he can go and get wasted and act up safe in the knowledge that good old Jamie will keep things safe for him, but now he's on his own.

He's still there when I wake up, looking like a corpse and we get on the plane to take us back down south with no trouble, I'm out of it and asleep for the duration, in fact the wheels hitting the tarmac is the thing that actually wakes me up I'm that far gone. Our time at Malaga couldn't be in greater contrast to how it was on the outward flight, all that happy drinking in the warm sunlight gone, replaced by freezing cold darkness and crushing fatigue with another couple of hours to wait for the flight that will finally take me home. I realise that Tom has disappeared at some point during this wait, amidst my tired and post-drunken stupor, I wonder if he will actually make it onto the plane if he's left to his own devices.

It's not until I'm strapped into my seat on the return flight along with everyone else on the plane that I see Tom again, he is the last to board by far and very nearly misses it. He ignores the funny looks in his direction from some of the other passengers and slumps into his seat next to me, massive dark bags hanging under his eyes and sweat covering his brow making some of his hair stick to his face.

"Sorry." He says pathetically, but I ignore him, I can't believe what a state he's become. Taxiing begins very shortly after he sits down and as we turn onto the runway with the sun coming up, he starts moaning and gasping, I look over to him and have the disgusting sight of his nose exploding once again, a plume of blood gushes through his fingers and down onto his jacket that is folded across his lap.

"Jamie lad, help me I'm dying." He minces, stuffing the jacket up against his nose which surely ruins it. "Oh God, fucking hell I'm dying." He carries on and I just watch him, not really knowing what to do, then think back to how he and everyone else reacted back in the hotel when this last happened and shake my head. Now all roads have led us to this; after his misery over Christmas, the way he was up at Newcastle and his unusual behaviour of the last couple of weeks, a perfect storm here in Madrid of warm sun, alcohol and a shed load of coke – leaving him sat on a plane hurtling down the runway with his nose spewing blood out uncontrollably.

It is at the exit to the terminal at Manchester Airport making our way back to the train station when I next say anything to him after a silent flight home once his nose had finally stopped pissing blood and he had been to the toilet to clean his face and hands up. Still staggering about looking like the "addict" he told me he was back in Madrid, I turn to him and get in his face.

"Look at the state of you, you fucking loser." Who knows whether he's taking any notice or not, his eyes are miles away. "Nice one for using me to sort out your flights and hotel so you can go and take the piss. Stay away from me, I've had enough." I leave him standing there and turn away to walk to the train station feeling numb and hoping I don't see Tom again for a long time.

CHAPTER TWENTY THREE

Sunday 24th February 2008

I sack Blackburn away off today, can't be arsed with Tom and my toys are well and truly out of the pram. I've heard nothing from him and I think he probably expects I won't be bothering especially after what I said to him in the airport. He's got the match tickets so he can do what he wants with them, I plan to spend the day sitting at home, might listen to it on the radio, might not. Knowing my luck I'll miss an away victory yet again, last season when we played Blackburn it was the day of Mum's 50th birthday party and so I decided to go out with the family and gambled on missing out on Blackburn. Predictably, it ended up being one of the great Wanderers away days of recent times. Tom went and witnessed Ivan Campo head the winner right in front of a massive travelling Wanderers support of around seven thousand followed by Jaaskelainen unbelievably saving two late Blackburn penalties and I believe the celebrations in our end were unreal.

I've been to Blackburn a few times – seemingly drawing on every occasion – they were dire affairs. I can mentally picture the images from today too; an almighty crush to get onto the train at Bolton Station followed by anxious faces of those trying and failing to get on further up the line at Hall i'th' Wood and Bromley Cross. Lads crammed into every available space of the train quaffing cans and singing songs then an exodus at Darwen, hordes marching down the long road to Ewood, or a hardy few staying on the train to alight at Blackburn itself and embarking on the deceptively arduous walk from the centre of town to the stadium. Either way I envisage the masses converging on the famed away pub The Fernhurst, filling the bars, the numerous large rooms and the car park. It's a drizzly day so maybe the festivities will be a little more muted than normal but still in our end it will be a good atmosphere especially with the jubilation of Madrid still there, loud and lively in the stands and the cramped concourses down below.

 Of course it's easy to say in hindsight that I made the right decision not to go, but I am glad I missed out to be honest. It was a game which by all accounts we looked capable of getting a result from for long periods which makes the 4-1 scoreline in the Dingles' favour hard to take and after the week I've had it would have been one sickener too far. I sit in the living room for much of the day looking dazed and feeling like a bomb's gone off in my head. I'm still fried from Madrid and fed up about it all, reflecting on it constantly and also trying to stop Flick dropping into my consciousness as she often attempts to do.
 Holly lazes about with her head flopped into my lap as I talk over things with the parents, I know they've long been unsure of Tom's behaviour although they're always civil and friendly with him anytime he's round, but Madrid seems to have been the last straw. They tell me in no uncertain terms that he's not welcome at the house anymore which only serves to make me feel more miserable, I want to keep out of Tom's way for a while sure, but that makes it seem just that little bit more final and irrecoverable. I can't believe how a trip that was supposed to have been such a great event has turned into the calamity that it has – but then this whole season is crashing down around me; it has been a disastrous few weeks.

Monday 25th February 2008

"I need a fucking change man..." I moan to Dan as I ram home another file into its slot at work, a trolley full of these to put away then a further basket overflowing with loose papers awaits at my desk to do the same with when I'm done. He's been stood here listening to me whinging for about ten minutes now either because he actually cares or because he can't be arsed doing any work of his own. At any rate I've told him about everything that went on in Madrid as this is the first time I've been back in since then. I begin to reiterate what I've been saying for what feels like forever now about feeling like I've no real direction in life when he sighs loudly and interjects.

"Mate, you know what? You've got to figure out what and who you are." I scrunch my face up at him as if I've not got a clue what he's on about. "You're trying to do this 'lad' thing, getting wasted every weekend and fucking about all over the place, but then you're spending the next four or five days in here moping about regretting it. You gonna do that forever or what?" He's right, obviously, but it's hard to break out of the monotonous trap.

"Well what else am I gonna do?" In frustration I manhandle another manila folder into the gap which tears it right down the front but I just leave it as it is.

"Fuck knows, I dunno, mix it up a bit or something. You seem to have hassle pretty much every time you're out with Tom, stay out of his way for a bit. Go travelling again, whatever." The thought of travelling sounds perfect, moving abroad even, but it feels too much like hard work right now.

"I wish, I'd go mad saving up to do that again. Even at home I'm fed up as well, it's alright but I'm sick of getting back there and having to decide how much I tell them about what has been going on. Most of the time I can't be arsed lying or dodging stuff, so just tell them the lot. They don't wanna be hearing that." Dan's jaw drops dramatically.

"You mean you've told them about all this shit you've told me?" He cackles as I nod my head. Yeah, they know most things, some details are left out that are a bit too colourful but I've kept them in the loop with a lot of it.

"The way I see it is, they're going to end up finding out about something daft that happens at some stage so rather than have to go through the whole process of starting from the beginning and telling them everything, I may as well keep them updated as it happens. See what I mean?"

"No. Fuck no!" He responds instantly. "Oh hi James, what have you been up to tonight? *Oh well Mum I met this rotter off the internet and shafted her in front of her two sleeping kids, but now I'm bothered I might have knocked her up."* He mimics a thick Fred Dibnah accent and rhymes off a load of other activities I've confessed to him about.

"Alright, alright calm down, I don't go into that much detail, they just know the general issues."

"The *general issues*." He sniggers. "Poor parents." It makes me feel guilty about telling them my problems, I'm glad I can talk to them about stuff and there's no way I'll tell them the literal ins and outs of everything but I suppose they don't need me unloading all my shit on them. It's a lesson to learn.

"Anyway as I was saying, I need a change of scenery, some different company and some new faces, I'm bored of Bolton." I move the conversation away from parental disclosure and Dan rubs his hand across his chin for a moment, over a beard that has been growing out for a couple of weeks and has turned from being the same tone as his sandy coloured hair into a shade of ginger. It definitely needs a trim.

"Right, well, you might be in luck. The lad I live with, Will, is going away with his missus at weekend. A few of us are off out on Saturday, tag along and crash at mine if you want?" I'm taken aback at first, me and Dan get on well at work or on staff do's but haven't really hung around together much otherwise, certainly not been round to his flat or out with his mates. It's a great chance to do something different though.

"Yeah man, that would be ace, cheers!" I exclaim, just what I needed.

"Fair do's, it's no problem." He replies in his usual easy going manner. "No bringing any married or dodgy birds back though, my mate probably wouldn't appreciate that in his bed, fella."

He's nothing to worry about on that front.

Saturday 1st March 2008

So I spent yesterday evening stood on Dan's balcony six storeys up in the centre of Manchester looking out over the skyline as countless lights shone from the high rise buildings around the city. It was awe inspiring, a couple of beers with a mate after work watching the world go by and I could only imagine what this would be like on a warm summer's day. We worked our way through a pack of bottles whilst battering *"Pro Evo"* on the Xbox all night in his gigantic wood floored living room; a smart kitchen in one corner, sound system in another churning out a medley of Death In Vegas, Primal Scream and Feist, a widescreen telly in front of us and massive patio windows opening out onto the gated balcony with the cityscape beyond, it is intoxicating.

Today after a few in the afternoon, now me, Dan and four of his mates are making our way to the Northern Quarter just a few minutes away from the flat for an assault on the numerous bars in the area. This is the life.

Our first stop is Trof and we are lucky to find a bank of chairs and a sofa to take up residence on as the venue is otherwise packed, it is hot and loud in here but the atmosphere is great. Four lads and two girls make up our group; all of them Dan's friends for years, all of them stylish and well turned out, funny and confident, all of them graduates from some degree or other yet all of them obviously making a better fist of the post-grad thing than me. I'm envious and fond of them in equal measure in no time.

They're all down to earth too which isn't always a given round these parts by any stretch and I'm instantly accepted, making them laugh by taking the piss out of Dan at work and all of us ribbing him about City drawing 0-0 with Wigan earlier in the day. Kate, one of the two girls in the group and inevitably gorgeous too, chats to me for ages about travelling and I lay it on thick about my exploits around Europe, though of course when the beer starts to flow I end up regaling them with the tale of turning the bar over in Munich and even some of the scenes from Madrid but I don't expand on that trip too much.

A few rounds in here then we move on up the street to Odd for another but it is very much standing room only, before crossing over into to The Bay Horse where we get on it big time. I'd need a lottery win to be a regular around here though as I'm paying nearly four quid for every pint, rifling through cash like there's no tomorrow. I don't know how Dan does it on the same wage as me though I suppose he's not financially burdened as much by shelling out on clothes and going to football, he's more of an occasional attendee at City and rarely travels away. You'd be stumped paying the rent he does at that gaff anyway.

Cold air hitting me when we leave the pub brings home the fact that I am very much drunk, but on to another couple of places we go; Tib Street Tavern and Cord, via a cash machine and I'm fucking hammered, everyone laughing at my accent which has come out in force now but the others aren't exactly in control either. Sian, the other bird, has managed to drop two glasses of wine in the past half hour yet laughed her arse off on both occasions. All five of us are on top note and I'm loving it, I'm told I should come out on the piss with them more often and I wholeheartedly agree every time it's mentioned, I'd love to but I hope they like mixing it up by going to Spoons now and again to lower the costs.

Sian falling over at the bar is our cue to call it a night, one of those comedy tumbles where with no-one anywhere near her she just leaned then slumped to the floor like a falling tree but she sees the funny side again, the girl is tatered. A massive take-away each is bought in Hunters on the way back through the Northern Quarter then me and Dan see everyone off in a couple of taxis before stumbling back to the apartment. I must tell him that it is amazing he lives so close to this place at least a dozen times on the short journey back. Eating – and keeping down – the entire pizza that I came away with is ultimately however too tall a task to master.

Sunday 2nd March 2008

It's another hangover, but it's a righteous hangover. I come-to on Dan's couch with the light breaking through the blinds onto my face, feeling rough but I had a great night and for once one without any regrets or lingering paranoia. It is past eleven now and Wanderers kick off against Liverpool at half one, there's no way I can be arsed to get up and out to that now, but I'm not fussed. I drift off another couple of times during the morning before I'm woken by Dan shambolically stumbling into the living room looking wasted and going for the fridge. He crashes onto the other settee chugging from a bottle of orange juice.

We just sit there for ages, slouched and watching some food program before I slope off to get sorted. I find out that Wanderers are getting beat within ten minutes as well, so the league woes continue. I go and stand on the balcony to let some fresh air liven me up a bit and watch one or two people walking about down in the largely deserted streets below, a leisurely Sunday underway in Manchester.

"You and Will have got it made here mate, it's a top place." I tell him.

"I know yeah, not for much longer though I don't think..." Dan says from the couch behind me and I swivel round with a frown on my face.

"Why, what you mean?"

"I reckon Will and his bird are going to move in together soon."

"Really?"

"Yeah. They've looked at a couple of houses already just casually but I think they'll start properly going for it soon. They've been going out for about five years as it is and he's always up at hers, he talks like they'll be moving in together all the time. They're probably best off in their own gaff to be fair."

"What will you do, will you have to move on?" The prospect of having to give up a decent place in a really good area of town is a great shame.

"Well maybe yeah, but..." Dan tilts his head in my direction with a sort of loaded grin on his face. "I could also just look for a new flatmate to replace him. What do you think?" Ever slow on the uptake, it takes a while for the penny to drop. Then it dawns.

"What, as in, *me*?..."He scoffs at my numbness.

"Yeah mate, you said you wanted a change didn't you, so how about taking over Will's contract whenever he does decide to go?" Wow, that's massive, a life changer. A buzz of nerves, excitement, or *something* pulses through me. He continues before I can say anything further. "I'm not pushing him out or saying he's going in a couple of weeks or owt like that, but I'm fairly sure he'll be looking to go in the near future. So when he does, the offer is there if you want it."

"That's fair enough, but yeah I'll definitely be up for it, that would be brilliant!" It has been a great couple of days here and the idea that I could live like this is mouth-watering, what an opportunity. "Saying goodbye to all the commuting every morning and night, back home from work in no time and being able to chill out in a place like this? That'd be quality." I go into one for ages about what it would be like to live in the middle of the city and Manchester nights out, the balcony in summer time, watching films on the big screen telly with a beer. Dan laughs at me, I'm sold already.

Back in my own bed later and home feels boring now after the weekend just gone. Alongside the irresistible prospect of living in Manchester and flat sharing with Dan who I've really got along with these last few days, I feel more than ever a resolve to have a fresh start. Tomorrow I'm going to splash out on a load of new clothes for work and join a gym, get myself in shape, feel sharp in time for summer and all that shit. I keep thinking about the undying humming sound in the city that emanates from the combination of cars, people and life that can be heard virtually all night long and the likes of Dan, Kate and Sian making the most of their lives. Lying here I decide that there's no need to allow myself to be dragged down anymore by the antics of Tom or by scraping the barrel getting involved with any girl I can get my hands on, getting wasted on the same street in the same town every weekend. There's more to life than this.

    That's what I keep telling myself as I go through the process of deleting the names, numbers and email addresses of the litany of girls I've been involved with recently and it feels significant to me to be doing this. I suppose there's nothing stopping them getting in touch with me, but they won't be getting a response. Flick is a tough one to let go of though and I leave her till last. I miss her face very much, but it's done.

CHAPTER TWENTY FOUR

Barclays Premier League - Thursday 6th March 2008

		P	W	D	L	Pts.
15	Sunderland	28	7	6	15	27
16	Birmingham City	28	6	8	14	26
17	Bolton Wanderers	28	6	7	15	25
18	Reading	28	7	4	17	25
19	Fulham	28	3	10	15	19

Bolton's reward for overcoming Atletico Madrid in the UEFA Cup is a two legged tie with Sporting Lisbon of Portugal in the Last 16 and the potential of meeting Glasgow Rangers in the next round if they were to win. In the Premier League a 4-1 defeat at Blackburn and a 3-1 home loss to Liverpool leaves the side out of the relegation zone on goal difference only.

Still communication between me and Tom remains non-existent, no calls or texts and his Facebook which admittedly he doesn't go on much anyway hasn't been updated since we beat Atletico at home on Valentine's Day. The build up to this next round of the UEFA Cup has been far less exciting than either Madrid or Munich was for me partly because of recent events but also because there was never any chance I could have afforded to travel out to Lisbon for the away leg at such short notice. If we somehow manage to find a way past these though we could end up facing Rangers and that would just be an absolutely daft state of affairs home and away and I would find a way up to Glasgow, no doubt about it. I don't hold out too much hope for this next fixture though, as I haven't in any round of the tournament so far in truth.

Unfamiliar seats for this game and unfamiliar company as I've persuaded Dan to come and sit in the North Lower with me behind the goal. A few drinks in Manchester after work then straight up here on the train was how I prepared for tonight, so different to the sickening nerves I felt before some of our other European games this season compared to the calm I feel tonight, expecting defeat home and away in all competitions now. We're in before kickoff and there seems to be quite a decent crowd on, though not with the same fervour there was in the previous round.

"Looks an alright following for Sporting..." Dan looks out the lower tier of the opposite stand. "A thousand perhaps?" It's great to hear the unusual chants of a foreign team in our stadium and the prospect of seeing players who might end up going on to be well known throughout Europe. A thousand might be a bit optimistic though.

"Ah I wouldn't go that far, they've only got that bit on the right of the partition, they're Wanderers fans on the left." A few hundred I'd say, but they're enjoying themselves at least.

"I bet some of those lot never imagined they'd be watching their team in Bolton one day." Dan goes, making a rather unimpressed face.

"The Middlebrook Pleasuredome is one of *the* prime European football destinations mate, don't knock it." I tell him then join in with a rendition of *"Walking Down The Manny Road"* as the game gets underway. The atmosphere and feel of the whole event is so much different to Atletico but we do at least look in good shape, having a go at Sporting and Al-Habsi – in goal in place of Jaaskelainen – has very little to do.

The rather subdued stadium is brought to life mid way through the first half though. A cross is pumped into the Sporting area which is headed down and Matt Taylor has a go at goal, it's blocked but the ball rolls out to

Gavin McCann who passes it into the bottom corner of the net as calmly as any seasoned centre forward would. Three and a half sides of the Reebok Stadium roars out its appreciation and the arms and clenched fists go swinging about again as we show another European team how it's done.

"Get in there badger head! Get in!" I shout into Dan's ear, with him standing there politely clapping, sure enough on the big screen McCann is shown wheeling away in celebration with the distinctive stripe of white hair running through what's left of the dark patch on top of his swede clearly visible. It was a top finish really, made it look easy. Sporting have a chance almost immediately after the kick off to restart but otherwise we remain in control and I'm surprised at how well we are playing considering the run of defeats we've had in the league. Half time comes and the players are cheered off enthusiastically, leading 1-0 against another continental giant.

Again we go at them in the second half and at times look desperate for a second goal, Helgusson has me jumping out of my seat and about to climb all over the shoulders of the bloke in front when he smashes a header against the bar and I'm left with my heads in my hands, a massive chance. More opportunities go begging all through the half and after a few periods where the crowd really does get into it there is a definite return to the sag in atmosphere, Sporting suddenly begin to get a foothold. They hit the bar themselves with a cracking shot from Vukcevic, then just minutes later the same player finds himself with the ball bobbling at his feet just outside the area, it's a move that resembles something we could easily have conjured ourselves with a direct ball flicked on quickly into his path and he emphatically leathers it past Al-Habsi on the half-volley.

Their support goes wild, the rumbling howls of their goal celebrations that sound so different to those of British supporters echo around the stadium and the players pile over the advertisement hoardings to rejoice with them, Sporting fans clamber down the seats to get to the front. It beats the stuffing out of Wanderers on the pitch and whatever belief there was off it appears to evaporate too, our positive play that looked like bringing us a second goal earlier on disappears and Vukcevic nearly scores again with a shot that Al-Habsi saves well, the keeper impressing me again just as he did in Munich. One final half-chance from Matt Taylor is missed and then the final whistle blows which Sporting appear to be very happy to hear, a decent result for them.

Dan looks at me gravely after we finish applauding Wanderers off, we did play very well at any rate for a team near the bottom of its domestic league but a win here was crucial really.

"I think you're screwed now pal." He says, patting me on the back.

"I think you might be right I'm afraid." I respond miserably. One apiece it ends and we trudge off into the night with Portuguese voices making all the noise in the ground.

Thursday 13th March 2008

So this is our day of European reckoning. I'm pessimistic about our chances and have spent most of the week mentally preparing for the knockout and perhaps a fairly big defeat in the process because Sporting looked quite classy when they wanted to last Thursday. With the tie at 1-1 we must score to have any chance, as it stands we are heading out on away goals. All day I trawl the supporters' forums online as people begin to upload their tales and photos from Lisbon so far, they all involve a lot of sun and an awful lot of Super Bock. I envy those who made it but it's tempered by knowing I couldn't have afforded the trip even if I just went for the day with the club. The next round will be a different story, if it comes to that.

It is as low key a setting as I can imagine for me watching the game; work then gym and now at home alone as Mum and Martin are away, looking after the dog and with no alcohol in sight. Telly on, fire on and sat on the couch watching the coverage. It soon becomes clear that Gary Megson's team for tonight bears no resemblance to our strongest side; no Davies, no Diouf, no Taylor, no Campo, no Nolan, no Steinsson, no O'Brien, while McCann and Gardner are out injured too. I can't believe my eyes when the lineup appears on the screen, it's an almost second-string eleven and I feel flattened by it, now we really have no chance.

Every time the presenters mention the lineup I shout and swear loudly at the telly, filling the empty house with noise, then when the teams eventually emerge from the tunnel to begin the game I moan even more. Those who have actually travelled to Portugal for this must be doing their fucking nuts over there about this.

"And what's that fucking bench about as well?!..." I scream at the television, Holly jolts up from her slumber and wonders what the hell is going on. I've just seen the substitutes list go across the bottom of the screen and even I've never heard of half of the lads on there; Harsanyi? Sissons? Jamieson? Woolfe? It's a fucking youth team that, in the Last 16 of the UEFA Cup. I'm apoplectic, stood up now in the living room, eyes wide, my cheeks burning. I wish I was pissed up.

Ricardo Vaz Te, our very own footballer on ice and leading the line tonight, smashes a half chance into the side netting but otherwise we look sterile. Slow, defensive and just booting the ball upfield hoping something will stick. That often doesn't work in the Premier League when we field our strongest side so how it is expected to succeed here I'll never know. We are let off the hook only because Sporting seem to be dragged down to our level and offer very little themselves, it's a shit game in a half full ground with the only positive being that I can hear the constant sound of Bolton Wanderers' finest singing their hearts out in one corner of the stadium.

The match stumbles into half time goalless and I take Holly for a quick walk as an apology for nearly deafening her for the last three quarters of an hour, I'm sure I'm forgiven seen as I'm finding all sorts of treats in my parka pocket for her to snatch out of my hand on our way around the block. I'm back home with the game a couple of minutes past the restart and the same story unfolds, with the odd shot coming in from Sporting and very, very rare forays forward from the Whites which of course come to nothing. We have absolutely no presence going forward all, not even from the likes of Stelios or Helguson who are more recognised first teamers.

Just as happened at the Reebok last week, Sporting begin to take authority of the game but with no options or by the looks of it even any will to fight for it, Megson's only response is to throw on forwards Daniel Braaten and Nathan Woolfe and they don't make an ounce of difference. Despite us needing to score to avoid away goal elimination it's Sporting who continue to go for one of their own. More chances and more long range drives keep Wanderers hemmed in and then with just five minutes remaining, in acres of space on the right, Pereirinha runs into the box, cuts inside JLloyd Samuel who is nowhere near close enough to put a challenge in and curls the ball into the far top corner of the net via the crossbar. It's over.

Our longer than expected and very memorable European run comes to an end as the final whistle goes and I know that is almost certainly the last time I will see Wanderers play in a competition like this for a very long time, I'm depressed and angry. Why couldn't we have given this second leg a go tonight? I knew the result from the first game wasn't a great one but it feels like we've just thrown the tie away here, I expected a bit more from Stelios, Vaz Te and Helguson but above all I expected more from Megson. Yes, Wigan is massive at weekend, a must win game, but it makes me wonder about what the point of qualifying for the UEFA Cup in the first place was. Sure, it wasn't Megson's team when we originally qualified but this was a chance to make a name for himself as much as it was for the club.

I spend the night sat there mulling over that very question. To me this shows that our ambition is 17th in the Premier League every season, early cup exits and very little else. Negative play and scrapping for everything. The state of football today. I'm not saying we should be Arsenal or United and I know that financially and culturally we will never be near that level and I'm comfortable with that, it's what makes teams and fans like us different. But we got to the UEFA Cup by being *us* twice now and it feels like we've disrespected our own achievements. I hope the Super Bock flows freely tonight for the Wanderers fans over there – even the European Away Snob – they'll need it.

Sunday 16th March 2008

Wanderers have played Wigan at their place three times since they were surprisingly promoted to the Premier League; twice in the league and once in the cup with two defeats and a win, no prizes for guessing which of those three was the one I didn't attend. As local derbies go this is the closest to home for us, you can even see eachother's ground on the descending aerial view that *"Match Of The Day"* does before a game at either the Reebok or the DW Stadium. It's a rivalry that goes back a long way but until a couple of seasons ago we hadn't played them for many a year and so for the fans that came into the game from the mid-nineties onwards, such as me, there's hardly any experience of fixtures between the two.

They don't like us and we don't like them but I wouldn't call the games between us passionate affairs, not derbies of the like you see on television between other local rivals, in fact ours are played out in front of far from full grounds with the only real noise coming from whoever populates the away end. It's a curious one, but games between us and Wigan aren't exactly a great spectacle.

Wigan are coming in for some quite serious stick for the apathy the town has shown for their football team being in the Premier League, attendances are almost exclusively sub-20,000 save for the visit of one of the top teams and a trip to the DW is not an inspiring experience. I like the day out that surrounds a game there but the ground is a joke, surely whoever designed it has never actually been to a football game – not as a regular punter sat in the normal fans' seats at any rate. The away end is a steep, one tiered affair that can hold something like 5,000 people yet below the stand is just a single narrow concourse housing all the bars, food outlets, toilets, entrances and exits into which those 5,000 have to cram. The scenes down there at half time in particular are chaotic at best, often plain dangerous.

Tom and I went to our league and cup games here in Wigan's first season up, both of which were woeful defeats, but the fact that it's only a short bus ride from

Horwich meant that we could start and end the trips in our regular Lee Lane haunts and not be too knackered or skint to carry on long after the game. Today though it's just me. A first ever away game that I've gone to alone; no Tom, no Chris or Paul, no-one. I feel like an outcast today on the Wigan bound train, a proper Billy-no-mates sat here on the rattler with a miserable look on my face and no-one to talk to. If I bump into Tom at the game today then it's going to be pretty awkward, but I don't know if he'll even go to be honest, no idea what he's been up to. I intend to keep a low profile anyway, in and out, via a quick drink somewhere.

  Emerging from Wallgate, chin buried down into the high collar of my jacket, I feel even more vulnerable and conspicuous now in unfamiliar surroundings but I make a beeline for The Anvil pub just by the bus station as I can see Wanderers shirts around there so I decide to go in and at least be around friendly forces, as it were. I've been in pubs alone many times before abroad and at University so this sort of thing doesn't bother me, I quickly find myself stood with a pint in one hand and a bag of fanny fingers in the other chatting to some Bolton fans, obligatory Sky Sports News coverage on the screens above providing our subjects of conversation.

  The drink begins to work its way into me along with the excitement that comes with being at an away game no matter who you're with – if anyone – and I'm trying to stop myself from texting Tom about it. Asking if he's here or making some sort of point that I'm here and he's not is just not what I should be doing really, it's only going to make the situation worse. I put the mobile away and zip it into my coat pocket, got to leave him to it for now. After a few in The Anvil I walk out into the streets and follow the crowd towards the ground.

There is, to me anyway, a feeling of experiencing a "proper" Northern away game on the walk to the DW

Stadium; through tight terraced streets, past derelict warehouses and gnarly pubs, under dark railway bridges last used an age ago and on towards a wind-blasted wasteland to be crossed en route – spoiled of course only by the abomination of a 21st century football stadium at the end of it all.

There's some half-hearted chanting directed at eachother once the singular crowd of people heading to the match splits and it becomes clear who is a home fan and who is going to the away section, before this there was just an unsure hush amongst the group but now with distance between them the youth following each team find some courage and begin trading obscenities. I walk on up the side of the stadium past mounted police and burger vans towards the turnstile indicated on my ticket, glancing around and behind me quickly just in case Tom happens to be there with his mates giving me daggers.

I'm in with only minutes to spare before kick-off so opt to give the vastly over-subscribed bar a swerve and stride directly up towards my seat and once out in the open I'm presented once more with this dump of a stadium, four single-tiered stands open at each corner and framed by ribbed metal back walls and roofs. The Reebok is often slated by visiting supporters for its sterility and a lot of the time they're right, but this really is the pits.

With the teams out and ready to go I look around me and think of the images and sounds of those great derbies and *Clásicos* around the world of Association Football; the stand-sized banners of the Milanese *tifosi*, the surges and choreographies of the Argentinean *barras bravas*, the flares and fireworks of Belgrade's Ultras. Then I bring myself back to this, the sight and sound of a few hundred men, women and children chanting *"Your mum's your dad, your dad's your mum..."* at eachother on a windy day in a Wigan retail park.

Seemingly this away-curse I've got following me around like a bad smell isn't going anywhere either, I watch the game stood up near the back of the stand feeling detached and disinterested, it's fucking dismal and being played on a complete mess of a pitch. Wigan have a man sent off with only a few minutes gone for nearly snapping Cahill in half and their fans look livid with it but I could clearly see from where I was that it was a shambles of a tackle so I don't know what they're moaning at and for all of five minutes hope spreads across our support that we can get a win here but then it becomes apparent that once again we are going to be let down.

Despite resting almost the entire first team in Europe during the week in preparation for this today it appears the time off has done nothing good for us and Wigan don't look like the depleted team by any means. About half an hour in, a Wigan throw in floats into the box and there's Emile fucking Heskey to smash it into the goal right in front of us. Cue the predictable scenes of delight amongst the natives and I just stand there watching it all shaking my head.

We offer nothing, *nothing*. The referee doesn't help by disallowing a Diouf goal on one of our rare forward ventures but there just appears to be no plan, no strategy to take advantage of their ten men, get by them and build some sort of comeback and worst of all it looks like some of the players don't even *want* to make a go of it. Megson brings on Rasiak just before half time which is an invitation for most of us to do one downstairs because if one thing is for sure in this relegation fight that we are now well and truly in, he isn't going to be the man to get us out of it, he is undoubtedly fucking gash.

A horrible atmosphere prevails on the concourse throughout the interval and this carries over into the majority of the second period as Wanderers continue to labour and begin to look like they're accepting defeat, we barely threaten. As was the case in the first half we don't get much help from the referee but we don't help ourselves either and with around ten minutes remaining with no springs of hope on the pitch, I decide to leave.

    I retrace my steps of earlier on heading for the train, maybe if Tom was here I'd have stayed till the bitter end and seen it out but I'm bored and want to go home. Luckily enough there's a Bolton-bound train still in the station so I'm on it and on the move not too long after the game should have ended and away from the town before the crowds return sat in silent thought about the day. I can't just suddenly turn round and appear at Tom's door saying everything that's happened is forgotten about because it isn't, not for me anyway, but there's no doubt that going to football especially away games isn't half the fun that it is when I'm there with him.

    I stood in that ground today with my hands in my pockets watching the game glumly and silently with no-one to bounce comments off and enjoy the experience with despite the result, it was bleak. Then I think about the anger and frustration I saw amongst the travelling support and it carried an edge that I haven't seen before with an element of real menace in some of those present, most vividly by those saying they were at the Sporting game, or by those wearing the distinct green scarves worn by fans of the Portuguese side undoubtedly picked up whilst over there on Thursday.

    I'm angry and confused at what the whole point of striving for Europe was in the first place and the lineup we used over there, so who knows how aggrieved they feel. I'm also pissed off that we were shit – yet again – against Wigan and that we're in deep relegation trouble now, but many of those who were in that stadium today were fresh, or not quite feeling so fresh, off the plane from Lisbon where they had spent hundreds of pounds and sat many an hour waiting in airports to go and watch one of the most important fixtures in our history only to discover that the team selected to go and win on foreign soil comprised of, for the most part, our Reserves. So to attempt to justify it, Gary Megson said he took the decision so that our "big hitters" could be fully rested and ready for today – then they don't even turn up and perform. It has been an absolutely scandalous few days.

Wednesday 19th March 2008

Despite how miserable going to Wigan alone was on Sunday, I find myself at Old Trafford on my tod again just days later for Manchester United away. I can't really explain why on Monday I just decided I might as well go, especially as the maelstrom from our UEFA Cup exit and subsequent defeat at Wigan continues to rage but I got a ticket anyway then failed to talk Dan into coming too, although at a fucking ridiculous £39 it was hardly surprising. I'm there in decent time after staying on a bit later in work then going for a few on Deansgate and getting the tram to the game, arriving at my seat while the players were still warming up on the pitch as I refuse to spend any more money in this place and buy anything from downstairs.

I don't really do hate, especially when it comes to football, it's a waste of energy. I certainly dislike and consistently wish the worst on a variety of clubs for a variety of reasons; Tranmere, Wolves, Ipswich, Oldham, City, Blackburn, Bury, Everton and United to name a few, their varying stature showing just where we're at and where we've been in the relatively short time I've been watching Wanderers. I sense I'm in the minority in this corner of Old Trafford tonight though, there's a number of Whites in here absolutely foaming at the mouth.

We've been rocked by the news this week that Jussi Jaaskelainen has been ruled out for the rest of the season with a back injury. He's been one of the best keepers in the league in previous seasons and has played a massive part in keeping us *in* this league for years so it was a shock to find out about it but it's probably the one place on the pitch that we actually have able backup, in Ali Al-Habsi. His performance against Bayern will live long in the memory and I rate him highly so I'm not too worried in that department.

It doesn't take long for United to get into us once the game starts and we go a goal down within ten minutes, but it doesn't stop the noise from our end, in fact it intensifies as we take the piss out of how quickly the home fans return to near silence moments after they scored. The stewards are busy being pricks with us too, in someone's ear every few minutes and ejecting lads all over the place. Fair enough, do as you please if people are standing there doing all the Munich shit which I've never been into, but from what I can see, some of the people being man-handled out of the stands with their arms up their backs have barely done anything.

Kevin Davies almost gives us a moment to celebrate wildly as out of nothing he's presented with a chance that he doesn't take – and then we're virtually finished by the twentieth minute when Ronaldo batters a free kick into the top corner, prompting a couple of minutes worth of noise from the home end and another wave of ejections. So with the game gone already I just stand there watching it play out, near constant noise from our support including a group waving their trainers in the air singing *"Shoes off for the Wanderers"*.

We have a good spell in the second half with a few chances and even a disallowed goal from a Diouf free kick that the referee makes out was taken a moment before he blew the whistle, the arsehole. In truth though I know our efforts would end up being futile but I shout myself hoarse nevertheless and carry on singing for the Wanderers right until the end in a half empty Old Trafford that has looked this way since about the eightieth minute. Final whistle goes, I offer a few last choice expletives to the stadium and its residents then head off into the night with us stuck right in the relegation zone and with time running out.

  After what seems like an eternity I'm finally stood in the bitter cold on the busy platform at Manchester Piccadilly and a malaise sweeps over me as I peer down at the tracks, the Star & Garter pub and the red light district beyond on the streets below, waiting to go home. Feeling insular with my head down and music playing shutting out everyone else around me. Predictably I don't get a seat when the train does finally come, stood up until Bolton then I'm straight into a taxi and sit up till late with a brew watching telly. What a shit couple of aways they were.

  The fact dawns on me that I haven't actually seen us score a goal away from home since last year.

CHAPTER TWENTY FIVE

Barclays Premier League - Saturday 22nd March 2008

		P	W	D	L	Pts.
16	Birmingham City	30	6	9	15	27
17	Sunderland	30	7	6	17	27
18	Bolton Wanderers	30	6	7	17	25
19	Fulham	30	4	11	15	23
20	Derby County	30	1	7	22	10

Bolton Wanderers are eliminated from the UEFA Cup after a 2-1 aggregate loss to Sporting Lisbon who go on to meet Glasgow Rangers in the Quarter Finals. Successive away defeats to Wigan Athletic and Manchester United send Bolton into the relegation zone with eight games remaining.

A huge bear hug from Tony greets me when I return to my regular seat at the Reebok Stadium for the first time in what feels like months to watch our game against Manchester City, he seems genuinely pleased to see me and I'm chuffed about that. Could really do with a permanent bear hug today actually, it is so cold and despite layering up in all sorts of Fjallraven and Barbour and doubling up on socks I've still spent most of the time since I left the house shivering.

"This is a sight for sore eyes!" Tony enthuses once he releases me. "I thought you two had given up the ghost, where have you been?" Tom didn't come against Liverpool or sit here for the Sporting game either, it seems.

"Oh I was sat over there for the UEFA game..." I waft a gloved hand towards the goal at the North end of the stadium. "But I gave that Liverpool disaster a miss.

Tom's not been here either then has he not?" Tony shakes his head, puffs of white breath rise upwards as he exhales. "Ah well, we're not speaking at the moment. I've not seen him either." Tony frowns and Anthony leans in to listen too as he picks up on that last comment.

"Bloody hell, you're joking? You're usually on great terms the pair of you. What happened?" I sigh and say nothing for a few moments wondering what, if anything, to tell him. In the end I tell him about the Madrid fall out and him acting up but leave some of the finer details out.

"Ah don't be daft, you can't let that drag on and on. The worst bit is you'll end up never talking again and forget why..." Tony's raises his voice over the sound of the crowd as the teams are applauded onto the pitch accompanied by the booming music from the speakers. "Put it to bed, otherwise you'll regret it!" He shouts and I nod agreement while half turning away to see the players. Anthony grabs my shoulder and turns me round.

"Besides, why miss out on all this entertainment?!" He opens his arms out wide and gazes around as if to survey a scene of great majesty before him, then starts chanting *"Come On You Whites"*.

It's beginning to register with me that I'm going to have to make contact with Tom again at some point soon, I probably need to redress how much my social life revolves around him, but has all that has gone on since Christmas really been enough to drop him for good?

Wanderers make a promising start, we even hit the bar, but before long the game subsides into another dull affair. Our tactics are defensive but we do at least hold firm and I enjoy watching Gary Cahill play in particular, for a team struggling so much as we are he doesn't half look calm on the ball. Calmness on the ball was one of the truly special things that Ivan Campo had in his prime for us, a joy to watch at times, but he again worries me a lot today playing poorly and looking a serious weak link.

"What was that about entertainment?" I say to a bored looking Anthony as half time arrives, he sticks up two fingers at me in reply. Down on the concourse slowly sipping my way through a volcano-hot Bovril I think more about Tom. There's no doubt that I miss him and miss going to games with him, Wigan and United away proved that doing games like that alone is no good at all and I miss having a laugh on nights out with him too. But I can't abide seeing and putting up with him when he's fucked up on coke and nor did I enjoy being made to look like the loser when I was the only one *not* on it

Back up at pitch level we endure another half of insipid football from both sides, we look unbelievably slow on the attack. How I would love to have Okocha or Djorkaeff in their prime teleported into the centre of this pitch right now and watch them unlock City's defence – a pass or a darting run, some impetus and a bit of hope. But, there's nothing apart from the cold and the quiet. It finishes goalless and we stay third from bottom.

Sunday 23rd March 2008

I'm lying in bed with my eyes on a documentary I've recorded but not really paying much attention, yet another embedded camera crew following a British platoon around Afghanistan. This particular one spends all day fighting tooth and nail to take control of a village then has to pull out at nightfall leaving it to the Taliban to move in again as soon as they turn their backs. Thoughts are again on what to do about the Tom situation as they were last night while I sat at home doing nothing, alongside wishing I could be in that apartment in

Manchester – I'd even take sitting in doing nothing there, at least it would be *there*.

      Dan's words about *"this 'lad' thing"* keep coming back to me and it's clear I'm not cut out for it, not to the level that the likes of Tom, Paul and Chris are anyway. If I'm going to knock about with Tom again then I have to accept what he's going to be like and get on with it, it's either that or let it slide on and on like Tony said could happen. I don't want the latter so basically I'm going to have to find a way of putting up with it when he goes off on one despite the fact he's virtually impossible to communicate with, just let him crack on and try to enjoy my own nights regardless.

      I'm not sure how feasible that actually is but I'll give it a try, we would have laughed about how shite yesterday's game was and gone for a pint then forgot about it but instead I could only wallow over the match and our predicament miserably. Going to home games is bad enough as it is these days let alone doing them on my tod.

      That makes me think about how poor it has become going to the Reebok in the last few seasons, the atmosphere is more often than not dead apart from the really big games and on the whole it has nowhere near the same sort of feeling of togetherness and spirit that watching matches at Burnden Park did. I was only fourteen when I last saw us play at that brilliant old fossil of football and only got a few seasons' worth of pleasure out of it but even then I could feel that unique pull of watching Wanderers there whether it was full or – often – not. I wish I could have been at drinking and going out age back then; drinks in town, walking down Manny Road to the game, then back in town again afterwards in no time. Now it's not just the physical distance away from town that has diminished that match-going feeling, or the all-seated, all plastic and breezeblock design of the stadium, but leaving Burnden seems to have turned Wanderers into a different football club entirely.

    I suppose it doesn't help when we're not exactly up to much on the pitch though, because there was a fairly brief time at the Reebok when it seemed like everything had come together and the place was at last gaining a soul of its own. After our promotion through the Play Offs in 2001 and just about surviving the following year in the Premier League, the ground was regularly hosting 25,000+ crowds and some of the best footballers ever to wear a Bolton shirt. I'm often ridiculed about this especially at work but I still maintain that for a few months in the 2002-2003 season we were graced by the best player in the league at that time bar none in Jay Jay Okocha.

    The team was still struggling in the lower reaches of the table but individually Okocha was at times singlehandedly destroying opposition sides. The standout moments immortalised on YouTube are obviously unforgettable – making Roy Keane and David Beckham look stupid with a series of delicate mid-air touches over their despairing tackles, or the way he kept possession at a corner against Arsenal by flicking the ball over his and a defender's head from behind them both – but there were countless other examples of brilliance from the man in almost every game, it was to be awed at. Then, ultimately, he helped keep us in the division once more with a goal of the season contender against West Ham and a free kick against Middlesbrough on the final day.

    Alongside Okocha were Youri Djorkaeff, one of the great attacking players of the modern game who could also produce not just skill but effective brilliance out of nothing and Ivan Campo who was beginning to find his classy feet in the team. Between them – in front of an often full stadium – and with a belief running through the team and fans that we could survive again, the Reebok enjoyed some of its finest hours to date. In patches that feeling came back in the following years with these players continuing to work their magic and the side developing into an actual force in the Premier League; bolstered by even more high quality signings, a League Cup Final and our first European adventure but even then there were long periods of time where games felt flat. Now with the team struggling to inspire and struggling to survive, with crowds tailing off and little to excite, our home games have again returned to the humdrum.

  I go downstairs when the documentary finishes and look for Martin, with thinking about my own past watching Bolton which are all relatively recent memories it makes me want to go and hear some of his again. Years ago Martin followed them everywhere as they toiled through the eighties in the arse-end of the Football League in a desert of an era between Frank Worthington's time and John McGinlay's, Andy Walker's and all the rest. Top division football, a brand new stadium and a stint in the UEFA Cup were all not a consideration or even a distant dream back then yet he still went all over the place to see the games, but then all of a sudden just stopped going and I've never understood why.

  Get him reminiscing though and you could be there for hours. I've seen the photos of him from the 80's, sun-drenched joy outside Wembley. Him and a dozen mates at least, the Twin Towers in the background, pissed up lads wearing shiny Bolton shirts with Normid emblazoned across the front and Martin stood in the middle of it all, beaming from behind his oversized tash. They'd all gone down in hired minibuses and set off from a pub in town with scarves and flags flying from the windows all the way down, it must have looked like the

England van that drove around Turin in *"The Italian Job"*. A great day to be a Wanderer he told me, after so many years of misery.

He used to have a vintage Bolton Wanderers scarf and a rosette from that day watching the 1989 Sherpa Van Trophy Final, a 4-1 win against Torquay United. Now though, he sometimes asks how we got on, sometimes watches *"Match Of The Day"*, but never does anything more than the absolute minimum to keep up to date with the latest news.

I don't think it's to do with "The Modern Game" that has put so many of those lads of the 70's and 80's off. I've met a few of those types and most of them burn with an intense fire and passion about how the game has been lost and how much better it was back in their day. They speak of how the players have become celebrities, mercenaries, that the teams have become totally disconnected from the towns they represent, longing to love the game again and reclaim those Saturday 3pm's but hold out no hope for its future. Some have taken up watching non-league football, some still back their teams but stay away or don't even watch in protest, but at least maintain some link to their club and perhaps return for the very biggest games, I know there were many in Munich and Madrid who haven't attended a Wanderers game in years.

Martin though isn't one of them, he's simply given it all up. From where I stand I don't know how that would be possible, how could I lock away years of emotion, travelling, expenditure and memories and simply forget about them? If it's true that clubs were more community orientated back then, that teams were more "worth" supporting, that it was cheaper and easier to get to games then I'd find it even harder to say goodbye to it all but on the surface at least, none of this is a problem for my Step-Dad.

Football just stopped existing in his life. He met my Mum in 1992, they fell in love immediately, married quickly and settled into life together very early on but from what I can gather he had stopped going to Wanderers before all that. Bolton had spent most of the 1980's very much in the doldrums, even slipping into Division Four at one stage before slowly, slowly, rebuilding – eventually culminating in our renaissance in the 1990's but only after heartbreak in the Promotion Play Offs more than once. Attendances at a dilapidated and crumbling Burnden Park were woeful, rarely scraping above 10,000 but the way he talks about those days when prompted, you'd think he would surely be one of those hardcore who would stick it out regardless. I don't think he has an explanation, he just moved on somehow. I don't envisage that befalling me in the future though, I've invested too much in it all.

"Hey Martin…" I plonk myself down on the couch in the living room opposite where he's sat watching a black and white film on telly. My idea of hell, a shit old Western on the television on a bright early spring Sunday with sun shining in through the windows onto dusty furniture with no plans to go outside. "Was talking to a mate's dad the other day, he was on about how many pubs there used to be in town, didn't there used to be loads or something?" I know exactly what I'm doing, I've not spoken to anyone's dad at all, but this might prompt him to tell me some more stories about the past.

"Oh aye." He goes, attention breaking from John Wayne. "You were looking at over 300 pubs in and around the town centre, all types of place too and none of this crap you get on Bradshawgate now."

"Three hundred?!" I exclaim, that's a lie surely, I can't imagine that. "Never, there must have only been about four people in each bar then?"

"No really, three hundred at least. Everyone went out then, everyone. Friday nights you couldn't move for people everywhere you looked, there was nothing else to do was there? We used to start at the top of Deane Road then by the time you hit town you were already leathered." I can see it there in his face, some flickering excitement about it all just waiting to burst out, he's on a roll. "Trotters Bar was our pub on a Saturday, we used to wait in there for the away fans coming past then we'd all pile out and chase them up Manchester Road. It was a right bloody dump though, but it was our pub so it was our dump, you know what I mean?" I know exactly what he means. He's laughing now, I've heard this one before but I love it, listening to him going into one about how the journey from town to ground was often a running battle.

"Team was rubbish though wasn't it?" I offer, teeing him up once again.

"Oh yeah, absolutely shite. But that didn't matter to us, the entire week was all about the match especially if it was away. Work and then off in someone's car or the train Friday night or Saturday morning to Shrewsbury or Plymouth or wherever, it was just what we did. They got beat more often than not, I can't describe to you how bad some of them teams and some of them grounds were that we saw, but it was brilliant."

We then go on a whistle-stop tour of his memories of being a Wanderers fan in the 80's; from Pele being linked with the Manager's role, to part of the ground being removed to accommodate the Normid superstore, to Aldershot relegating us to Division Four. "That day at Wembley in '89 felt like a reward for sticking with it through all that though. It was only the Sherpa Vans like, but it was better than we'd seen for ages." Hearing about all this again from him is so much better than reading it in one of the many Official Club History books I've accumulated over the years on my bookshelf and I can't help but feel enthused about supporting the team again, continuing that legacy.

"I don't get why you stopped going though. It got so much better after that..." I tell him. "You earned the right to see all the cup runs and promotions we had in the nineties!" He laughs when I say this.

"Ah, I'd served my time by then, I left it to you younger ones." I still don't get it, he was hardly decrepit, he still isn't.

"Come off it! Too old? What made you stop going, why?" He looks back at the telly playing around with the remote and looking a bit stuck for what to say, sighing.

"Well I suppose I changed jobs around that time, stopped seeing a lot of the lads I used to go with and we lost touch. I ended up moving to this side of town and after that there was no fun in going anymore especially on my own."

"Didn't you miss it, miss travelling or even being at the ground?" Martin regards me almost pitifully at that and smiles.

"No not really. You'd be surprised Jamie how quickly it stops mattering when you don't go. You find out there's more to life and other things you can be doing and spending your money on." I shake my head at him, that is simply not computing. I give him a joking dig about giving up on the side and missing out on some great times but he's not for budging, tells me it just doesn't mean anything to him anymore. I leave him to it after calling him a turncoat and saying the film he's watching is crap to which he says he'll belt me if I carry on, returning to my room to fire up the laptop.

I saw mentioned on one of the forums recently that the company that used to produce our season review videos from the late 80's and 90's are still running and are converting them into DVD's to sell. After this day of reminiscing about better footballing times I'm totally inspired, there'll be no giving up on the Whites for me like Martin did that's for sure. I trawl through the online threads to find the phone number for Roadrunner Video and save it into my mobile. It will be getting called during the week, time to see some of those Endsleigh League games again that I haven't seen since the actual days they occurred on at last. Plus it's now glaringly obvious to me that I need to get in touch with Tom again, if one of the only reasons Martin can come up with for stopping watching his team and missing out on great experiences is that he lost touch with his mates, then I can't let that happen to me.

CHAPTER TWENTY SIX

Wednesday 26th March 2008

I was actually a bit apprehensive about phoning Tom out of the blue so instead sent him a text on the Bank Holiday Monday just gone asking how he was and if he wanted to meet up. In addition I also called the number for Roadrunner Video when I got back into work and ended up chatting for ages to a thoroughly nice chap who does all the copying and delivering about how I got into watching Wanderers. I place an order for copies of two of the most important season reviews from my formative years as a Bolton fan; 1993-1994 and 1994-1995, I cannot wait for them to arrive.

Not giving much away in his eventual reply, Tom said I could go up and see him at his house this week and so I stay on the train after work past my usual Bolton stop to alight at Horwich then traipse up past the stadium to the Brazley estate. Ray lets me in and asks how I am, it's been a while since I last saw him but maybe he doesn't even know me and Tom have barely spoke recently, he says nothing out of the ordinary. I go upstairs to Tom's room and knock on the closed door before sheepishly letting myself in.

The nerves are there as I enter, not sure what to expect and when I finally see him he is sat on his wide windowsill looking outside. To be honest apart from not being covered in blood, he doesn't look all that much better off than he did stepping off the plane from Madrid. Tom slides off the ledge and turns to face me and he looks fucked, addled, with dark bags clearly visible under his eyes and dry lips. His oil slick black hair covers part of his face and his shoulders are slumped. In the background I hear he's got The Libertines on, which suits.

"Alright." I offer, simply. "Been a while hasn't it?" Tom sniggers and agrees.

"Yeah man, ages. Been up to much?" He turns the music off and I stand next to him at the window.

"Er, not a lot really. Went to a few games, I've forgotten what winning feels like. Not been going yourself?" He shakes his head.

"Nah... Fuck was all that about in Lisbon, playing a reserve side?" I knew he would be pissed off about that like I was, of all our recent results I could tell that would be the one still doing his head in.

"Don't even get me started on that. And then getting beat by Wigan a few days after as well, we're a fucking shambles. What have you been up to then?"

"Not a lot either, been to a few gigs and that recently with Paul and Chris. They keep asking after you." Yeah right I think to myself, I'm sure they do.

"You look wrecked man, were you on it last night as well or something?"

"Ha, no long weekend really I was out Bank Holiday, you know how it is up H-Town."

"Horwich's favourite day!" I picture how on Bank Holidays the streets on the village are usually empty as everyone is in the pub, he laughs and agrees. "Listen..." I continue, getting to the point. "I know we've not really spoken recently and that, but how do you fancy going to the game on Saturday? Gives us a chance to catch up." I didn't know how else to put it really so may as well use the match as a way of getting back on terms again somehow.

"Yeah alright, sounds good to me. You not in a mood with me anymore then?" I raise my eyebrows, wasn't really expecting that.

"No, well not if you're going to start spraying blood everywhere or getting your knob out near me again that is..."

"Ah I was only having a laugh, just enjoying myself away that's all, soft lad."

"Yeah but you could have proper fucked yourself up, you were acting a right tit. Fair enough, pissing about in the airport and having a load of drink yeah but come on mate you went way too far doing all that coke. It sent you daft, just like it did last time." This seems to annoy him and he shakes his head, pointing a finger at me.

"Kin' hell this is a bit rich ain't it?" I frown as he goes on the offensive. "You could have ruined birds' lives or your own in the last couple of months the way you've been fucking about, don't tell me about acting like an idiot." Tom goes, not shouting but sounding agitated, touché I guess. "What's worse, me having a mad one in Madrid for a couple of nights or you knocking someone up and being stuck with a kid for the rest of your life?" I see his point to an extent, a stern look dissolves into a bedraggled smile as he sees I've not much comeback to that.

"Alright yeah, fair one. But come on Tom you have to admit it's going a bit far when you can't stop blood coming out of your face..."

"Look, it happens, but I'm fine aren't I?" That sounds a lot like what Paul said in Madrid, but who's to say which of us is in the right here I'm clearly on ground I'm totally naive about. "Fuck me, you'd have had trouble stopping blood coming out of *your* face if that woman's husband found out you were shagging her behind his back, wouldn't you? Thinking you might have got that tramp pregnant, shafting someone you work with... I tell you what, I know whose shoes I'd have rather been in around that time."

There really is nothing I can say, no point me lecturing him about acting responsibly or thinking I had any sort of moral high ground because I don't. I look a bit sorry for myself, gazing away out of the window at the legions of street lights shining across Brazley, but Tom smiles and punches my shoulder.

"Oi pal, it's nothing to get mard about, we're both cunts you just have to deal with it!" He actually sounds quite cheerful about that. "I've known for ages what I'm like, once you come to terms with it things get easier. I still fucking love you." And with that, we shake hands. So it's as simple as that, I'm a cunt, Tom's a cunt. I'm just going to try and do something about it, that's all.

"Well seen as you put it like that..." I say and we both stand there laughing together like madmen at nothing in particular, just happy to be on terms again I suppose.

"There can be no forgiveness for going with a bearded woman though mate." He tells me, cracking up even more and I close my eyes in anguish.

"*Don't.*"

CHAPTER TWENTY SEVEN

Saturday 29th March 2008

  I felt excitement this morning as time approached my first game back with Tom and the first tentative opportunity to put my new attitude to use; I'll have a drink and a laugh with him but I'm also ready to just chill out a bit, we're not responsible for eachother, both free to do as we please. At any rate, today will be slightly curtailed as I'm out in Manchester later on with Dan and his lot. Regardless of anything though it does feel really good to be sat back in The Greenwood having a pint pre-match. Arsenal are today's visitors.
  "Look at the state of them loafers he's got on..." He nods in the direction of a group of people who have just come into the pub, all of them piss wet through from the rainstorm in full force outside. "They've had it them!" Tom chuckles, the brown suede on the fella's shoes looks to have turned into a dark and patchy mess which no doubt squelch when he walks. Tom himself looks a lot better than he did when I saw him at his house the other day; well dressed, clean cut and sounding a lot more lively, it's good to see. "Anyway, Villa away next week, still up for it?" He asks, there is no doubt about it.
  "Definitely." I reply instantly.
  "Good man, I'm going to drive. I'm meant to be working the day after but at least it means we're there and back sharpish, alright?"
  "Yeah that's cool, should be a goodun." It seems like a decent way of getting back into the aways with him as well, no prospect of us getting leathered if he's driving although it does mean we'll be going in his mad little car that has about a hundred things wrong with it. He spent a

good few weeks driving round with a broken handbrake not so long back, it just moved up and down freely and uselessly after he pulled up too hard on it. Proper death trap it is.

We talk about his car and our last visit to Aston Villa on the walk down to the ground following a couple more drinks. Our last trip to Villa Park was for the Carling Cup Semi Final in 2004, where we carried a 5-2 first leg lead down there and very nearly ballsed it up with a 2-0 defeat. I'll always remember finding a dropped ticket on the floor of a pub we had packed into beforehand and the extremely relieved owner buying me a pint of Diesel which I very nearly puked up all over him not long after. We came so close to losing that Semi, the last few minutes were pure torture.

This game today would usually be seen as a bonus fixture as it is against a top team, one that if we were to get anything from it would be a surprise and a boost. The problem is that we're now in a situation where we need points and can't treat any match as a bonus; I'm convinced we'll get beat though and that would leave us in even more dire straits. Both Tony and Anthony are pleased to see us once we are back in position but are as pessimistic as I am about our chances in the match, tension can be felt all over the ground.

Instead though Wanderers come out and go for it from the off and we look miles more up for it than Arsenal, playing in their unusual rugby style hooped away shirts. With the rain coming down heavily and the pitch causing players to slip all over the place, our opponents seem to visibly wilt before us just as they have done time after time in previous seasons here.

I'm reminded a bit of the Atletico Madrid home game in the way we don't allow the other team to settle but this time it takes far less time to break the deadlock than it did in that one.

Diouf sets Steinsson free down the right wing who has no-one near him to challenge and he hammers a cross into the box, the type of low, curling and fast ball that you know is going to cause mayhem in a defence whoever comes into contact with it – and majestically Matt Taylor is the one who makes sure it's him who gets that contact. He heads it low into the net and the whole move and finish was done at such pace that Arsenal had no answer, we are jubilant in the stands, a proper flying arms and bodies moment.

The pattern continues, Bolton once again harrying Arsenal at every possible opportunity and we're making them look ordinary, fucking up another title challenge for them. Proof that they're rattled comes as one of their players goes right through Steinsson head on with one of those horrible high challenges – studs into shins – and he's sent off. It happened dead level with our seats on the opposite side of the pitch and you could hear him get hit, Steinsson's lucky to get up and carry on after that; it is a terrible attempt at a tackle. Abuse for his assailant is in full flow and fully deserved.

We aren't finished. Again we press Arsenal, again we manage to bully them out of possession around their box as they fail to clear, Diouf slides a pass in line with the area and there is Matt Taylor once more who places an angled shot along the floor into the far corner. Closing in on half time and we are running away with this. Taylor races over to our side of the ground where we're all going wild, brilliant stuff from Wanderers.

I feel proud through the break that it looks like we have at long last turned a corner and managed to reconnect with our old selves somehow and I'm taken back to years gone by as the concourse is filled with chants and songs which me and Tom join in with wholeheartedly. Into the second half and we just carry on from where we left off, not giving Arsenal any chance to settle or get their game together and the likes of Fabregas, van Persie and Hleb don't influence the game whatsoever.

Arsenal make a couple of changes with an hour gone and everything going against them, then in no time they force a corner and manage to get a goal back from it. It shows how deeply damaged my confidence is about us that even despite still being in the lead and despite how great I felt up until that very moment, the goal going in makes me feel sick to my stomach and I instantly fear the worst. You can clearly see a balance tip on the pitch as Gallas, the scorer, is there rallying players and the travelling fans. His colleagues run into the net to retrieve the ball to get the game going again quickly with reinvigorated roars from behind the goal.

"Look at this we've backed off, we've backed off!" I can hear Anthony's familiar cry behind me minutes later as Arsenal come at us. He's right, where earlier we were into them straight away, now they're passing it around us and everyone is dropping deeper towards our goal. *"We've fucking backed off!..."* He shouts again as they maraud into the box and get a shot away which Al-Habsi saves but just as the rebound is about to be pounced upon, Gary Cahill scythes through the player and takes him out for a penalty "... Oh no, fucking no!" Anthony concludes desperately and Tom is busy kicking the shit out of his seat looking livid, I look around me and no-one can believe how this has turned on its head.

I've no doubt they'll score the penalty and they don't prove me wrong, van Persie sends Al-Habsi the wrong way and their fans erupt, players flooding into the net for the ball again and now it is all Arsenal. They begin to play the type of flowing football that has impressed so many people in recent years and we do our very best to let them. It's unreal to see how much of a different side we look, miles away from them every time they get the ball moving.

Our only hope now is the clock as it ticks away towards ninety, suddenly delighted to escape with a draw when at one stage I thought we looked good for a three or four goal victory. Standing there with my hands on my head I watch Arsenal come at us yet again as stoppage time begins with a move that looks exactly like the one that helped win them the penalty; down the left, into the box and a cut back for any one of the wave of attackers running onto it.

The result is inevitable, our world is about to come crashing down. Into the area they go, there is the cut back and there is Fabregas to tap it home. They go utterly berserk behind the goal when the scorer runs over to them. It's a sight like no other watching an away end going mental, it is just a pity that it coincides with disaster, they're climbing over seats and running down the stairs to the front screaming and shouting.

We are stood in stunned silence as a mass evacuation from the East Stand is in full swing all around us; the result feels like a relegation in itself. Me and Tom do one as soon as the final whistle goes and Arsenal act like they've won the cup, not really saying much to eachother on the way out, I feel totally shocked. We part outside the club shop and he heads back towards home while I walk on solemnly and drenched in the direction of the train station for my ride to Manchester and eventually take my place in line outside the gates with Arsenal taking the piss across the road.

It is late on into the night when I find myself sat propped up against the bare brick walls of Sand Bar, just off Oxford Road and deep in Manchester's student district. Already under our belts tonight are a shortlist of pubs that constituted the bulk of my student life for my final eighteen months at University; the likes of Joshua Brooks, Thirsty Scholar, Font, Revolution and the Footage & Firkin have all been visited so far tonight since I arrived in Manchester from the game. I'm quite nostalgic at the best of times, so this particular pub crawl has brought back all sorts of memories for me and taken my mind off the defeat.

Dan and Sian are at the bar while Kate, Dan's flatmate Will and another lad I haven't met before are with me. I've only spoken fleetingly to Will before tonight but he seems alright enough despite being yet another of *those* kind of United supporters, an avid yet never-present at games type. He puts it down to the Glazers' takeover of the club making him feel disconnected from it.

"We were fuckin' awesome today against Villa, man." He tells me. "You should have no problems against them next week, they're crap."

"Oh yeah? We don't have the likes of Rooney and Ronaldo up front mate, I think you'd turn most teams over with them..." United hammered Aston Villa 4-0 at the same time we were surrendering against Arsenal this afternoon.

"You should have enough though against them, I watched it on Al Jazeera earlier on and they looked all over the place. I reckon you can win down there." I grimace into my half-full pint and tell him I wish I shared his enthusiasm.

Kate and the other member of our group are locked in conversation at the corner of our table and Will must sense they're not listening in at this point. The other lad is one lucky fucker – I think Kate might be into him, she is absolutely top.

"So has Dan mentioned to you about me possibly moving out then?" The question throws me momentarily,

I had been under the impression that it wasn't something being openly discussed at the moment.

"Erm, he said something about it the other week, yeah…" I feel my way through the sentence, wondering what's coming. "Why, was he not supposed to say owt?"

"No it's fine mate, fine. I've brought it up a couple of times recently and he's just said you might be interested in moving in my place if I were to go, that's all." Clearly all this wasn't just something Dan had a hunch about when he spoke to me about it in the flat on the weekend I stayed over.

"Well, obviously only if you were to move out, but yeah it would be great. It's about time I moved out of my parents' house and out of Bolton really." I still sound wary.

"Fair do's. Fair do's…" His Manc accent suits that phrase well and he leaves a pause for just long enough to make me think he's not going to say anything else. "Me and the missus are looking around at places now, she wants a house I think she's had enough of sharing a flat with her mate. I reckon we will be sorted by summer." I fail to stop the wide grin that appears on my face. "Chuffed with that aren't you?!"

"Yeah, yeah I am."

"It'd be a shame to be moving out, it is class living in that flat but it's time to move on. Better to have someone Dan knows moving in rather than having to advertise a space." It sounds great to me, yet to consider any financial or physical practicalities to do with the move, but already sold on the idea. We clink our pint glasses together and as Dan returns with Sian the group returns to a single melee of noise and laughter. I'm far down the road to being severely pissed but so is everyone else and I feel at home with this gang. Could get used to this.

CHAPTER TWENTY EIGHT

Thursday 3rd April 2008

Brian is infuriating at times, he's got the attention span of a goldfish. We've broken up the start of the day by chatting about retro football shirts and have been discussing the old adidas kits that had three giant stripes coming over the shoulder and how good Bayern's red shirt with blue stripes was. But just as I'm talking about Papin, Klinsmann and Matthaus, he just suddenly interrupts with "That Gabriella Cilmi is fit as fuck ain't she?", a whole passage of conversation ignored – and he doesn't even notice it – I walk off shaking my head calling him a dick and a dirty old man, he doesn't understand what's up. Cilmi's *"Sweet About Me"* plays on the radio in the background for about the hundredth time this week while I drift away into the bowels of the file library.

"Anyway..." Brian's voice booms from behind me barely a minute later, he's followed me to carry on chatting, no work in hand and clearly very little intention to do any. "B & B is sorted for my stag do, thirty quid when we get there so that's not bad is it?" Ah yes, Brian's stag do. I'm joining him and a load of his mates in Chester in a couple of weeks in advance of his wedding which isn't until after the season has finished, nothing elaborate, no messing about on quad bikes or clay pigeon shooting or fucking about in trees, just a piss up. He can't be arsed with any of that stuff and I'm glad of it.

"Yeah fair enough, sounds good to me."

"Nice one, we're aiming to get to Piccadilly for about ten so will meet you in that sports bar, should be enough time for a quick drink." I tell him that's fine, thinking to myself that I'll no doubt be completely out of it by nightfall, but looking forward to it all the same.

"Heading for anywhere in particular in Chester or just going wherever?" I ask, my work dumped on a shelf now also.

"Just playing it by ear, as long as we can stop for a curry at some point later on I'm not fussed." I'm glad the only stipulations on this particular stag do will involve a curry, that will do for me.

"Excellent, I'm looking forward to it mate, ever been to Chester before?" Brian stands there silent for a moment with a blank expression on his face then looks back in the direction of our desks.

"Did you hear what Graham was moaning on about this morning, that bird he'd seen outside?" And with that, his attention is gone again. Absolutely impossible this bloke.

With another day of work successfully navigated by switching off and going into standby mode until four, I make my way out to Salford Central Station and onto the train back to Bolton so I can go home via the gym. I exit the Interchange once alighting the train and again find myself wondering where the pride and love for the team I support comes from, when the town they represent is in a state like this. To get to the gym after leaving the station I have to walk from one side of the town centre to the other but it really is a depressing journey. I mean for a new visitor to Bolton the first things they are confronted with when they leave the station and turn towards town is a near-derelict pub, a ridiculous looking bridge and a fucking porn shop, followed immediately by discount stores and charity shops, it's dismal.

Onto the precinct I go, the concrete elephants that I used to climb on when I was little are still there but again everything else is just a sorry tale of depression; of closed down businesses and of urchins populating the pavements, young scallies hassling pedestrians and eachother, street-mentalists gobbing off about God and people trying to flog tat from shaky trestle tables. Into the main square, I trek past the foothills of the steps leading up to the Town Hall, a tall totem of the town's history standing above all the misery below but even this is looking like it needs a good clean.

Next I walk on in the direction of the main post office, bypassing more defunct outlets and old buildings left empty for years. There are features and landmarks in the town which offer a nod to what is good about the place; Churchgate, the Octagon Theatre, Le Mans Crescent with the library and museum, the Town Hall itself, plus the fact that the suburbs surrounding it offer some great countryside and historical buildings – but it is being overtaken by decline. The place feels like it's on its arse and everyone knows it, you'll hear few good words about the state of Bolton Town Centre from the locals at the moment.

I finally emerge at the other side of town and the gym appears in view beyond some trees as I walk down a road passing between a downtrodden Gypsy's Tent pub and a little further to my left, the site of the long-since closed down Hawthorns nightclub. This was the scene of some of my finest and most treasured early nights out even though its best days were probably behind it when I was going. I always smile to myself when I pass that place and think back to some of my experiences in there either on its Thursday metal nights or Saturday indie sessions. Fledgling times as I began going in town and experiencing proper nights out, initially in its almost pitch-black, sticky-floored original guise then afterwards when it was done up and renamed Indie-Go, brightened up and made more colourful – though we always preferred how it was before. Varsity bar, Hawthorns, takeaway, home. Glorious, innocent times. The whole town is crying out for a revamp.

Saturday April 5th 2008

Well, we've been due a twatting and sure enough Villa go to town on us. Will's prediction that they weren't up to much was miles and miles off the mark. We've been getting beat or scraping draws recently but no-one apart from Blackburn and Liverpool have really hammered us so far since New Year. However today Aston Villa smash four past us in one of the most one-sided games I've ever had the misfortune to watch.

There has been a distinct feeling of anger and disillusionment – even revolution – in the air for the last few weeks amongst the Bolton fans in a way that I've never experienced before. I wasn't sure how to handle it at first, of course I'm used to us struggling with relegation and promotion, enjoyed the cup runs and been depressed by the play off defeats and ten-match winless runs in the Premier League, but this is different – a genuine hatred for the manager and a total loss of hope and belief in our players.

For a while I just ignored it and expected it to fade out but then we lost to Blackburn, Liverpool, Wigan, United and Arsenal in amongst going out of Europe, we have taken just one point from a possible twenty-seven and the vast majority of our support today saw it as the last straw. In my lifetime we've always been a fairly stable club in terms of the hierarchy, not the sort of team that has a new manager every other season but now all of a sudden there is a clamour for more change, a new manager, a player clearout, a change of style. Exactly what was supposed to have happened last summer.

Apart from the terrible result and our impending doom though I have had a decent day out, Tom drives us there and back but despite him only being on soft drinks we have a good laugh. A large chunk of the journey home is taken up with talk about potential away games to be done next season once the inevitable relegation happens.

"Well for a kick off you've got Preston and Burnley, they're a must." I look at the Championship table in the back of the paper that I bought this morning yet didn't even open until now. It takes us a while to get out of Birmingham but once we hit the M6 we manage to cruise along at a fair pace, leaving the Villa Park debacle behind.

"Definitely!" Tom replies emphatically. "Both Sheffield clubs, *yes*. Wolves, *yes*..."

"Blackpool." I see them languishing near the bottom.

"Oh fucking yes, that is *happening* I'm telling you now. Messy that one lad, messy." I could make a case for the majority of these teams on here to be worth a visit to be honest.

"Bristol is a top night out, so Bristol City. Cardiff. Charlton..." I continue, he nods through all of that.

"What about Leeds, how are they doing?" I drop down another league and see the names in there.

"Play Off positions in League One, so they could come up. That's another one. Forest are there. Tranmere are seventh."

"Bollocks to that, Tranmere aren't going anywhere." Shame that, I'd like to renew acquaintances with them someday, the fucking tramps.

"You've also got your grim ones. Coventry, Barnsley, Scunthorpe..."

"Fuck it, we'll do the lot." Tom goes, hitting the horn a few times with us both laughing hysterically. "You can stick your United and your Liverpool and your

Arsenal, it's Barnsley for us now!" And so we speed on up the motorway loudly singing *"Barnsley away on a Tuesday night... Blackpool away on a Friday night..."* to the tune of *"Ring Of Fire"*, adding a new team to each verse. At this rate, expenditure on Munich and Madrid will be small fry compared to our plans for next season.

CHAPTER TWENTY NINE

Barclays Premier League – Saturday 12th April 2008

		P	W	D	L	Pts.
16	Reading	33	9	5	19	32
17	Birmingham City	33	7	9	17	30
18	Bolton Wanderers	33	6	8	19	26
19	Fulham	33	4	12	17	24
20	Derby County	33	1	8	24	11

A 0-0 draw with Manchester City represents Bolton's only point from their last eight league fixtures. A 3-2 loss at home to Arsenal and a 4-0 reverse at Aston Villa consolidates their place in the bottom three heading into the final five matches.

    A fully packed Jiffy Bag deposited in the post box this morning with my name on it is handed to me by Martin; I know exactly what this is. Joyfully I open it to reveal the two Wanderers season review DVD's, their covers exact replicas of what would have been seen on the VHS tapes back in the day, I cheer and rush up to my room to put them straight on. Warm rays of sunlight reach into the bedroom broken up by the half-open blinds and just the very thought that we are finally moving away from winter lifts my spirits even more, I'm pretty much jubilant by the time I load the 1994-1995 disc into the DVD player. A great start to a huge day.
    At first I'm confronted by a black screen that lingers on for just a little too long and I begin to worry that I've been given a dud, but all of a sudden a mad and piercing noise that sounds like something off *"Space*

Invaders" blasts out of my telly accompanied by a notice warning me that this is an "Electronic Sync Pulse" that has been edited onto the cassette and can only be removed by the copyright owner. What the hell is the point in that, I curse as I hit mute until it's gone. Absolutely baffling.

Then we're straight into it and within seconds I'm transported right back to my childhood and the mid-nineties, my first ever game appears not long into the review and I get to see again Bristol City despatching us 2-0. I always imagined through the years that the Lever End in which I sat was full but it is clearly shown to consist of more empty faded aqua-green seats than occupied ones.

What follows after this is a breathless tour de force from John McGinlay and co bagging left, right and centre in game after game. Mixu Paatelainen, Richard Sneekes, David Lee, Alan Thompson et al finding the net at regular intervals with the legendarily partisan commentator Dave Higson ecstatic after every goal – in his eyes every single strike is brilliant, regardless of whether it's a tap in, a screamer or whatever. I'm also struck by how sizeable many of our away followings look too, the footage from Grimsby, Port Vale and Wolves all show large contingents of Wanderers fans who go bonkers each time we score.

Stadiums either gone forever or revamped beyond recognition flash by with each encounter as I plough through the DVD, I'm fully aware I've had a massive grin on my face since the very first goal went in. The Burnden pitch begins to turn into a quagmire with the months rolling on, amber street lights of Bolton are sometimes visible in the background if a night match is played and I try to imagine what it was like at that very moment in different parts of the town. Premier League Norwich City are dumped out of the Coca Cola Cup as David Lee skips past four defenders and lashes home to put us into the Semi Finals, our legend grows.

Then the game I've been waiting for and the reason I bought these discs finally arrives, the 5-1 against Wolves that started all this for me. Richard Sneekes puts us a goal up with a twenty-yard drive, then Simon Coleman heads us back in front at half time following a Wolves equaliser. Burnden Park is packed out, the away terrace is heaving, the pitch is like glue.

And then Jimmy Phillips. The scene appears quickly and I feel myself jolt as I know this is *"The Moment"* happening right here in front of me again, Alan Thompson lays the ball off to Phillips and sure enough he takes aim from miles out and it flies in. Behind the goal the Lever End is going mad and I know I'm in there too somewhere leaping around and falling in love. Off Phillips runs to celebrate, the camera panning around to follow him which shows how delirious everyone in the ground is, just how I remember it.

A replay from behind the goal shows that alas the ball more elegantly swerved into the net rather than changed direction three times as I'd imagined and that it wasn't quite the top corner that it hit, but it is still a thing of beauty. Owen Coyle has a shot massively deflected in to make it four then Thompson weighs in with one of his own, drilling in from outside the box which finishes it off and there it is, game over. I'm almost welling up at the sight of all that, a cherished memory plucked from so many years ago and presented to me now which hasn't lost any of its glory.

On it goes, Bolton progress into the Play Offs via defeating Swindon Town in an epic Coca Cola Cup Semi then losing to Liverpool in the subsequent Final at Wembley, despite Thompson half-volleying in one of the all time great Wanderers goals. I remember watching that and thinking he was surely the best player in the world if he could do that versus a team like Liverpool, totally ignoring how Steve McManaman had ran the show and won it for them.

However it's not our only appearance at Wembley that season because after Wolves are again done away with in the Semis, the DVD ends with the famous Play Off Final win against Reading. That is probably the game I most wish I could have been at in my lifetime, money for tickets and travel for that just weren't something I would have been given back then by my parents so as friends and classmates set off for Wembley, I watched it at home on TV.

The rest is part of Wanderers folklore. I watch us go 2-0 down in the first half then Keith Branagan saves a penalty and we go on to win 4-3 after extra time to be promoted to the Premier League and into a whole new era for the club. The final scenes are of Dave Higson interviewing the travelling fans outside afterwards, all of them beaming and delighted in the sunshine outside Wembley, just as Martin would have been six years earlier. Once I've switched the player off I sit back in my seat feeling completely elated and refreshed at seeing all that again and totally motivated for our game at home to West Ham this afternoon, this has set it all up and I can't wait to get there. I wouldn't swap supporting Bolton Wanderers for anything.

With this new found inspiration I arrive at the ground excited about the game and strangely optimistic, I'm convinced we will win today, not felt like that all season really and with good reason to be fair. Even Ray has decided to come to this one, there was little trouble getting him a seat next to ours so the three of us have a couple of hours in the pub beforehand and go to the ground, via a look round at the front of the stadium where some sort of protest has been organised.

We see a crowd of probably no more than forty or fifty people and it will hardly have the owners of the club or the chairman quaking in their boots, they're just stood around really not making much noise or doing anything in particular. I doubt they would sack yet another manager off after such a relatively short time in charge, if that's what they're gathered for and they're definitely not going to suddenly force anyone higher up the chain out with a show of force like this.

It doesn't dampen my enthusiasm for the day, into the ground we go and I'm shouting and singing as keenly as ever. Despite the way things have gone recently we do look ready for a battle again on the pitch and just as we did against Arsenal we dominate them first half, just minus the goals. Kevin Davies, as always an absolute force of nature up front is terrorising West Ham, the crowd gets more and more into it as he flings himself into his headers and tackles, their defence can't cope with him physically.

He has a header cleared off the line and then another blocked from not much further out, it has us jumping about and cursing everything in sight in the crowd, then Davies gets his head to yet another ball into the box and Diouf turns it into the goal. The cheers and celebrations are manic, me and Tom mob his Dad who looks like he doesn't know what's hit him and I feel the hands of either Tony or Anthony grabbing at my back in the melee. Then the jubilation is gradually replaced by expletives and frustration and more and more of those around us catch sight of the linesman with his flag raised for offside and our players having a go at the referee rather than returning to the centre circle.

The way the players and fans with a decent view of the angle down at that end are complaining it seems the goal should have stood and it is a feeling of injustice that takes us into half time, but although most of those around me on the concourse are pissed off I'm still convinced we'll win this one especially if Kevin Davies carries on running the show up front, the opposition don't know what to do with him.

We are sometimes, well more than sometimes, quite tardy getting back to our seats after half time but Ray doesn't want to miss any of the game. I'm glad he came today. More dominant play from our centre forward forces a corner and from that, Diouf's centre causes confusion in West Ham's defence, their keeper flaps at it and it makes the ball drop right down at Kevin Davies' feet. He blasts it home from point blank range and again the place erupts, but with no premature end to the celebrations this time. I see people flooding out of the stairwells to rush back up to see what's going on all over the ground, so many people take extended half time breaks that there's probably as many people downstairs as there are pitch side. I nearly fall forward as I hang over the seats in front cheering, with Tom's arm pushing into my back, going wild as well. Brilliant from Davies, he's deserved that today big time.

Our goal seems to wake West Ham up somewhat and they start to get into the game more with a few shots at Al-Habsi but to no great effect and we fight on to the end, I don't expect it's the most exciting game in the world to watch for an outsider but I'm totally enthralled by it and so glad to see us really looking like we have some passion in the side still.

Of course, Davies ends up getting himself booked which seems to be obligatory when he plays and the opposition whinges all game to the referee about the way he puts himself about, the fucking soft arses, the man is a giant today. Tony tells us that he's suspended for a couple of games now because of that, missing crucial matches for us and it's gutting considering the lack of options we have up front and certainly no-one in his class for leading the line. Thankfully though we do see this one out and there are great scenes of relief at the end, our first home league win since the second of January, I just knew we would do it today.

I finally get home later on in the evening after a few celebratory drinks with Tom and Ray, the win today and other results going our way were massive for us. I've enjoyed spending time with them both, we've had a laugh and took great delight in listening to his stories of following Wanderers in the seventies and eighties, getting away with a minor telling off by police for things that would almost certainly mean an end to liberty today.

Watching *"Match Of The Day"* later I revel in seeing Davies' goal and performance again, it seems he even dislocated his finger in a sickening direction today but just had it realigned on the touchline before playing on, he is very quickly becoming a living Wanderers legend. As a centre forward he's never really scored loads of goals and I remember when he first signed for us not exactly being blown away by the news – *"MOTD"* tells me that was his 100th career goal today yet he's been playing about fifteen years – but it is his presence up front, the way he bullies defences and brings other players into the game that most impresses me. Fair enough, we've been mostly shit and he's only scored four goals this season but one of them was the equaliser in Munich, a moment that I'll still be reminiscing about long after the current players and staff have all left, so for that alone he can do no wrong.

I find myself struggling to sleep tonight and it is hope that is doing it. We've given ourselves a *hope* of staying up.

CHAPTER THIRTY

Barclays Premier League – Saturday 19th April 2008

		P	W	D	L	Pts.
16	Reading	34	9	5	20	32
17	Birmingham City	34	7	10	17	31
18	Bolton Wanderers	34	7	8	19	29
19	Fulham	34	5	12	17	27
20	Derby County	34	1	8	25	11

Mixed emotions today as I sit in amongst Brian and his mates on a train to Chester for his stag do. I can't wait for what lies ahead, a pure and unashamed day of boozing far away from home and familiar faces, but I'm also forfeiting a trip to Middlesbrough with Tom for our crucial game at the Riverside Stadium in the process. He's gone up there with someone he works with and assures me that Paul and Chris are most definitely not going with him but to be honest I'm not fussed either way on that count. I feel like I'll be able to switch off or compartmentalise my reactions to his antics whenever he's with them from now on after all the time I've spent thinking about it in the last few weeks, he can do what he wants as long as it doesn't impact on my own enjoyment.

We are booked up ready for Spurs next week anyway so it's not like I'm avoiding doing aways with him still and I suppose that will be the acid test of my new mindset about Tom and what we're both like when we're on the piss. The club laid on free coach travel once again for fans travelling to Middlesbrough today hoping to boost our attendance up there which is usually fairly sparse and if we can get a good result then all of a sudden we are back in the mix.

I've never met any of Brian's friends that are now filling this particular train carriage with noise and laughter, could have done with Dan coming on this do too but he wasn't interested so I'm going to have to be unusually sociable today or else I'll end up having a miserable time of it. To be fair to him, Brian is involving me in his conversations and did a good job of introducing me to everyone at the bar on Piccadilly where we all forced down a breakfast pint to begin the festivities.

The plan for today is simple; get to Chester, check in and drink till we drop around the town centre. Brian's not due to get married for another month but this was the weekend that most of his mates were free and so here we are, though I cant help but feel some envy in the pit of my stomach as I think about Tom making his way to the North East – something like today is exciting, but it's not quite the same buzz as it is when you add a match into it all as well.

The hotel, when we finally arrive, is nothing more than a B & B close to the train station but at least it's got a pub attached to it and most of the lads go straight in there, a few of them haven't even brought bags with them but I head upstairs to my room to dump my stuff and quickly change. I expect that after I leave this room I won't be back until the early hours so may as well take this chance to smarten up rather than leave it till later.

I'm not up there long and soon enough I'm making my way into the pub to kick all this off, I've turned out wearing the burgundy and sky blue knitwear and polo shirt combination that was *so* popular on the Newcastle trip and a new pair of Wallabees, feeling good and sharp, a spring in my step. My recent hard graft at the gym has definitely paid off, I've dropped over half a stone already and it has enabled me to actually get into a pair of fairly tight fitting, straight-legged Nudie Jeans for the first time, they've been lying dormant for weeks.

"That's fruit..." Brian goes as I walk into the bar, it's all very basic and outdated, but I don't mind it. I actually like rough around the edges places like this; old frosted windows, wood panelling on the walls, hammered brass-topped tables, seats bearing cigarette burns from times gone by and a giant oval-shaped island bar dominating the middle of the beige lino floor. Everyone turns to regard me making my entrance and a couple laugh along with Brian as he stands at the far end of the room pointing at my attire.

"What?!" I exclaim, arms out wide. "Oh sorry, I thought this was a night out lads, not a painting and decorating job." I nod over to Brian stood there in a massive checked shirt – he is a big lad but it takes the piss – and baggy pale blue stonewashed jeans, topped off with a shocking pair of plain white trainers. His mates aren't much better, sporting an assortment of age-old woollen jumpers, nondescript fleeces and the odd t-shirt with various slogans blaring off the front of them saying shit like *"Professional Drinker"* and *"Beducated"*. "I'll nip back and fetch my portable radio and a Daily Star if you want?" I shout over sarcastically as I reach the bar, they laugh, it's a good start and already I can feel the familiar excitement and adrenaline rising up and enveloping me that comes right at the start of a long session.

There are about fifteen blokes here in total and though I know none of the others, I know that in this mood once I've had a couple of drinks I'll be chatting and laughing along with the lot of them. One of them, an absolute mountain of a man who's leaning heavily against the bar already has a number of empty shot glasses next to him and a pint in his free hand. He catches me looking over and grinning incredulously at his empties, they've only been down here about twenty minutes.

"Sambuca pal, God's own drink." He bellows at me, his whole frame bouncing with his laughter and I laugh along with him but shake my head, he's bang wrong on that count.

Our timing is impeccable, within ten minutes we're all stood in a large crescent shape around the room staring up at a television showing *"Soccer Saturday"* though it's on mute and despite only our group being in the pub, the young barmaid has already said she can't turn it up. Good organisational skills from Brian and his mates as City don't play until tomorrow at home to Portsmouth, but no good for me of course.

It's torturous just looking up at the screen waiting to see if a goal update from Wanderers' game flashes up at the bottom and then when the program focuses on our match and a pundit talks about it, I've no clue what they're saying. We could be getting battered for all I know. I text Tom and tell him to keep me updated for the third time today, a reply once in a while wouldn't go amiss.

Things start to go Bolton's way quite early on, updates from Fulham show they're a goal down to Liverpool then just before half time I at last hear from Tom who tells me we're doing alright, brief, but at least it's not bad news. It seems like most of the others have taken the Wanderers cause to heart too as the afternoon progresses and they see how important the result is to me, the silent TV is doing my head in, but another text comes through from Tom saying simply *"Just hit the bar and the post!!"* yet as soon as I put the phone away I look up and the screen has flashed to the game and there in huge font on the screen it proclaims *"Middlesbrough 0 – 1 Bolton"* and I throw my arms aloft and cheer loudly, downing my beer.

McCann is the scorer and within moments my phone is vibrating with texts, capital letters about heroic badger heads and the away end going wild. I'm jealous

I'm not in amongst it but elated with the score, feeling about ten feet tall. Then we revert to the agony of watching the screen flick all around the grounds and back to the talking heads as the effect of the goal dies down, more alcohol consumed though I do turn down numerous offers of Sambuca from Brian's mates, no need for that just yet.

Reports from The Riverside become more and more sporadic with full time approaching, just when they should really be going there more often I think, I must look at the clock a hundred times once it gets past twenty to five, it just doesn't seem to be moving at all. I can't drink anymore; don't know what to do with myself, fidgeting, not taking any notice of anyone else, willing the FT to scroll up from the bottom of the screen. Other teams around us are finishing their games and getting beat. This is agony. It's 16:55.

The picture returns to the presenter looking animated – ranting on at something silently – and then we're taken live to Middlesbrough, where the Wanderers players are charging over to the away end which is in raptures. The team are mobbing one another, jumping on eachother's shoulders and the camera pans to the crowd where they're celebrating that much that it looks like a full scale riot has broken out. I punch the air and shout along with the delighted fans at the game, one of Brian's mates slaps my back firmly and some of the City clan cheer for my sake too.

The league table comes up next once we're taken away from the players continuing to party and incredibly it shows we have moved up to sixteenth, results couldn't have gone any better for us today at all and I'm absolutely over the moon. More texts, predictably triumphant and I respond in kind, realising this is yet another away win Tom has seen without me. Another Sambuca comes my way – can't turn this one down – and I neck it immediately, this is going to be a great night.

With the important football out of the way we finally leave the boozer we've been in all afternoon and fan out into the streets of Chester. Making our way through town we have another couple of stop offs, the kind of pub crawl that only leaves enough time to hang around for one drink before piling back out the doors again, stragglers having to down their pints or leave them as the mob move on. I can barely keep up, I've never been on a proper piss up with Brian before and he can really put it away yet doesn't even seem that drunk, he leads the charge stopping only it seems to reminisce with one of us about some other Manchester City related memory.

A slightly longer stop comes at a pub that backs onto a picturesque garden and river, pleasant surroundings but the interior is packed out with people watching the late kick off between Blackburn and United at Ewood, the majority of Brian's lot are City though and there are some very unimpressed looks on their faces. It's a bit bemusing, we could easily have gone elsewhere if they're that bothered but it looks like we're here for the duration of the second half now especially as Blackburn are playing well and are a goal up.

My phone rings, I expect to see Tom's name and be filled in on the day's events but it's Dan on the other end.

"Alright mate, how's the do?" He asks, I go outside and away from the noise.

"Pretty good yeah it's a laugh, Brian's a fucking sponge man he's been on it since morning but is acting no different than he does at work!"

"I thought he might be, any City stories?" Dan laughs.

"What do you think? It's like walking about with a Wikipedia page on the piss mate."

"Haha, nightmare, what are his mates like are they the same?" A rumble of shouting comes from inside and I crane my neck to see inside but am just greeted with a giant sign for cheap food offers obscuring everything.

"Some are yeah but there's a good mix, they're all decent lads to be fair. They were buying me drinks for Wanderers winning as well so it can't be bad, can it?"

"Oh yes! Survival?!" I snigger in response, I know he's taking the piss.

"Steady lad, steady." He laughs again for a couple of seconds then goes quiet.

"Anyway, serious card now mate. Will's moving out at the start of July they've found somewhere to live. Want to replace him then, do you?" I feel like falling over.

"Fucking definitely!" I shout down the phone, brilliant news. "What do I have to do now?"

"Nothing just yet mate not till summer, just thought I'd let you know it's all yours." A gigantic grin is plastered all over my face.

"Well, cheers it's made my day that has. Well, that and Gavin McCann..." My body is shaking with adrenaline and excitement.

"No worries pal, looking forward to it." I tell him I am too and he hangs up, leaving me to go back inside still wearing the grin. Struggling to get my head around the enormity of this new chapter in my life that's about to begin.

The pub is still a swamp of tension when I get back to our group and within seconds United snatch an equaliser at the death so half the pub erupts in wild celebration. Glares are exchanged between some of the City lads and the more vocal United fans, it looks like a standoff is about to ensue especially as the Sambuca loving mountain starts slowly advancing like an old Panzer but thankfully Brian steps in and suggests we move on for the curry. Good call.

Strangely, although it isn't my most favourite of foods, nothing makes me feel more hungry than the thought of having a curry with all the trimmings and our stop off at the first Indian we came across – Brian's only wish for his stag do – turns out to be a feast. I can't contain my delight at the result, Dan's news and being here with all these lads on the piss as we plough through almost everything on the menu between us.

I deal with the inevitable bloatedness in the usual way in the next place we come to later on, the gang beginning to lose one or two of its number as the day and the food takes its toll but still a good seven or eight of us soldier on, even Brian has started to look a bit wasted but remains by far the most coherent of the lot of us. The night begins to slip into that blur of faces, noise and lights that only comes after serious and prolonged drinking and it ends with Brian wearing a wedding veil and us standing together as a group, lost on a dancefloor singing *"Sally Cinnamon"* at the top of our voices, arms aloft in triumph. An absolutely legendary day.

CHAPTER THIRTY ONE

Barclays Premier League – Saturday 26th April 2008

		P	W	D	L	Pts.
14	Middlesbrough	35	8	12	15	36
15	Sunderland	35	10	6	19	36
16	Bolton Wanderers	35	8	8	19	32
17	Reading	35	9	5	21	31
18	Birmingham City	35	7	10	18	31

It was decided within ten minutes of leaving Middlebrook that we will never get the coach to an away again, especially a long distance one like this. Now over two hours into the journey down to London for the Spurs game the conditions are almost unbearable. It's developing into a hot day and being cramped together on here with Tom's elbow sticking into me and the other seats occupied by a mixture of not-rights and idiots sweating into their fancy dress costumes is a sad existence. All of us are taking advantage of the free travel laid on by the club again, a fine gesture which sounds great at first but is far from it in practice.

"Honestly, I'm paying top dollar for the train to Chelsea, I don't give a fuck. It's not happening again this." I inform Tom and he's in agreement.

"Yeah definitely, we'll sort it tomorrow. There's a grown man down there dressed as fucking Spiderman, I can't take this anymore." I just can't get my head around the whole wearing fancy dress at football thing. We haven't stopped moaning about this journey since the wheels started moving and despite the astronomical figures we'll get quoted for the train back to London in a couple of weeks for the last game of the season at Chelsea, it will be a bargain compared to this.

"Good, at least we'd be allowed to actually have a beer on there as well, I'm parched." Despite having the blower above my head on I'm sweating into my Fred Perry polo and irritated that I won't be able to turn up at the game feeling fresh. A still, heavy heat hangs like a fog down the aisle.

The first series of *"Phoenix Nights"* is being shown in its entirety on a screen hanging from the rafters down at the front of the vehicle and though it's still piss funny, I think everyone's seen it about a thousand times now so the reactions to the best moments are quite muted, with people just desperate to get off this coach.

"Not seeing anyone at the minute then?" Tom asks, after a few minutes' silence and an abandoned attempt at going to sleep.

"Nah." I reply, dragging the word out. "I feel like I've had my fingers burnt at the moment really."

"That'll be where you've been sticking 'em." He comes back straight away.

"*Nice!*" I wipe my hand on his shoulder which makes him recoil, calling me a dirty bastard and that he doesn't want my germs.

I've not given all that stuff much of a thought recently. It's not like I'm not looking at girls – far from it – but I've been quite happy to not have to deal with any fallout from it for a while, waking up in the morning without crushing paranoia is definitely the future. Most of my thoughts recently have been about moving into Manchester and now it has been properly confirmed it can't come soon enough, Mum's getting used to the idea now and it sounds like Martin can't wait to get shut of me.

At long last the coach arrives and deposits us sorry looking bunch of supporters off behind the stadium, with not much longer than an hour until kick off there's very little for us to do other than to file into the nearest offy and get a couple of cans each to drink on the street.

"How rough is this place mate, 'kin hell." Tom mumbles warily to me after we take a turn into a small road leading away from the shop and High Road, by the stadium. Just somewhere to hang about for a bit while we have the cans and away from police or stewards.

"I know yeah, it's like we've walked into another world." The scene on the main road outside the stadium was one of hustle and bustle, people and cars and noise everywhere yet after taking a few paces up a street leading directly off it, all the noise and all the traffic has gone. We are on a run-down terraced street; houses with their fronts covered in chipped and peeling coloured paint, one or two with all sorts of junk and furniture in their gardens, cars parked bumper to bumper from top to bottom of the road. We stop about a quarter of the way up, the pair of us leaning our backsides on a skip that is full to bursting with masonry and giant shards of plaster and glass, drinking our tins of some completely unknown, but cheap, Polish grog. I smile and start laughing to myself and Tom clocks it.

"What's up with you?"

"Of all the places we've drunk in this season, this has got to be the worst hasn't it pal?" It makes him laugh too, we must look a state here, tired and bedraggled after a long drive in the heat, leaning on a skip drinking beers in some poor souls' front street.

With our empties dumped we make our way to the ground and are forced to wait a while in the queue at the turnstile, our allocation is small today but I know we've sold it out. The brightness of outside gives way to a dim interior which my eyes take some time to adjust whilst climbing the steps to the upper tier and our seats. As the pair of us head up and out of the stairwell and into a barrier of stewards pointing us up into the stands, I look up behind me to see our small but packed enclave of support in full voice and it is a fine scene, all with arms out wide singing for the team.

At our seats, beneath the giant UFO-looking police control box, we are offered some relief from the glaring sun which totally envelops the pitch. It seems fairly close and compact up here with not much of a partition between us and the home support to speak of but then this is hardly a high-risk game and from what I can tell everyone is in good spirits. It's all short sleeves and end-of-season leisureliness for the Spurs lot, many of whom just sit there watching us fret our way through every single second of the game and probably feel relieved that their poor early start to the season is long forgotten.

Their team appear to be feeling less carefree however as they set about carving us up from the off, we are given a lesson in pure dominance as Tottenham stroke it around the perfect looking pitch, finding one of their own every time. Their footballers look nimble and skilful in tight, pure white kits, gliding past any Wanderers player in the vicinity before floating another pinpoint pass to give someone else a chance to have a run with it. Our only respite from what looks to be a sure-fire hammering is that for all the possession and intricately constructed passing moves, they don't actually decide to shoot very often.

We continue to back Bolton loudly and constantly from our corner of the ground but it is clear there is nervousness coursing through everyone of a Wanderers persuasion. It is intensely frustrating to see that whenever we do get a sniff of the ball we elect to smash it upfield towards the hapless Rasiak, in for the suspended Davies and seemingly expected to play a similar role as him, who is snuffed out at every opportunity. This is completely ineffective football, so Spurs just continue to toy with us. As the half continues, for every chant or shout of encouragement there begins to be one of anger and dismay at the way we look to be inviting a battering.

A breakthrough very nearly comes through Steinsson hitting his own post trying to clear a free kick, but somehow we make it to the interval unscathed. Tottenham are applauded off enthusiastically by their fans who must be pleased to have watched their team play so well and I'm sure will be expecting them to turn all that dominance into a large, goal-infused victory in the second half.

"It's got the makings of another Villa this has..." I grimly begin to get into the two plastic beers each we get at the interval.

"Too right, we are fucking shit." Tom responds. "That Rasiak is an absolute donkey, we might as well be a man down." True, though no-one else has stood out for us either really. The half-times from other matches with a bearing over our position are not promising, especially as Birmingham are winning.

"How the fuck are they beating Liverpool?" I shout at the screen. "That's typical that is." I launch an empty bottle into the bin.

"Bollocks ain't it. Bastards." Sunderland are beating Middlesbrough and Wigan and Reading are drawing at least though which is slightly better, it'd keep them down near us, but a Birmingham win is the last thing we want. "Basically we *need* something out of this today. I don't fancy getting owt at Chelsea on the last day and that's after us having to beat Sunderland too." Our plight is currently pretty dire which shows how crucial our last few results were just for keeping us alive at all. The remaining drinks are necked and it is with a horrible feeling of impending doom cramping my stomach that I begin to climb the stairs just as the teams restart.

 Again we are pointed up to our seats by stewards and I'm about half way up the steps when I look over my shoulder to see a cross from Steinsson smashed low into the box which makes me stop and turn round fully, everyone else on their way up doing the same, the ball careers into a group of players massed in the box. It is our substitute Stelios who gets the next and crucial touch though and the following few seconds are a haze of unbridled joy. It doesn't quite register that we have managed to do this in the first instant – with the ball trickling over the line into their goal after three-quarters-of-an-hour of Spurs being the only team present – but Wanderers are somehow one up.

 It's in the goal closest to us and Stelios races over with his arms skywards, mouth wide open and bellowing. There is complete chaos in our end and where I'm stood, I jump to my right to mingle in with those at their seats to avoid a tumbling crush on the steps and every single person is going absolutely wild. Down at the stairwell the stewards are fighting against a tide of Wanderers fans pushing against the barrier to hang over it, even though we are in the upper tier and there's nowhere to go. Up here with me, people are stood on seats or falling over the ones in front, which is pushing me into them too whilst my arms are around a total stranger who is doing his best to deafen me with his delighted screaming.

 This is an unbelievable and potentially life-saving goal, from a player I have always liked and who I've wished could have been given more of an opportunity this season. Seeing him being mobbed by the rest of the team is a great sight. Once some sense of normality returns in the Bolton end it turns out that I'm about ten rows away from where I should be and I high-five with the bloke who gave me a perforated eardrum. Tom's there when I get back, laughing his head off at the shambles of the last few minutes and my disappearance down some other aisle.

Our euphoria turns out to be a freak island of positivity surrounded by more of the same of what we were subjected to in the first half, making the whole thing feel even more bizarre. Tottenham resume their dominance, back to passing it around the park only this time with the added spark of an unjust deficit to put right and scoring our goal begins to look like one of the worst things we could have gone and done. Barely five minutes have passed since the Stelios goal and Robbie Keane, often a thorn in our sides down the years, sets up Malbranque to tap home the equaliser.

Tom and I share a look that says we both know the floodgates are about to open and Spurs can smell blood. Attempts on goal rain in and our defence goes into last-ditch survival mode; Al-Habsi saving well on a number of occasions, Gary Cahill standing firm like his life depends on it making blocks and clearances just when it seems his attacker has surely passed him by. It is our Alamo. There is no hope or even any intention of an attack from us with any glimpse of the ball being used as an opportunity to smash it away from yet more danger but of course this only serves to invite another Spurs sortie.

They are so dominant that it is plainly ridiculous for them not to be ahead, more attacks come in and it is left to our rearguard of ten Wanderers players to repel them. With a front three of Berbatov, Keane and Bent, Tottenham have an almost unfair advantage, every assault containing at least five or six players coming at us at full pelt. It remains like this for the entire second half and I am absolutely shitting it throughout.

Four minutes extra are signalled as the end approaches after the worst marathon of football spectating that I could have imagined and it is of course capped with more clear chances on goal for the home team. Guthrie clears one off the line then right at the death with many in the Bolton end close to breaking point, Berbatov somehow conspires to head over the top when unmarked in the box. It is relentless and it is shattering. The final whistle is a gigantic relief, miraculously spared a massacre for a reason I'll probably never know – but who cares.

We go to look at the other final scores on the screens downstairs after applauding our knackered and dazed looking players off the pitch but to be honest I'm so drained that I don't really know what I'm supposed to be looking for and it's Tom who provides the running commentary for my benefit. Birmingham have ended up drawing 2-2 after being 2-0 up over Liverpool, Wigan and Reading have drawn and unfathomably Fulham have come from 2-0 down at City to win 3-2 on what looks to have been a crazy day of football away from the slow torture we have endured here.

Back on the coaches we are able to try and piece together what everything means today with such a mixed bag of results. We come to the conclusion that although playing Chelsea away on the last day of the season is far from ideal – especially as the last time that happened we got relegated in 1998 – next week at home to Sunderland and the results of the other teams around us that afternoon are going to provide the answer to where our future lies. We are out of the relegation zone by just a point, after next Saturday we could either be virtually safe or almost certainly doomed.

CHAPTER THIRTY TWO

Barclays Premier League – Saturday 3rd May 2008

		P	W	D	L	Pts.
14	Wigan Athletic	36	9	10	17	37
15	Middlesbrough	36	8	12	16	36
16	Bolton Wanderers	36	8	9	19	33
17	Reading	36	9	6	21	33
18	Birmingham City	36	7	11	18	32

  All I feel today is nervous, all I've felt in the past week is nervous. The possibilities and permutations of everything that could happen today have been laid out, dismantled, examined and re-examined on a daily basis since the draw at Spurs which has served to gradually increase the discomfort inside me as my stomach, now seemingly replaced by some sort of internal cement mixer, has churned more and more. Wanderers' season-defining game with Sunderland doesn't kick off until quarter past five, just after everyone else's games finish, a quirk of the televised fixture schedule that means we will have a crystal clear picture of what we have to do to achieve our salvation by the time we get going. Basically though we just need to win it, regardless.

  At lunchtime I'm at the gym but despite the fact I feel as fit as I ever have, the Michelin Tyre gut I once sported now reduced to almost nothing, my mind isn't on it and I just sit in the sauna instead, a slight trembling running through me constantly and an ache in my legs. All I can think about is the game, Sunderland are just about safe but won't make it easy for us and I don't know whether an opponent with nothing to play for is better to play than one with a prize still to be attained, you could make a case for both I suppose.

I didn't think I'd still get so worked up like this about football, I thought those days had gone after the last-day drama against Middlesbrough in 2003 and didn't believe anything else would come close to that again, but here I am just as bad once more.

Against the clock I taxi it up to The Greenwood to meet Tom and I'm there just in time for kick off in the three o'clock matches. He asks me if I'm feeling confident whilst handing me over a pint he's just bought and another to his Dad, I shake my head and tell him I'm shitting it. I say he must be feeling a bit off too if he's getting rounds in like this but he laughs and calls me a wanker, insisting it's my turn next. We shuffle off to one of the very few spare tables, the pub is busy and so is the outside drinking area, it's a bit sweaty in here today. Tom concedes that he is actually cacking it as well as we sit down stony-faced, neither of us relishing this at all. The drink provides slight relief from the anxiety I've been feeling and it is obvious there is a lot of tension in here among everyone else gawping at the updates on the projector screen taking up the majority of the back wall as well.

Ray chastises us for being so nervous when it's obvious we're not going to survive this season, clearly not afflicted with the same tension – or hope – that the rest of us are. His default setting usually is Negative though, so it's no surprise. *"In the end they'll always let you down Wanderers, always have"* he concludes. I note Tom rolling his eyes sat next to him and I just snigger, there have been countless times in my life where they haven't let me down, some as recently as the last week or two so I don't share his opinion, perhaps it's just his coping mechanism for days like this.

No reply to Ray's comments ever comes though because within moments the presenter on the television is flapping and shouting and we cut to Reading where

Tottenham have taken the lead and the majority of those in here jump up in simultaneous celebration. One of the games central to our survival swings in our favour and it is treated as if we've just watched Wanderers themselves take the lead, me and Tom out of our seats, shaking his smirking Dad's shoulders and trading gestures of pumped fists and shouts of *"Come on!"* with other drinkers. It is just the start we needed.

That early boost helps to siphon off some of the nerves in the room and a hubbub of more cheerful sounding chat begins to rise up, we talk about my move to Manchester and the prospect of him maybe doing the same sometime and finally quitting the job at the bookies. He really does sound much more positive than he did a few months ago and I'm pleased he does, but even more pleased for myself that I'm moving away. It's only twelve miles physically but symbolically for me it's so much further than that.

There are not many more goals before half time other than Middlesbrough scoring which probably ensures their own Premier League future but they're not really our concern today. We go outside at the break to stand in the sun to discuss tonight and we settle on returning here after full time, but I sense we are aiming to end up in town and hopefully with something to celebrate.

We return to our table fairly tardily after the half times and as soon as we set foot back on the well worn carpet another cheer goes up with the news that now Fulham are in the lead against one of our other closest challengers Birmingham, the day is going exactly how we would have wanted to so far and my spirits are raised through the roof. The pair of us even manage to coax a smile from Ray as we celebrate in front of him. Talk of the prospect of a great night out later increases as the second halves roll on and a journey up Bradshawgate to see off the last home game of the season.

An avalanche of goals across the divisions fills the update screen for the following three quarters of an hour, none of which have any bearing over Bolton but with the campaign at its conclusion many of them have some sort of critical impact in one of the leagues; Forest getting promoted to the Championship, Gillingham and Bournemouth getting relegated to League Two and the Forest promotion prompts some more talk about potential post-relegation opponents next season.

Still though my overwhelming hope and desire is for us to survive, I can't deny that there is a small part of me that has thought about what a year or two in the Championship would be like now I'm of a mind to go to multiple aways, with so many varied places around the country to visit. Those thoughts have increased a little as our struggles have continued but really, I want us to stay up, we must stay up.

Fulham add a second goal against Birmingham which coaxes another large cheer, it seems the team from London are mounting a survival bid like we are so that goal is vital for them and it means Birmingham will remain below us going into tonight's kick off. My eyes are trained almost exclusively on the Reading scoreline though and just as was the case stood in the pub in Chester watching silent updates from our match at Middlesbrough, this is an excruciating experience.

Also just like that day, magnificently, the full time whistles at both games so important to us go at about the same time and we celebrate, drink up and get ready to rush down to the ground in one movement, a very excitable exodus begins. It is left up to us to control our own fate.

For the final time this term we follow the same well-trodden path down the back of St. Joseph's School playing fields and onto Mansell Way to bring us onto

Middlebrook, walking at a brisk pace to get in by kick off. Hundreds weave their way around parked cars on the retail park in the direction of the stadium before choosing to descend either the steps or grass bank to get down to the turnstiles and by this time I just want to get to my seat and get this over and done with.

The crowd is seemingly overcome with nerves, most of the noise comes from Sunderland's travelling support who can enjoy their final away of the season and think themselves lucky not to be in our position. I clap and shout the players onto the pitch which is bathed in epic golden sunlight but I'm in no mood to sing just yet, I feel sick in my throat.

It starts slowly. Wanderers look slightly anxious and seem to want to overcome this by just keeping the ball and not doing anything stupid with it, I'm happy with that for now, last thing we want is to go behind early on. Sunderland appear to be in no mood to push the boat out either when they get the ball which I'm sure makes for a pretty dull spectacle for the live television cameras but for me and all those around me every second is enthralling and the tension is horrific; pleading for something to drop for us, dreading a Sunderland chance, heart pounding constantly.

We advance a little. Our attacks are of course dominated by the long and high ball into the Sunderland area looking for Davies – thankfully back in the team – and Nolan, playing the percentages and just hoping something comes off. We try over and over, looking for the angle which might just catch Sunderland out and with about half an hour gone we finally find that angle. El Hadji Diouf lofts in a cross which bypasses the first man or a towering defensive clearance and makes its way to Davies at the back post, straining and climbing to reach it before his marker, which he does, connecting with a header from inside the six-yard box and he somehow manages to knock it over the bar. Springing around at my position in the stands with my hands covering my face I fear our best chance of a reprieve may have gone skywards with the ball.

Half time approaches. I'd have been quite happy to go into the break level beforehand but seeing Davies balloon that header begins to make me feel more nervous than ever, my knees are actually shaking as the game plays out before us. Kevin Nolan on the far side of the pitch to us begins to advance towards the corner of the box and a teammate sprints off him into the corner, I scream out for him to pass it and have us clear down the right, but Sunderland back off giving him room to look for a cross of his own. Into the box it goes again, perfectly weighted to drop right at the feet of Diouf and at last their defence has switched off, he's unmarked but at a perilously tight angle to the goal. I quickly shift my vision around hoping for someone to be running into space for him to lay it off to but I'm not given time to pick anyone out.

Diouf's first touch is to kill the ball, his second is to fashion a shot that curls around and beyond two defenders and the goalkeeper into the top corner, a magnificent goal. There are scenes of jubilation all around me and the ground is engulfed in a wave of noise, Diouf is mobbed and wrestled to the ground by teammates nearby to us in the East Lower as I lean against the seat in front shouting profanities in angry ecstasy whilst being manhandled by those around me. Everywhere I look there are Wanderers fans going off their nuts in celebration. Tony and Anthony both standing on their seats swinging their arms around whilst simultaneously trying to stop the other from toppling from their perch.

"*The scorer... El Hadji Diouf!*" The stadium announcer exclaims to further loud cheers and thousands of people shouting his name which sounds like booing to the untrained ear. Delighted singing and chanting takes us through to the interval with Wanderers half way towards virtual safety, incredible. There's a vibrant feeling down on the concourse with optimism in plentiful supply and even Ray looks like he might say something positive for once. We talk about Diouf and his impending exit from the club and the goal in this, his last home game.

That he announced he was to leave Wanderers at the end of the season before it had even finished and while we were in the middle of the relegation scrap has not gone down well with some of our fans and only serves to reinforce a lot of others' opinions of him as a thoroughly unpleasant bastard. I couldn't claim to have been his biggest fan over the last few seasons with some of his spitting antics but his actual football and goals have been priceless to us. If his goal today keeps us up then I doubt many could argue about his contribution to the club, after providing us with other crucial strikes against the likes of Newcastle, Manchester City, Lokomotiv Plovdiv and Atletico Madrid down the years.

Into the second half. The same story that occurred in the first period begins to unfold in this, Wanderers with more of the possession but using it predominantly to simply launch it long and high. Sunderland look totally anodyne, it is strange to see a team led by someone usually so aggressive and combative as Roy Keane playing without any hint of their manager's character. They opt for the long ball too whenever they get the chance, which Cahill and O'Brien deal with perfunctorily. All the time though my anxiety continues to gnaw away beneath the surface, hopping from one foot to the other, chewing on my bottom lip.

A triple change for Sunderland is Keane's attempt to revamp his side, I can't say I've ever seen three subs at once come on for the same team and for a few minutes it looks like it could have the desired effect. Their long balls finally begin to hit their target, namely the giant Kenwyne Jones, being employed in much the same way we would use Kevin Davies. A chest down and shot from him is blocked, then for once Sunderland go out wide and manage to fashion a cross which is headed back right in front of our goal and Jones slides in looking certain to score but misses the ball by a matter of inches, a massive let off. All of a sudden the dark clouds of worry reform and pack in over us and I glance to my left to see Tom's face has gone bed sheet white, but I don't have it in me to say anything reassuring to him.

  The final ten minutes. We have gone from looking quite comfortable to a team that has suddenly remembered the grave danger they are in, more balls are flighted into our area, all of which come to nothing but every single one of them to me looks like it has goal written all over it for sure and I nearly heave. Their fans have returned to full volume and roar Sunderland on, shooting towards them and pleading for some sort of quality to break out from somewhere. Bolton find some respite by winning a corner and at least as long as it is down that end we can't concede.

  Matt Taylor swings the ball in close to the goal, Davies and Nolan charge in but it's a Sunderland defender who gets his head to it and only manages to direct it backwards and beyond the goalkeeper. Wanderers fans burst to their feet to celebrate, Andy Reid who is stood actually in the goal boots it clear and we are halted mid-leap and unsure of the outcome, awaiting confirmation, but up goes the linesman's flag and away go our players waving their arms aloft. It's given! The goal is given!

  At last we can celebrate, at 2-0 the game is over with and the stands are alive with Boltonians revelling in what is surely now our Premier League survival. There have been crazier reactions to goals this season; this one is more of relief with the three of us locked in a bouncing hug, all doing our best to deafen eachother and backslapping furiously. Finally I'm released and there we stand in a close bunch singing *"We are staying up!"* with the players pumping fists towards the crowd and jumping around deliriously. We *are* staying up.

    Myself, Tom, Ray and a number of random lads we know from our numerous visits to this pub over the years and from Wanderers stand and sit around wooden picnic tables outside The Greenwood an hour after full time and the celebrations in the ground enjoying the last hour or so of light, the low sun casting long shadows from our beverages across the table tops. The lot of us are on a high, I feel like a weight has gone off my shoulders and the sick feeling I had carried in my stomach for so long before today has now gone completely, evaporated within seconds of full time. With Ray going home after a couple of drinks with us and a firm shake of the hand from him, me and Tom decide on heading into Bolton as soon as, recruiting a number of the others to join us.

    We fill the minibus taxi with Wanderers songs belted out on top note all the way down Chorley New Road into town, hands in the air, heads poking out of windows and we're deposited on Nelson Square so we can pile straight into McCauleys to hit the shots. Town is awash with people and a high proportion of them are wasted, perhaps out all day enjoying the weather. I throw two shots down my neck in quick succession whilst crushed in shoulder to shoulder at the bar then swipe up the bottles of beer I've got and attempt the hazardous trek back to the others, navigating through swaying people and spilt drinks. Tom's getting to work on a fish bowl full of neon stuff which I have a few swigs of and my teeth feel instantly furry.

Refills are purchased in no time, I want to be leathered and am well on the way, clinking glasses with random drinkers shouting *"cheers!"* at them, telling a bird at the bar how fit she looks in that dress she's wearing and just laughing at the scowl of a response I get from her. Fuck it, we've survived. Another fish bowl of Chernobyl effluent for Tom, another couple of shots and bottles for me and they're dealt with swiftly too before we're back onto the street and bouncing into Barracuda across the square. Our group has fragmented a bit already but it's no matter, everyone is off doing their own thing.

The atmosphere is brilliant, full to bursting and just what we want. The music blasts out at us, weaving through happy dancers on our way to the front, it's a throbbing mix of anything and everything that is big at the moment from the likes of *"Black and Gold"*, to *"American Boy"*, to *"Wearing My Rolex"* and on it goes, none of which I'm especially into but it soundtracks a night out like this pretty well. That said, I do find myself miming along to The Ting Tings by the time we're finally served after an age, there is no order at all to the queue here it is just one heaving mass of thirsty folk.

I'm drunk and at the peak of the buzz that comes from it, laughing and dancing around with Tom, the whole place is jumping. It is not even spoiled by the appearance of Paul and Chris from nowhere, they just seem to materialise in front of us and we shake hands and embrace like long lost friends. I've not seen them since Madrid but for me it feels like water under the bridge now and long gone. We stand drinking and talking with them for a while, I hold nothing against them for what went on or against Tom for that matter, they were just getting on with enjoying themselves how they wanted to and it didn't matter what anyone else thought. I understand that now, even applaud it really, why should anyone else matter? I could learn some lessons from that. Tom looks pleased to see them too but not hanging on their every word as he once was, good for him.

    They're away and heading off with whatever group they've come with once they empty their drinks, with no appetite to go back to the chaos trying to get served here and we say our goodbyes. There are no promises to meet up soon for a drink as lads often make with absolutely no intention to actually do so, I'll just bump into them another time. I tell Tom we should move on too once I finish off my umpteenth bottle, via a piss.

    The toilets are up at the back of the bar so it is another struggle of near Captain Scott proportions to get through and up the steps then the agony of a wait just to get to the urinal for some relief. Once I'm done I emerge from the loo and as I'm descending the steps I glance over towards the scene at the bar and glimpse a shock of blonde and a familiar face amongst the hordes of mingling and crisscrossing heads and I double-take, seeing for a clear second or two, Flick. Our eyes meet and there's a flash of her smile before another melee of human traffic sweeps in between us and she's gone.

    I do nothing other than smile to myself and pick my way out of the place towards the side door where I meet my mate to continue our journey up Bradshawgate, my head swirling quite wonderfully with alcohol and the random treat of seeing Her. Triumphantly we bounce from bar to bar, feeling fantastic in the heart of this town that I love and loathe in equal measure, driving on towards an inevitable rendezvous with the smoke and lasers of Ikon. This is my Bolton.

CHAPTER THIRTY THREE

Sunday 11th May 2008

Tom tells me to hold up a minute as we thread our way from Fulham Broadway Station towards a pub in Parson's Green that has been recommended to us by some people on a Wanderers forum I use. It is turning out to be some walk but I don't mind as it's a sweltering afternoon in London, so I'm enjoying the stroll. While he crouches to fasten his laces I look around me at the impressive terraced townhouses that line both sides of this street, complete with small but brightly flowered gardens and perfectly manicured trees punctuating the pavements at regular intervals.

I peer through the front windows of the house nearest to me giving a view right through the length of the building and catch sight of a number of people in the back garden enjoying a barbecue in the sunshine, a bloke in a lilac polo with the collar turned up tends to the coals as others stand grinning nearby cradling slim champagne flutes. The large square window I look through frames a momentary snapshot of this seemingly perfect and extremely affluent lifestyle in SW6, but it is washed away quickly as Tom walks past my eye-line and shouts *"twats!"* in their direction.

There's due to be thousands of us here today, using the free travel again which has slightly softened for many the disgraceful price of £48 for a match ticket. Regardless of this incentive though we have come by train and I'm glad of it, I have made a promise to myself that next season will be all about getting the train to aways no matter whether the coaches are free or not. It is the *only* way to travel really, not slumming it on a bus full of kids and pensioners. Watching the countryside fly by on the train down, a couple of drinks near Euston at The George and a tube over to West London all at our own pace was excellent and I am beginning to fall in love with the capital.

We finally arrive at our destination – aptly named The White Horse – and are straight onto strong cold lagers standing in the busy beer garden talking football with the locals and generally feeling pretty good about life. There was no need for the jackets we brought along with us today so they remain draped over chairs, I've been soaking up the blistering sun in my brilliant-white OTS polo and have already started to sense the prickling sensation on my arms and the back of my neck as they began to burn the moment I left the station. I was even considering shorts at one stage this morning but seen as my shins are still ripped to shreds and scabbed from celebrating the goals last week, it was wise to keep that nasty little sight out of view.

Tom's been giving me a ribbing all day about the adidas Jeans in Tahiti colourway I'm wearing on my feet but although they're half a size too big for me I spotted them on eBay and decided I had to have them, in all their lurid two-tone blue brilliance. They only arrived yesterday, just in time for this. Tom's piss-taking is rooted in pure jealousy, I think they look fucking mint and so does he, it is obvious.

They'll tide me over for now until the main event comes around this summer as those rumours about adidas reissuing some of the old City Series classics that kept me awake at night before Christmas have turned out to be totally accurate. Dublin, Stockholm and London will all be released and available before the start of next season and I intend to buy all three, I'll break the bank to get the lot in one go and there's probably no looking back now with my spending on clothes and footwear. Something in me has changed I can tell, I have a shopping list as long as my arm already and I'm not really arsed about the cost.

We join up with some of the characters from the internet forum and it is good to meet them, discussing the team as if we've been mates for ages and none of us can quite believe how we survived this season. It has been one long and hard slog where we've just battled and scraped and fought to get over the line. I doubt we will get away with this again next term. There is unanimous agreement that our European tour was something special though and each person adds their own nostalgic anecdote about what happened where. There are stories of getting held up at U.N. checkpoints on the Macedonian border, of basking topless in Lisbon fountains and of masterminding escapes from lockdown in Serbian hotels – and Munich bar heists, missed goals and burst noses all take their place in this pantheon of legendary tales.

I am sure of two things, one that we will still be talking about all this in years to come and two, that it will be a very long time until our next foreign adventure.

All of us walk to the ground together chatting and laughing along the leafy streets, a mixed gang of Bolton fans many of whom had never physically met until a short time earlier and now getting along famously. It provides a fitting end to the season for me as I was doing a similar thing on the way to Birmingham so many months previously. Mine and Tom's seats are up near the back of the top tier of The Shed End and it takes some hard labour to climb the steep steps, we are in shade but it still feels like being inside a greenhouse and is very uncomfortable.

I've always thought Stamford Bridge had something unusual about it, in a good way. Any time I see old footage of Chelsea playing in the 70's and 80's I notice the large three-tiered East Stand then a mismatch of odd looking terraces curved around the rest of the pitch, sometimes even with cars parked up behind the goals for some reason. I also noticed how it always looked well attended, that's why I never join in with the quite embarrassing *"Where were you when you were shit?"* chants that we often aim at their fans.

I've always considered Chelsea to be well supported both home and away through thick and thin, it's just their recent success has brought with it a fair few hangers on which is natural I suppose. Obviously the place has been totally redeveloped since but I'm glad that the East Stand seems to have retained some of its original character, there's few grounds left in this league that can say that.

We are demob happy in the Wanderers end and the atmosphere is brilliant, celebrating our virtual survival and not having to come here looking for a life-saving result. As for Chelsea, they know they have to beat us and hope United don't win at Wigan for them to claim the title so I think deep down they know the game is up and despite some good vocal support at the outset, they soon quieten down. The game plays out like a friendly, it is quite dull and lacking an edge but I'm not bothered, I'll take this over nearly vomiting watching us against Sunderland last week all day long.

Half time Heinekens are shared, along with rolled eyes at the masses of fancy-dress-clad supporters down on the jubilant concourse, then back up to our seats for the final half of football this season at last. Latest scores show United lead at Wigan so Chelsea know the title is gone for sure now and they will just have to console themselves with the small matter of the European Cup Final next week in Moscow, oh the poverty. I also notice that Fulham, in the middle of trying to achieve an escape even more improbable than ours, are currently 0-0 at Portsmouth and needing a goal to survive on the last day and it serves to make me feel even more relieved about not having to go through all that again after 1998 and 2003.

Chelsea do seem to want to have more of a go in the second half at least though and begin to fire some shots at Al-Habsi. They show an impetus which suggests they've had something of a bollocking at the interval and Wanderers come under an increasing number of attacks. With an hour gone a Chelsea corner floats beyond the packed box and is met with a cross-shot half-volley from some distance out and at an angle, it is shielded by our defence but the rebound goes straight into the path of Lampard who repeats the action. He drills the ball right at Shevchenko who turns it into the net from point blank range and they have their fairly meaningless breakthrough after all.

Regardless we just continue to sing and dance in our corner of The Shed, I'm sure none of us would choose to have any hand in United winning the league of course but after the season we've had it is just a relief to still be in this division at all. News eventually comes through that they've scored another anyway so it's irrelevant and it is clear to see that the hopelessness of it all takes the wind out of Chelsea's sails again, their morale sapped and their energy stolen. Back we come to take advantage of this, firing our high altitude bombs into their area, one of which manages to evade everyone including the keeper and it smacks down off the crossbar and straight to Stelios standing only yards out, but it's too fast for him to take control and tap it in. It looks like we will ultimately end the season with a defeat.

Into stoppage time and the dying seconds of 2007-2008 we go. Wanderers launch a gigantic last throw into the Chelsea box aiming for a flick on which is just about won by Kevin Davies, forcing a panicked clearance from their defence along the floor but this just leaves the ball rolling out invitingly towards Matt Taylor for the final kick of the campaign. He slams it back where it came from, into the goal via a deflection and it sends us into absolute meltdown, men dressed as Batman falling down through the seats, coloured wigs flying into the air and me mobbing Tom with a tear in my eye, done and dusted. All the emotions of the season and its events well up, the marathon complete.

We stand together with 3,500 others, our arms out wide, loud and proud: *"They all laugh at us, they all mock at us, they all say our days are numbered. Born To be a Wanderer, victorious are we..."*

Barclays Premier League Final Table – Sunday 11th May 2008

		P	W	D	L	Pts.
14	Wigan Athletic	38	10	10	18	40
15	Sunderland	38	11	6	21	39
16	Bolton Wanderers	38	9	10	19	37
17	Fulham	38	8	12	18	36
18	Reading	38	10	6	22	36

Bolton Wanderers survive by a single point to compete in an eighth straight season in the Premier League after remaining unbeaten in their final five games. Victories against West Ham United, Middlesbrough and Sunderland plus draws away at Tottenham Hotspur and Chelsea ensure the team's safety at the expense of Reading, Birmingham City and Derby County.

EPILOGUE

The left wing of our chock-a-block Airbus wobbles slightly as we climb away from Manchester Airport, beyond Jodrell Bank and into an endless, uninterrupted blue sky before it drops and we bank gently to head south. *"Getaway"*, without doubt the soundtrack to my season plays in my ears yet again as I activate the iPod and think about closing my eyes and trying to sleep for some of this journey to Ibiza. The week in the sun I daydreamed about all winter is finally here. It has been a crazy few months and so much has gone on, some of it I regret, much of it I don't. Now I'm out on the other side of it I can look back and laugh.

    I think about Amy, wondering how many more times Tasha has covered for her since I last saw her. I think about Steph, virtual strangers in the same work place with barely a word or even a glance shared in months. I think about The Virgin, her with the beard, The Hen I kissed in Newcastle, the Bergeracs thief, Joanne... shards of memories still lingering on. I made a real cock of myself with a few of those and I'm not proud of myself. I think of Flick, hoping she's well and missing her still.

    On the pitch this has been such a strange campaign in many ways. It has been a learning season for me, never seen anything so brilliant, never seen anything so poor. The unforgettable highs of Munich, Madrid and the late survival push mixed with the crushing lows of the consistent beatings and lame performances in between. Learning more about aways and the perpetual grind of nine months travelling the country following a team. Learning about mates and about myself. I'll have to start packing my bags and boxes quite soon after I return from holiday ready to move in with Dan in Manchester and start off a new chapter in my life and I can't wait for it all to begin.

It has been a relentless and draining few months and this break can't come soon enough. A tap on my shoulder puts paid to my rambling thoughts and any immediate designs on sleep and I look to the seat next to me, removing a headphone from my ear.

"Got any of that throat medicine on you mate?" Tom asks, poker faced. And I hope to Christ he's joking.

Printed in Great Britain
by Amazon